A Company of Three

A
Company
of Three

A NOVEL BY

Varley O'Connor

ALGONQUIN BOOKS
OF CHAPEL HILL
2003

Published by
ALGONQUIN BOOKS OF CHAPEL HILL
Post Office Box 2225
Chapel Hill, North Carolina 27515-2225

a division of
WORKMAN PUBLISHING
708 Broadway
New York, New York 10003

This is a work of fiction. While, as in all fiction, the literary perceptions and
insights are based on experience, all names, characters, places, and incidents are
either products of the author's imagination or are used fictitiously. No reference to
any real person is intended or should be inferred.

Library of Congress Cataloging-in-Publication Data
O'Connor, Varley.
    A company of three : a novel / by Varley O'Connor.—1st ed.
        p. cm.
    ISBN 1-56512-373-5
    1. Actors—Fiction.   2. Actresses—Fiction.   3. Friendship—Fiction.
4. New York (N.Y.)—Fiction.   I. Title.
PS3565.C655C66 2003
813'.54—dc21   2003051893

10   9   8   7   6   5   4   3   2   1
First Edition

For my parents,

Louise M. Varley and Donald H. Varley

"The only true voyage of discovery, the only really rejuvenating experience, would be not to visit strange lands but to possess other eyes, to see the universe through the eyes of another, of a hundred others, to see the hundred universes that each of them sees, that each of them is. . . ."

Marcel Proust, *The Captive*

A Company of Three

LEADING PLAYERS

Robert Holt—the narrator
Patrick O'Doherty
Irene Jane Walpers

Part I

1 The Cowgirl

Patrick and I had been friends for a year when Irene appeared in our acting class, as if she had raced to New York expressly to meet us. There she finally sat, all luminous prettiness and hypnotic, smoky blue eyes. Someone sitting beside her must have cracked quite a joke, for with a toss of unruly brown hair she dissolved into laughter that shook her small frame, and rippled over the rows of students, infecting the others. She finished, then coughed. A rather raucous, I-don't-give-a-damn cough. Then she quieted, turning her exquisite attention again to the room before her. Bring it on, her face seemed to say. Hello world, I'm here! Patrick for one, and I for another, would never be the same. She had the ability to so pour herself into what she was doing—life, laughter, a role—that for me there was something awesome about her from the beginning.

Patrick and I were veterans. Acting had drawn us together. Irene, the last potent elixir, entangled us hopelessly.

Youth is the time when we are most easily influenced, and usually one or two people most deeply affect us, and, not to put too fine a point on it, set the tenor of our lives. But life is full then, teeming with people who come blazing in and then vanish, often as not. Still, it wasn't long before I knew that Irene and Patrick were my two people.

WE'D ALL COME TOGETHER in scene-study class, which took place once a week in the studios over Carnegie Hall. People tried out six and seven times to get in in those days—but I was fortunate. At my audition the notorious Andre Sadovsky had sat sneering, trimming his nails with a clipper as I gave Tom's farewell speech at the end of *The Glass Menagerie*; my best audition piece, or so I thought.

When I was finished he'd said, "Give me some Shakespeare."

I did Mercutio, and about ten lines in he interrupted. "Yes, yes. Oh please. Stop. You can come to the class but—" he looked down at the picture and résumé he had tossed on the floor. "Mr. Holt. You can come, but don't do anything. Understand?" I stood glued to my spot in amazement, expecting that he would have more to say. He whispered to the beautiful blonde in a tiny tube top who sat at his side.

Andre reclined in three folding chairs pushed together to form a chaise lounge. His lank hair was gray, his face swarthy, his eyes like two chips of coal pressed into dough. Not innately prepossessing.

"Mr. Holt?" He'd looked up. His voice was a high nasal whine. "Did you have a question?" I'd been dismissed. "Samantha will tell you when the class begins," he said as I left. The lovely Samantha floated out of the room behind me. "That was wonderful work." She gave me her hand and I shook it. "You're only the second person he chose today." Patrick had gone in before me and had already left.

"I thought he hated me," I said.

"No, he just hates auditions. He acted too, years ago."

"In Russia?"

"No, Brooklyn." She winked, and sat down to fill out a form.

"What did he mean when he said I shouldn't do anything?"

"Oh. Don't push. Just say the words."

My heart sank. It had happened again, I had pushed, I was *over-acting*.

My experience in the class, though, was better than what I'd expected after my audition that day. Andre liked me. He liked Patrick, and we found ourselves in the enviable position of protégés; meaning that Andre watched us closely, took our work seriously, and brought out, I think, what was best in our talents. Others were not so lucky.

"Darling," he said to a sweet, earnest woman named Maryann Bosco from Memphis, who always wore hats, "it is simple, it is natural, you want an award? It's boring." He crossed his arms and leaned forward. He never raised his voice. "Nothing gets through your head. Here in this class I tell you and tell you what isn't enough. This is the theater, yes? You are doing a scene from a play. In the movies you can maybe be boring because they have got those explosions around you, not here. Even life, at least my life—" here he cast a droll look at the class "—is not so boring as that. Sit down, please. Go back to Lee Strasberg."

"Mr. Holt," Andre said, the first day I worked in his class. "Do you tend to be a repressed, conservative person?"

He'd thrown me again. "No." I could feel myself color.

"You wouldn't see it," he responded, and to my dismay people laughed. "With you there is an abundance. You don't need to try. Do it again without trying."

It went better, of course.

"What did you mean when you said I was repressed?"

He shrugged. "Actors who push often are. They've been saving it all for the stage. Don't look so distressed. Your talent is fine."

I lived in a fourth-floor apartment in a crumbling brownstone on West Forty-sixth, between Ninth and Tenth Avenues. The street stank in the summer, and as I walked home from the restaurant on the East Side where I worked, it got hotter and hotter, until I felt I was entering an oven; I understood, firsthand, the origin of the name Hell's Kitchen. But I loved the apartment, its proximity to the theater district, to Restaurant Row—even though, in those days, I couldn't afford to eat there, with the possible exception of Joe Allen on special occasions—and to the strange sign I saw by a doorway just several blocks away:

THE ACTOR'S CHAPEL. I never entered the place, but as I trudged home after auditions, the sight of it comforted me in an unacknowledged, peripheral way.

It was a steep walk up the stairs to my apartment, steps listing away from the wall and turning up in a zigzagging spiral from floor to floor. Inside it was cool, from the rasping air conditioner in the living-room window that I kept on full blast—my haven: cheap wood-paneled walls, orange-shag carpeting, the dresser and the door to the bedroom closet painted in blinding shades of bright blue and green. It had come furnished, and it was my own. There were roaches, and the kitchen swarmed with them before I finally called the super.

On the heels of our first year in Andre's class, Patrick and I had been sure that we would be invited to Crispins, Andre's theater, to work for the summer. But we were not. Patrick went away to work at a dreary resort in Rhode Island, and I stayed in the city, disappointed by the abysmal production of a Neil Simon play I'd been cast in that May. We performed the play at a Ramada Inn in East Orange, New Jersey.

One matinee performance fell on the Fourth of July, this being the bicentennial year. Afterward I took the train home, rode the subway two stops to Times Square and found it completely deserted, everyone gone, evidently, to some version somewhere of the day's festivities.

The summer of that year had its moments. But with the resumption of Andre's class in mid-September, I began the graduate directing program at NYU. I'd done this as much for my father as for myself. He'd never liked the idea of my being an actor. As the son of an academic—he was a professor at Columbia—I had learned that the logical thing to do if you felt stalled was to go to graduate school.

Patrick had gone to emcee a weekly seaside variety show and spent most of his time washing dishes and restocking liquor in the cantina. When he came back he said he would *never, ever* return to Rhode Island.

Patrick was tall, but for an actor he was inordinately tall, six-foot-seven. And, *factually,* he was unattractive, although at first sight, awaiting our Andre auditions, he'd looked to me like a tall Fred Astaire: He leaned with one shoulder against a blank wall, head downward, studying a script. I studied him as I usually studied my competition, and he felt my eyes and looked up. I saw a ruddy, peeled-looking face, a thicket of sand-colored hair erect as a brush; his head in total formed the shape of a hatchet or a wedge; his eyes were a shocking cornflower blue. Then he spoke: "Gotta match?" And animate, reaching into his pocket and crossing to me, he changed, became fluid, dashing— gorgeous, I had to admit.

Patrick took up and enthused over everything Andre said. He had begun in the musical theater and "real" acting was new and mysterious for him. He read ceaselessly, he watched people everywhere, making notes in a spiral-bound notebook he kept in his pocket, and if he were up for a part, he would *be* the person in his own life as preparation, dressing like a dandy or a colonel, speaking in a Latvian accent to friends on the phone. But alas, despite his determination and commitment, he was not very good.

What Andre saw in Patrick was a presence, a style that was odd, but riveting. You may have thought his work unbelievable, arch, straightforward to a degree that verged on the bizarre—but you couldn't stop watching him. Often, when Patrick was up in a scene Andre would laugh at the end, but delightedly: "Oh dear, oh dear, oh dear, that was *terrible*, Patrick. What is this you have done?" But he'd say this with such tremendous enjoyment.

In Patrick's first incarnation as a dancer he'd been a huge success. He'd arrived in the city from Boston at the age of eighteen, and in three years he was featured in two Broadway shows, a national tour, and several stock and industrial shows. Then he'd wrecked his right knee, ending his dancing career. After that he left the city for a while, coming back just a week before the day I met him at the audition. He never said much about his old life. Very few of his friends were friends from that life—there was Maria Valdez, a flashy woman I'd met once or twice, and Benton, who had no last name, a shadowy figure Patrick mentioned occasionally, mostly without explanation, and so elliptically that at first I thought Benton was a place.

How Patrick suffered over losing jobs. He would take to his bed for a few days or a week, depending on the magnitude of his disappointment. On the day in October when Irene was first scheduled to go up in class, Patrick was, again, holed up in his apartment. I'd been calling him for days without getting any answer and I stopped by to see him that afternoon. I leaned on the buzzer outside of his building and waited.

I stepped back, ready to leave, when I heard a thin voice: "Who is it?"

"Robert."

"Robert." I heard him sigh. "Come up then."

He lived in an attractive four-story brownstone in the Seventies on the Upper West Side, quiet by city standards, genteel, smelling of gardens if the wind was right. That day it was. We sat out on his fire escape overlooking the tangles of growth at the back of the building: his neighbors with garden apartments had created a veritable jungle, and it sparkled with sun.

He leaned back and lit a Gauloise. "I really can't go out, I have a touch of sore throat." He wore a red flannel plaid bathrobe; in winter he wore brown leather slippers, the kind grandfathers wear.

"Well, you'll want to come to class," I said. "The cowgirl is up today."

"Irene Jane?" Tempted. "Well, I can't."

"If you were sick, you wouldn't be smoking."

"You know that's not so, I never stop smoking. I have no restraint," he said, blowing fumes of blue smoke through his mouth and nose. He snatched the newspaper I was holding and scanned the front page.

"You can't have it." He never bought a paper of his own; he liked to steal mine. "Come on, Patrick. Get dressed."

"Oh my God." He had opened the paper. "Chairman Mao died."

"Weeks ago. You know who she's stuck with?" I asked, resolute.

"Who?" he said, rustling pages.

"Irene."

"Irene *Jane*," he corrected.

"She's doing a scene with Clarence."

"She is not. I can't conceive of what scene it could be," he said, tongue in cheek, and setting the paper down, started to rise. As he did, I saw the white scars on his knee, hundreds of tiny raised scorings that circled the joint so it looked as though someone had sewn it back on.

"I'm weak," he called, going inside to get dressed. "If we walk, we'll have to walk slow."

I had called Irene the cowgirl because she always wore cowboy boots: thus far I had seen her in three different pairs. Patrick was shocked by her name, Irene Jane Walpers. "Walpers?" he whispered after Andre introduced her. "Tell me he didn't say *Walpers*." She sat in the back of the class, taking copious notes, and although I'd been hoping to strike up a conversation with her, she managed to slip in every time, just as class began, and then slip out the minute it ended.

We walked over to Broadway, then south through Columbus Circle. Patrick had brought my newspaper. "Why don't you just buy one?" I said.

But his attention had drifted up to the sky. "Don't you love New York on a crisp autumn day?"

CLASS MET FROM three to six on Mondays. When we arrived Clarence was setting up his props: a metal frame suspending a punching bag, gloves, two benches, a jump rope, and a stack of white towels. Only the towels were a new addition. His brown head was as smooth as his face, freshly shaved for the scene. He was stripped to his Everlast trunks, his white socks, his black high-top sneakers.

A shy, gracious man from Jamaica, Clarence was obsessed with *The Great White Hope*, a Pulitzer prize-winning play about the doomed life of Jack Johnson, heavyweight champ of 1908. He had been in the class since the previous January, and whenever he was up he did the same scene from this play. This would be the fourth time. No one understood why Andre let him do it over and over, without much progress that any of us could see.

"Clarence," Andre said, months prior to Irene's debut. "There is someone with you in the scene. Ellie is there."

"Yes," Clarence replied. "Jack ignores her. Jack's working out."

"What you do is work out. What *she* does is attempt to get you to stop."

Clarence blinked.

"Isn't there anything she does that distracts you?" Andre asked. "You get angry at her, yes?"

"But Jack keeps working out."

"But obviously, Clarence, other things are going on. At least you have to stop for a bit, just to get her to leave, so that you can go *back* to working out."

Clarence nodded, and then next time would do the scene exactly the same. I had heard from Samantha that his audition for the class was extraordinary—"The best audition," she told me, "I've seen." Perhaps he had been the victim of the idea that playing a scene was all about sticking to your initial intention.

Two vultures, Patrick and I, took front-row seats. Clarence jumped rope; he liked to break a nice sweat before the scene started. Irene was not yet manifest.

Andre appeared wearing his standard Brooks Brothers jacket draped over his shoulders, white dress shirt, gray slacks. He absorbed the sight of Clarence and his gym, and took his seat farthest from the door, by the grimy windows overlooking Seventh Avenue.

"Clarence," he said. The rope stopped with a swish. "Keep in mind, please, at the end of this scene your wife is in such despair she goes out and throws herself down a well. Understand?"

"Yes, sir." Clarence looked confident.

"Irene is ready?" Clarence went and stuck his head out the door, came back and said, "Scene," then put on his gloves and pounded the bag. I was admiring his footwork when Irene came in.

She wore round spectacles and a shabby gray dress, and today she seemed frail, even though I had assessed her figure as slender but strong. She wasn't very tall. After a pause, she began to speak and Clarence ignored her, belching out his lines between slams at the bag. She kept speaking to him, but without much insistence, seeming too tired for the urgency that what she was saying demanded. It put a new, interesting twist on the scene. Nonetheless, Clarence just boxed. Irene talked almost as if she were talking to herself, as Clarence took off the gloves and went for the jump rope. He stopped to tell her he wanted her to leave, not just for now, but for good. And then, suddenly, she hauled back her arm and slapped him with a force you couldn't imagine she had. *She's fearless,* I thought, and I realized that everything she'd been doing had led to this gesture. It was both unexpected and absolutely right. I looked over at Andre. His palms were pressed to his cheeks in his pose of concentration. Clarence was stunned, and then superb for the remainder of the scene.

"Goddamnit," I whispered to Patrick, "she cracked it."

Andre applauded, so everybody did.

"And now we can put the scene to bed? Robert, go get Irene before we have lost her to the well."

She was sitting on the floor in the hallway, her arms wrapped around her bent knees. "That guy's gonna kill me," she said.

"Who, Clarence? Oh no, he's ecstatic."

"He is?" I detected a stronger twang in her speech than I'd heard in the work. It was charming. Her eyes were silvery: they were dry.

She picked up her boots, they were black ones that night, and followed me back in. How could I casually invite her for coffee after class?

I needn't have worried; Patrick took care of that.

We'd seen her go into the rest room to change. We both waited outside.

"Are you waiting for Irene?" I said.

"Of course," he answered, "aren't you?"

"Patrick—"

"Let's do a scene with her," he said. "She's smashing."

"All right." I had had something else in mind, but saw it was hopeless, for tonight.

"May I buy you a cheesecake at Wolf's?"

"Wolf's?" she said. "Isn't that famous?"

"Yes it is, so you must," Patrick said. He took her hand—he was shameless. "I'm mad for your work."

"I like yours. That was funny, that scene you did."

"Thank you." His last scene had been an adaptation from a Salinger story. It wasn't a stretch—it being basically how he behaved in real life.

"Yesterday," she was saying, "I had bagels and lox."

Where was she from? I couldn't quite get it.

Patrick said, "How lovely for you."

SHE WAS FROM Coffeyville, Kansas, she said after class, and had been in New York for three months. She wore a short white dress that in the deepening night drew light from the sky. The three of us carried our jackets. A student played the flute outside Carnegie Hall and Irene dumped the change from her purse in the open case at his feet. Her cowboy boots clumped on the sidewalk.

"How was working with Clarence?" I asked.

"Oh listen," she shook her head, "he ignored what I did, said, *didn't* do," she rolled her remarkable eyes.

I glanced up at Patrick, who was trying not to smile.

"But this morning I figured it out." We stepped out from the curb to cross Fifty-seventh at Sixth, when the light turned green; Irene ran and we followed, horns blasting. "I said to myself, now really, what do I see? And I said back to myself, well, he's crazy, y'know? And *yes,* by this scene in the play he *is* crazy. He's beside himself, trapped."

A waiter with hair like a blob of black paint directed us to a table at Wolf's.

"All he knows is how to fight," Irene continued, "and he clings to it, hoping it will save him. Though it won't. But when he sees I've become as bad off as he has, he still has enough love to try to get me out, even if he can't save himself. So okay. If he's so obsessed with his own thing, how would he notice how bad I am too? I had to be crazier somehow than he is." She smiled, and picked up her menu.

She was wired. Her face was flushed. "Though I shouldn't have hit him," she added, "not without warning him." Her hands were very small, the fingernails bitten. I thought she was wonderful.

She looked at Patrick, who was giving her his undivided attention, chin propped on one hand. "I can talk to you easier while you're sitting down," she said. "Is your height a hindrance in finding work?"

"No," he said, "all my producers build sets to scale." He watched her as though he had fallen in love. When Patrick decided he liked someone he adored him, all out, no holds barred. He did it with me. On his first visit to my apartment he circled the rooms, looking at all of my ordinary things, saying "So this is your kitchen. (Here is your table, is this your chair?) Here are your weights. (Do you use them here, or bring them out to the open space of the room?)" I had the feeling that if I weren't there he'd have been going through drawers.

We got our cheesecake and Patrick watched scrupulously as she ate. "Irene Jane," he said, "eating cheesecake."

She put down her fork. "Are you making fun of me?"

Patrick blushed; his hands fluttered up to his hair, trying to arrange it, and then he got up and walked off toward the phones.

"What did I do?" she said. I began to explain, but she got up and went after him. The first woman I'd liked in months and I had to be with Patrick. She probably thought we were lovers.

They returned a few minutes later, smoking Gauloises, behaving like old, old friends.

"No, I know what you're saying," she told him. "I had this acting teacher once, well, that's not how it sounds, she was my *only* acting teacher." She sat down, touched my hand, leaning close: "I'm practically an amateur, if you want to know the truth." She looked back at Patrick. "But Rose, God I loved her. She taught me to act. She made you be in your body and somehow it came. She was old and fat, with a horrible cough, carried cartons of Salems in her bag. But she was the best Juliet I've ever seen. She was trying to tell me how to do it one day and I couldn't, so she showed me. She took off her glasses, shut her eyes, said the lines, and I swear it was like she was young, beautiful, in love." Irene's voice had softened. She laughed. "Rose was a hoot. Once she said to this guy, Get it up, you look like a limp prick."

"Oh my," Patrick said.

We sat drinking coffee and talking until the bright lights, the dazzling chromes and the voices around us felt like a permanent part of my brain. Outside, the night rush of the traffic was soothing. Irene's dress looked like snow. "So what scene will we do?" Patrick said.

"Am I drunk?" said Irene. "I feel like I'm drunk." She leaned her head for a heartbeat against my shoulder. "We're doing a scene?"

"Of course," Patrick answered. "The three of us, aren't we?"

"I thought it was a foregone conclusion," I added.

"Great!" she said. We exchanged numbers, then she dashed across the street, late for a dinner engagement, heading to the Sixth Avenue subway. I watched the motion of her legs in her boots, the sway of her hips—and my breath felt shallow.

"Oh no," Patrick said. He had turned back and seen my stare. "I've committed a major misdemeanor."

"Forget it," I said, as we started west.

"You could have told me."

I stopped and said, "What did you do with my paper?"

"God, I don't know, left it in class, or *somewhere*. It's only a paper, don't be a bore. I'm sorry."

"Anyway, you have excellent taste," he said. We passed the Winter Garden Theater. "What is it about her?"

"She doesn't wear black."

"Yes, very refreshing."

"She's not anorexic."

"Even so," Patrick said, "I thought Melinda was a very nice girl."

I'd met my old girlfriend, Melinda, at a Macy's White Sale. Four years of Carnegie Mellon had left me fed up with actresses. I'd roamed the corridors of Bloomingdale's, Alexander's, Saks, running my hands over luggage or shoes or shirts I had no intention of buying — perhaps a dishonorable system of meeting women, but I've heard worse. My results had been fairly good. Melinda, however, had left New York for six weeks in June and returned weighing eighty-two pounds. One morning she cried for three hours after eating a doughnut and I just lost my patience. I also liked stewardesses. I'd met a fantastic Asian woman named Candace on a plane the Christmas before, and we had maintained a bimonthly fly-in affair.

"What scene shall we do?" Patrick asked.

"I don't care."

"I'd like to do Coward. But, really, we don't have to." Patrick was good in Noel Coward, and he knew I knew it.

"That would be fine."

"You probably want to work with her alone."

"Patrick, I'm only attracted to her. Besides, she may be engaged to her sweetheart in Kansas, who knows?" We were standing outside of my building. An elderly woman passed by us, and peered up at Patrick as though searching for the top of a very tall tree.

"You know we're both frauds," he said. "We thought she was cute because of her name and her boots, but now we're intrigued because of her acting."

"True," I said, "true." There was nothing worse than getting a crush on someone and then finding out that their acting was atrocious.

"No matter," he said. "I hope you marry and have thirteen children. I'll be the lonely avuncular friend who dines with you Sundays."

"Shut up. You have any auditions this week?"

"No, nothing. You?"

"I can't even try for a while, too much work for school."

"Are you learning anything?"

"I suppose. I better go." Patrick was lingering. "What are you doing tonight?" I asked him.

"I don't feel like going home. . . ." He surveyed the street, withdrawing. "It's a beautiful night. I'll go walking," and he set off.

"I'll give you a call," I said to his back. He lifted an arm and dropped his fingers in a wave. I stood, momentarily pondering his extremist habit of either staying excessively inside, or never wanting to be at home at all. I felt guilty. I should have suggested dinner. I thought of how hard it must be to start over, given what he had already achieved. I went into the foyer, wondering fleetingly what had become of the man Patrick had met in Rhode Island. But I had Irene's phone number out by the time I got in my door. I laid it down on my three-legged telephone table—one side propped up by a nail hammered into the wall—and tried to remember if she had touched Patrick tonight. Was she a "toucher," or could I safely interpret her touching of me as flirting? I went into the kitchen for a beer. No, I wouldn't call her. She wouldn't be home, I recalled, and I'd see her soon enough. Through rehearsals our romance could evolve at a natural pace. I imagined her cowboy boots lined on the floor of my closet, her face on my pillow.

I opened a window, leaned out: the super and his wife sat on lawn chairs in front of the building; a black man with a paisley valise in his lap sat on the stoop across the street. The cool air flowed over my eyebrows. *The theater,* I thought, reminded of nights when, from my parents' apartment in Jersey, I'd gaze at the lights of the city and think like a corny movie actor or a song—*just wait.*

TWO NIGHTS LATER I sat up reading for class at two in the morning, the radio turned up to drown out the resound of a car alarm. It was only when I became aware of another sound, the apartment's buzzer, that I realized the car alarm had stopped. Cursing, I rose from my bed and turned off the music. Drunks liked to sleep in the building's foyer and they buzzed down the row of names on the intercom to be let in. When the ring sounded again I went into the living room, peeked between the slats of the venetian blinds, and looked out at the street. It was eerily quiet, then a figure stepped away from the building and into my view, and I saw it was Patrick. I raised the blinds, opened the window. He looked up, holding something white to his face, and after pushing the buzzer to let him in I grabbed my keys and ran down the stairs.

"Oh, you're dressed," he said, sighting me. "I didn't wake you." He had progressed a single flight and leaned heavily with one arm on the bowed, pitted wall; his words were uncannily precise, coming as they were from under a bar rag he pressed to his mouth and nose.

The stairway was dark enough that I didn't see the blood until I stood beside him. Even then, I couldn't see much. There was blood near his eye and soaking through the rag; I thought I could smell it. I smelled liquor too.

"What happened? Were you mugged?"

He let me help him up the stairs, said he'd been kicked in the ribs and the hip. Inside the apartment I saw that the cut at the top of his cheekbone wasn't bleeding anymore. He took the rag off his face and revealed that the blood from his nose had stopped too; it was swelling, and he dabbed away redness from there and the side of his mouth. He touched his nose.

"Is it broken?" I asked.

"I'll just use the bathroom," he said, turning to it. "All right?"

"There's some stuff, a first-aid kit," I said to the door. "Under the sink."

"Thank you," he answered.

"You don't need to go to the hospital, do you?" He must not have heard.

When he emerged he'd put a Band-Aid on the cut and wiped off his face; his features looked blurred, and the front of his shirt was splattered with blood. We went to the kitchen for ice and sat down at the table.

"I was walking," he told me. "I may have stopped at a bar. Or two."

"How many were there? Did it happen in the street?"

"Three. There were three."

"Were they armed?"

"No, but what could I do?" He didn't seem angry.

"*Goddamnit,*" I said. "How much money did they get?"

He patted his pockets, withdrew his wallet and opened it. "None. I didn't have very much."

"Did you resist? Were you drunk? Are you going to report it?"

"Robert, don't," he said sharply. "Really." He caught me off guard. I felt chastened, a child interfering in an event I had neither capacity nor experience to understand. He arose from the table and at the sink dumped out the ice I had wrapped in a towel. "Let's talk in the morning," he said, his back to me.

"You want to sleep here?"

"Yes, thank you," he said.

I got him a pillow and a blanket for the couch and then went to bed myself, less bewildered by the way he had spoken to me than by the strange passivity of his reaction. The Patrick I knew would have fought back, and told me about it with great indignation. He was physically strong. Although he didn't dance anymore he swam, he lifted weights, played tennis—thrashing me soundly the few times we played. He'd spent his youth fending off bullies because, from the age of thirteen, he had taken ballet. Furthermore, he had told me, he was too tall not to know how to defend himself—his tallness, instead of deflecting aggression, provoked it.

But what I had seen that night was an air of defeat, then an annoyance with me for being its witness. Maybe, I decided, I was reading into what had to be a humiliating, frightening experience. We would hash it all out eventually. But in the morning he was gone, and we never spoke of the incident again.

2 Casting

Our first rehearsal was scheduled to be conducted at Irene's apartment. That afternoon Patrick had called to say he would be late. Would I call Irene and reschedule for one hour later? I said that I would and then didn't. I put on my leather bomber jacket. Patrick told me I looked like a hood when I wore it, but someone who wore penny loafers was no one to talk. He probably had the largest pair of penny loafers on the eastern seaboard.

I had been downtown that morning to pick up my belongings from where a play I'd been doing had closed. It had barely been a part. I came on in act 3 in a letter sweater tossing a football and grinning like a fool, the director's idea of a boy at sixteen. But it had provided a modicum of salary. My parents were paying my tuition and rent. Soon, I thought, I would have to get another job. I walked over toward Sixth on West Fourth Street through quickly moving pedestrians in the brisk air, and the more modest street sounds of the Village compared to Midtown, when I saw Irene alight from a gleaming black Jaguar in front of her building: the boots, the beautiful legs, a red dress that went whipping around her as she pushed the door closed. Over her dress she wore a thin jacket, and she clutched her arms as the man in the car, leaning over the passenger seat, talked to her through the open window. I was practically upon them when she turned and said, "Hi!"

She took me by the arm to the window. "Neal, this is Robert from my acting class. Robert, Neal Parks." He had wispy blond hair, small features crowded together at the center of his face, and ears that, somehow, looked pointed.

"Tell me," he said. "Is she any good?" I honestly didn't know what he was asking; I feared a sexual inference. "Can she act?" he clarified.

"Oh. Absolutely." I stepped back on the sidewalk, realizing that he looked slightly familiar. His car was so shiny I could see myself in it.

"Thursday then, sweetheart?" he said to Irene. "Nice meeting you, Rob," and he pulled away, nearly hitting a cab that zoomed by on his left.

We were outside of a coffee shop; beside it was where Irene lived. If my building was crumbling then Irene's had already crumbled. It was an old tenement, inhabited, mostly, by aging hippies and fifties bohemians. Across the street was an erotica store, the Pink Pussy Cat Boutique.

Irene pushed open the broken front door and we trod up the rickety stairs. "Neal is terribly successful," she said. "He's on a soap and has all these commercials. We rendezvous at the Waldorf-Astoria. He's stuck in a *terrible* marriage." She smiled dazzlingly, then unlocked number six.

A black cat sat waiting inside, purring as loudly as an outboard motor; she scooped him up in her arms.

"St. Martin," she said, kissing him on his short snout, "who his mother loves more than any creature in existence. This is Robert," she said very gently. To me she said simply, "He doesn't like men."

I followed her down a dim hallway, passing by several small rooms, to a living room at the front decorated with a shaggy yellowish rug, books crammed into milk crates, Salvation Army–type furniture; on the far wall was a makeshift curtain sectioning off another room, and from behind it came the sound of copious weeping.

"Ruth!" Irene said. Giving the cat a last kiss on the head, she set him down. "Excuse me."

She slipped behind the curtain. The room had a fusty, unventilated smell, and the weeping got louder. At least she didn't live with a man, I thought. She reemerged, took my arm, and led me back down the hall.

"This is my room," she said, showing me into a space about as big as a cell; she was now somber and abrupt, like a nurse dispensing with an unwanted visitor. "I'll be right back."

"Look," I said, "I'm early, I'll go out and come back later."

"Oh, please don't."

"Patrick's going to be late."

"Then we can talk!" Once more she shot off her sparkly smile, and left.

St. Martin was stretched out at the foot of her bed, his chin on his paws. He rolled up his gold eyes without moving his head, indicating he wouldn't much like the idea of me sitting down on the bed as well. There was no place else to sit since the bed took up half the room. I went over to inspect the photographs resting on a footlocker under the window. One was of a middle-aged woman, hands folded primly, standing in a field. Looking closer I saw that she had the same eyes as Irene. They were almond-shaped, long, so far apart and deeply set that in the shadow that fell across her face, she looked almost as though she were wearing a mask. I picked up the other photograph and gingerly sat down on the bed near the pillow. St. Martin slowly lifted his head and regarded me.

"Too bad," I told him.

The photo showed Irene in a pink spangled suit and a ten-gallon hat, swerving a horse by what looked like a barrel, two-thirds of the picture hidden by great clouds of dust. A real cowgirl, I thought.

She reappeared, sans boots, and shooed St. Martin away. She sat down beside me on the bed with her legs crossed Indian-style, the skirt of her dress bunched up around her. I thought she smelled faintly of cinnamon. There was a run in the foot of her stocking and her hair was tossed from the wind outside. "Oh, that's me," she said, taking the picture—I had just realized, too late, that I was still holding it—"doing rodeo." She studied the picture. "I set a record in Tulsa, and in my hometown I was rodeo queen. That may sound funny to you, but where I come from it's a very big deal."

"I don't think it's funny," I said.

She kept looking at the picture. "That's my horse, Mercury." She got up and put the photograph back in its place on the footlocker. "He's dead now." She stared down at the other pictures, then picked up the one of the woman in the field.

"This is my mother," she said.

"She looks a lot like you."

"My mother's dead too." The words hung in the air. I felt I was wrong in thinking that I could get to know her. It wasn't just Neal or the cat or the roommate—the whirl of activity I had been waiting to settle since I arrived. It wasn't even her general demeanor—which always, since I had first noticed her in class, suggested that hers was a full, complete life, and that she, at the center, was thoroughly involved and not waiting for anything new. It had more to do with how she'd handled the pictures, how she had positioned them on the trunk like a shrine. She seemed older, like a woman with a past, although she was barely twenty-one.

I wanted to tell her I was sorry her mother had died (I didn't quite know what to think about the horse), but to say it seemed trite. She sat back down on the bed, again pulling up and crossing her legs, and the deep blue of her eyes, her body—the energy and heat that seemed to emanate from her—loomed larger than anything she said. The light slowly drained from the room, and as she turned on the lamp, a glow fell over us.

She poured us glasses of wine from a gallon jug of Burgundy she kept in her room. Because her roommate was an alcoholic, Irene couldn't keep wine in the kitchen. "Ruth," she explained, "lives a life of catastrophe." Today, for instance, at a go-see for a print job, she had opened her portfolio on the photographer's desk and out scurried a frantic, undaunted swarm of cockroaches.

"Oh God," I said, "that's disgusting."

"Yes, but it isn't the end of the world. That's why she was crying. For Ruth it's representative of her entire life, that's what she told me. I told her tomorrow we'd set off another bomb, but that didn't cheer her up."

I laughed, and so did Irene. We both stopped on a dime, however, when Ruth—a bone-thin woman of maybe thirty, draped in long hair the color of an Irish setter—poked her head in the door.

"Irene," she said, "I'm going out," and disappeared down the hall.

Irene poured us more wine. "St. Martin, darling," she said, "come and see mother." The cat had slinked back in the room. He jumped up on the bed and settled down, curled by Irene. "Ruth's had some wonderful work. She's up for a play at the Kennedy Center. But she says she's too old not to be more well known."

"What about you?" I asked.

She shrugged, looking shy. "I have an agent, well, just for commercials. Lynn Singer, do you know her?"

Of course I knew Lynn Singer; she was among the better-known agents in the business. "Sure I do. Irene, that's great." So much for the concept of me as her mentor. Neal had undoubtedly gotten there first.

"And I got a play. Well, for now I'm the standby, but I'm supposed to go in by the end of November."

"What's the play?"

She leaned over, reached under the bed and brought out a script and handed it to me. "It's not Broadway, but I think it's pretty good."

She was the standby for one of the leads in the most popular off-Broadway play of the year. Patrick had seen it five times, I'd seen it twice. It had both a cult following and the respect of the mainstream theatrical community. It was funny, stylish, tough, and nostalgic; one of those shows that charms everyone. How did she even *get seen* for the play? Lynn Singer had nothing to do with the stage.

Patrick arrived, stooping into the room and delightedly scanning its meager contents. "What a dear little den," he said. "You could hibernate here for the winter. Tonight, though, we're reading the scene over champagne at One Fifth. Please, I insist. It will put us in the mood."

Afterward, he and I walked Irene home, and then continued to the uptown subway.

"You're quiet tonight," he said as we waited on the platform.

I was despondent; equally envious of Irene's success and desirous of the death of Neal Parks.

"Do you like the scene?" he asked me.

The choice was typical Patrick; a bright, witty triangle play about love among artists, by Noel Coward, of course. In the scene I was Leo, a playwright, the close friend of Otto and Gilda, a painter and his beautiful consort. I appear unexpectedly at their garret in Paris, finding Otto out of town and Gilda alone. The following morning Leo and Gilda must break the news of their tryst to poor Otto, who does not take it well. The tone is theatrical and chic, and despite how much they rant and rave, and who sleeps with whom, you know that the three will yet carry on.

"The scene is fine," I told Patrick.

"Would you rather play Otto?" he asked.

I turned away and bought a paper, gave him half. "Here. No, I like playing Leo."

I looked away from him and down into the tracks where water had settled from the rain the night before; slow drips continued falling over the tracks from the ceiling above. I loved the subways in New York: the cool lonely tunnels, the sudden vibration, the sound of the trains in the distance, the lights against the wall—then the huge rush of wind as the train pounds into the station, the pfft! of the doors sliding open, and the assurance of delivery from one part of town to another, one world to another.

Jimmy Carter was running for president and I scanned the headlines about the upcoming election. I looked over at Patrick, seated on a bench and happily reading. His unending legs were crossed at the knee and again at the ankles. He had on a black Lacoste shirt and an expensive-looking herringbone jacket. His script was rolled and tucked in the pocket. Penny loafers. In spite of his various neuroses, Patrick had a beautiful dignity.

Patrick never competed with anyone. I, on the other hand, endlessly stacked myself up against others. For as long as I could remember, I'd had the sense of all things being just out of reach. I thought of all the times I'd waited for my father—not my stepfather, David, but my real father who'd left my mother and me when I was four and she was just twenty-two. We moved out of the city to New Jersey, where my mother's parents lived, but every so often the first few years after he left, my father would call wanting to see me. My mother would get me ready for a weekend or a night with him. I can still remember the smoke from my mother's cigarettes wreathing the air as we waited, the swish of her slippers on the linoleum, back and forth to the phone in her efforts to reach him; and her crushing disappointment. Me anxiously checking her face for the signs of what I soon learned was inevitable, that he wouldn't ever come. When I was fifteen, I found out that he had moved back to New York. In an attempt to avoid child support—even though he could damn well afford it—he had been living in Atlanta. I was determined to be an actor by then and had my eye on an expensive apprentice program. He was a Broadway stage manager and I resolved to look him up and ask him for the money.

"He isn't your father," my mother said. "David is your father, and if he ever hears what you're doing, I'll—" She didn't finish, but glared at me, expecting that I would relent.

I did not. I took the bus across the bridge and then rode the A train downtown. He met me at the stage door of the Longacre Theater and brought me inside, where he introduced me to the actors as their rehearsal dispersed for the day, the director, the stagehands—and then we went out to a bar and everyone, as in the theater, knew my father there. He had curly gray hair and although he was heavier than I had remembered, he was handsome. He patted me on the back and told me what a nice kid I had turned out to be. Men stopped by our table. I drank Cokes as I explained my interest in acting and the apprentice program I hoped to attend. "Sounds good," he said, smiling, but people kept interrupting. He'd mentioned dinner on the phone and I thought that at dinner it would be quieter and I could ask him for the money. But he had forgotten dinner. I finally said that I needed the money and told him how much. "I haven't got that kind of money to spare," he said, laughing. A couple approached and sat down.

"This is my boy," my father said. In a little while I said that I had to go, and he told me to come back and see him anytime. I never saw him again.

My mother married David when I was ten. She referred to him as "our savior." We were constantly to remember how much he was doing for us, what he saved us from. I developed the conviction that my mother and I did not belong with David as his wife and son, that we lived our new lives only by a strange operation of grace and that anything—a lapse in duty, an unconscious look—could send us back to the time my mother hated, when we were continually disappointed.

Looking down into the subway tracks I felt scorned by the universe. I was enjoying my black mood too, though, because in the script I had so far composed of my life that I expected to be overlooked, misunderstood, and then to succeed to an extent that surpassed all my hopes. I would achieve tremendous acclaim as an actor, I would be rich. I would eventually marry a ravishing genius of an actress and we'd be the modern-day Lunt and Fontanne. We would live in the Dakota, having drinks with the Bernsteins and the Lennon-Onos on quiet nights at home.

Patrick assumed he was *at least* as fascinating as the Lennon-Onos, just as he was. I looked back at him, still reading the paper, sitting as gracefully on an uncomfortable bench as he might in a French drawing room. And at the sight of him I seethed with sudden, ashamed, covert resentment.

• • •

THE NEXT DAY I called him and we talked about Neal. He reminded me that the best women often had the worst taste in men. If possible, I should accept her as a friend. And so I bided my time, watching Neal on his soap whenever I happened to be home at 1:00 P.M. (his acting wasn't bad, but his ears were definitely pointed) and putting together the puzzle of Irene Jane Walpers as much as I could. Through our rehearsals, a background emerged. Her mother had died of uterine cancer when she was twelve. Her father had bought her a horse to distract her as he threw himself into his own apparently unceasing grief. He turned Irene's upbringing over to her great aunts, Wilma, Jean Rae, and Bonnie Lorraine, none of whom Irene had ever been close to. In high school she started to act, but upon graduation she only did rodeo and kept house for her father. Then she had a relationship with a tough, older cowboy-type guy named Hank and saw that she'd have to do something constructive with her life or she'd go crazy. Most of her friends were marrying men like Hank, having babies right away. In her town, she told me, you wouldn't know that the sixties had ever happened. Guys went off to Vietnam, they came back or they didn't, but nothing changed. Irene enrolled in Coffeyville Junior College, where she met Rose, her acting teacher, and everything shifted.

Six weeks shy of her twenty-first birthday she got on a bus for New York. Rose had told her about the Actors' Equity Association, where one could make contacts for places to live. On the day Irene met her roommate, Ruth was playing Handel on the stereo and reading the recently published diaries of Anaïs Nin; she lounged around the apartment in a gorgeous kimono. She was the *fantastic opposite* of Coffeyville, Kansas. The day Irene moved in, the black cat materialized on the fire escape outside of her window, underfed, an obvious stray. Irene called him St. Martin, in honor of the Academy of St. Martin in the Fields, whose name she had seen on the cover of the Handel recording. The name represented the endless potential of her new life. She wasn't exactly a hick, she said, but New York—*New York!*

She walked herself ragged through the hot month of August, making the rounds to theatrical offices. She was pretty and talented, but above all she was bold. She wasn't aware of how hard it was to do what she was doing and so, very simply, she just forged ahead. She had, for example, auditioned for Andre's class because she was there in the building and saw the auditions going on; she had no idea of Andre's reputation or of what he could possibly mean to her career.

It had become difficult to be seen for plays in New York on your own; having an agent was increasingly imperative. Most agents had signs reading, DON'T KNOCK! (I HAVE A DOG, HE WON'T LIKE IT) PUT YOUR PICTURE AND RÉSUMÉ UNDER THE DOOR AND WE WILL CALL YOU, and PLEASE, KNOCK AND IT'LL ONLY RUIN BOTH OF OUR DAYS. DON'T LEAVE A PICTURE, WE KNOW THEY'RE EXPENSIVE AND WE'LL ONLY THROW IT AWAY.

I'd managed to get an agent, an old friend of my mother's from when she was a chorus girl years ago. Harry White was about two hundred years old. He looked like his name: wavy white hair, skin so white it looked dusted with powder. The walls of his office were plastered with autographed head shots of famous dead people. I would call on him once or twice a week and we'd sit in his dark cluttered office and talk about the good old days. He was kind. Harry kept a sign posted on his door warning actors not to knock without an appointment. But if they did knock, or called on the phone, he heard them out. There were towers of résumés stapled to head shots stacked on his desk. In a passive way, he tried to get me auditions. I called him whenever I heard of a part I was right for, and he sent my credentials and picture in an envelope stamped with his name, and, nearly always, that was where it would end.

Patrick refused to subject himself to this treatment. He attended the appropriate open interviews and auditions listed in *Back Stage;* he did a lot through the mail. Irene, however, had been instructed by Rose to make the rounds every day, nine to five—by 1976, an old-fashioned approach in most people's minds. What the new approach was no one could quite say, but it had to do with connections established in vague, roundabout manners.

Irene had made a list of every agent, casting director, nonprofit theater, and producer, and called on each one. If she failed to get an appointment she'd go back until someone would see her. She believed she belonged in the business; in her mind, there was no doubt about it. And as far as her campaign succeeded—as it did fairly well those first months in New York—her success was largely attributable to this very forthright air of entitlement and expectation. People could smell it, as they can smell doubt and trepidation. She seemed in so many ways then refreshingly unscathed, and people were drawn to that quality.

I couldn't be envious of Irene for long because I was also drawn to her. Once our rehearsals began, the three of us grew close, almost immediately. We skipped the interim steps of friendship and jumped to calling each other on the phone most days, seeing each other three or four times a week. We went out after class and rehearsals to Jimmy Ray's, the Buffalo Roadhouse, the Collonades, often to Wolf's and One Fifth. We went to parties in spacious white lofts, dingy storefronts, apartments crowning the cold black glittering rivers. Each week we saw one or two plays, despite our scant disposable incomes. We would "second act" plays, mingling with the sidewalk smokers at intermission and slipping into the theater among them, hoping to find three vacated seats.

But before I accepted this triumvirate that was, on one key level, as unsettling as it was rewarding, I had to test, as it were, the romantic waters.

PROBABLY CLOSE TO three weeks from our first rehearsal, a few days before we put up the scene, I went by the theater on East Fourth where Irene had a read-through of her play. This was her first standby rehearsal. She'd said they would be out at three.

"Hello!" She held her script, bound in a folder, to her chest. She said good-bye to the women she had walked out of the theater with and kissed me on the cheek. "What a nice surprise."

"I had a class," I told her. Behind her, through the outer glass doors of the lobby, I could see the banner spread above the doors to the house, covered with quotes from reviews, and to the sides blowups of pictures from the show. Irene's eyes, dark blue in the clear cold air — her eyes always changed — glistened with excitement. "How'd it go?" I asked her. Boys were yelling at the gas station on the corner, and music drifted out to the street from somewhere nearby.

"I'm too happy," she said. I barely heard her; she spoke in a breathless stage whisper, furtively, but insistently.

"What?" I moved closer to her — cinnamon, the warmth of her breath for a moment against my neck and ear.

"I'm too — *run*." She was off, barreling down the sidewalk, her coat like a billowing sail. I ran with her, our breaths getting louder than the sound of the traffic — the music behind us, the shouts of the boys fading into the distance, gone. We ran across Bowery and up Lafayette, west along Eighth, weaving in and out of the crowds, and I thought, God, she can run, while everything spun, my head throbbed, and I listened to the pounding of her boots.

She cut south, in the direction of Washington Square. "Irene!" I called, falling back. How did she run in those boots? I had on heavy leather shoes and my feet felt like bricks, my cheeks warm in the air. We turned — I was running beside her again — and were in a cobbled alley, an enclave just north of the park, of converted stables and cottagey homes. Irene collapsed against a gray stuccoed wall near a door, and I staggered up to her. It was quiet. We were both breathing hard. No one else was around. Her coat was open and I didn't think, just putting my hands on the wall at either side of her, bent my head down to her face and kissed her. I felt the cool air in my hair against my hot scalp, the heat of her lips. The wall under my hands was hard, gritty, cool; my hands were damp.

I don't know how long it lasted before, gently, she pulled away. She turned her head toward the door and I moved slightly back. "I wonder who lives here," she said. "It's quaint, isn't it?"

"Yes."

She didn't look back at me. I put my hands in the pockets of my jacket. She began slowly walking, watching the doors. She'd taken the strap of her bag from her shoulder and wound it around her wrist and then let the bag drag on the ground, and the dragging sound irritated me.

"Irene, don't."

"What?" She stopped and looked at me and I thought of grabbing her and pushing her back against the wall and kissing her again, but her eyes were too guarded and I couldn't. Ahead of us, at the end of the alley, where the cobblestones opened out to the street, I saw the cars on Fifth Avenue going by.

"Should I not have kissed you?"

She shrugged, looked away.

"Irene."

I took her arm, she looked back at me and I let her go.

"You know I'm attracted to you, and I think you're attracted to me too." I knew it from the tiniest extra beat that existed between us, circling, albeit subtly. A clump of her short wavy brown hair, which she wore parted on the side and pushed back, had fallen over her forehead, and I wanted to put it in place with my fingers.

"I'm already involved," she said.

"But are you attracted to me, that's all I'm asking."

She sighed. "I'm involved." We stood facing each other.

"He's married," I said.

She unwound the strap from her wrist, put the strap back around her shoulder, turned. "I knew you'd say that."

We simultaneously started walking toward Fifth.

"Doesn't that matter?" I said.

"Not really."

"Not really? Are you in love with him?"

"No." She was putting her script in her bag.

Then what, I thought, was he that great in bed? She had a father complex? He had to be forty. We had come to the sidewalk.

"You spend more time with me and Patrick than him," I reminded her. "You see him, what, for an hour or two now and then if you're lucky?"

She stopped walking again, as angry as I was, and to avoid people passing she moved to the edge of the sidewalk, near an iron fence and a building. I followed her.

"Well?" She looked away, at the Washington Square arch and the park.

"Patrick never does this," she said.

"Does what?" I laughed. "Patrick's gay, of course he doesn't."

"I know he's gay. That's not what I meant." But it was very Irene to skip over a detail like that. Bright as she was, being fresh out of Kansas, there was an occasional gap in her knowledge of life that you could drive a bus through.

She turned and looked at me fiercely, her eyes very dark, her mouth taut. "I thought you liked me."

I laughed again, "I like you fine, I—"

"No. I thought you liked me." Her face had softened and I softened inside, but I still felt driven, and sad then, I realized, almost despairing. I wanted to say, Oh, I like you, I like you so much, I'm afraid I'm falling in love with you.

"Robert?"

"It's okay," I said.

"We could, I mean, we could sleep together if you want to, but. . . ."

"What?" I wasn't sure I had heard her correctly.

"If you want to sleep together, then—"

"Irene, don't." I said it too harshly; I touched her arm, said softly, "Don't, okay?" I hadn't wanted her to say it, especially not like that. I had wanted it only to happen and it hadn't, and now I wanted to forget it.

"Okay," she said.

"You wanna walk?"

"Yes."

I didn't know if I had in a sense forced her to say what she did or whether it was her way of telling me that she *was* attracted to me, Neal or no Neal. But rather than analyze it, I did what I usually did when my pride was offended: I covered my tracks, I changed the subject, and I mentally erased the whole incident. I'd gotten so good at this, I didn't even quite know I did it, it was that second nature. We entered the park and stood watching the children and the mothers at the swings. One little kid was wearing a stocking cap and when he'd go up on the swing the tassle would rise, so at the utmost arc of his ride the cap would stand straight up from his head like a cone.

THE PALL OF THE argument faded. Somehow I knew that already a bond had been forged between her and Patrick and me and that, whatever happened, I wanted her in my life. Already, we had become a family. For a thousand reasons. For one or two. We were living the scene we rehearsed, that was one. We wanted to be Leo and Gilda and Otto. We all had a need for closeness, continuity, and we all hated our childhoods. On this last point Patrick lied, claiming, "We're insanely happy. There are eight of us. We're rather like the Kennedys." They were Irish Catholic and lived in New England, but I suspected, based on his family's turnout at a showcase he'd done the previous year—one lone tall sister—that that was the family he wished he had.

3 The Beginning

In early December Irene went on in the play on East Fourth. It was only for a night. That night, for some reason, Gina Lloyd, the girl Irene was standby for, couldn't make it and Irene called me that morning to ask me to come. Then she called Patrick. Then Patrick called me. "Look outside," he said. I went to the window and peered out the blinds: it looked gray. "Okay, what?" I said, back on the phone. It was a Saturday morning and I wasn't quite awake.

"They have predicted six inches by tomorrow," he said. "It isn't enough that she got absolutely no notice, so there isn't time to get anyone to come. Now, it will snow."

"Maybe it won't."

"Well, it *will*," Patrick answered. "Just pray, or whatever you do in emergencies, and maybe it will wait until eleven-thirty-five." On Saturday nights they did two performances, at eight and at ten. Irene had instructed us to come to the ten o'clock show since she'd need the first show to warm up. He and I discussed having flowers delivered before the first curtain.

"She's nervous," Patrick said, "so she's being a drip. She isn't worried about the snow and said that it might be better if nobody comes."

"She doesn't mean it."

"She won't even call Andre, I'll have to call him."

"Can he get a ticket?"

"Well, if it snows that won't be any problem. But no, they're sold out. Fortuitously, she has three comps."

"You want to have dinner?"

"Yes, if I can eat."

We agreed on a time. I hung up, put on the water in the kitchen, and pulled up the blinds. The sky looked metallic, a silvery gray with a hard, brittle light, and its density did not bode well. I looked at my watch: in less than ten hours she would be onstage. I wouldn't have liked going on as she had to tonight, with only the two weeks of standby rehearsals the previous month. And Gina Lloyd was good. But of course all of this made the night more exciting.

After dark the sky turned into a wadded, purplish mass. Patrick rang the buzzer at 7:35. He was wearing a suit and tie and his cashmere overcoat. I had on jeans and a sweater and my bomber jacket. "I'd tell you to change," Patrick said, "but we have to pick up the flowers in Chelsea," and he headed back down the stairs. "You said you were having them sent," I called after him.

"I'm getting a cab!"

I caught up with him and we got a cab on Ninth Avenue.

"Twenty-first and Seventh," he said. "Then we'll continue on to East Fourth."

"We'll never get there in time," I said.

"We'll make it," he said. "I know this incredibly artistic man, he used to be a dancer but now he's working in flowers. If you wire, it's always the same old thing. Reginald is creating an original."

We got out in front of what looked like a closed discount plant store. Patrick knocked on the door. It was 7:40. "Don't worry," he said.

Someone opened the door from within a darkened space.

"Reginald," Patrick said, "you got fat."

"You didn't," Reginald said, cuffing Patrick affectionately on the arm. "You look exactly the same."

"Well, cut down on the sweets," Patrick said. "This is Robert." He lit a Gauloise. "Where is it?"

"I just finished." We followed the broad back of Reginald, practically all I could see, through a path between trees. The rich smell of wet soil and evergreen reminded me of the snow that hadn't come, and I felt a good prescient jolt of tension in my chest, telling me that tonight would go well. We entered a small lighted workroom to the rear of the store. "Momentarily," Reginald said, holding a finger next to his wide pinkish face. He turned to open an aluminum door in the wall and brought out a tall arrangement and set it on a counter.

It was awful. The vase, a tubular shiny black ceramic, was about sixteen inches high; from it shot two parallel sticks. Another stick was propped horizontally between them, and at one of its ends was suspended a row of red berries. Three long-stemmed red roses and a burst of evergreen effectively floated among the sticks, and one snowball mum, propped up with wire, nodded off to the side like a pale, recalcitrant sun.

"I thought, something festive," said Reginald. "You know, for Christmas."

"Yes," Patrick said. He looked at me.

"Yes," I agreed. "It's sort of—Oriental." I glanced at my watch.

Reginald told us the price and I nudged Patrick. "Pardon us," Patrick said. "A brief conference."

We stepped out of the workroom and into the darkness. "Tell him to take out the roses," I whispered to Patrick, "give us nine more and let's go."

"I can't do that. He'd be hurt."

"Is anything wrong?" Reginald called.

"We'll be right there," Patrick said, "go ahead and wrap it up."

"Okay," I said, "I don't care." It was too late to argue.

Back at the counter Reginald said to Patrick, "You haven't seen Benton, have you?"

"Who?" Patrick asked.

"God, I just think of him and I never miss dancing," Reginald said.
So Benton was a person, I thought.

"Stay away from him," Reginald said.

"I'd love to chat," Patrick said, meaning exactly the opposite, "but
we must run." We signed the card, paid, and dashed back to the cab.
But we got stuck in traffic and when we pulled up in front of the theater, they had already closed the doors to the house.

We stood on the sidewalk. "This isn't our night," I said.

Patrick looked up at the sky. "Come on, let's get dinner," he said.
We walked away, Patrick holding the red and green tissue-swathed
arrangement. We had a couple of Bushmills, straight up, at the restaurant on the corner. A pipe had broken in the kitchen and they weren't
serving food, which made us postpone our dinner; we'd eat with Irene.
We had another drink. The arrangement sat on the chair between us
at our table by the window.

"So who's Benton?" I asked.

Patrick pulled away enough of the tissue so that Reginald's master-
piece was fully revealed. "Robert," he said, after digesting the thing for
a minute or two, "should we still give it to her?"

I was aware that he had pointedly ignored my question, but I decided not to pursue it. "The vase isn't bad," I said. "We could dump
it all out and just give her the vase." This, Patrick considered.

"Frankly, Robert, Reginald wasn't much of a dancer either," he said.
We each took a rose and left the arrangement in the chair.

Outside the sky hung low and the cars moved smoothly and strongly
beneath it, like sharks underwater. A crowd was collecting in front of
the theater. The first show had let out, but they hadn't yet opened to
seat for the second one. Two limos pulled up; people leaned off the
curb, hailing cabs. We went into the lobby and didn't see Andre.

"Oh, I'm so nervous," said Patrick.

We shuffled around, hoping to overhear comments on Irene's performance, but everyone chattered away about everything other than
the play. The house was nice, with plush seats and a red curtain. It was

an eclectic crowd: college students, lumberjack men, East Village divas in feathers, leather types, and nondescript people craning their heads toward the flamboyant. The show's hard-core fans called out to each other in shrill, excited voices, embraced, blew kisses, waved scarves so their bright colors leaped and shot through the air like party streamers. The room pulsed at the edges of my mildly drunk consciousness, and, as the house lights went down, broke into scattered bursts of applause and shouts and with a crinkling of papers and coughs settled into a smooth, breathing mass as the illumined stage blazed through the darkness.

Patrick sank into his seat, in fear. Andre was whisked down the aisle and seated beside us. When the star entered, with Irene in tow—she had to be dragged on the stage like a limp, helpless kitten—and stopped, struck her pose, and slowly, deliciously, spoke her first line, the stage was already so hot that the laughter went on for a minute or more. Irene played the role differently than Gina Lloyd, with a dead-on earnestness, and she played it precisely, her reactions as full and funny as anything she said. As soon as I could tell that the house had accepted her, were delighting in her, I relaxed.

Then, in the tradition of seventies theater, at the end of the first scene Irene's character had to be totally nude. It was quick, a flash in the light before blackout. I knew it was coming but even so—there, white in the darkness, in the big block of light underneath the proscenium arch, was her body. It was uncanny. I thought that my sexual feelings for her had been tucked away for the day in the future when she would tire of Neal Parks and come to her senses and love me. But when I saw her I felt myself jump. What I felt wasn't sexual; I felt a shock at how she was exposed, and I wanted to protect her. I wanted to tell her to stop, to come down, to be sensible and to choose another life. Then it was gone, her body suspended above us like an image, or a sacrifice; and what I'd felt was still lurking in my skin. I told myself it was the Bushmills. I should have had dinner.

The production surged on, rolling over us, pulling at us with its pace, its bright wit, its harsh edge. Irene's character changed, like an old Hollywood heroine, from the amazed little girl we had seen at the beginning into a tough, steely "dame." I thought clearly—yes, she would soon be a star. At the end she ran up the aisle to the back of the house and rushed into the arms of the director. Then she ran back to the stage and Patrick was laughing and stomping his feet—then we were all standing and clapping. After the bows the cast formed a tableau, a silhouette of arched backs and cigarettes; the stage lights blacked, and then the houselights came on. There was an inaudible collective sigh.

"In the future," Patrick said, "Gina Lloyd may stay home."

A man in the row ahead of us with a handlebar mustache and a brown leather vest turned and said pensively, "I don't know. . . . She's good, I'll give you that. The new girl is good."

"She's not good, she's fabulous," Patrick replied. "It's an absolute case of the Carol Haney-Shirley MacLaine syndrome, dear."

Knitting his brow, the man turned away, thinking about it.

"Mother of God," Patrick said. "To be in a *hit!* I am so thrilled I'm about to explode. Well?" he said to Andre, who had started to file up the aisle; Patrick and I may as well have been clinging to his back as we followed, awaiting his pronouncement. But he only spoke when we reached the lobby, where I saw, through the glass, the start of the snow.

"Unfortunately, I must be off," he said.

"No," said Patrick, "you're not going backstage?"

Andre hadn't even taken off his coat, in his characteristic way. I'd never seen him arrive at the theater except in a rush, and at the end of a play he always darted for the door.

"Thank you for inviting me, Patrick," he said. "Tell Irene I am pleased with the work and on Monday I will give her a note on the end of scene four." He pulled up the collar of his London Fog coat, and hurried off in the gathering flurries of snow.

"Well, he came," I said to Patrick, who looked let down.

"Thank God we're here," and he turned to the box office, "or she'd never know how brilliant she was."

We retrieved our roses from the usher, who'd kept them for us in a tin can of water. As we waited outside of the dressing rooms Patrick said, "When I went on in the Fosse production a friend of mine came back and told me, 'All right, I have suggestions, but I know what you need to hear first is that you were good.' So I'll tell you, to start, you were good, you were very, very good."

"What was the criticism?" I asked him.

"Oh, I don't remember. That wasn't important."

She knew she'd been good. On her dressing-room table was a spectacular multicolored bouquet from Neal Parks.

We went to Lady Astor's, beautiful in the window seats with the snow falling outside. Long velvet drapes, candlelight, and the tinkling of glasses. We ate red steaks and drank a bottle of good red wine. Our conversation—of Andre, of the show, of how Irene's life would be changed, once Gina Lloyd had moved on and the role became hers—was buoyant, overlapping, until sated on food and liquor and the excitement of the night, we subsided against the cushions of the booth, none of us talking, while Patrick smoked. I watched the black night through the tall rectangular window, made blacker by the whiteness of falling snow.

Irene took my hand across the table and then took Patrick's. "Do you know, it's the beginning," she said. "I know it now, there isn't anything I would rather do."

"I wouldn't mind being kept by somebody fabulously wealthy and attractive who adored me to distraction," Patrick said.

"Oh, be quiet." She lifted his hand and then put it back firmly on the table.

"Soon it will be a new year," she said. She was feeling fervent and sentimental and this was her night. She looked almost plain in her street clothes, face clean of stage makeup. "And this is the year we will always remember, since this is the year it is all going to start."

She poured what was left of the wine into our glasses and offered a toast, saying too too dramatically, her head high, eyelids at half-mast,

"It will be heaven in seventy-seven." We laughed and drank. We got into our coats and went out in the snow and walked in the middle of the white street, where the snow was thick and there weren't any cars. Patrick whistled a plaintive tune, testing the air, and Irene ran up ahead trying to slide, ran back and told us that it wasn't slick enough yet, and made Patrick give her a ride on his back. She climbed up on the hood of a car and put her arms around his neck and wrapped her legs around his waist. He groaned, but she could not have weighed more than a hundred pounds.

4 Histories

"You had to be a tea bag?" Irene said. "How'd you do that?" She relit the joint and passed it across the table to me.

"I don't know, you hunch down. You sort of—expand."

"Like they're putting you in the hot water?"

"Yeah. Oh, I remember. My arm was the string." I took a hit off the joint and got down on the floor and demonstrated. We were at Patrick's, and Patrick was ignoring us. The table was littered with half-eaten cartons of Chinese takeout and Patrick sat apart from us, in an easy chair near the couch. I had been telling Carnegie Mellon stories to Irene; Patrick was listening to the John Coltrane/Johnny Hartman rendition of "Lush Life" for about the tenth time, looking dour. He never smoked dope. The ashtray on the small table in front of him overflowed with butts. I got up from the floor. "Hey," I said. "Hey, Patrick."

Irene turned in her chair and looked at him. "Hey," she said.

He didn't answer and she looked back at me and shrugged.

"How many times you gonna listen to that song?" I asked him. It ended, he got up and put it on again, sat back down and lit another cigarette. I sat down at the table again and relit the joint. Patrick's place was one large room, with an alcove for his bed. He had a cut-glass decanter for sherry, silver flatware, a subscription to the *New Yorker*. The apartment was exactingly neat, except for the shelves on brackets surrounding his bed, which were so overloaded with books that they threatened to topple and kill him in his sleep. Dominating the main room was a glossy painting of the Ansonia Hotel, bought during the run of his first Broadway show.

"What was I saying?" I said to Irene.

"Um . . . I don't remember." She dug an egg roll out of a crumpled paper bag.

"Isn't that cold?" I asked her. "Tea bags. Then I had to be a block in a baby's playpen."

"I don't get what that has to do with acting." She studied the egg roll. "This is gross, why am I eating this? Robert, why am I eating this?"

"How should I know?"

"You want it?"

"No, I don't want it."

"You want it?" she said to Patrick. He glowered; she giggled. He ate practically nothing, subsisted for days on champagne and Häagen-Dazs coffee ice cream.

It was mid-November, several weeks before Irene went on in the show. That evening we had performed our scene in Andre's class to unanimous acclaim. Andre said Irene was a "marvelous, magical little gamin," I was "coming along," and Patrick "was better here than in anything we have seen him do yet." We weren't surprised. But after Andre spoke to us, he dismissed Irene and me and left Patrick sitting alone in front of the class. Patrick looked happy, loving the extra attention. Andre said, "Isn't it so that if an actor has a quality, naturally he should let it be? That is, if he comes to me and I see that he can be sensitive, let us say, at the drop of the hat, this we will not need to work on." Patrick shifted in his chair. "It would be fair for me to say please, do not bring in scenes in which you are sensitive, yes? I would want him to work on the opposite quality." Patrick agreed. "You are very good at style," Andre said. Patrick said, "Thank you."

"Many actors," Andre said, "do not understand style. From now on you'll please bring me Odets, or Miller. Maybe some nice Michael Weller."

Patrick inclined his head as though he couldn't quite hear. "Realism?"

Andre nodded, "The kitchen, the sink. It is time."

Patrick's great shoulders drooped; his chest caved in toward his spine.

"Or," Andre said, "give me kings. Give me Shakespeare, but please. Do not do any longer what all of us know you can do."

Irene put back the egg roll, got up from the table, and sat on the arm of Patrick's chair. "Oh, c'mon." She wrapped her arm around his neck and patted his shoulder. "There, there."

"Watson," I said. "Elaine Watson." Earlier, we'd been discussing new names for her. I picked up our list and went and sat on the couch. "Walters isn't bad."

"That's practically Walpers. Maybe I should just leave it."

"Maybe you *should,*" I said, as if she had come up with a wildly original idea. I had briefly tried Bob just because my mother hated it, but soon I'd switched back.

"Scrunch over," Irene told Patrick. She sank into the space between the arm of his chair and his lean right hip.

"Darling," Patrick said, "you know I love you, now get up and go sit on the couch." Instead she went to the window by the door and opened it wide; a cool rush of air swept into the room.

"We should go out," she told us.

"Go ahead," Patrick said, disinterestedly. His song had ended and he didn't move to play it again; the cigarette smoke drifted out of the room. He stood, took the list from me, and ripped it up, then took it and the ashtray to the trash in the kitchen corner.

"You don't have to do Weller or whatever," said Irene, sitting down beside me on the couch—she took off her boots—"just do kings."

"Yes," Patrick said, returning, "I'll have to do kings."

"Richard two and three," she said, "then the Henrys."

"Introduce me to your father," Patrick said to me.

"Why?" I said quickly, suddenly tense.

"Well, for obvious reasons." My stepfather was a Renaissance scholar, and I understood that Patrick wanted to confer with him about the kings. David would be flattered; he would spend hours with Patrick and they'd become friends. I could see it, the two of them sitting up past midnight in the study, my mother looking fetching in her emerald robe, plying them hourly with steaming Turkish tea and exquisite finger snacks delivered unobtrusively, geishalike, to the door.

"No," I said. He'd been trying to meet my parents for months. In most instances I found Patrick's rapacious curiosity amusing, but not here. I intended to keep the different portions of my life *separate*, cleanly divided, one from another. There was my life in graduate school, then my life with Andre, Patrick, and Irene. My restaurant life three days a week was in a drab Ukrainian restaurant on the Lower East Side. There was my sex life, consigned to the depths and shadows of department stores. Distinct, things were easier. It was difficult, for instance, to believe I was an actor destined for greatness while wielding a sponge across the slimy surface of a table at lunch hour. I told people I was a student of law. I sat back against Patrick's couch and acted impassive. Irene sat closer to Patrick, her denimed legs tucked neatly underneath her. They started to speak as though I wasn't there. Patrick propped his chin on the steeple he'd made of his hands.

"Has he told you anything about his parents?"

"Not much," she said, frowning and trying to look like a scientist.

"His mother is supposedly young and incredibly beautiful," he said. "Name of Marilyn, as in Monroe. She was a chorus girl when *he* arrived," he continued, nodding at me. "He was practically born in a trunk."

"Oh, Jesus," I said. Irene looked rapt.

"His stepfather is eminent for his knowledge of Shakespeare, they travel all over the world. These are sophisticated, interesting people and yet—" He lowered his voice. "*He* keeps them hidden away in

New Jersey. They live in Fort Lee for God's sake, and I've never even seen them."

"Well, Robert, really," she said to me, playing along.

"Oh, you'll see," Patrick said, as if warning her of the fatal defect in my character. "The next time he has a good part in a show, heed the way he encourages you to come on a Thursday, and how Thursday will never be the night the parents appear."

"Why?" Irene said as herself.

"I don't hide them away," I said to Patrick, annoyed.

"He does," Patrick said to Irene. "You begin to imagine huge walk-in closets with padlocks, filled with skeletons, or cash. . . ."

I HAD TO GIVE in or come off as a hopeless neurotic. I promised to take him along to Fort Lee at the end of the month, amends for Thanksgiving when I had to work. Irene was to go too, but when the day arrived she was shooting her first commercial, a before-and-after bit for a cold medication.

A little stack of annotated Penguin editions of plays about kings rested on Patrick's knee on our trip out of the city. He studied his notes and then, from the bus, looked pacifically at the scenery. It was a vigorous November day, the sky full of wind and blustering clouds. As the bus rolled over the George Washington Bridge, I watched the boats gliding across the water below us, above us the shining cables soaring into the sky. "I might have liked the life of a scholar," he said. "Long hours in the library, only the whispering sound of pages turning."

"I'd have to get out," I said. "I only lasted through college because I was an acting major and hardly had to study."

"I suppose I'm imbalanced. All those years of staring at my body in the mirror, you know, at the expense of my mind."

"Do you miss it?" I was thinking of my mother.

"Dancing?" He looked away, out the window. "I don't think about it. It makes me too sad." We rumbled past the toll booths and into Fort Lee, past the shops in back of the thick, wind-filled air, emblazoned with light. My mother had given up her own dancing after my father had left us, and her bitterness over that and all my father had cost her was still with her. He had died just last year. True to form, she'd decided it was inconsequential that I know. He had stepped out of a bar, as he did every night after leaving the theater, and into the path of an oncoming taxi. It swerved but he fell, hitting his head sharply on the fender of a parked car, dying instantly, they said. I heard five days later, when David called me against my mother's wishes. Since then, I'd kept a layer of coolness between her and myself. As a child I'd been crazy about my mother. I couldn't remember being unaware of her beauty: her straight dark hair, cut at an angle so it sliced across her face, her sharp brown eyes, her lush body.

When I was in school, she'd pick me up and we'd often go into New York. At five and six I was obsessed with all things medieval. We'd go to the Metropolitan Museum. I loved armor, and she waited patiently as I circled glass cases enclosing the impressive metal men. Once, going home as the sun set—the gold light tinting her red coat orange— she stopped, touched my shoulder, and said, "I have to sit down." We were walking along Fifth Avenue by Central Park and I followed her to a bench. She was crying. I held her hand, hating the stares of people passing by.

"You don't have to worry," I said. "I will take care of you. I am your knight."

"Oh, baby, no, I take care of *you*. You're my little boy," she said, pulling me to her.

I remember collapsing against her with relief. I'd forgotten that I was still a child, and as we got up and walked on, the world looked distinctly lighter, more hopeful than it had in all of the time that I could recall.

She'd taken a job in New Jersey selling makeup and doing runway modeling at a local department store. She'd talk about dancing again, and took classes to stay in shape. But once David, her savior, came along, dancing was "what she did as a girl." She dedicated herself to the marriage with a fury I couldn't understand. Suddenly our lives were thoroughly shaped by what she perceived to be his needs: We must always be quiet while David was reading; we must never make a mess because David isn't used to children; we mustn't speak at the table since David is accustomed to adult conversation.

When I was nine, I remember wandering into the living room where I heard their low voices. They stood facing each other, in profile. She had on her silk pajamas and he was still dressed. She moved close to him, taking his arms, and slid down along his body, dropping to her knees. "I would do anything for you," she said, pressing her face to the base of his stomach, her arms encircling his hips. How could she? I'd thought angrily. *Pledging* herself to this stranger who seemed to have nothing to do with *our* twinship, our doubled lost lives?

My PARENTS' APARTMENT was in the town's first residential high-rise, on an undeveloped expanse of brown land. It had a spectacular view of the city, all glass and cool light. As we knocked on the door I warned Patrick to take off his shoes, since my mother had covered the floors with white carpet. She herself had on four-inch heels, but these were a pair of her "indoor shoes."

"You must be Patrick," she said. "I'm so glad to meet you." Her dark hair gleamed, chopped into a fringe above her eyes and just north of her shoulders; she wore a stylish formfitting pantsuit in a soft shade of gray.

"Hi, Mom," I said, kissing her cheek. "Where's David?"

"What a beautiful home," Patrick told her. "May I have a short tour? I've heard *so much* about you." He followed her into the living room. He wasn't being polite, he really liked corny middle-class things. He thought they were sweet. After poking my head into David's study, I went to the kitchen and opened the refrigerator.

"David's gone out for snacks," she announced, walking into the kitchen with Patrick smiling beatifically behind her. She put on tea, and shortly thereafter, David showed up, rumpled, a caricature of a

professor. He had misplaced the list she had given him and lost a button on his best cardigan sweater in the car. "My," he said, shaking
Patrick's hand, "you are certainly tall. I have an associate, in the history department, Saul Tabor—Marilyn, you know Saul. Saul is six-
five. I believe you are taller than that." David was five-nine or ten, a
shade taller than my mother.

"Yes," Patrick said, "I'm taller than that."

"How tall is your father?" David asked. He took his glasses out
of his pocket and put them on, for a better look at Patrick. He
stood shoeless in the doorway to the kitchen in his coat, still holding
a bag.

"Not as tall as I am," Patrick said.

"You have any brothers?" David said.

"Yes, I have four."

"How tall are they?"

"David, please," my mother said, "you're embarrassing Patrick."
She took the bag from him and attended to the snacks. The plan was
for my mother and me to run errands while David and Patrick discussed the kings. We left them in David's study with a snack table
laden with tea and an assortment of biscuits, cheeses, and nuts.

As soon as we got out the door, she started in. "You never call me
anymore."

"I've been busy."

"Where did you get this horrible jacket?" She reached out to touch
it—my leather—then squeamishly withdrew her hand and finished
tying the belt to her trench coat. Her high-heeled boots clicked on the
floor of the elevator.

"Patrick is lovely. I've seen him dance. What was it, some tacky little show by that person who thinks he's Michael Bennett—? Anyway
it was Broadway and your friend was featured. He would have to be
featured, that height." She may have had to quit dancing but she remained an expert. "You say he was hurt?"

"Knee, on a jump."

"Shame." We headed out of the elevator and into the parking garage.

"How was he?" I asked.

"In the show?" She unlocked the car, paused, put a many-ringed hand to her mouth: "He was—oh, very good." She sighed. "Here, drive," she said, tossing me the keys. "Take me to Teaneck."

"Teaneck? What for?"

"I've got something to show you."

I pulled the Dodge out as she took an Aquafilter from her purse and stuck in a mentholated Benson & Hedges; I heard the snap of her lighter. "Mom, open the window," I said.

"Oh, sorry." She cracked it.

"I thought you quit."

"Well I did, I only smoke two or three a day." I cranked my window all the way down. "Robert," she said, "why do you insist on treating me like a leper?" I rolled it back up. I was looking forward to the drive, if we managed not to bicker. I liked driving and missed it in the city. I took a scenic route through neighborhoods nestled into hills, sloping down into a valley of parks and schools and autumn-swept woods, the streets flooded with leaves.

"Honey, are you happy?" she said.

"Mom. What kind of question is that?" As usual, she was wearing Shalimar. The smell of it was faint in the car, and mingled with the lingering scent of cigarette smoke and the smell of burning leaves outside.

"Are you seeing anyone?"

"What, like a girl?"

"I suppose you wouldn't tell me if you were."

"I don't like girls," I said.

"Sure."

"You know me so well?"

"Yes, I do." Good old Marilyn, basically unshockable. "Honey, you know," she said, "you don't have to work. Now that you've gone back to school, David and I are willing—"

"You're paying tuition and rent, that's enough."

"You should focus on your—"

"You want to leave me some pride here, Mom? And while you're at it, am I allowed privacy? I know what I'm doing. I really don't need you to dictate my life."

"God, you're touchy. What's wrong, did you have a bad audition or something?"

"Stop it."

"Stop here." We were coming into Teaneck and there was a strip mall to our right. "I just need to pick something up."

I parked, and watched her walk into a stationer's store. A guy maybe in his thirties with shoulder-length hair, who had come out of a bakery several doors down, looked her over, very openly. "Fuck you," I said, through the window.

Men were always looking at her and making comments. When I was younger it thrilled me. But lately I wondered whether it would ever end. I rested my arms on top of the steering wheel. The wind had died down, the light weakened in the late afternoon. What she had implied was that if I didn't work I could see her more often. Which I had no intention of doing.

She got back in the car and told me to turn left at the next intersection. Just past the Dairy Queen and an Interstate Bank we pulled into a parking lot, shielded on one side with a coppice of trees; on the other a cinder-block wall, demarcating an area for junked cars by a service station. But at the center was a small low building with shingled facing and a freshly painted sign reading MARI-JEANNETTE'S. The "s" swept back and underlined the letters, the "i" was dotted with a star.

"Wow," I said, genuinely pleased. "Is this what I think it is?" For years she had hinted about starting a dancing school with a friend; I had never believed her.

"Jeannette put in bigger money so she gets her whole name. But I'll do more teaching so I come first."

Inside it smelled of wood and varnish, the tang of fresh paint. "They're doing the floors," my mother said, beaming. But no one was there. The larger of the two studios was finished; rays of light from the windows glanced off the wall of mirror and shot down onto the lustrous honey-colored floor. She knelt at the door, checking the floor for tackiness with her finger. "All right," she said.

"It's beautiful," I told her.

"What this room needs is sweat," she said.

"I'm proud of you, Mom."

"Oh, well," she said, brushing my compliment off with a hand, "I need occupation. You'll be required to come to recitals of course. Three year olds dressed up like daisies and falling all over the stage." A phone rang. "Phones," she said, "they've put in the phones! Be right back."

I went up to the mirror, curious as to how it attached to the wall. Bolts. Two pieces. *You know what I did in those studios?* Patrick had asked me. *I learned to fly. Oh Robert, the work it takes to fly. Cracked feet splitting open and bleeding. Bones aching so you couldn't remember what it felt like to live without pain. The life of the body. When I didn't dance anymore I had so much free time. I didn't know what to do with myself. There were nights I'd wake up thinking No, I missed class. You couldn't miss class, it was worse than missing Mass, if you'll pardon the rhyme. And then I'd remember. There were days I would fear that my body was rotting. Slowly weakening away, at last hopelessly atrophied. I wasn't used to it being this case that only served to carry me around.*

My mother had danced from the age of three and hadn't stopped—"not for more than two days, except for when you were born"—until my father deserted her.

I backed away from the mirror, abruptly cognizant of my own reflection as she came heel-clicking back down the hall and her figure filled the doorway. "Why didn't you tell me?" I said. "Why couldn't you have told me he died?" I stepped back against the wall, felt the barre dig into my waist.

She put her hands in her coat pockets and said, "Well, it's good you're asking me, you've been thinking it, obviously, for so long that—"

I felt my heart opening up like a flower; I tried to stand casually and as I waited it seemed that finally something would change. But then she leaned into the door frame so that she looked tough.

"Robert, he destroyed my fucking youth."

"Forget it," I said.

"Forget it? How can I forget it?"

"I've heard this before," I said weakly.

"Really. Then why did you bother to ask?"

"Can't it for once be about me and not you?" I was shouting.

She turned and walked off down the hall. The barre at my back, I bent toward the floor, my hands pressed to my thighs, feeling crushingly lonely, dizzy with all of the things that rushed in my soul, bits and pieces of the past that would not lie down.

She sat at the edge of the desk in the reception area, about to light a cigarette. "No," I said, taking it from her and putting it back in the pack. Since she couldn't smoke she pretended to cry; dabbed at her eyes with a balled-up Kleenex fished from her purse. "Today of all days," she said.

AT HOME, DAVID and Patrick had switched from snacks to cocktails. I sat with them in the study, nursing a beer and stifling yawns while my mother fixed dinner and David held forth on the War of the Roses. But at dinner I must have come to. As we sat beneath the chandelier—the dimmer turned low to set off the lights of the city in the distance, the glow from the white couches and chairs of the living room, like ghosts afloat in the darkness—David said, "Marilyn, Patrick's a Harvard man."

"Really?" she said. "What a small world."

"Well, Avery's Harvard, fifty-two. Walter's twenty-nine. In the math department," he explained to Patrick, "old as the hills." David was a

Cornell man, forty-four. He launched into one of his favorite stories of how he'd chosen Cornell over Yale.

Patrick smiled at him, entranced, and delicately nibbled at the tiny wing of his Rock Cornish hen. With the hens we had almond wild rice and cranberry relish, which struck me as suspiciously reminiscent of Thanksgiving. Patrick had dressed up, wearing a tie, his herringbone jacket, and a new pair of gray flannel trousers with razor-sharp creases. But his hair had grown quite long and didn't stand up as it usually did; he'd tried to grease it into a style with a part, but as stiff and coarse as it was it had partially escaped, so that he looked vaguely electrified.

"You never told me you'd been to Harvard," I said to him later, as we cleared the table.

"But I must have," he answered.

"No, when?"

"After I left New York," he said.

"But I thought you went to Europe."

"I did go to Europe, but later."

"Oh. When were you in California then?" I was sure he had mentioned California.

"Briefly," he said, with a sniff. "California. Cowboys and Indians and the movies, there isn't much to do."

"And where did you have the operation?" I asked. On his knee.

"Why, in Boston, Robert. I'm sure I told you. Freshman year I was a handicapped student at Harvard. It worked out fine. All these smart, well-groomed people offering to carry my books."

I loaded the dishwasher while my mother showed Patrick her scrapbooks in the living room: my mother as a ballerina; with Agnes de Mille; as a Rockette. ("A Rockette!" I heard Patrick exclaim.)

The second Patrick and I hit the lobby I shouted, "Jesus, *Goddamn.*"

"Was it awful for you?" Patrick said.

"No," I said, but the brisk night air felt good, bracing. There were faint stars in the huge black arc of the sky.

"I'm sorry, but I like them very much."

"That's all right. They like you."

"Do they?"

"Oh yeah. Harvard, huh?"

"It's not such an outstanding achievement. My father and brothers went there. If they didn't, I wouldn't have even gotten in."

"What do they do?" I said.

"Something terribly boring. I don't remember."

"Business?" Patrick lived off a small trust. He strode steadily forward, his eyes fixed on the lights of the bridge up ahead.

"Marilyn looks a lot like you," he said. "A feminine version, of course."

"Do you see them much? Your family. You ever get up to Boston?"

"Not often." Typical, I thought. He replied to questions about his past with terse answers and let subjects drop.

"Who's Benton?" I asked. We had come to the bus stop, a bench underneath a blue plastic kiosk. Patrick sat, and took out his cigarettes.

"Did you hear me?" I said.

"I heard you." The beam of a street lamp cast a bluish tinge over Patrick's face, enhancing an appearance of strain and exhaustion.

"The florist, Reginald," I went on, "said you should stay away from him. Why?"

"I'd prefer not to discuss it," said Patrick.

"Reginald said he had something to do with dancing." Then lucky for him, the bus pulled up. Equally lucky, two girls seated across from us were coming home from what seemed like a party. They laughed and talked drunkenly, making our conversation impossible. They wore tight pants with tremendous bell-bottoms, sported shags with pieces of hair directed out at their cheeks and down onto their necks like tendrils. Patrick smiled fondly, but he looked drawn and disturbed. I wondered what in the world I had inadvertently hit upon. I recalled the night he had shown up at my apartment, bloodied—recalled his distracted responses to my questions then, his abrupt dismissal.

At the terminal we headed toward the downtown subway and the girls stumbled off in the other direction, singing a Cher song.

"Ah, youth," Patrick said.

All of the newstands and snack shops were closed. We went down the ramp, the sound of our footsteps echoing off the tiled walls of the tunnel.

On the platform he said, in tones of tender appeasement and strange, wistful apology, "Benton is no one. Benton is more—a bad frame of mind. To be avoided at all costs, you see."

The train sounded close by in the bowels of the earth and I had a quick, dreadful vision of my father's death, the swerve of the cab, his feet flying out from underneath him, the strike of his head against the fender and the fall to the street where he lay on his side, his cheek pressed to the asphalt, next to the tire. We got onto the train, where an old man was sleeping. Above his head was a horizontal poster of one of the last "Miss Subways." She had an old-fashioned hairstyle, teased at the crown and curved into a flip at the ends, and the copy said she lived in Far Rockaway, Queens. The train lumbered into motion, started picking up speed, and for an instant lost its lights so I couldn't see Patrick beside me: I felt a grip in my gut. We rushed ahead into the dark as if we were rushing toward something voracious and unstoppably real.

5 Winter

Winter was eternal that year. The snow and the cold were relentless, and as the weeks and months crept along I began to forget that the trees had been green, and it seemed we had always lived in this stripped barren place, rushing from one lighted shelter to another. In January, a young and newly successful comedian named Freddie Prinze stuck a gun in his mouth and blew out the back of his head. Patrick did Henry IV, Prince Hal, and the Richards, but none of them succeeded. I could see that he was going through the motions. Acting was not the departure from myself that I had hoped it would be, but rather a journey into the very parts of myself I thought it would rescue me from. And Patrick held himself at a remove, walking trippingly among the mines. Irene and I sat at the back of the class dying for him. After each monologue he'd sit and listen to Andre's criticism, a pleasant expression on his long reddish face, his hair cut again to its normal upstanding length, as tall sitting down as many of the class standing up. And one day as I watched him it occurred to me: How will he survive? Who will *hire* him? But more than anyone I'd ever met, Patrick was who he was *in spite of.* Who knew? I said to Irene. Maybe the air he breathed was thinner than ours. Maybe it took a while for things to reach him, up there where he lived. If anyone should have been able to play Shakespeare it was Patrick. What are the kings if not gigantic, glorious inventions?

Irene's work, on the other hand, had gotten so raw you could hardly watch it. One snowy day, the wind howling outside, the sky dark at 3:30 in the afternoon, our classroom so cold we were all wearing jackets, she showed up in a wisp of a nightgown and did a Maggie in *After the Fall* I will never forget. In the scene she becomes frightened; she imagines smoke billowing out from the closet, and by the time Irene got to the speech she went pale, white as a sheet. What, Andre asked, had she put in the closet to achieve that moment? "I saw myself dead," she answered.

My own work felt glib. I turned to directing in graduate school— and I began an affair with Brenda, a sexy, complicated woman I picked up at Saks.

I met her at the end of January, the same day I had my first big fight with Irene. Irene had remained unflinchingly devoted to Neal. Neal was a gambler. Poor Neal, she would say, he owes all this money. He also had a child with an expensive disability. We were stomping through snow on Great Jones Street after attending a call for a show that was already obviously cast. I was in a bad mood; I didn't have time for dead ends. Irene's descriptions of the roles had tantalized me into coming.

There were faint gray smudges under her eyes. Gina Lloyd, her unwitting nemesis, continued on in the show on East Fourth; might never leave, and this stroke of bad luck was consuming Irene. Her hair was shoved into a red felt hat and the rest of her was draped in an enormous black woolen cape. I hated the cape; she looked like a kid playing dress-up.

"I'm beside myself, Robert," she said. "I've tried not to think of it all morning, but Neal called me last night and it's bad. The bottom fell out on pork bellies. He owes thousands and thousands of dollars." A red-mittened hand appeared from the recesses of the black cape to smite at her heart. "He's already in debt, as you know, and—"

I stopped, snow whirling around us, and said, "I don't care."

"What do you mean?"

"What I said. I don't care. I don't know Neal."

"You're selfish, Robert." She looked like a waif, a match girl, a worker for the Salvation Army.

"I'm selfish? Here's a guy with a wife and child and a girlfriend on the side—I'll let that one slip by, all right?" She was glaring at me. "What I won't let slip by, what strikes me as nearly obscene, is how Neal, who's got half the ad agencies in the city begging him to take more of their money, who's got the whole network of CBS under his thumb, is determined to throw it all away." I took a breath. A bit hyperbolic, but the point had been made.

"I mean everybody I know," I addended to my previous statement, "with one-eighth of what he's got going would think they were in paradise."

"But I care about him."

I motioned in the direction of Broadway. "I'm going uptown," I told her.

"You said you had a class."

"I do. I'm skipping it."

"To do what?"

"I'm going to bring my possessions out to the street and hold a yard sale for Neal."

Christ, it was cold. I walked to the corner, and she followed me. He could sell his Jaguar, and Irene could sell the presents he'd bought for her too. Now gracing her living room was a big fat color TV. (On which to watch Neal?) He'd given her a set of *Encyclopaedia Britannica*, for research, in a bookcase with a "genuine walnut-stained facade." It was pathetic how unimpressive his gifts were, as though he knew it wouldn't take much to keep her. I wondered whether he still took her to the Waldorf-Astoria.

"What's wrong?" she asked. We had stopped again, at the corner. I wanted to go. "Nothing."

"We'll be by the restaurant tonight." She and Patrick often stopped by for a drink near the end of my shift.

"I'm worried about Patrick," she said. "Let me know later how you think he seems."

I looked at the gray patches under her eyes; the small bones in her face looked sharper, like she'd lost weight.

"Y'know, you look terrible," I said.

"Thanks."

"Why don't you slow down? There was no reason to go to that call."

"You didn't have to come if you didn't want to."

"You wanted me to come."

"Thanks for the favor." Her eyes were a hard crystalline blue. "You have the loveliest way of showing you care."

She turned and started down Broadway, calling back, "I just remembered, I can't make it tonight."

Snow was packed at the collar of my jacket, was melting down my neck in icy rivulets. I had lost my damn scarf. Some guy with a briefcase knocked into me and I shouted, "Excuse me," then headed uptown. I went about three snowy blocks before hailing a cab. Extravagant, dumb, skipping class, taking cabs in the middle of the day.

The driver was a woman, with beautiful smooth chocolate skin. She had the heater full blast, and we traveled slowly in the snow. She glanced at me in the rearview mirror and I smiled. Here was the problem: you couldn't be friends with a woman you'd once had a crush on.

People labored along on the sidewalks. The light was weird; fuzzy and bright. The greens, reds, and yellows of the stoplights glowed through the falling snow; I watched the sweep of the wipers, the windshield filling with whiteness and then clearing. The driver had a bushy Afro. I wondered what it would feel like to touch: springy, soft, like the stuffing used to pack china. On Lexington Avenue headlights went on and the snow, the quiet cars, the hurrying people—the women in their pretty coats—became otherwordly, eroticized, slow, like a setting in a movie.

We pulled up beside Saks. I smiled at the driver again and tipped her hugely, letting my fingers brush the skin of her palm as I gave her the money. It wasn't natural, I thought, to live without love. Even the mannequins in the windows looked good. Of late, I had had one torrid night with Candace the stewardess who told me in the morning that she was engaged. I went inside Saks and down the wet aisles between the women selling makeup and perfume. I got on the escalator, rising up among the junk, all of it looking superfluous, tainted, forlorn with the holidays gone, like the day after an expensive failed show.

I'd come to the men's department. There was a fabulous head of long hair bent over an underwear rack: dark, glossy, as sleek as the hair of a violin bow. I couldn't see her face. Married. Yes, that would be fine. She looked up—a face like a Siamese cat, compact, finely wrought—and, damn, if I didn't know her. I walked over to her anyway. She stared at me, trying to place me. Brown eyes, almost black. White, white skin.

"Robert Holt."

"Brenda." Rough, sexy voice.

"Drama crit," I reminded her. "How come you're not in class?" I asked.

She sized me up a second longer, replaced a package of Jockey briefs, said, "Exhaustion, despair." She lifted her brow in a look that said, You?

"I needed socks."

"I'm married," she told me. "Unhappily so."

I must have come upon her at the perfect psychological moment.

"You want to get coffee?" I said.

She shrugged.

I bought a pair of socks for verisimilitude, and we went to the store restaurant and sat at a table that rocked whenever I changed my position in the slightest. Brenda ordered water; coffee, she said, gave her the jitters. She kept her jacket on.

"What made you decide on directing?" I asked. She looked bored, sitting low in her chair, her long legs stretched under the table, cramping mine. "Are you an actress?"

"God, no."

I set my elbows on the table and it wobbled prodigiously, so the coffee sloshed out on the saucer; Brenda's water tossed in the glass. "I've worked in film," she said. "I've done sets. . . ." Her eyes said, I've been around. "I'm going into directing for power."

"Oh." At least she was honest.

"I'll probably fail and wind up as somebody's secretary."

"I don't think so."

"Why not?" She waited for an answer.

"Well, I was being polite but—" I was paralyzed, my hands now in my lap, not daring to touch the table or go for the coffee. "You're obviously a determined person—"

"You know what I'd like?" she said, interrupting. I had no idea. "I'd like to be the head of a studio. I'd like to be William Paley. I'd like to fire people and sign checks for millions of dollars."

I imagined her body, lean, paradoxically pliant. I took a chance and slunk down in my chair, stretched my legs out alongside of hers. She didn't move.

"You're nice," she said. How would she know.

"You're gorgeous." A pause, her eyes studying me.

"I'm thirty," she told me.

"Oh, really?" I pressed my leg against hers; the table shivered, stilled. "You have some time?" I asked her.

"You have an apartment?"

David had given me a MasterCard at Christmas for use in emergencies and it was burning a hole in my pocket. We went to the Waldorf-Astoria.

After that we established a schedule: Tuesdays and Thursdays, 1:40 to 2:55. We both had a break between classes and we met at school, in an obscure costume storage room to which Brenda had procured a

key. It was hot there, and dark, the windows blacked out, the only il-
lumination coming from a droplight we found near the couch. As soon
as we got the door shut we'd be pulling at each other's clothes, feeling our way to the couch, knocking into the dust-smelling garments
hanging heavily around us. One of us would reach down to turn on
the light and then it got slow, languid, our bodies slick from the heat.
Having skipped lunch we'd be hungry, and I'd bring bags of nuts we
fed to each other, still locked together.

Leaving was hell—the mad dash to the rest room, where I attempted to clean myself up with the wood-chipped industrial paper
towels, under the glaring fluorescent lights.

Brenda was as different from Irene as a woman could get. She'd
grown up in the Village, the child of communists who had marched for
the Rosenbergs in the fifties. Her husband was a public defender, and
I enjoyed imagining her on the edge of great danger, the target of a kid-
napping plot being devised by thugs her husband had sent to the
Tombs, as I held her in my arms. She and her husband were embroiled
in a struggle for power, she explained.

I was finished with my longing-for-love phase. My new passion for
directing had me in a focused-on-nothing-but-work phase, with
Brenda taking care of my libido. Irene proclaimed that after the high
moral tone I had taken with her for sleeping with a married man, I was
acting like a hypocrite. When she met Brenda her eyes went straight to
the ring, and she gave me a withering stare. By then, Irene was driving me crazy. As the winter wore on, her angst, and her yearning for
justice in a business that had promised her near-instant glory and then
reneged on the deal, began to grate on my nerves.

THE NEXT STEP in Gina Lloyd's precarious career had fallen
through, leaving Irene behind, stuck where she was. One night around
six she showed up at my door, drawn and mournful, that now familiar darkness beneath her blue eyes. I'd had a great day with Brenda,
then running lights for a play I'd designed. I can't say I was happy to

see her. Lately I hadn't called her as often, and I would sometimes cancel when the three of us had plans.

"I didn't know what to do," she said. "I've been walking."

"Come in," I said. "I'll make coffee."

She removed her wet cape and spread it over a chair in the kitchen. She stood near me at the stove sighing, rubbing her arms desultorily; she sat down in one of the chairs, put her hands on her knees, and gazed at the floor.

"I went on in the show last night. Gina was sick." Her head sank lower. "I was terrible, Robert, I was *terrible*. I was stiff. Everyone knew, they felt it. I hadn't had rehearsal since when? November." She got up and went to the window above the sink: it faced a wall, and falling snow. "I hate winter," she said.

The kettle whistled. I poured the water over the coffee grounds.

"Today, know what I did?" she said. "I'd had an audition for some pilot at CBS—well, they taped the audition and sent it to the Coast, but then changed the part I was up for to a man. However, they thought I was lovely, or *somebody* thought I was lovely because I was summoned today, to this cathedral of an office." She chewed on a thumbnail. "This woman casts for the movies in LA. She'd like me to call her when I go on in the show, or have a part on TV, it doesn't have to be much, ten or twelve lines. Or when I'm on Broadway." She laughed. "I wanted to tell her that I can't get seen for off Broadway, let alone Broadway!"

She turned from the window. She held herself, at the sink, and I focused on her sweater, tight at the midriff. Her waist looked so small, I thought I could encircle it with my hands. "All of these things are happening to me," she said, "and yet nothing happens." She sat down at the table.

"It will," I said.

"*Oh God*," she stretched her arms out along the table and slapped it—"I was *terrible* last night, you can't know." She sat up straight. "It was humiliating. . . . 'Be patient,' Lynn Singer tells me today, 'you're a good commercial type'—forget the fact I don't *get* commercials. You know it's much harder to get a theater agent as long as I'm tied up with Lynn." She picked up her coffee, set it back down. "I just walked in the snow." She looked back at the window distractedly, then at the clock. "God, I gotta go." She got up, packaged herself in the cape.

"I've gotta go," she said again. And that was that. Two or three days went by before I heard from her again. She called me one morning about eleven o'clock.

"Listen, I can't reach Patrick. I've been trying for days. I've left messages on his service and he won't call me back."

It was a Sunday. He'd had a general audition for the Manhattan Theatre Club on Wednesday. It probably hadn't gone well. He had been optimistic, had read an entire script to me on the phone as a rehearsal.

"He's probably in bed," I told her.

"Why? Is he sick?"

"I doubt it. Sometimes he just goes to bed. Like for a week."

"Don't you worry?" she asked.

"Tomorrow is Andre's class. He'll show by then."

"I don't like this. . . . We should go up there."

"I can't. I'm working tonight and I've got a thousand—"

"How would you feel if something happened to him? We'd never know, no one would know."

"You're overreacting."

"You're underreacting."

"Irene—"

"I'm going. Come or don't come, it's your choice." She hung up. I kicked a leg of the telephone table and the whole thing collapsed.

"Oh, terrific," I said.

I grabbed my jacket, looked out the front windows: another beautiful day. There was a little wind, and it raked up the top layer of snow from the ground, swirling it over the street. If she wasn't feeling hysterical herself, I thought, she assumed everyone else was. I picked up the phone again and called Patrick, but he didn't answer.

When I got to his building she stood at the top of the steps, studying the roster of tenants. "I rang him forever," she said.

"Try it again," I told her.

She pressed the buzzer. He lived on the fourth floor, at the top. "Could he hear us if we yell?"

"He's in the back."

"Oh, that's right. What if I can get one of the ground-floor neighbors to let us out to their garden, y'know? We could throw stones." She rang a few of the buzzers and nobody answered. Finally a man stuck his head out a window on the second floor.

"Whaddaya want?" he called down.

"I'm sorry for bothering you," Irene said. Then she looked back at me, "We could ask the—"

"It's freezing, y'know that?" the man said.

"Would you mind telling me where we might find the super?" she said.

"There aren't any apartments here," the man said. "Everybody's lived here for years." He had a black beard and he pulled at it, nervously.

"We don't want an apartment," she said. "You're the super?"

I realized she was about to ask him to let us into Patrick's apartment, which I thought was an inexcusable invasion of privacy. But by now she'd succeeded in freaking me out. "We're a little concerned about our friend," I said, "one of the tenants. Patrick O'Doherty?"

"O'Doherty?" said the super. "I don't know O'Doherty."

"Very tall?" Irene said.

"Oh, *O'Doherty*. What's the matter?"

Irene explained, and the super shut his window and appeared a minute later at the front door. "Okay, c'mon." We trooped up the stairs.

"What's he got," said the super, "mental problems?"

"We just want to be sure he's all right," Irene said.

"Sometimes," said the super, "an old lady falls down. Sometimes it's drugs. I got six buildings here on this street and sooner or later, couple times a year, something's gonna happen." Cheery guy, I thought.

Judging by his darkly restrained excitement, these calamities were the high points of his life.

He shook his head ominously, and banged on the door. There wasn't any answer. "Okay," he said quietly, "I'm gonna open it up."

He unlocked it and the door swung open.

We stepped in. "Patrick?" Irene said.

"Patrick," I said.

He peeked timidly around the corner of the alcove, "Robert? Irene?"

"I don't have better things to do," said the super, looking disappointed. "O'Doherty, answer your phone," and he left.

"Thank you!" called Irene. "We're terribly sorry."

Patrick sat weakly back down on his bed. "I thought he was a burglar, I thought I was through."

"Guess I'll go," I said to Irene, annoyed. "She was worried," I said to Patrick.

"I'm depressed," he told her.

She sat down beside him, "But you can't just lie down and give up." I looked at the book he'd been reading, *Vanity Fair*.

"You don't understand," he said. "I hate myself when I'm like this."

"It isn't *your* fault," she said.

"I'm going," I said.

"I'm depressed too," she said, "Robert's depressed."

"No, I'm not."

She ignored me. "Everybody's depressed. It's winter. No one I know has gotten a part in anything for months. It's not only you."

He lay down again, folding his long pale hands on the lap of his robe. "Go away."

She stood, and, changing her tactics, said, "Patrick. How many days have you been in this bed? Since Wednesday?"

"I think so," he answered her tentatively.

"Get up," she said. "I mean it. Go take a shower and get dressed. We're going out." He didn't move.

"Go on," Irene said. "We'll go to a movie, I'll make us lunch."

When I left, the shower was running and Irene was in the kitchen opening a can of chicken noodle soup. If she had convinced my super to open my apartment I would have been livid. And yet I had to admit that she was good for him. But her inference that I didn't care irked me. If *I* had ordered him out of bed he would have never spoken to me again. And why did she say that I, too, was depressed? *Was* I depressed? Last night I had dreamed about my father—a dream in which everything was pervaded by the murkiness of his absence. I roamed the earth in a perpetual fog, where objects and people kept dissolving into mist.

The thing I liked about directing was that it was not about me. Not as acting was. As a director I had to step back. Only then could I distinguish the meaning of the parts. Directing was about concept, about surfaces as well as depths; it was formal and even logical. Being submerged in a *self* could never be.

IN MARCH, PATRICK appeared in a Sam Shepard play. It was poor, both the production and his performance, but my parents came opening night, Patrick's old friend Maria, and Irene and me. Then we all went out to a gloomy basement bar near the theater. My mother wore what I called her Ethel Merman fur, and got on quite well with Irene, who was charming, if thinner than ever. Maria had come with a very young, very handsome man named José, whom she ignored.

"So, tell me," Maria said, turning to me, "how is he? Really."

She wore her hair pulled back tightly, had a long thin nose, liquidy eyes, nails like talons. Maria had taken care of Patrick when he hurt his knee, and he had said he would die for her. He'd known her since he had first come to New York, when they worked together as dancers. I'd seen her on Broadway; she was wildly successful.

"How, really, is Patrick," I said cynically. She leaned forward, wrapping her hand with the red daggers around her glass. Her blouse bared the tops of her small, lovely breasts and I found it difficult to keep my eyes on her face.

"How do I say it," said Maria, "he's well? He's happy?"

"Yeah, sure."

Her eyes dropped to the table, mine to her chest, she looked up, my eyes leaped to her face—and I saw that her expression could not have been any more serious.

"As far as you know," she said in a low voice, "he isn't seeing Benton, is he?"

Who the hell *was* this guy? "Benton who?" I said. "I don't know him." Something about Maria made me cautious.

"Oh . . . Really?" She opened her purse and took out a card, held it out to me. "I want you to do me a favor. Just please, if Patrick sees Benton—as far as you know, call me, yes?"

With, I'll admit, a wolfish leer at her breasts, I accepted the card.

My mother and David got up to leave and after they'd said goodbye, Maria called to Patrick. "Patrick, I want to *dance*." She arose from the table like a queen and he took her hand.

I looked at José, who was shredding a napkin, and said, "So, José, what do you do?"

"I'm a dancer," he said without looking up. What a night.

Maria and Patrick started lightly, doing disco, but got gradually stagier, adding complicated moves, swing steps and lifts, and soon the others on the dance floor sat down and they took over the space. It hit me with a jolt, with a visceral shock of adjustment, that Patrick was dancing. He was amazing. I had always thought of him as elegant, but disembodied somehow, willfully detached. Now I could see him as he must have been on the stage: elemental, immediate. I had this strange feeling of seeing him for the first time, or of discovering a person that until now I had only glanced at. Patrick hoisted Maria from one side of his body to another, spun her away from him, spun her back, turned, let her drop, caught her at the last second with his arm; she threw back her head and laughed, and they were in motion again.

I turned to Irene and said, "Hey, wanna dance?"

She laughed. "Oh yeah, sure."

The song ended and a new song began, with a slower, irregular beat.

Maria and Patrick did a syncopated Ginger and Fred. At the end Maria returned to the table sweaty and flushed, lifting Patrick's arm in the air like after a knockout: "*This* is a man," she said, "this is a *dancer.*"

"Thank you very much, Maria," he said, limping. "I'll be in agony tomorrow." She barked something in Spanish to José, who put money on the table and gathered their coats. She hadn't let go of Patrick's hand; she half sat, half leaned against the end of the table and pulled him to her. It was settled that Patrick would share a cab home with Maria and José. I would wait for Irene, who had disappeared and was taking forever coming back to the table. The three of them left and took with them the life of the place. Irene showed up and wanted to finish her beer.

"So what did you tell him about tonight?" she said, after a pause.

"What, about the show? Not much, I liked his entrance."

"What else?" she said. "What else are you planning to tell him?"

"Nothing," I said.

"For God's sake, Robert."

"What?"

"He was shitty in that show tonight, and you're not going to tell him?"

"Why should I?"

"He has more talent than both of us put together," she said. "But it won't amount to anything if he doesn't take it seriously."

"Why don't you tell him?"

"I will. But he needs to hear it from you."

"Why from me?"

"He listens to you."

I stared at her, miffed. I did not feel like getting sucked into Irene and Maria's dire need to look after Patrick. I hated how everything this winter was a crisis. Apparently he had an affair with the mysterious Benton that did not work out well. Why should I watch for his re-appearance? I didn't even know Maria, and as far as I did, everything about her struck me as exaggerated. Patrick was already given to drama and posturing; he didn't need any encouragement.

"Where do you think he went at Christmas?" Irene asked.

"He went to LA," I said.

"But that isn't where his family lives," she said, "and why was he so secretive about it?"

"He said he went to visit a friend, Irene. Friend, I imagine, meaning lover. And despite his protestations, you have surely figured out that Patrick doesn't get along with his family, yes?"

"Why wouldn't he say he was visiting a lover?"

I picked up her beer and drank it, then beckoned for the check. "Oh c'mon, you know how he values all things—genteel. It fits in with his general attitude, as if he's above sex. Christ," I said, "can we get a check?"

Irene wasn't in a hurry. "I just feel so worried about him, since Christmas. He doesn't seem right."

"Why don't you stop it. Why don't you stop worrying about Patrick and Neal and the business—God, Irene, sometimes these days I don't even know you."

"Well, I don't know you," she said stonily.

"Translation?"

She looked off at the empty dance floor. "I can't talk to you anymore. You're not interested in talking to me."

"Oh, right, *I'm* the problem."

"I make you deeply, fundamentally uncomfortable, don't I, Robert?"

"What's that supposed to—"

"Forget it," she said, "can we forget it?"

"Fine with me." We got the bill and paid it and left.

The night was bone-crushingly cold. We walked in silence down Broadway.

"You're getting a cab?" I asked. I could walk home.

"Yes," she said.

I turned west, but feeling guilty checked back and saw a cab go shooting right by her. She hadn't hailed it, only walked onward, small in her long black cape.

I ran to catch up with her, "Irene," and she turned as though I had slapped her. "Aren't you getting a cab?" I asked.

"I'm walking."

"It's cold, it's late," I said. "You can't."

A cab pulled up and I opened the door. Once she was inside I leaned in. "Drop it, will you?" I said. "I'll call you."

She turned away.

I walked home as quickly as I could, but I couldn't sleep. My mind raced. I didn't know who was wrong or right. I fell asleep and then a snatch of conversation replayed itself in my head. Maybe I was wrong for distrusting Maria, but I didn't see why I should trust anyone. Then I couldn't feel at all who I was or how I felt and my pulse and my heart boomed in the dark. I put on the light, listened to a couple of Lou Reed songs on the radio, stared at the walls of my ugly, ugly room.

IRENE AND I TALKED on the phone the next week and ended up fighting again.

"Give me your opinion," she said. "I want to break with Lynn Singer, and I'm thinking of quitting the show. Lynn's doing nothing for me, and Gina will die in that show."

"There's an expression, Irene," I said, sighing. "A bird in the hand is worth—"

"You don't understand! I can't take this anymore! I have to do *something*."

"Calm down," I said.

"Calm down," she repeated, and quietly seethed.

"This business is hard," I reminded her. "Did you just get that news?" To her silence I added, "Look, if you didn't want my advice, then why did you ask?"

"You're so fucking selfish, Robert. I think you've found your true niche in directing. Egomaniacs seem to flourish there," she said, and hung up.

As it happened, her show closed three days after our disagreement. There was a small fire backstage, damaging props and a section of the curtain, and management used it as an excuse to cancel.

It closed during the first week of April when everything had thawed. The city was liquid and then there was one final freeze, a shower of snow and a few days of suspended, soul-testing cold. Brenda's husband had gone out of town and we'd planned to spend the night together alone, but Patrick had tickets to a new show for all of us and Brenda wanted to go. Afterward, at Jimmy Ray's, Patrick was courtly; Brenda liked him as I knew she would. Irene, chain-smoking, carried on about how rotten the show was—the acting, the directing, the acts were too long.

Outside it was too cold to even walk a block, and Brenda and I got into a cab. She said, "Boy, the play wasn't that bad."

"Irene isn't herself lately," I said. "She isn't usually negative. She's been under stress. Career stuff. I think you'd really like her if you got to know her."

Outside the door to my apartment, Brenda said, "You're a little in love with her, aren't you?"

I got her inside, pulled her to me, and said, "I'm a little in love with you." We stood kissing, leaning against the door, still in our coats. "Put on music, light candles, distract me. I'm feeling guilty," Brenda said.

My spirits sank, momentarily, with the thought that there wasn't an act in the world that did not carry with it complications.

I had a radio and plenty of candles. I lit a dozen of them and set them around the room. I'd bought champagne, and while I poured it she put up her hair. It would come down, littering the bed with the bobby pins she'd used. But we tried to keep it up since frequently, in the heat of passion, I'd flip her over, and the next thing I knew she'd be crying "Ow, don't, you're pulling my hair." I wondered if this occurred with her husband, though I assumed that it didn't. I pictured him as supernaturally graceful, making love in a suit.

Before we fell asleep I got up and blew out the candles, and as bluish light leaked through the blinds and I felt her warmth, we drowsily made love again. Then I awoke and the room was fully lit from the open blinds in the living room. She slept soundly, her hair scattered darkly over the sheets. I put on my shirt and went to close the blinds, when the phone rang. It was Irene.

"Robert?"

"Just a sec, okay?" I set down the phone; I was standing in the freezing cold foyer without any pants.

I shut the bedroom door gently so Brenda wouldn't wake up.

"Were you asleep?" Irene said.

"No. What's wrong?"

"Well, last night Patrick and I, we went to Bradley's." I glanced into the kitchen at the clock; it was already noon. "So it was late by the time I got home." She heaved a long sigh. "You know, usually, Patrick comes in and walks me to the door, but it was really late and I told him to go on—" I thought she'd been attacked, hurt. "And I went in," she said, "and. . . ."

"Irene? Are you okay?" My heart pounded.

"Oh yeah, yes. But, you see, I came in last night and Ruth had tried to kill herself. I found her, and I had to get her to the hospital, and now, really, everything's okay, and I came back here and cleaned everything up. But then I thought I should try to sleep—I don't feel like I can."

"You want me to come down?" I said. I was already calculating how long it would take.

"Would you?"

"Yeah, listen. Give me half an hour."

"Thanks, Robert. I'm just—"

"I'll see you soon."

"Okay, bye." Clean it up, she had said. Then there had to be blood. I took a quick shower, then I sat on the bed and kissed Brenda lightly.

"Oh, hi," she said, putting her head in my lap.

"Brenda, wake up."

She blinked, "Why are you dressed?"

I told her and she sat up, hugging a pillow to her chest, "But why do you have to go? She's not lying there and dying at this moment, is she?"

I stood and said, "I'll see you later."

"No, you won't. I'm at tremendous risk being here, you know that. I don't have all day."

"Then I'll talk to you later."

Brenda got up and strode past me and into the bathroom. I followed her, but the door closed and was locked.

The shower went on and I left, thinking, well, that could be that. I didn't give a damn. There was crunchy ice on the front steps; the air was very cold, stinging my face, and I felt that freezing sensation inside my nose. The scant row of trees lining the street, each one small, ever struggling, wore icy jackets that sparkled in the sunlight.

Irene opened the door to the freezing apartment in a T-shirt and jeans. I looked down at St. Martin and saw the short fur on his back being ruffled by air coming from somewhere behind them. "Hi," she said.

"Hi." I kissed her on the cheek. I heard a sound like the tinkling of bells. "You have the windows open?" I asked, closing the door. I went past her to the first room off the hall, a sort of cloakroom, and saw the long curtains flapping. The window was open wide; next to it hats hung on the wall, and many scarves were waving in the breeze. I shut the window, and as I did, saw that one of the scarves had tiny bells sewn to its hem; when the window was down the sound stopped. She stood in the doorway. "Go put something on," I told her.

"I felt I should air out the apartment," she said.

We went to the next room, her room, and while I closed the window she took the photographs off her footlocker and rummaged for a sweater. "Look what Patrick got me last night," she said, indicating a bunch of violets in a small crystal vase.

I closed the rest of the windows, and in the bathroom I saw that the shower curtain was missing. I knew that whatever she had done she'd done here, although there were no other signs. It smelled of disinfectant.

Irene sat on the edge of her bed, in a sweater and socks, St. Martin looking up at her with what so appeared to be a sympathetic expression that I almost liked him. I sat at her other side, put my arm around her. She felt tense and was shivering. I got her back against the pillows and pulled up the blanket, dislodging St. Martin, who screeched at me and hissed. "Glad to see he hasn't changed," I said, and she laughed a little.

"I'm so happy to see you," she said. She had her knees drawn up and she buried her face in the blanket that covered them.

"Are you warmer?" I asked her.

"Yes," and she looked back at me.

"You could have called me last night," I said.

"No."

"Or you could have called Patrick to come back."

"No, well, he said that he wasn't going home. He was planning to stay out. I wouldn't have called him anyway. There wasn't time. She'd —cut her wrists. She was lying in the bathroom, out cold." She shuddered. "I thought she was dead, and her hair . . . her beautiful dark red hair . . . was matted with blood."

"I'm sorry," I said.

"I reached her mother on the phone," Irene said. "She's flying in tonight."

"That's good," I said.

"Yes." Her eyes were glassy, steel blue; their light flickered, dimmed.

"What is it?" I asked.

"It never crossed my mind that she would do this," she said, "that she was capable of this." She gazed at the floor. "I mean, there was always something wrong with her, one thing or the other. But she's had a good career—she won an Obie, did you know that? A few years ago. Things hadn't gone well lately—*God.*" She bit off the word, made a fist of her hand, pressed it to her mouth, and brought it down; when she looked back at me her eyes changed again, suddenly wary. She had wanted me here, but all that had happened between us over the winter came up like a wall.

A lump rose in my throat. "Can you sleep?" I asked her.

"I think so."

"Look, I'll stay though," I said. "I'll just sit in the living room for a while to be sure you're okay."

"You will?"

"Yes." I stood.

"Robert? Thanks." She settled into the bed and I shut the door gently.

I thought of Ruth's hair. I thought Irene was strong and brave. I thought that whatever our differences, every time I saw her act I fell in love with her again. It all made me sad. I looked out the windows down to the street. Shadows lay on the sidewalks. People hurried by, bent from the cold. Watching her act was like watching a girl out in dark space alone. Fearless. Electric with life. I thought of the violets Patrick had bought her, and how he had said he was staying out. And then I realized what should have been obvious. He'd been going to pick someone up. I had never really considered how it was for him being gay, and now as I did the idea of shame rose in my mind; shame co-existed with secrets. It didn't make sense in reference to Patrick, and yet it did.

I thought again of Ruth's hair, which was thick, very rich in color, and remembered once thinking that it didn't fit her, her paleness, her thinness—as though it were heavy, as though all of her strength had been sapped to sustain it.

Now everything seemed deflated, drained of hope, by what she had done, and I hated her for it.

• • •

I LEARNED SOMETHING that night. I started to see how much my love for Irene had to do with what she was and what I was not, with her goodness, her generosity. She was, in fact, hopeful, as it was so hard for me to be. It was her hopefulness that let her down—her gorgeous, unbridled sense of expectation.

Spring came, and then it was June—the streets clean and golden. One day Irene and I went to the island park at Hudson and Bank to rehearse a scene. She wore a blue-and-white flowered halter dress, and the traffic and the bench we sat on all became part of the scene. Later we walked to the river, where people sunned on the piers.

"Irene," I said, "Patrick and I are going to Andre's theater to work for the summer." I'd dreaded telling her.

"Oh," she said, solemn, but seemingly fine.

"You're okay?" I said.

"I'm okay." I walked her home, went uptown—and as I opened my door the phone rang.

"Hi," she said, "it's me. I'm going too, he just called."

"Did you have a premonition?" I asked. "You took it awfully well."

"No, I didn't. Patrick told me yesterday morning. I threw things and cried for two hours."

"Well, he could have *told* me he told you, or you could have told me."

That night we sat out on Patrick's fire escape, the metal still warm, the smell of onions and garlic wafting out from the kitchen where he was cooking dinner. From the gardens voices rose and the sweet scent of flowers and trees. She was still wearing her blue dress, pulled up and bunched at her thighs so her legs were free—both of us hanging our legs off the side, holding the rail. Patrick was whistling. She had a sweater draped over her shoulders. Her knees were tan in the semi-darkness. The light behind her haloed her hair. It was a night perfectly free and open, cut loose from time. I thought that she felt as I did, as though the building behind us, the rail at our arms, the slats under our legs, were the flimsiest props and sets. Only we were real, suspended together in the clear, windless night: "Oh God," she said. "Robert, it's summer."

6 Summer School

Crispins was part of a summer arts festival scattered across three villages in Litchfield Hills, Connecticut, a bucolic place of rolling hills, farmland, and picturesque country inns. We bought bicycles, and rented a house down the lane from the small sign in the shape of an arrow reading DRAMA, THIS WAY. The house was at the edge of the larger of the three villages, where the theater was located. The arrow pointed the way to the yellow brick building that housed the stage and the theater's offices, not far from our rehearsal space in the town community center. The costume and scenic shops were closer to the main street, back doors flung open to an arbored walkway, in a huge white barnlike clapboard structure, a former hotel, whose upper stories housed apprentices and staff. The total area of Crispins covered only a mile, but in summer it jumped with activity. And in the mornings or the long afternoons, you would see Andre in his jaunty summer cap and jacket with the epaulets strolling his domain.

The attention he had lavished on Crispins for thirty years—people called it his wife and child—had paid off in its steady, quiet success, its understated prestige. Actors would kill to work there, but if Andre didn't like a person for whatever reason, even murder couldn't get him a job. Once there, we were all members of a quasi-extended family in a sort of summer camp for actors. "Here," Andre said in his opening address to the company, "star and novice alike, young and old, work together shoulder-to-shoulder for the love of the play." If the egalitarian ideal was not the reality, there was nonetheless an atmosphere of camaraderie. Everyone had left their regular lives and lived together, and, because Andre had handpicked each of us, we were a congenial group. Too congenial, perhaps.

We didn't all last until the end of the summer, as it turned out.

OF THE THREE OF US, my contract was the best going in. I was hired as a member of the Young Company, and did six roles that summer, the most valuable acting experience I yet had. Andre employed Patrick for the Main Stage. Bryan Johannes, the summer's leading man, was quite tall (*not* as tall as Patrick), and was breezy and dapper. Patrick was his standby—though in a stock season of short runs, Andre never intended Patrick to go on in Bryan's roles. Patrick was there for insurance, but mostly to play several bit parts.

To work at Crispins, an actress of Irene's age and experience had to be either non-Equity or famous, and Irene was neither. But Cynthia Brown, the ingenue lead in the opening Shaw, had been ill, and Andre needed a strong standby capable of playing the role. So Irene was hired, with the rest of her summer left up in the air, but with suggestions of two ingenue roles for later in the season that Andre hadn't yet cast.

As a director Andre was a wizard, masterful with actors, bringing halting scenes to life with a few whispered words. His black eyes darted from one cog in the Crispins' machine to another, the wheels in his largely impenetrable mind turned sixteen hours a day.

Patrick made it to Crispins because Andre liked him so much. Andre believed in his talent, believed it was there, only hiding. But Andre also drew sustenance from Patrick. By day two he had Patrick sitting behind him in rehearsal; in a frustrating moment Andre would turn and say, "So, Patrick, what do we do?" or "Where does that leave us?" And Patrick, knowing he was *not* being asked for a solution but for respite, would respond with a witticism or an encapsulated story, and Andre would laugh and turn back, refreshed, to the work.

Our house was a one-story brick-and-wood cottage on an acre of land. There was a small forest of birch, maple, and oak in back, and a farm down the road; we heard baying sheep and howling dogs at night from our screened-in back porch. Irene took one bedroom and I took the second. Patrick requested the handsome living room, using the cushions and an extension mat to sleep on the floor. Privacy wasn't an issue with him, since he rarely slept more than five hours; the last to bed and the first awake, he would, annoyingly, greet us in the morning, bright-eyed and showered. After rehearsal, we'd bike to town and buy groceries for dinner and linger in the twilight over beers on the porch, and these evenings were close to idyllic—ideal, complete.

One night a car pulled into our driveway as the last of the light vanished in the trees, and Irene, standing and tugging at the back of her cutoffs, said, "See ya later. I'm summoned to Andre's." She put on her socks and boots and departed. She looked gorgeous. Patrick got up and opened the door, peering out after her.

"I think it's Morris," he said.

"Not *Morris*," I answered.

"I'm sure it was Morris."

Andre didn't drive, and each year chose a minion from among the apprentices to serve as chauffeur. Morris was a skinny obnoxious guy who liked Fleetwood Mac; I couldn't believe he'd been chosen. Being chauffeur was a cushy, coveted job, a position of trust, and always led to another better job the following summer.

Someone in the office had leaked the details of Irene's unusual contract and there was talk that Andre was "interested" in her. I'd heard about this and was sure Patrick had too, but we hadn't said anything about it. Being summoned wasn't strange. Andre spent days in rehearsal and conducted business at night, at home. Since Irene's fate had not yet been determined, it was logical that he'd invited her to his house to discuss it.

We were running lines at the kitchen table when Irene returned: we heard the back door, but she attempted to walk down the hall right by us.

"Hi!" Patrick said cheerily.

"Oh, hello," Irene answered. She came in and sat down.

"So tell," Patrick said, lighting up a Gauloise.

"There isn't much to tell. Maybe Hermia in *Midsummer,* Masha in the Chekhov."

"Oh my God," Patrick said ecstatically: " 'I am in mourning for my life, I am unhappy. . . .' And you'd get to dip snuff."

"I know," she said, "it would be great."

"But he didn't say anything definite?" he asked. "You'd be a marvelous Nina—" and he recited, " 'Men, lions, eagles and partridges, all living things have completed their cycle of sorrow, are extinct. For thousands of years the earth has borne no living creatures on its surface, and this poor moon lights its lamp in vain.' "

"I'm going to bed," Irene said.

"Pleasant dreams, dearest!" he said to her back. "Something happened," he whispered.

"So it seems."

But in the morning we all went off to rehearsal as usual. I found Patrick on the green behind the community center at the end of the day, talking to Bryan. There was something distinctly movie-starrish about Bryan—a mild noblesse oblige, shades, and capped teeth. But his face was comfortably craggy, and I had seen him pacing the lobby of the theater one afternoon with his Shaw script, nervous, intent, and I'd thought: the work never changes then, despite fame—it springs from a central, universal place.

"I should go," Bryan said to Patrick, "I'll see you tomorrow," and nodding a friendly farewell to me, he crossed to the sidewalk that led to the street.

"Where's Irene?" I asked Patrick.

"She got a note telling her to see Jan in the office. We're to meet her at home."

We waited on the porch, and she came in presently, sat down, and looked out at the trees; I went to the kitchen and brought her a beer.

"Thanks," she said. "Let's eat out tonight, huh?" She took a long pull on the bottle. "Like a special occasion."

"What happened?" Patrick said.

"I don't know," she answered, "I honestly don't." She brought up her legs, and hooking the heels of her boots on a rung of the chair, propped her arms on her knees. "I go back to the city tomorrow. I was informed that with Cynthia, well, my services are no longer required."

"Shit," I said.

"Was Andre there in the office?" Patrick asked.

"Oh no," she said. "This is via Jan." Patrick and I were rendered momentarily speechless. "I feel funny," she said. "I've never been fired from anything. I've never imagined myself as the *kind* of person who is fired. . . ."

"Irene," Patrick said, "what happened last night?"

She was silent, then the pitch of her voice dropped. "He said he was attracted to me."

"No," I said, "are we in a movie?"

"Well, but it wasn't like o-o-o, sleep with me, baby, and you're in luck. He was acting uh, sexy, lounging on the couch, like in class with the chairs put together. God, I don't know . . . and asking me questions about myself." She set her beer on the floor. "Hinting at the roles, telling me he thought I was talented. We went outside to look at his pool and he put his arm around my waist and said I was pretty. I thanked him and he kissed me, but nice, like a father. I wanted to be gracious, and as soon as I could without being obvious about it, I moved away. I guess I wasn't supposed to do that."

"Irene," I said, "like a *father?*"

"Never mind," Patrick said, "go on."

"When I left," she said, "we were as friendly as when I arrived. But we were supposed to discuss the rest of my summer and we didn't."

"You don't seem surprised," Patrick remarked.

"Or shocked," I added.

"Because it goes back to last fall," she admitted. "He called me at home after my first scene in class. He got me the audition for the show on East Fourth. Sometimes we had drinks and dinner together, but I just felt flattered. He seemed interested in me as an actress."

"That's naturally part of the attraction," said Patrick. "Remember Samantha?"

"It's perfect," I said, "in a really disgusting way. It all fits."

"But he's such a cultivated person," she said quietly, sipping her second beer. It was dark and we had put on a light.

"Irene," I said, "he got you here hoping to get something going. He couldn't, so he's sending you home, and that isn't right."

"No, it isn't," said Patrick.

"But Cynthia really *was* sick," she protested. "And it's true that since I'm Equity they can't afford me, and maybe he didn't tell me that he had to let me go himself, because he feels badly about it."

"I think that Andre and Crispins will do fine," I said to her, "without you defending them."

"If only it were clearer," she said.

"It never is," Patrick replied.

"I feel awful," she said.

We all did.

"Now listen to me," Patrick said, sounding unusually adamant. "You are going to be perfectly fine. Because none of this has a thing to do with you or your abilities."

Overnight Patrick drew up a pact that we all signed in the morning.

"It says," he announced, "that in this ravaging business we must stick together. Therefore we pledge that whomever of us becomes powerful first will look after the others." I thought it was melodramatic, but Patrick seemed deadly serious about it and it seemed to make Irene feel better.

"In blood," Patrick said after signing, and producing a safety pin from his pocket, he pricked his thumb and then pressed it to the paper.

Irene giggled, and did the same.

"No," I said, when she handed the pin to me. "It looks dull. Get it out of my face, Irene. I signed the stupid thing, didn't I?"

Patrick looked stricken. "Oh, great," I said, "oh, brother. Okay, come on, give it to me," and I stuck the pin in so deep that blood ran onto my palm.

"Thank you, Robert," Patrick said.

Irene laughed. "Extremist," she said. "Next time try keeping it simple."

THERE WAS A FLURRY of gossip for two or three days, but attentions were soon diverted by an endless supply of more proximate scandal. Stacey, an apprentice and the daughter of a famous Broadway star, seemed determined to sleep with the entire company. That was only one of many offstage dramas. It was nice to get away and go out on tour to the Berkshires and then along the coast.

I found myself calling Irene. I told her about the towns we passed through, the details of the day's performance. The night she told me she had broken up with Neal, I hung up and said to myself: "Don't." I refused to set myself up for another rejection.

In a dream that night I made love to her on my mother's dining-room table, our images reflected in the luster of the wood, the light from the chandelier falling on our naked bodies. I awoke in a sweat, cursing my own imagination.

I began to flirt with a woman in our company named Alix. Alix reminded me of a young Katherine Hepburn. She was from Vermont and had a refreshing no-nonsense way about her—like Brenda, very different from Irene.

Mostly I lived through the summer drawing each ounce of passion spent on the stage back into myself, preternaturally aware of the faces of the other actors, their voices and motions, the constantly increasing and diminishing levels of the audiences' attention; I was alive in the moment of the play as I had never been before. I'd come out of the theater after a show, and the joy, the acute sense of life I'd feel, would spill over onto the world so that whatever my eyes alighted on—a rock, a tree—shimmered with significance. I stood by the harbor in Mystic so struck by the deep, white-capped green of the water, the nets of the fishermen spread across the decks of the creaking, rocking boats, that I fantasized about signing myself on to a ship. One afternoon I ate lunch on a grassy hill near the campus of Williams College and then lay back, hands under my head, to look at the sky. There was a crackly, restless quality to the air; the gigantic fluffy white clouds gathered and grew dark, moving and changing so rapidly, it was like time-lapse photography of a storm, like an old biblical film I had seen of the Creation. It was too beautiful to leave, and I lay watching until the entire sky was black and the thunder crashed and reverberated in the ground and the rain, at first softly and then in a torrential shower, soaked my whole body.

We returned to Crispins in July to rehearse a new cycle of plays, in time for the last performance of *A Midsummer Night's Dream*. Patrick had been cast as Starveling, one of the rustics. He and I were in the kitchen the next evening when Irene called. Patrick talked to her, "What? Oh, it isn't." He covered the mouthpiece and said to me, "There's a blackout in the city." Back to Irene, "Where are you? No, *do not* go up to Times Square. . . . I know it's exciting but stay in the Village, do you want to talk to Robert? All right, he'll call you tomorrow. Prudence! Good-bye." He shook his head and sat down at the table. "She hadn't considered that it could be dangerous. She thinks she's still in Kansas riding bucking broncos."

I went back on the road for ten days. When I called Irene, she'd broken from Lynn Singer. No matter what Lynn thought, Irene was not really a good commercial type; she wasn't ordinary looking enough. Her eyes were too far apart, watchful, changeable, deep. With those eyes you could never think she was exclusively any one thing.

"They make you look almost—sophisticated," I said.

"*They do?*"

"I said almost, Irene. Don't get your hopes up."

"Listen, I should meet you somewhere, see the shows, get out of the city. What I'll do," she said, "is come up for Andre's closing party and see you and Patrick both. I was a member of the company, if only for a week." It was a point of honor, to prove that she hadn't been bothered by what Andre had done.

WE WERE DOWN to rehearsing for our last cycle of plays. In the surprise of the summer, Clarence came out to act in the last two shows and moved into Irene's old room. Stacey, the promiscuous apprentice, had broken her foot, but gamely hobbled about on a cast with a rubber hoof and developed an embarrassing crush on me. I encountered her everywhere, looking up at me soulfully. I listened for her distinctive step-and-a-thump and ditched her when I could. It wasn't that she was bad looking; she had thick tawny hair and evocative, pale blue eyes. But she gave me the creeps.

Patrick thought it was a scream. "Stacey has been in lust many times," he told Clarence, "and we're talking daily. But never until Robert has she known love."

"Do you *mind*?" I said.

When Irene arrived she agreed to be my girlfriend for the party to keep Stacey at bay. "We'll stick next to each other like Siamese twins," she said. I picked her up at the bus stop alone. She disembarked, rumpled and pretty.

"Well then, you haven't been swallowed by the city," I said, and we walked to the theater. She didn't want to talk about herself.

"Later," she said. "For now let's pretend that my stupid life doesn't exist."

There was a shuttle service running to Andre's. We were picked up by Morris at six o'clock. We traveled down a dirt road and up a precipitous hill that veered sharply right through trees, throwing Irene, in the backseat between myself and Clarence, close against me. The road flattened out, running into a clearing that led to the house, and I said to her, "What's the story? Are we engaged? Are we living together? What?"

"Oh, definitely engaged, darling," she said, leaning into me. Clarence had a diamond pinky ring on and in the spirit of the evening, he lent it to her.

The house had manicured grounds, and the living room, opening out to glass doors displaying the pool, was elegantly appointed with Chinese antiques and a gleaming grand piano. It was already crowded, but much of the acting company hadn't yet arrived and most of the faces were strangers, people from the city. We spotted Andre, busy talking to someone, and passed through the dining room on out to the pool. Patrick and Clarence went back inside, leaving Irene and me alone by the bar.

"I feel awkward," she said. "Oh, not about you," she said. "Here, give me a kiss."

"Mm, good," I said, "Maraschino cherry."

She plucked another one off the bar and then slumped a little. "I shouldn't have come. I feel embarrassed."

"Andre is the one who should feel embarrassed, not you," I told her. "You want another drink?"

"Oh, all right." I turned and heard her say, "Take my hand, take my hand, I just saw Stacey."

Yes, there she was, pushing through people at the glass doors and heading, step-thump, in a beeline toward us. Irene wrapped an arm snugly around me, blotting out practically everything but the feel of her pressed to my side.

Stacey smiled up at me, sadly this time. "Hi, Robert. . . . Oh, hi, Irene."

"How are you, Stacey?" Irene said. "Have you had a good summer?"

"Yes," she answered. She plainly didn't know what to do with her hands; she folded and unfolded them and finally grabbed the sides of her dress. It was a nice summer dress; she'd clearly taken pains to look attractive.

"I'm sorry you hurt your foot," Irene said.

"Yes, well in two weeks I get the cast off."

"That's soon," Irene said.

"Good-bye," Stacey said abruptly, and thumped away.

"Let's get out of here," said Irene. "Let's go for a walk."

We crossed quickly through the house — pausing to bum a cigarette from Patrick for Irene — and ran down the front steps and off toward the road. As we went through the house we felt heads turn, and a group at the door stared at our linked hands. "They'll think we're off making mad, passionate love," she said. "Got a light?" I struck a match and touched it to her cigarette.

The paved drive turned into gravel and then a dirt road. "Can you walk in those shoes?" I asked. She'd traded in her boots for a pair of delicate high-heeled sandals; her legs looked good in anything, but in those shoes they were spectacular. "Sorta," she said, wobbling a little, and then she gave up, took off the shoes, and carried them.

"It's so pretty here, after being in the city." She looked up at the sun sinking into the trees. "Here, step." She threw the cigarette down and I put it out. "Robert? I didn't come to see you in New Haven because I was jealous. I still felt hurt and it would have been too hard to pretend I was happy for you. I'm sorry."

"That's okay," I said.

"If I'd just gotten a play in the city this summer, one measly play."

"There's less theater in the city in the summer. . . . How are things otherwise? How is Ruth?"

"Much better, very well really. She's engaged — like we are." She grinned, holding up Clarence's ring, and her face lit up like a lantern.

We rounded a bend and the road dead-ended. "Oh, look," she said. Where the road stopped was a guardrail, and beyond it the land opened out and down into a valley. We stood a while looking at a profusion of bluish green pines, and the color, the scent, the silence echoed inside me. Then I looked at her again, said, "I like your hair longer. Where'd you get the tan?"

"Oh, at my last, and final, commercial audition I met this man.

Nothing serious. He took me to his house in the Hamptons." Of course.
There would always be men to take her to the Hamptons, to the Waldorf.
"You know," she went on, "this summer, this year has been—I'd like to
get away. . . . Think about things, come back rested. If I could."

"What about Coffeyville? Can't you go home?"

"No. No, that's out of the question."

"Is it?"

"My father doesn't care for me, I don't care for him. It wouldn't be
restful."

"The air here smells so fresh," she said. A quick burst of it blew her
hair forward; I reached out and pushed a few strands off her face and
then felt I shouldn't have. I refocused again on the valley of trees, noticed the sky bleaching from blue to white.

"My father—" she said. "When my mother died—" She stopped,
folded her arms over her chest.

"Are you cold?" I asked.

"No." She gazed straight ahead, as if seeing something beyond the
trees. "When my mother was sick in the hospital, my father would
take me to see her after school. The last time she was sick he'd stay
with her all day and come back to get me in the afternoons. One day
I was waiting for him in my room, at the front of the house, so that
through my windows I could see the driveway, and one day he drove
in, but all the way in, not partway, and I knew it was over. I was so
scared, I stood waiting for him to come tell me it wasn't so. But when
I saw him as he came up the walk, he looked up at me through the
window. Yes, she was dead, I could see that. But also what I saw in his
eyes was this, this hatred, like he wished it was me who had died. And
that's when I thought, I'm alone." She stopped. "Later he said he hadn't
seen me, that on that day he'd been blind and hadn't seen anything.
But I was right, anyway; from then on he was never a father." I touched
her hair and she leaned into me, put her head against my shoulder,
turned into my chest and I put my arms around her and held her. In a
minute she pulled back. "You know what else it felt like?"

"What?"

"It's getting dark—" she stepped away. "We'd better go." We looked once more at the valley and then started back. She took my hand and I didn't think anything about it except that it felt good and warm.

After a while I said, "What else did it feel like?"

"Well, I remember thinking for the first time that you really couldn't have anything. That you could never truly hold anything in your hands. And if anyone said that you could, it was a lie."

"I know," I said.

"Yes." We saw the lights of the house, saw it was crowded; people cluttered the front steps and yard.

"Are you all right?" I asked her.

"Just fine, I think I'll get drunk. We should mingle, but if Stacey harasses you give me a whistle." Outside the front door she put her hands to the sides of my face, kissed me, and said, "Bye, chum, see you later."

Inside, the party extended down a hallway and into the kitchen and bedrooms; loud, bright-seeming, and smoky, and someone was playing the piano. Alix, svelte in a great long brown dress, introduced me to an agent she knew, who said I should call her the next time I performed in New York. I took her card, thanked her, and backed away, going out to the pool for a drink. Clarence stood by the other side of the pool with a fantastically beautiful woman, the actress who would play his wife in *A Raisin in the Sun*. She had very large eyes, and the extreme whites of her eyes glittered against her dark skin. Tazzia something. This was Clarence's summer. He'd grown out his hair into little incipient dreadlocks, and wore a set of brass beads.

On my second beer I headed into the house, and as I did, Irene lurched and then stumbled out of the house, after her shoe skittered over the patio and nearly fell into the pool. Automatically I reached out to take her arm and she straightened. "Lookit that, almost flipped it in the drink. *Robert*, hi!"

"Take it easy," I said. She smiled, patted me on the chest, and walked away. I saw Andre in the doorway, watching her. I managed to get inside without having to talk to him; the costume designer was singing a torch song by the piano. I shared a joint and had a long, boring conversation with one of the techies in the kitchen. Bryan, who had seen our first dress yesterday, walked by and gave me the thumbs-up sign—only, in an odd gesture, raising the thumb he put it to his mouth and kissed it. How typically Bryan, supportive, but hard to read.

I wandered out of the kitchen and back into the living room, where the pianist was playing Scott Joplin. There was Bryan and his girl-friend and Cynthia's TV-producer husband. Strange, I thought, that she should be married to a TV producer, or was it? But then I saw Irene and Andre, and incredulously observed that the lower halves of their bodies were absolutely glued together—at the sides. They were talking intently and her hand was positioned possessively on the center of his back.

I went outside looking for Patrick, first to the back and then to the front yard. I spotted him sitting on the front steps, smoking and talking to skinny one-eyebrowed Morris, of all people.

"Patrick," I said.

"Pardon me, Morris." He rose and came out to me on the shadowy grass. "If you want to know anything about anything," he said, "talk to Morris, he's a fount of information."

"Irene's coming on to Andre."

"She isn't. Where?"

We went up the steps past Morris and into the house, slinking away to the outskirts of the room where we wouldn't be seen.

"Over there," I whispered.

"Yes," he replied. They had moved and he was sitting in a chair and she sat on the arm; one of his hands rested casually on her thigh. "Well, such is life," Patrick said.

"We should do something."

"What? I hardly think it's any of our business, Robert."

"We should just let her do it?"

"Well, certainly," and with that, he turned to go back outside.

I watched him leave, then I stared at the happy couple and finally stalked noisily past them—they didn't flinch—and out to the bar. And as I ordered a beer there she was, with her impeccable timing and her thump: Stacey.

"Hi, Robert, how are you? Where's Irene?"

"Stacey," I said, "will you leave me alone?"

"What?" she asked, somewhat surprised.

"Just *leave me alone*," I said, and stomped off to the front yard, where I found someone who was about to drive back down the hill.

AT HOME I SAT on the porch in the dark, illogically, stubbornly waiting for Irene to walk in the door. Pictures crowded my mind—their heads together, hers brown and his gray, her hip pressed to his. Andre wasn't even someone you thought of as having a *body*. But of course he had one.

What was she doing? Who was she? I thought of how whenever we would come out of a movie or play she would change, taking on the mannerisms of one of the actresses in the story. It didn't seem like she was trying to do it but more like she'd been overtaken, as though this larger personality coming at her in the dark was irresistable. Andre, the pig, had once told us that most good actors did not have sharply defined personalities of their own, that they were vaporous and highly suggestible. When Irene worked, she studied the script very consciously; then she thought about it for a long time; and lastly, she hypnotized herself. "What do you mean, hypnotize yourself?" I had asked her. "I can't explain it any better than that," she had said. It was eerie. Even Patrick said once, "It's scary how good she is already, having done close to nothing." Who was she *beneath* the acting? And why, whenever I thought I'd begun to get near her, did she slip away?

I must have been stoned because, on the porch, I began to believe that she didn't have a soul, that losing her mother had wreaked irreparable damage. I gave up waiting for her, believing in her, and in bed I thought of her saying you couldn't hold anything in your hands, and no one, it seemed, existed but me. There was only this house and the wind picking up outside and this summer that was nearly over and therefore itself nearly ceased to exist.

In the morning Patrick and Clarence were home and Irene wasn't. Around noon Patrick went off to a picnic, and I got ready to leave again on tour the next day. Presumably, Patrick would return to the city the following day, along with Irene. She hadn't called, which I thought rude, since she was supposedly visiting *us*.

About six o'clock I was in the kitchen ironing a shirt when Patrick came back. "Where's Irene?" he asked, sticking his head in.

"How the hell should I know?"

"Excuse me for living." When I took the shirt to my room I saw that he'd gotten a book and was reading on the porch. Shortly, the screen door swung open and I heard them talking, then her voice coming closer to me in my room, calling back to him. The door to the bathroom closed; opened.

I went out to the hall.

"Hi," I said.

"Hi." She wore a T-shirt and cutoffs and carried her outfit and shoes from last night. I followed her into the living room where she knelt by her suitcase, and began folding and packing her clothes.

"What are you doing?" I asked.

"We thought we'd have a beer and then go out to dinner, okay?"

"No, I mean, what are you doing?" I repeated.

"Oh." She clicked the suitcase shut, and picked up her boots. "Well. I'm moving into Andre's."

"You're what?"

She very deliberately set down the boots and unrolled her socks.

"What about your cat?" I asked her.

"Ruth will take care of him."

"You don't have enough clothes."

She shrugged. "We'll send for some, he'll buy me some."

"Why are you doing this?" I asked, ineffectively disguising my anger.

"Why? Because I want to, why not?"

"That's an intelligent reason," I said. "It seems to me your IQ has been dropping ten points an hour since you got here."

"Fuck you, Robert."

"Fuck *you*, Irene." She'd been sitting in a straight-backed cane chair by a window to put on her boots. Now she stood, and the angle of light from outside cast a shadow over her face so that her eyes and brow became dark, volcanic.

Patrick came in and said, "What's going on?"

Without turning I answered, "We're having a private conversation."

"People having private conversations don't shout," he said.

"Don't you think," I said to Irene, "that you should have done this earlier in the season when it would have made a difference?"

"*What is wrong with you?*" she shouted.

"Me?" I said. "What's wrong with *me?*"

"Oh, Robert," Patrick said, "don't carry on."

I wheeled on him: "Don't you ever, *ever* use that tone on me again."

"What tone?" he said. I glared at him. "Why don't we sit down," he said, "and discuss this in a civilized fashion."

"I don't see anyone civilized in this room," I replied.

"Then stand." He gave Irene a look and she sat back down; he took out his cigarettes, gave her one, lit it, lit one for himself, and sat down in the other chair, tossed the matches on the table between them. I went and leaned against the mantle.

Nobody spoke for a minute. "There's nothing to say," she said. "He just insulted me to my face and I refuse to discuss anything further."

"In my opinion," I said, choosing my words, "you are confused, and you are wrecking your life."

"What he's saying," Patrick said, "is that he's worried about you."

"How does he know what will or will not wreck my life? I think not doing this is more likely to wreck it."

"Oh," I said, "you admit it's calculated, you admit you're doing this to get something out of it—"

"Yes," she said, "damn straight I am."

"Then 'confused,' " I said, "may be the wrong word."

"Listen," she said, "I am so sick of hearing all the time how *provincial* I am, whereas it's you who's provincial. Maybe, maybe the *core* of this is that I realized, over the summer, that my first reaction when I left in June wasn't genuine, just automatic. I was *supposed* to be shocked and I was. I thought I was. All year when he showed an interest in me I thought, No, he's my teacher, he's older than my father—I can't. But why not? Who else makes more sense? I'm an actress, my acting means more to me than anything, and acting is what he knows, more than anyone I've ever met. He's who I should be with, who I want to be with." She had grown very calm, very sure of herself. She took a deep drag on the dregs of her cigarette and put it out.

"That," I said, "was an amazing justification."

"Oh Robert, grow up!" She'd lost it again. "You're such a romantic. Haven't you gathered that *anyone* who's attracted to someone wants something from them? Looks, or just to be near someone who behaves—"

"You are beyond justification, Irene. You're in *The Outer Limits.*"

"Forget it," she said to Patrick. "He's dead to me."

"Have you forgotten that Andre," I said to her, "who-you-should-be-with, *fired* you from the-thing-that-means-more-to-you-than-anything?"

"He's apologized for that," she said, "he admits it was a mistake."

"No, it wasn't. He got what he wanted."

Enter Clarence. Well, he didn't enter. The guy was making a break for the exit. But we had forgotten his presence and hearing him in the hallway we were taken aback; our three sets of eyes pinned him like a rivet where he stopped, just outside the room. "I want you people to know that I haven't heard any of this, yes?" he said.

"Yes," Patrick said sadly, "we know you haven't, Clarence." Clarence went on, and we listened to the squeak of the screen door as he left; Irene tried to stare me down, but I didn't give in, and she looked away.

Then I said to her, as kindly as I could, "You don't think much of yourself, do you?"

"Whatever," she answered, "has convinced you that you're so intrinsically valuable?"

"If I'm dead, you're deader," I said to her.

"Please," Patrick said, "you're both getting far too esoteric. She's having a dalliance and a nice vacation. And if Andre turns out to be good for her career, lovely!"

"Yeah, you would say that," I said. He had taken her side. "I'm not exactly surprised you would say that since everyone knows you've been sleeping with Bryan all summer." The reddish shade of his face darkened, and one of his hands leaped to his head in a self-conscious combing motion.

In fact, the Bryan affair was a recent development and I had thought little about it. What painted it lurid was the arrival of Bryan's girlfriend last night, in for the party from California.

"I don't know what you're doing," Irene said. "I don't know *what's* going on here, or why."

"You do too," I said, and I walked out of the house. I headed into the forest, plunging headlong down a path, slapping aside the stray branches that struck at my face. But then I tripped on a log that lay at the side of the path. I picked it up and heaved it into the dense thickness of trees to my right, and when I looked down at the dirt where it had lain I saw it was moist, teeming with dark, wet things that I had unearthed. Feeling dizzy I turned and retraced my path. If only I'd never met her. A girl with a father fixation, all the way back to that guy in Coffeyville; Hank. I had one desire, I wanted to get my bike and get out of here. It leaned against the wall by the porch door. Patrick came out of the house.

"Robert—"

"I'm leaving."

"Come inside," he said.

"No."

"Does this have to do with last night?" he said sweetly. "How the two of you were pretending to be lovers, and then she was with Andre? I wouldn't blame you if you felt embarrassed in front of the others—is that what's bothering you?"

I shook my head and laughed. "I didn't think of that," I lied. "But now that you mention it, that was shitty of her too. But no, that's not it." I kicked up the bike stand. "You know it isn't."

"I don't."

"Oh, Patrick." He was dissimulating, I knew he was.

"And why did you say what you said about Bryan?" he asked. "It isn't so."

I was dumbfounded. "It *is* so." Was Irene contagious?

"I've always appreciated, Robert—" now he was acting *hurt* "—how, in most circumstances, you respect people's privacy."

"Do you honestly believe that if something isn't said, it isn't there, Patrick? It isn't real?" He averted his eyes. "I don't care about you and Bryan. I don't think you're seeing Bryan in the way Irene's chosen to see Andre, and even if you are, I don't think it's quite the same. But don't lie about it."

"I'm not."

"Patrick. He drops you off in the morning, I've seen him. I don't *care*, but I won't pretend I don't know." He was picking at an imaginary piece of lint on his jeans. I walked my bike to the driveway, turned back, and he looked at me straight, head-on, seriously, and I thought I could see in his eyes that he knew he'd been wrong, but I didn't stay to find out.

THAT MORONIC PACT we had signed, what good was looking after each other someday if we didn't look after each other now? Daylight waned and night began reclaiming the road and drawing the houses into its dark breast. I decided to get a drink at the bar that adjoined a hotel in the next village over, a place where the three of us didn't go. I pumped the bike pedals vigorously, soothed by the feel of sweat breaking out on my brow, as if something were finally being released.

There was nobody at the bar, just me and the bartender. The walls were papered with raised red chevrons, stinking of gin and despair. The mirrors were cloudy, the banquettes vinyl and worn. I ordered a boilermaker and carried it to a booth. I would get drunk, get a room in the hotel. An older couple came in and sat at the bar. I got another drink. Two youngish women took a table by the door. A barmaid came on shift and stood sharing a newspaper with the bartender. I gazed, mesmerized, at the rows of strangely bright-colored bottles in such a dim place, and on my fourth drink I changed my mind; I'd go to Stacey's. I scraped back my chair, downed the remainders, and went outside. It was still warm. A nearly full moon lit the road.

Stacey lived with another girl in a rented house not far from ours. I rode home leisurely, admiring the scenery with boozy sentiment. I was singing and riding no-handed by the time I got to the sign that said, DRAMA, THIS WAY. It struck me as hysterically funny, then it pissed me off, and I stopped and took it. I pulled it out of the ground—it came up with jolting ease—and tucked it under my arm. I rode quietly up the driveway, humming a couple of bars of "Goodnight Irene." Irene and Patrick's bikes were gone. I went inside for a hammer, and planted the sign near the porch door so it pointed to the entrance.

Stacey's house was closer to the farm and smelled strongly of cows. The curtains were closed but a light burned behind them. I knocked on the door.

"*Robert.*" She had on a striped robe and it looked like she'd just washed her hair. "Robert, hi. How are you?"

"Okay, Stacey. How're you?"

She appeared to be in shock. She kept blinking.

"I—uh, I'm sorry about what I said to you last night at the party."

"Oh, that's okay." She gripped the sides of her robe and said, "Well—do you want to come in?"

"Yeah, sure. Thanks." She thumped inside and I followed her into a comfortable room of colonial furniture and overstuffed chairs, but ended up sitting down at the dining-room table to its side, under an amazingly ugly wagon-wheel chandelier. I was suddenly stone-cold sober.

"You want—can I get you something?" she asked.

"Yes, do you have anything to drink? Anything with alcohol, I mean, or any grass?"

She smiled. "I have both. Here," indicating a liquor cabinet, "help yourself. I'll be right back."

She thumped into a dark passageway. She was actually kind of cute, I thought. She had sort of full, pouty lips. I found a bottle of scotch and poured myself two or three fingers. On top of the cabinet was a photograph of her and her famous father standing beneath a marquee. What was it with these girls and their fathers?

She came back and sat at the head of the table and rolled up a joint, lit it, and gave it to me.

"Wow," I said, "pretty good. You want some?"

We passed it back and forth a few times. I sipped the scotch.

"You're really a good actor, Robert," she said.

"Yeah? Thanks."

"You study with Andre?"

"Yes."

"For how long?"

"Two years." I felt mellow; the room was getting soft and blurry. I could still smell the cows and they smelled good.

"I would love to study with him."

"He's a good teacher." Her hair was drier. I noticed her eyes again, what a light blue they were.

"So you live in the city?" She had her chin propped in her hand, her elbow on the table, watching me.

"Yeah."

"Me too, with my dad and my stepmother on Riverside Drive. Do you know my father?"

"Yeah—well, I don't *know* him, I know who he is." I took an involuntary gander at the photograph to my side. Stacey just stared at me. She was funny, she didn't seem to mind silences at all.

"Why don't you come over here and sit next to me?" I said.

With that same peaceful acceptance she got up and thumped over, stood next to me, her hips against the table. Oh, I'm gone, I thought. I hadn't believed I would go through with it; I'd thought I would get stoned and then ask to sleep on her couch. But her robe had come loose, or she'd loosened it so it gaped, and she didn't have anything on underneath: I could see her crotch, for God's sake. I reached out and pulled her onto my lap and we started kissing; I opened the robe, and said, "Where's your bedroom?"

We got up and I followed her down the hall. If anyone else was home there weren't any signs. Her bedroom was neat, one narrow bed, a dresser, a chair. She took off her robe, laid it down at the foot of the bed. I came up behind her and ran my hands down her body; she had very soft skin, and the sight of her unclothed from behind was very exciting. But then she sat down on the bed, lay flat on her back, swung up her big foot—and looking down at her, she looked very small, much smaller than she had on my lap or in her clothes. It was either the cast or her body in contrast to the cast, but how she looked startled me—her smallness, her foot, as though this small girl was attached to this tremendous affliction. I sat down beside her and saw this tiny blue vein jump at her temple. I unbuttoned my shirt. She sat up, opened my belt and my jeans, and I stood up and took off my clothes, and lay down on her. Since she had laid down, there wasn't anything even moderately romantic in it.

Then—it must have been the moonlight—she swiveled her head away and upward, and her light blue eyes got even lighter, so pale they looked almost white, like she didn't have any irises, and it frightened me. I took her chin with my thumb and turned her head back down and then it was okay, but my heart was pounding and suddenly the trick of her eyes and her body underneath me excited me incredibly. I lifted her hips, positioned myself, and drove into her deeply. She moaned, but I didn't want to hear her.

"Be quiet," I said.

It wasn't making love and it wasn't even sex and soon she wasn't even a part of it, and it was fantastic, I thought I could do it forever, going faster and harder until, from what seemed a great distance, I heard a high, shrill sound that I didn't want to hear, that wasn't me, but it got louder and I had to stop. She was crying.

"What," I said. "Stacey." She turned her head away. "Stacey." She wouldn't look at me.

I pulled out and rolled over to the side of her.

"Hey. Stacey, come on. Stop crying. What's the matter?"

"I'm sorry," she said.

God, I wanted to get up and leave.

"I'm sorry," she repeated. She sat up and wiped her face, and then she went down on me, and I let her. But when it was finished she stayed sort of lying on my legs and kissing them.

"Stacey, come here."

I felt terrible, I felt sorry for her. I got her to come up beside me and I put my arm around her so that she was lying against me, her head against my neck. I smoothed back her hair; it was still damp and very soft, really soft silky hair; she smelled like soap and the sweat of a very young girl.

"I'm sorry," she said, "we can do it again in a —"

"No," I said, "that's all right."

"Sex makes me cry," she said.

Great, I thought. Fabulous, and as I stroked her hair, which she seemed to like so much and appreciate, I thought, What happened to her? I imagined all kinds of things, and the longer I lay there the worse I felt. I was falling into a long black tunnel of pain and if I kept lying with her and stroking her hair, I would never get out. She nuzzled me and sighed.

"Stacey. I have to go home."

"Now?"

I got up, and as I put on my clothes had a horrible thought.

"Did I hurt you?" I asked. "Did I hurt you before?"

"No, it's me," she said, moping and putting on her robe. She walked me to the door.

"When you get back from tour the summer will be over. If I give you my number in the city, will you call?" Oh, what to say. Then she said, "Irene went with Andre, didn't she?"

I looked into those pale blue eyes, and knowing that she could be cunning and hurtful like I was, made my answer easier.

"Stacey, I won't call."

"Oh—"

Then I saw that her question hadn't been badly intended, that she said it because she liked me, and felt for me. I thought I should say something—you're nice? You're pretty? Don't do this anymore with people you don't know? Instead I said, "Well, good night."

"Good night." The door shut and I heard her thump back to bed. It was cooler outside. Not much. My head hurt. Fuck it, I would go home.

The sign remained where I'd put it. One of their bikes was parked by the porch door. It wasn't that late but the lights were off and I went straight to my room and to bed. In the morning when I left they were both gone.

ENDINGS WITHIN OUR knowledge are poignant for everyone. But actors are always walking away; from jobs, groups of people, not knowing what will be next, when we'll be acting again. At the close of our last show I returned to the empty theater, stood on the stage, and looked out at the house. It was modest but old, with a certain faded grandeur: a golden-fringed olive green curtain; a floral carpet—the original worn thin, threads showing through; plaster carvings in the shape of chariots on the box seats; ceiling fixtures like twelve-pointed stars. I took it in like a deep cold breath. The theater was my home. This stage, like all of the others, was where I belonged. Having this home, this life, this work, I could walk confidently in the world. I took one last look, turned resolutely, and left.

I didn't call Patrick and he didn't call me. But in late September I saw him in the Drama Book Shop, perusing the uppermost shelves of the Restoration aisle. He had on a white shirt, opened at the neck, and a partially unknotted tie; his jacket, hooked on a finger, swung over his shoulder. I approached him, so happy to see him that my smile felt ready to crack wide open. "Patrick."

"Robert," he smiled back.

"You look great," I said.

"I had an audition."

"How'd it go?"

"Fine. It went fine. You're looking well too."

"I feel well."

"I missed you," he said.

"I missed you too," I said, relieved.

We talked about what we'd been doing since Crispins. He'd reactivated his Screen Actors Guild membership and was going up for bits in film as well as theater. We both thought that we should enroll in a new acting class. Andre's was canceled through December, as it was every third year while he traveled "for respite and inspiration." I'd heard that he always brought along a pretty woman. This year, then, Irene was the lucky winner.

"Look," he finally said—we'd been in the aisle for half an hour—"you want to get coffee?" We went to Joe Allen, then back to my place and talked for hours. By the end of the night we'd decided to get an apartment together. I was fed up with mine, he was tired of living alone, and we could afford something nicer together than we could on our own.

WE RENTED A LARGE apartment on Fourteenth Street between Fifth Avenue and University Place, smack in the middle of a thronged discount shopping district and the spillover from Union Square Park, a hangout for junkies. Close by were the tree-lined blocks of brownstones where we had really wanted to live.

"We can either afford a tiny brownstone apartment or plenty of space in a building with no character," Patrick had said.

We were on the sixteenth of twenty-one floors, at the quiet back of the building, facing north: we had a view of the Chrysler Building and the Empire State, its lights changing colors for holidays, and we could see into about forty windows of another large building.

"Good grief," Patrick said, "throw out the TV."

It must have occurred to me that by moving in with Patrick I would see Irene again. But he and I hadn't discussed her. He tried; I wouldn't listen. Patrick and I had, of course, been friends *before* Irene Jane Walpers. My one stipulation was that we would get a subscription to the *Times* and he would pay for half.

"But that's such a commitment," he said. "I like to read it religiously, but if it's there *in* the apartment and I'm busy and I can't, I am ravaged by guilt."

"You just like to steal mine," I said.

"Don't be absurd," he replied, but I won.

By day three we had our belongings in place. That afternoon we went up on the roof with chaise lounges we'd bought at one of the stores on the street. There was a call in *Back Stage* for actors "of all sizes ages and shapes" for a pool party scene in a film that would shoot on Martha's Vineyard the following week. The one catch was that you were required to be tan: we had four days.

"We're insane," Patrick said. "Battalions of copper-toned men have been marching back from Fire Island since early September."

"Here," I said, "have some lotion." He was whiter than me, Irish white, wearing shades and an oversize swimsuit with seahorses on it.

We had a great view from the roof, twenty-two stories up, and it was late in the day and the heat had abated.

"I like your lotion," Patrick said, "it smells like a piña colada." After he'd used half the bottle he opened the *Times*, holding it away from his body. "Do you have any idea how many important people have died this year, Robert?" he asked.

"Don't read the obituaries," I said. "You always read the obituaries first. It's morbid."

"I don't. It's an article. Elvis. The *divine* Joan Crawford. Groucho

Marx, Nabokov, Ethel Waters—*Zero Mostel*. Maria Callas. . . . It's
the end of an era."

I got up and walked to the edge of the roof and looked out at other
people sunning on terraces, patios, small islands sticking off concrete
hulks—at the complicated rivers of traffic, the spires, the smokestacks,
the miniature trees. I stared, feeling powerful, certain, and strong. I felt
ready to take on all of it.

I lay back down, read a section of the paper; traded with Patrick,
read another; took a nap. When I awoke it was cooler still but my skin
clung uncomfortably to the plastic chair.

"Do you think we're getting anything?" I asked Patrick.

"No—the sun's gone. It's nice up here though."

"I'm going down," I said. I folded the chair. "It's getting late. You're
staying up?"

"For a little while, yes. With my eyes closed I am lying in the trop-
ics." A siren wailed from down in the street. I felt edgy, hungry, as if
some part of myself already knew which of the two of us—of the three
of us—would finally make it, and why, and what would happen then.
I went to the door that led to the stairs, but before I opened it I turned
and looked back at Patrick, his feet hanging way off the end of the
lounge, and at the lights of the city behind him as they started coming on.

Part II

7 Return

On the morning of the day when Irene dropped back into our lives, a postcard of Westminster Abbey arrived. We'd gotten the Tower of London, Red Square, and a grisly image of the dead Lenin in his glass coffin. I'd glance at the side with the writing, never actually reading what it said, and deposit her missives on Patrick's desk in his room. If one came when Patrick collected the mail, he always left it on prominent display, lately propped against his new lapis lazuli cigarette box on the coffee table in the living room. That morning, about to put Westminster Abbey faceup on his desk, I read the first line: *Dear Robert and Patrick,* interesting order, I thought, *How's everything there?* "A-OK," I answered, setting it down. "Since you asked, things are going exceptionally well." I grabbed my jacket and went off to a day of classes.

Truthfully, things could have been better. I'd been going at the business for more than four years, I was nearly twenty-seven, and where was I? Crispins had been my best job, but it changed nothing, did not make the job of *getting* jobs any easier. Still, I prided myself on being a realist. Life went on, and yet sometimes, alone—mapping a scene, dressing hurriedly for work or for school—I would suddenly lose track of where I was and what I was doing for no apparent reason, and feel such a disassociation from everything I thought of as myself that it was as though this blankness, this *freeze* had come from outside, instead of arising from within.

Patrick got work as an extra in films or TV. With his arresting physicality he often got an upgrade—a single line, or a silent bit, all of which seemed to end up on the cutting room floor, except a burglary scene in *Kojak*. But he had his own methods of sustaining himself. Occasionally he would leave the apartment abruptly at night and be gone for several hours. I had an idea of where he was probably going, but one night he asked me along—and we walked at a backbreaking pace all over Manhattan, down side streets, along avenues, by the rivers and parks, where it was populous and where it was deserted, where only distant reflections lit the ground beneath our feet, to the Battery Tunnel and then up to the Nineties on the East Side, stopping once to use the john in some seedy bar on Avenue B. By the time we headed home it was 3 A.M. But Patrick still did not look relaxed, and so we went to an after-hours joint and got drunk in a way that we never had before. I slept through the entire next day; Patrick was out of the apartment as early as ever, off to the gym.

Living together, our lives began to fall into a kind of rhythm. But portions of his life still seemed mysterious. I took a book of his off our shelves in the living room one afternoon and saw written inside on the flyleaf: Benton Millston Caruthers III. For a second I looked at it as if I had come upon any other name, one I hadn't heard of, and even laughed. (I thought, What kind of affected jerk writes his whole name with *the third* in a paperback copy of Jackie Susann?) Patrick sat reading on the couch. In a loud voice, I read out the name. He looked up and I said, "Maria told me to call her if you ever see him. Everyone wants to protect you from him."

"Yes, well, they can't," Patrick said, shortly.

"Do you see him?" I asked.

"Not in years," and he stood and left the room.

Another time, searching for a stamp, I discovered in Patrick's desk a drawerful of Catholic paraphernalia: rosary beads, a missal, even a painted statue of Mary. He had rehung the tiny gold crucifix from his old apartment by the light switch inside our front door, but I'd always judged his attachment to it as ironic—he had made a crack once about the decorative value of a good hanging Christ. It would be very Patrick, I thought, to embrace the trappings of the Church without buying its doctrine, and since he had been raised a Catholic he might be keeping the items in the drawer for sentimental reasons, relics of a childhood he liked to remember, or imagine, as happy. But the drawer was the one to the right of the center, as close at hand as the stapler, the pens, the Scotch tape.

Then in December, only days before Irene reappeared, a travel agent called for Patrick and asked me to tell him that his airline ticket for San Francisco was ready. He had said he was going to Los Angeles for the holidays, as he had last year. When he came in that afternoon I gave him the message.

"San Francisco?" he said. "I'm going to LA, not San Francisco."

"The travel agent said San Francisco."

"She made a mistake," he said quickly, with an annoyance disproportionate to a mere mistake.

I took Patrick's secrets personally, as signs that he simply didn't trust me. Then too, every friendship has its codes, its unspoken agreements, and vital to ours was the cushion we allowed each other: the longer we were friends the more we both knew what we should and shouldn't press.

That night—a clear, cold night in December, I got home at seven. I had a guilty appreciation of the lobby of our building, whose decor Patrick called Las Vegas East. I entered through the sliding automatic glass doors, strode past the uniformed doorman at his circular desk, and caught a satisfied glimpse of myself in the mirrored back wall while pressing the "up" button at the elevators. Angel Jacome was on duty, head doorman, a compact martinet who would go down with the building like the captain of a ship. Charles worked most nights, mournful Charles, in his late fifties, with an ashy complexion and a soft lisping speech. If murderers came while Charles was on duty, well, those were the breaks. With Richard, a big Irish guy who worked afternoons, you might do better. Richard liked playing the horses and hit Patrick up for a loan every two or three weeks.

Patrick wasn't home. I took a long steamy shower, prior to going over to Brenda's. She had separated from her husband just after I had returned from Crispins. We had a love nest in her new West Village apartment. The last time I was there I'd gone over early, at about five. She rang me in, and upstairs, there was Norm. The husband. He wore an old-fashioned tweed suit, a thin man who possessed such pronounced cheekbones they looked like they hurt. She opened the door and kissed me, and led me in with her arm looped through mine.

"Norm, this is Robert," she said. "Sit, we have a few minutes." She nodded for me to sit too.

Her apartment was tiny and Norm had been sitting on the bed. I sank into the one nearby chair, a canvas beach chair so low that my ass skimmed the floor. Brenda hauled in a chair from the kitchen for herself and Norm sat back down, and there we sat as Norm became visibly nervous and upset. He'd started trembling, and she had to have noticed but she kept talking.

Eventually I got up and went to the bathroom and didn't come out until he was gone.

"Well, that was Norm," she said then.

"Why did you do that?" I said. How was he in court? I thought. A guy that nervous?

"Norm's a basket case," she said, "that's how Norm is."

"Are you still seeing him, Brenda?"

"Yes, I see him, I have to. We're in the process of getting a divorce. Do you not want me to see him?"

I didn't know what to say. "No," I said, "just spare me having to socialize with him." I wasn't in love with Brenda. But the view I had had of the messiness of her marriage unsettled me. That sort of messiness was exactly what I didn't want in my life. All the same, I wasn't in a hurry to call it off. It was all too convenient.

WHEN I SAW HER, her cheeks flushed, the smell of the dinner she was cooking an effusion of warmth, I stepped inside the apartment —that rich capsule—and took her in my arms.

"Oh," she said, "you are amorous tonight."

"Every night," I said.

"Let me go, I'm getting dinner."

She wasn't a very good cook and I'd had a sandwich beforehand. She had brought the small table and chairs from the kitchen into the main room, but the bed and a fire in the grate at the foot of the bed were the feast. Although the stuccoed walls were a stark white, a colorful quilt was spread on the bed and the fire threw gradations of light.

"Sit down," she said, coming in with a large dish wrapped in a bath towel. She set the dish on the table, poured wine, and returned to the kitchen for a basket of bread.

"Good wine," I said.

"Get drunk and you won't know what you're eating." She took an edge of the towel and lifted off the cover of the dish. "It's a casserole."

It had smelled a lot better than it looked.

"You don't have to eat it. Here," she said, and passed me bread. "It's fresh, I got it on Bleecker this morning."

"I'm not very hungry." I drank more wine. "You know, you don't have to cook, Brenda."

"Oh, I should. Norm and I—" she looked down at her wine glass, touched the rim with a finger, and followed the circle of the glass slowly around. "We went out too often, it was profligate."

"He's obviously still crazy about you. Maybe you still have a lot to work out. Maybe I should get lost for a while." She raised her eyes, and held mine.

"I don't want you to get lost, can't we just go on as we have been?" She smiled, her face softening.

"Can I come over there and kiss you?" I asked.

She nodded, and I did, and in a minute she left me and went to the windows to pull the blinds. Then she matter-of-factly started undressing.

"Let me," I said. I slid her jeans down her legs, let them drop to the floor; pressed my lips to the lovely protuberance of her hip bone, across the soft flesh that led to the other.

Later, under the covers, restored to the plane we most comfortably occupied together — sexed-out, entangled — we lay quietly, enjoying the heat of the fire.

"Robert. Are you asleep?"

"No."

"Get up, my legs have gone numb."

"God," I said, "I'm exhausted." I sat up and lowered my feet to the floor and got dressed. She had developed sleep issues and wouldn't allow me to stay.

She came with me to the door, wrapping herself in the sheet. Her long hair fell over her arms, and touching her breasts against the sheet, I kissed her good-bye.

My legs felt detached going down the two flights of stairs and through the cold foyer. Sirens screamed from the direction of Seventh Avenue and on West Fourth a girl tripped and fell down on the sidewalk in front of me — Friday night, lots of kids from Jersey and the outer boroughs in town. The boy with her helped her up saying "Nancy, why the fuck you gotta be getting so drunk?" I crossed Sixth, thrust my hands deeper into my pockets while trying to hold my arms close to my sides for warmth.

I turned north at the Washington Square arch, heading up Fifth. I thought of the play I was leaning toward for my thesis production, *The Rehearsal*, by Jean Anouilh. It felt right, its tensions, its slide from a light bantering tone, with only the suggestion of danger, to the reality of what was at stake all along — that the players were playing for their lives, as we all were. And there was a part for Patrick. A key image rose in my mind, of a tall man with a shattered glass in his hand. I sailed into the lobby, past Charles, nodding off at his station, and into the elevator, hoping that Patrick would be up. He could fail, I could fail, it could be bad for our friendship, but I knew he could play this, it was perfect for him. He'd be fabulous visually, the height would be great. If I could create a rehearsal atmosphere in which he felt secure, he would probably make the production.

I opened the door, and there was Irene.

She sat on the couch, opposite Patrick, who sat in one of the chairs, at the far end of our living room, by the windows.

"Hello, Robert," Patrick said.

"Hi," she said, standing, but then in confusion — Patrick hadn't stood — resumed her seat. I walked toward them: she had on what looked like a pajama top.

"Hi, Irene," I said, "how come you're wearing your pajamas?"

"Oh, I stopped by on the spur of the moment." She laughed, picked up her drink and took a long sip — it stained her lips fuchsia. Her voice sounded shrill.

"Let me get you a drink," Patrick said, rising.

"What are you drinking?" I asked.

"Chambord."

I sat down in the chair beside Patrick's, facing Irene. Her hair was longer, darker; she was pale.

"How was Russia?" I said.

"Cold." She smiled, "London was nice though."

"Yes, I like London."

"I'd never been there before." She glanced around the room, at the windows. "This is glamorous, with the lights? I like it," she added.

"Me too."

"Patrick said you've been in a movie."

"Oh, well—"

"Oh, well?" Patrick said, coming back with my drink. He put it down, sat, relit the Gauloise he had set in the ashtray. "He is now a member of Screen Actors Guild, he won the role over sixty other aspirants, and earned two thousand dollars for three days' work."

"But it was a stupid movie," I said.

"It's a horror film," said Patrick, "it's supposed to be stupid. He had to be shot," he said to Irene. "They pasted two metal discs to his skin, connected to two small balloons filled with red liquid." Patrick had come along to watch the filming of my climactic scene.

"I had to be shot in two places," I said.

"Special effects pushed a button," he said, "which made a loud bang and set off a small explosion, a shock to the discs that burst the balloons, so the blood spurted out through cuts in his shirt."

"Did it hurt?" Irene asked me.

"The explosion? No. Just like a tap."

"He had to do the reaction though," Patrick said. "I thought you handled it awfully well, Robert. They got it in one take," he said to Irene. "First he was shot in the chest, then he tried to escape and they got him in the side."

"Sure to go down," I said, "in the annals of film history." I stood, and drained my drink.

"It's good to see you," Irene said.

"You too. Welcome back."

I left the room, their silence growing behind me.

In bed I thought, here we go again, and only a fool would feel as I do—I felt glad.

In the morning, going through the living room to get to the kitchen, I saw that the heap of blankets on the couch was Irene. I put on coffee, waiting in the kitchen for it to be ready, and heard her call. "Patrick?"

I walked out to where she could see me. "No, it's me."

"Oh." She sat up. "He was supposed to wake me."

"He'd be at the gym now, he'll be back soon. You want coffee?"

"Yes, thank you." She came and stood in the kitchen doorway, in her jeans and her pajama top. I pulled out a drawer and took out two spoons—as stiffly as I had behaved the first time I'd stepped on a stage.

"Robert, don't be angry with me anymore. I've missed you and Patrick so much."

I turned to her and knew, as I'd known last night, that she was very unhappy. I didn't know when she got back or where she was living, but I imagined her at Andre's, lying awake in his bed as she listened for his breathing to slow, and then getting up and coming here. For an instant every particle of my reserve was blasted away.

"You are a very difficult person," I said.

"I know, I don't have to be. Really I'm *not*." Her hair in a tangle, one bare foot on top of the other, an old, familiar gesture.

"Okay," I said. I picked up the cups, gave one to her.

"Okay," she said, taking it, still hesitant.

She'd folded the blankets neatly on the couch, but sat on the floor by the coffee table. I watched her take a sip of coffee, and then Patrick's cigarette box caught her eye: an azure blue box that opened on silver hinges, an antique, not much larger than a pack of cigarettes; its surface was a mosaic of lapis lazuli. "Did you see that?" I asked, sitting down.

"Last night," she said, picking it up, cradling it carefully in her small hands.

"We used to go visit it in the store. He loved it so much that I finally told him he had to buy it or I would."

"What's it like, living with him?"

"He takes Geritol."

"He *doesn't*. For iron-poor blood?"

"He does. He buys three bottles at a time." We laughed, "He chugs it," I said. "I found it in the kitchen and could not believe it. When I asked him about it he got insulted, said that some people looked after their health—this while he's dragging on his cigarette, right? And then he tried to get me to try it, and when I refused he wouldn't speak to me the rest of the day."

She fell back flat on the floor, laughing; sat up, wiping her eyes. "I'm so glad, Robert, so glad to be back."

AFTER THAT I SAW her once, twice a week. She didn't speak of Andre. She talked about London as though she had been there alone. She described how seeing the famous historical sites made Shakespeare real to her; she could imagine becoming his women—living as they had lived then. In most ways she seemed to be the same Irene who had left us, intensely committed, ever open to change. But a new self-doubt had crept into her manner. I had a sense of her grasping at us for comfort, clinging to Patrick and me almost desperately. She was living with Andre, but clearly they were not getting along.

In February, she worked in class for the first time that year. Andre kept stopping her.

"No, no, no, *no,* what are you doing?" he said.

The work wasn't even that bad; it was good in fact, better than other things he had praised her for extravagantly. She started again and he stopped her, and then dismissed her scene partner.

"Now," he said to Irene, "this is unacceptable, amateurish, and crass." He waved her away, flapping his hand repeatedly until she sat down.

I had never seen Andre so boorish and unfair before, but it was even stranger to see Irene meekly accept his treatment.

Patrick and I picked up a small single bed for nearly nothing and put it in our small extra room, so that she'd have a refuge.

"SO YOU'D DO the character of Hero," I said to Patrick, handing him a copy of *The Rehearsal.*

He didn't answer immediately; he extracted a petal from the flowers at the center of the table—irises that Irene had brought when she'd come to dinner—thought better of it, and tried to put it back.

"I'm not expecting you to decide until you've read it," I said.

He fished the petal from the water; got it out, dried it off against his palm, and set it atop the bloom.

"Hero," he said, enunciating with special care. "Then I take it he's a good character?"

"Good? It's a good part. I told you already."

"I'd like to play a good *person*, Robert."

Nobody liked to play good people, it wasn't any fun. Besides, you were supposed to look for the good in the bad guys and the bad in the good guys. But of course Patrick believed in absolutes, which was why Hero was the role for him to play.

"He's not good," I said, "he's a drunk, among other things. . . . But he's a drunk on account of regret. As a very young man he went against his ideals, and it's ruined his life—in the sense that he can't just ignore what happened as some people might. That's why Anouilh called him Hero, there's a purity about him. Look," I said, "read the play and then we can talk."

A few days later I came out of my room to the living room. He was acting out exchanges in the play for Irene.

He struck a pose: " 'Is there some double meaning behind your words, sir?' " He changed his position, taking the part of the other character: "Now I'm the Count," he told Irene. " 'Since the invention of language, Villebosse, there has always been some double meaning behind the spoken word. In fact, words were invented expressly for that reason.' "

"Patrick," I said, "you know the whole play."

"Yes," he said, "I suppose I do."

"How many times have you read it?" I asked.

"Well . . . I can't be sure, twenty? Twenty-five?"

Irene turned to the bookshelf where she stood, back to us, paging through a *Roget's Thesaurus*.

"It's January," I said to him, "we start in April. You'll get it too set in your head. I'd just *prefer* it," I said, "if you left it alone for now. Read it again in March, but just for yourself."

"Why?" he said, equivocating.

"You know as well as I do that it's different to play a part than to appreciate it from the outside. If you admire it too much, how will you play it?"

His expression was bland. "All right," he replied.

Two nights later, he was reciting again to Irene: "'One must ignore mirrors. They are traps for the weak. For my part I contemplate myself only in my old portraits painted by the best artists of the time.'" He turned to me. "Am I allowed to read Anouilh's *other* plays?"

8 Hero

Brenda helped me with the auditions. I had hoped to avoid them. The cast wasn't large, four men and three women, and I'd thought I could cast it with people I knew. But I was left short of two actors: the Countess, the most important woman's part, and Ville-bosse, which required impeccable comic timing. We put an ad in *Back Stage* and were deluged with actors, well over a hundred. At the end of the first day of auditions Brenda and I sat in the studio theater, with three stacks of pictures and résumés. The tallest stack was still "un-decided."

"This is ridiculous," she said. "You know who you want."

"I want everybody to get a good hearing."

She sighed, leaning back in her chair, and pinned up her hair—she'd been taking it down and putting it up since morning.

"See this stack?" she said, pointing to the "ins." "That's who you call back."

"Yeah, but—"

"You already transferred ten people from undecided to in. We're seeing twenty-five actors the day after tomorrow, that's enough."

"Brenda—"

"*Robert,* it's just a play, remember?"

"Right," I said.

"People fail, you know," she said. "Not just actors. People fail in business, there are failed teachers, failed politicians. I'm a failed wife. That's how it is."

I'd had no idea she knew me so well, nor that I was so transparent, and I didn't like it. My thoughts must have shown on my face.

At last she said, kindly, "I don't think who we do or don't call back Wednesday will make or break anyone's life."

I stared at her, studied those dark brown eyes I could almost fall into.

"Hey, Brenda. You by any chance still have that key to the storage room?"

"Deal," she said, collecting the piles.

The next day, Patrick told me that he needed a waistcoat. He said he had reread the play *once* since we last discussed it, and had discerned that in the play Hero remarks on the tightness of his costume as a physical correlative to Hero's psychological distress, and Patrick wanted to begin to explore the sensation. Our wardrobe mistress sewed him one out of muslin for rehearsals, and he began to wear it evenings around the apartment.

Just days before our first read-through I was walking east on Thirteenth Street and heard him call my name; I turned and saw him approaching, towering over people he passed, his brightly striped green-and-black cap shining out above the others like a beacon, an effulgence in the grayish early April day. He'd taken to wearing his woolen hat that winter after reading an article on a man who had gone mysteriously deaf following a brief unprotected exposure to the cold.

He had a scarf wound around his neck and pulled up against his jaw. "Hi," I said, "you know, it's fifty degrees. Are you coming from the gym?"

"I can't do the play," he said. "I'm sorry."

"You can't—?"

He glanced away nervously. "You know in the pool I always have my best thoughts. It came to me today. I realized that I can't do it."

"Come on," I said, "you want a drink, coffee? You have any appointments?" He shook his head no, and we went to the Cedar Tavern on University Place. We took a booth in back; Patrick ordered coffee, I ordered a drink.

"You can't quit now," I told him.

"Better I let you down now than later. I don't want to do it if I can't do it well." He took off his hat, leaving one side of his hair flattened, then ran a hand through it, fixing it with this single gesture; and in a continual arc from his head to the inner pocket of his jacket he got out his cigarettes, tipped open the package, slid one out with a finger.

"What you just did," I said.

He lit his cigarette and the smoke curled up between us. "Beg pardon?"

"A lot of the character you can do without trying. He's suave, smooth, y'know, he's got to be—irresistable."

"Irresistable? Oh Robert, to whom?"

"Shut up," I said. "Charming. All that shit you do."

His smile faded. "Exactly."

"But you're already doing more," I told him, "you're already thinking about it on a deeper level. With the waistcoat." He smoked, unconvinced. "Look, if you think you can't do it, use that, use the fear." I got more specific, "Hero lost what he wanted. He strikes out. Use your dancing, you know? What if that was the pinnacle? What if that's it?"

He stared at me. "Sometimes I think that."

"Sure, yes. Of course you do. Anyone would. So use it." I waited, feeling much less casual than I was acting.

"All right then," he agreed. "It wasn't that I didn't *want* to do it."

And it wasn't that I was so assured of my power as a director, of my ability to draw from him the performance I wanted. But I had an instinct about him; he had to play Hero.

In the play Hero destroys a young girl, in revenge against his friend the Count, who had once convinced him that Hero's first love, now dead, was beneath him. And so Hero cruelly seduces the Count's present love—the penniless governess of the Count's children—and she leaves the Count forever. Afterward Hero can't live, and he purposely challenges Villebosse, an expert marksman, to a duel with pistols.

The first day of our rehearsal, I thought, I can't pull this off. I looked around the table at my cast; the flaming hair of my Villebosse; the heavily made-up eyes of the woman playing the Countess; Patrick's green-and-black hat on the table. How ever would this group come together into the vision of wit, truth, and emotional catharsis I had imagined?

"I haven't directed much," I started. Fatal mistake. "I'm an actor. Which means that even though I have many ideas about *The Rehearsal*, what I care most about is the acting. We have to truthfully bring ourselves *up* to the material. The reality's heightened and the events are compressed, but it's very true to life. The thing to remember is that Anouilh writes people, first and foremost. To paraphrase Strasberg, you don't have to play a person, you already are one."

The reading went well. Patrick did nothing, which pleased me.

On the way home he said, "Robert, you should never devote yourself exclusively to directing. Acting is much too important to you."

"God," I said, "it has to be, doesn't it? Or why would we go through all the crap we have to in order to do it? I suppose it's incredibly helpful to men, having to confront our emotions . . ."

"Though it's not about emoting," he said. "That was a revelation to me, that you have to sneak up on the feeling, and that it is less about what you're feeling than what you do about it."

"I used to practice sense memory in chemistry class," I said.

"How very precocious," said Patrick. "Did you ever weep?"

"Weep? I think it's beyond me."

There were matters we couldn't discuss, but somehow we got at them through acting talk.

What I wanted from Patrick was his real involvement in the role, what I needed from him for Hero was his pain, the demon that resided in every actor. I had come to realize that a demon resided in each human being—a blister of pain, personal and tragic enough to fuel many parts. The difference between nonactors and actors was that actors learned to encourage it, mine it, like a treasure.

Slowly, he let down his guard. What inner material he used for Hero I didn't know. Any performance is a dense weave of associations, observations, old wounds, and desires. Eventually, too, the details become indistinct, as individual notes do in music, and from the actor's perspective, he and the role come together into a rushing sensation like life. He is swept up and carried off by the imaginary events unfolding around him. Then it's like skiing down a well-known but constantly changing terrain. I saw this happen with Patrick, and as it did, as his Hero took on this wholeness, this life, it threw out hints, flickers of light from the source. And I saw, as I had only intuited before, why I had imagined him as Hero, and what my own selfish reasons were for wanting Patrick. Patrick was sympathetic; no matter what he did you still cared for and felt for him. Hero was a wretched, malevolent creature, but the play could not succeed if the audience hated him. So here was Patrick, hurt, dangerous, real, and yet still innocent and magnetic.

The night after the opening show, in the loft where we had the party, I cornered Irene to tell her how well it had gone.

"He wasn't even nervous," I said. "When I went back, he was—" I didn't know how to describe it. "Just the usual Patrick, with that sort of sweet, eager expression he has, and then—to see him in the play. To see what he's doing. I couldn't believe it."

I kept having this double illusion of Patrick as my friend and Patrick as Hero—though I knew that I couldn't take credit for what he had done. He had worked hard, and he hadn't succeeded overnight. But the right part can free an actor; faith can free too. I felt proud of my faith in Patrick.

"He makes the sign of the cross," I said to Irene, "before going on."

"I'm sure with Patrick it's very sincere. Where is he?"

"Oh, gone. Off to some Irish bar uptown with Bryan."

"Bryan's here?"

"Yeah, he's in town to do a play."

She came with me to the last performance, three weekends later. She sat beside me in the darkness, exceedingly still. In the seduction scene, with the girl in his arms, he turned his face away from her as if seeing the other girl, his first love, and I almost saw her myself. And when he turned back to the girl in his arms he lightly touched his face to hers. Awful, as though he were passing his grief into her. It was his best performance.

The lights blacked and came up for the last scene, where Hero provokes Villebosse into the duel. Irene started to cry, to sob, loud enough that I was sure they could hear it onstage. The house was small, the audience level with the playing space, and I knew the effect was disturbed. *For once this is not about you, damnit,* I thought.

She didn't stay for the calls; she pushed by a group of people and ran out of the theater.

I found her at the end of the hallway, slumped against the dirty white cinder-block wall. I hadn't seen her cry in real life before and I was stunned by the spectacle of it, how she cried with all of her body, her shoulders heaving.

"Irene," I said coldly.

"I'm sorry," she managed.

"What is it?" Earlier that day she had presented the picture of a young glamorous actress in her beige linen suit and silk blouse, her gold earrings bolts of ultra-worldly light in her hair. Now her ankles fell off to the sides of her shoes, and her shoulders were as hunched and sharp as an old woman's.

"Did you find what he did so extremely affecting?" She caught my sarcasm, and looked at me.

"There is a quality in him," she said. "No, it's more concrete than that. I've felt it practically since the first day I met him, and to see him like that—"

"Like what? He was wonderful, wasn't he? This is what we've always wanted for him, isn't it?" I couldn't be patient.

"I said I was sorry."

"I'm going back." But as I left she said firmly, "You don't understand." I stopped and turned.

I felt thrown in a way I had never felt thrown by her before. Suddenly her reaction suggested depths I refused to acknowledge—in him and in her.

It would be years before I could finally interpret this night, and the ways in which I had so closely, unconsciously, aligned art with life. But I saw sparks of it then, in her eyes.

"What?" I asked.

"Go ahead," and she fumbled in her bag for tissue. "I'll be there in a minute."

"What did you mean?" I asked.

"Nothing," she said gently.

9 The Pool

It was the tail end of a depressing and stagnant summer when I met Patrick's sister for the second time, or rather I called her.

All of that summer I'd stayed alone in the apartment, stuck looking after St. Martin, while Irene and Patrick worked out of town. Weeks after *The Rehearsal* Patrick was cast in a show at the Goodman and then a new play at the Guthrie in Minneapolis. Irene spent the summer in Pennsylvania, doing stock. I stayed behind in the city waiting tables, dutifully lifting my weights, and sending out head shots and résumés to no effect. Topping everything off, Brenda went back to her husband. Then I was saved, temporarily, by a job at a theater in Boston, the Boston Classic. It paid very little, but I didn't care. I gleefully dropped Irene's cat at my parents' place and took off.

I explored the redbrick streets of Boston, and walked through Harvard Yard, thinking of Patrick. I ended up calling his sister, Margie. The family business, it turned out, was wool on the mother's side—the probable source of Patrick's trust. His father and brothers were accountants, not occupations I would have envisioned for male O'Dohertys.

Beneath the Boston accent Margie reminded me of Patrick, in her cheeriness and in the extremely interested attitude she took as she talked to me.

"Oh, I don't think Patrick's ever gotten over my parents' divorce," Margie said. "Well, they're technically separated, but they haven't lived together for years."

So much for the happy family, I thought.

"Ah well, Patrick is sensitive," she said, "as you know. But he's stubborn too. I can never get him to visit. Father doesn't understand him. Father did make an attempt last year, inviting us all to a benefit at his alma mater, Boston College, do you know it?"

"Not Harvard?" I said.

"Harvard? No," she replied. "Father and my other brothers attended Boston College."

"Did Patrick?"

She laughed. "Goodness, no. It was always dancing for him, he ran to New York as soon as he could right out of high school and he's never come back, not once."

I felt a sort of roaring in my ears. As she talked I wondered what wasn't a lie. I stared at the phone as one might an unfamiliar, vaguely threatening creature.

BY FALL IRENE was in North Carolina, playing the lead in a fifties comedy. Patrick remained in Minneapolis. He had become disillusioned. Derek, his director at the Guthrie, tormented Patrick with pages and pages of contradictory notes after each performance. In October, I received a letter from Irene.

Dear Robert,

I am thoroughly, from my toes to the tips of my hair, deliriously happy. There's got to be something perverse in loving our work as much as we do. I would not even TELL you how happy I am if you weren't working too. I wake up smiling. Okay, so it's a silly comedy, but playing it eight shows a week I learn all kinds of things. Andre says keep it

new, but I never have to try. And when I'm not working I loll in the
grass or read or cook—all of these lovely, ordinary things. I mean,
when I'm not at the theater I can live, because I'm not worrying about
looking for work. What a relief.

I have to tell you, and this is really the reason I'm writing, that
Patrick's unhappy. You probably know. Poor darling, he told me he
thought that in straight theater, as opposed to musicals, where words
and ideas are more important, it would be more refined. He didn't expect all the power plays and ego. Derek's a dog.

But that isn't what I want to say. I visited Patrick before I came down
here—did he tell you? One night we stayed up until four and he told
me that he did not hurt his knee on a jump. It was a car accident,
Robert. Somebody died. I don't have all the details. But he was on tour
with Maria in a show and their choreographer, Benton somebody (have
you heard the name?) who was also, evidently, his lover, was a total
beast and somehow initiated the accident. This other boy died, this
other dancer. Patrick could have died too. Benton basically set up the
situation that led to the accident. Then when it happened, he wasn't
even in the car. Patrick said I could tell you, but he was drunk. He may
not have meant it. But now you know. For me, it kind of explains things.
The loss of his dancing was worse than we knew. It's tragic, isn't it? We
have to be patient with him. He needs us.

On a lighter note, his new friend, Herbert, from the show, is an absolute doll. Ha-ha. I mean kind of literally. He's about my size and is
completely devoted to Patrick. It's an unrequited love (I mean, don't
even think of the height differential) and I can't help but feel a great
sympathy toward him. Unrequited or not, Patrick likes him. He teases
him constantly, about his size and Canada, where Herbert is from,
but if it weren't for Herbert, Patrick would be back in New York by
now.

So call me. I doubt you'd ever write. Have fun, be brilliant. I miss you
so much.

XXOX love, Irene

I put down the letter. I didn't feel anything. I was not even sure it
was true. Histrionics? Exaggeration? It just made me tired.

I HAD BEEN HOME in New York for a month, it was well into November, when one night Irene called. "Hi, guess where I am?" Her voice sounded breathy, excited. "I'm *here,* in New York."

"Really? How come?"

"Oh, well the star fell on his face and they closed the show. He went down right before my eyes center stage and didn't revive." She sighed, "They had to buy us out of our contracts so I got money. And here I am. I've been back five days."

I figured she was with Andre. Even as she proclaimed she despised him and would never, under any circumstances, see him again, there would be a relapse. Her work out of town had kept them apart, but it had also kept alive whatever was between them. Absence makes the heart grow fonder—or makes the heart forget.

"I'm not at Andre's," she said in a low voice, conspiratorially. "He has zero knowledge of where I am. I'm at a friend's."

"Are you drunk?"

She giggled, "Sorta. I've opened a bottle of Taittinger and I need you to help me drink it—can you?"

"Sure."

"Oh Robert, I have so much to tell you. I missed you so much. I would have called sooner, but I've been down, just generally crazy— I don't know, for no reason. I'm giving up Andre, I *am,* for once and for all and—I'll tell you when you get here." She gave me a Park Avenue address, and hung up.

The address was a massive prewar brick and limestone building on Park in the Eighties. I'd always wanted to see an apartment in one of these buildings, though I didn't expect anything on the scale of 2B.

I was announced by the doorman, and went up. There were only two doors in the quiet hallway. I knocked on B, she opened the door, and at first I saw only her, in a red satin robe, her face flushed and smil- ing, hair back, a few strands straggling prettily forward. Behind her there was a stretch of gleaming white marble and a staircase rising up into a blueness that was as expansive as sky. She threw her arms around me; through the satin of her robe she felt damp and very warm, almost hot.

She stepped back, took my hands and said, "Good, excellent haircut."

"You look great," I said, "where'd you get the robe?" She pivoted to show me the dragon embroidered on her back, "It's not mine," she said, "it belongs to the apartment." That's when I saw it: the faux-marble columns, the Venetian mirror, the pale silk-papered walls; I registered that we were standing in an entryway twice the size of my living room, and that the floor was, yes, real marble and the staircase, freestanding and leading up to another floor, passed a celestial blue ceiling adrift with fleecy clouds.

"What'd you do," I asked, "dump Andre for one of the Rockefellers?"

"Not quite." She took my hand and led me to a gilt claw-footed table, where she'd put the champagne and two glasses.

"Look at that," she said, pouring the champagne. She nodded at a small fountain with glycerine drops simulating water, a gilded Pegasus rearing up in the center. I caught sight of a grouping of sheep-sized bronze deer, pretend-grazing under the stairs.

"They stopped short of paintings on velvet," she told me. "Here, let's toast and I'll give you a tour." We clicked glasses: "To our return."

"Our return," I said.

It was decorated everywhere to the teeth. But amid the lushly cushioned sofas, endless antiques, Tiffany clocks, and the sheer number of rooms were reminders that whatever pains the owners had taken to impress, they were closer in spirit to Liberace.

"I have be-e-en vedy, vedy comfortable here," Irene said, coming back downstairs after viewing the bedrooms. We returned to the claw-footed table and polished off what was left of the champagne.

"What's in there?" I asked, indicating a set of double doors.

She whispered, "That's the outrageous thing I told you I wanted to show you on the phone."

"The whole place is outrageous."

"Here, wait," and she went and brought back a fresh bottle of champagne, and I popped the cork and we watched it bounce the length of the white marble floor and carom off one of the columns, spray bursting around us in a fan.

We went through the opening, which was dark, to the doors. "Okay," she whispered, "are you ready?"

"How come you're whispering?"

"I keep feeling like we broke in."

"Yeah, me too," I said, low.

"Here, cheers," she whispered. We clicked glasses and drank, and she opened the doors, laughing convulsively.

My eyes adjusted to the dim low-ceilinged space. It was a swimming pool, with a larger-than-life Romanesque torso at its far end, smoky mirrors at the sides, and a glowing cerulean-blue-painted ceiling. I walked closer and looked up to see that the ceiling was lit, from behind. It was painted with golden planets and stars and the symbols of the zodiac.

"Come here," Irene said, setting down the champagne and our glasses by the Jacuzzi—she pulled me over to a couple of doors reading GUYS and GALS beside cowboy-boot decals.

"Don't tell me," I said. "Your father struck oil."

"Not my father, but somebody's did." She raised her eyebrows mysteriously, opened the "Guys" door and said, "Find a suit and we'll get in the Jacuzzi."

The suits ranged from boxy trunks to skimpy Speedos. I found one midway between the two styles that fit and put it on and went back out to her. She was in the water, filling our glasses. She had on a black string bikini.

"Glad you came over?"

"Uh-huh." We sat opposite each other.

"So I'm waiting," I said.

She sipped her champagne. "His name's Floyd. Don't look like that, Floyd's a perfectly common name."

"I didn't say anything."

"You were thinking it."

"No, I wasn't." Her legs brushed mine under the water.

"He's very sweet. This isn't his, it's his father's."

"Oh, just a boy?"

"Thirty-eight."

"Well, for you—"

"Ha-ha." She grinned. "Irma's his mother. His father's named Dude." She giggled. ("Dude?" I could hear Patrick saying. "As in *ranch?*")

"You met him in North Carolina?"

"But really they're Texans. Old friends of Cal's, our star. Cal got Floyd a job at the theater, managing the house, because Floyd—well, he's sweet, as I said, but confused. He's never quite decided what he wants to do with his life."

"So he's trying show business," I said.

"Yes. Dude has bought him a play. Oh, it's fabulous, Robert, and they're doing it in New York and I can audition, there's a part that's just *perfect* for me." Oh Irene, I thought, but didn't say anything.

She rested her head on the tile behind her, then looked back at me and said, "I'm hiding." What was it about her tonight? All these levels, quick switches, layers of emotion.

"Hiding from what?" I asked.

"Andre. That's why I'm here. When the show closed, I told Floyd I was afraid to come back and he said I could stay here. They're almost never here. They won't be here for weeks, when they shop around the play."

"Are you sleeping with him?"

"Floyd?" She opened her eyes wide, as if to say, Are you mad?

"How are you feeling?" she asked, changing the tone.

"Just fine," I said quietly.

"If Andre calls me in North Carolina then I won't be there," her eyes fevered, wet lips slightly parted. It was still about Andre. "He won't know where I am," she said, "and I like that. Andre doesn't respect me." There were tiny beads of sweat on her upper lip and forehead. I had only half heard what she said; I felt the hot jets of water, soothing, stimulating.

She drained her glass. "Let's throw our glasses at the wall. They have boxes and boxes of glasses."

She pitched her glass at the wall by the table where the telephone was plugged in. It shattered and I got up—God, I didn't really feel how I felt until I got up, light-headed, floating. I turned and tossed the glass backhanded over my shoulder.

She laughed and said, "Race," and dove into the pool. I jumped and my skin contracted and opened to coolness, and my entire being flowed with the water around me as I swam to the far end behind her. She did a flip turn and I nearly caught her, my hand grazing her slick smooth calf, but she slipped away; I swam faster, using my strength, and beat her by half a lap.

"How the hell did you win?" she said, coming up from the water, panting, her hands on the ledge.

"I'm faster than you are. Why are you such a bad loser?"

"Can you grab the champagne? Have a victory drink."

With our backs to the ledge we took turns drinking from the bottle, looking off at the torso at the far end of the pool.

"If we got very drunk and stayed in the water," she said, "we could drown." She brought her hand down from her chest and ran it, with the fingers spread, through the water.

"But we won't," I said. Our voices were very clear, reverberant in the moist hollow chamber. The bottle was empty. I turned to put it up on the ledge; I faced her, my arms enclosing her. I kissed the side of her face and her neck.

"What are you doing?" she said.

I looked at her, "Do you mind?" Her eyes were a very dark blue in this light; with my finger I traced the line of her lips, kissed her softly, the side of her brow, and touched her hair, which was soft and wet, slick against her head.

She leaned back, looking up at the ceiling. "There's you. Aquarius. There's me. Leo the lion." She was being coy. She pulled away and I turned her around so that our positions were reversed, my back against the ledge, and pulled her in close.

"Robert, no—"

"Yes," I said. It didn't matter what she said, I didn't care about Andre or Floyd or whether she had meant it to happen, or whether I had
just finally chosen to push it. She pressed her pelvis against me, but
then she drew back a little, and I let her.

"I—" she stopped.

"You want me to," I said.

"But I don't."

"Yes, you do." I untied her top, and it fell in the water. "Irene," I
said. She didn't move. She just looked at me, and I ran my hand along
her breast, pulled her into me again with my other hand on her waist,
pulling her up higher, against me. We kissed, softly, but then she put
her hands behind my neck and really kissed me—I felt her tongue in
my mouth and was shocked at the sensation, together with the thought
that this was Irene I was kissing. I kissed her back. Again she pulled
away, just her head and her shoulders, and I saw and couldn't believe
how excited she was, her breath shallow, mouth open, her eyes half
closed, and I thought: Oh God, don't let me be too drunk to do it.
Then we were thrashing around in the water, slamming against the
ledge and the wall, the water sloshing around us, and I got off the bottom of her suit, and my own, and then we were trying to get out of the
water but we were both crazy with it, with lust, and didn't have any
control, so we didn't make it out of the pool but did it on the steps.
And I only really *know* this because of the scrapes I saw on her back
and my knees the next day. I didn't remember it, only flashes really—
the smell of the chlorine, my face in her hair, getting out of the pool
and somehow back out to the entryway and up the stairs, where again
we were overtaken and did it at the top of the stairs on a rug. I stood
then and told myself to calm down, thinking as we walked down the
hall to the bedroom of the things I would do with her when I got her
in bed—what those things were I don't know. Whether we *did* them
or not or did *anything* in the bed I don't know.

Maybe it was the Jacuzzi. But I woke up in a vast bed, in a room
that combined the decor of a Victorian parlor with an opium den:

ominous pieces of furniture, blood reds and golds, ubiquitous fabric, and fringe-dripping lamps. Somebody was driving a spike through my brain. Irene was lying beside me, I realized, and remembered enough to know where I was and why. We were under a canopy, thick red brocade. Irene was sleeping; she was a good sleeper, capable of sleeping through cataclysms. She didn't respond to my calling her name and so I got up.

I had this extreme urge to get out of the room. I found aspirin in a bathroom down the hall, and then urinated for ages. Then I remembered I was supposed to go to work, found a clock and saw that it was after eleven. How could I *do* that? I'd *never* done that. I should've been in at 9:30. Through Alix, my friend from Crispins, I had a more lucrative waitering job at a swank Midtown place that I couldn't afford to lose. I phoned the restaurant from a room with a moose head on the wall. The apartment was like a carnival fun house in which I was trapped. Fortunately Alix was working and told me she'd say I was sick. I went downstairs to find my clothes, traipsing stark naked down that immense staircase onto that gleaming floor, a huge frozen pond. Our suits lay in the pool like abandoned casings. The shattered glass glinted dangerously on the tile. I went to the dressing room and took a shower, and then sat down on a bench to rest, feeling grim.

I'd really pushed it this time, and for what? I had never in my life convinced a woman to want me, love me. When you did that, what did you have? Nothing.

I felt like a walking cliché and a sucker. When she had invited me over I had resolved I'd get her in bed. Because I wanted to get laid. Because I hadn't seen her in a while, which seemed to change things that hadn't changed. Because in Boston I had obsessed on that day I had first kissed her when she had said, "We can sleep together if you want," and back in New York I had thought, okay, I want to, give me a turn, huh?

What was *wrong* with me? This wasn't just any girl, this was Irene, *Irene,* and as I said her name to myself, all she was to me bloomed in my mind. She was brushed with a sort of magic. She was the hub of the wheel of our threesome. She had come to us at a time when I had started to feel the first burn, the first chill, of the knowledge that life might not work out as planned. But then she was there, and it seemed that our road was the right one, that we three were destined for great, fulfilled lives that others could only imagine. We would vault over the rest, confreres in a special society that no one else could understand. Exactly how she had reignited my hopes, I didn't know. She was just so incredibly warm, vibrant, gifted, and real—and there at the right time. *She was the real thing,* I thought. It had all felt so certain. I had felt that nothing could stop us, unless we made terrible, terrible mistakes.

I have to get out, I thought again. I took the keys I'd seen on the claw-footed table, found they worked in the front door, and left. I walked to Third Avenue and bought a bunch of yellow carnations, bagels, cream cheese, and a bag of coffee. Then went into a coffee shop and got a cup to go, but instead of going back to the apartment I sat down, and drank it while looking out at the busy gray street. Who are you? I thought, and why are you in my life? I could list her flaws to myself all day long and she wasn't diminished. Nothing she did altered anything finally. She was just always there, a force, a power, like a beautiful dream that lingers, coloring everything.

SHE WAS STILL ASLEEP. I put the flowers on the table beside her and went down to the kitchen and started brewing the coffee. There would be no more sex with Irene. I wouldn't watch while she relapsed with Andre, or some other old guy with money or fame, or the *son* of one.

I stomped up the stairs, hoping I'd awaken her. How dare she grab onto me, *use* me, as she did Floyd, a middle-aged cowboy living off his parents, as a replacement for Andre, because Andre didn't *respect* her —why should he? Oh, we were a fellowship; me, Andre, and Floyd. I felt closer to them in my anger than I'd ever felt to Irene. But then I saw her still sleeping, looking so innocent and young—it was remarkable to me that she was still asleep, so trusting, while I had been thinking horrible thoughts about her.

She opened her eyes, and I would rather have walked through fire than ever, ever hurt her again. I kissed her on the mouth, but it was a chaste brotherly kiss.

"You smell like outside," she said.

I pushed her hair from her face. She saw the flowers and sat up and the covers dropped down and I picked them up and draped them chastely around her. She gave me an odd look, but didn't say anything; smelled the flowers.

"Thanks," she said.

"I got breakfast too." I took her hand and held it lightly. "You know what? When I met you, you smelled like cinnamon."

"Cinnamon?"

"Yeah." I stared at her hand.

"Bad perfume," she said. "What do I smell like now?"

"Chlorine."

She laughed.

"Irene, let's not do that again."

"Okay."

"I don't think—"

"I agree with you."

"You do?"

"But don't go anywhere."

"I'm not going anywhere."

"I'm lonely. Stay with me today." She put her forehead down on my shoulder, resting it there. "Do you still love me?"

"Of course. Don't be ridiculous."

"I love you too."

"Okay, then."

She touched my face with the tips of her fingers. "I'm gonna take a shower."

She got up and walked across the room naked and that's when I saw the scrapes on her back, from her tailbone up past the center of her back.

"Irene—"

She turned around, "What? Oh c'mon, you know what I look like."

"No, your back." We went to the bathroom together and she examined it in the mirror.

"I'm sorry," I said. "Does it hurt?"

"Not really." She blushed and reached for a towel, and I left the room nearly faint with desire, confusion, and a salty taste at the back of my throat. Never before had anyone so affected me. She was treacherous, like an addiction.

WE HAD THE COFFEE and bagels downstairs. I teased her about the twang that had come back in her speech since North Carolina.

"You know me," she said. "In a week I'll be talking like I was born to third-generation New Yorkers."

We went for a walk down Fifth Avenue and over to Rockefeller Center, where they had put up the Christmas tree and a few skaters twirled to the piped-in music. Then we went back north again toward Central Park, crossed by the Plaza and the line of carriages parked near the fountain.

"Poor horse," she said to a mangy creature, its head hanging low, its tail switching lightly at the pavement.

In the park we went to the lake, then walked along the paths by the shore. Irene talked about Andre, about how he had locked her in a small room one night and did not let her out until morning, had sometimes given her money for a hotel. He hadn't wanted her to move out, however, that wasn't the point.

"There's something missing in Andre," she said. "I don't know why, whether he's lived too long for nothing but work, had a miserable childhood, he never told me. He could be terribly kind . . . I could tell he wanted to love me, but he had to keep making me into something, like he didn't know how to stop being a teacher. He said with me it was different. That it was serious and he wanted to marry me."

"Did you want to marry him?" I asked.

"No."

I could see she was flattered by the idea, may have flirted with it. What a catch for a girl from Kansas. Somebody so patently out of her league. The trouble was she had not reckoned on his seeing through her, which he obviously did. Why else would a young, beautiful woman go for Andre if not for his pull? She had outright admitted the move was careerist. Sometimes I couldn't help feeling when he'd treated her badly that she'd gotten exactly what she deserved. I still didn't believe that she was finished with him, though, and that made me feel slightly sick.

"Are we lost?" she asked.

We had emerged from a twisting pathway and the lake was nowhere in sight; a stream trickled by in a narrow ravine, and the trees here were dense, even stripped of their leaves, the sky crisscrossed by branches. "Oh God, we're lost," she said hopelessly.

"No, we're not," I said. She had stopped. "Come on." But her eyes filled with tears. "Hey," I put my arm around her. "We're not really lost. It's all right, we'll find the way back."

We went on, walking silently side by side for a couple of minutes, then we rounded a bend and there was the Delacorte Theater and we knew where we were.

"I've done such stupid, stupid things this year," she said. "I just get frightened. Here I am back in New York. I never feel that I'm good enough here."

"You're good enough."

"I was on such a roll, and now what? It felt so good, and I feel so hollow and useless without the show. It's the only place where everything about me makes sense, you know?"

"Yes."

"It's like what attracted me most to Andre. It was how he could *see* me, all of me, even my contradictions and the qualities in myself I despair of. He saw it all, and it was okay. He helped me to understand that my totality could be put to use. It was my capital. In acting nothing was wasted, and nothing was ever really lost. He was so good for me in the beginning. . . ."

We came out near Columbus Circle and headed towards Top-of-the-Park to look over the impossibly beautiful city. In the lounge, we sat sipping wine, enthralled by the wintery powder blue light cloaking everything gently. I thought that deep down she really didn't give a damn about that fancy apartment back there on Park Avenue and that she hadn't run off with Andre that summer just to secure her career. She was more complicated than that. That same tenderness I'd felt in the morning swept through me; there was nothing I wouldn't forgive her. And warmed by the wine we were light-hearted again, cocky, proud of ourselves for how well we had handled our tryst.

"I have the best idea," she said. "Come live with me! Why don't we go down to Fourteenth Street and pack you up for a week?"

I laughed and said, "I have to work."

"You can still go to work. Come on," she said, "as a kick, a diversion."

"A change of scene," I put in doubtfully.

What the hell, I wasn't planning to break off our friendship because of the previous night.

On the way I said, "Irene, remember that day you came out of rehearsal for the show on East Fourth?"

"Yes," she said.

"What did you mean when you said you and I could sleep together if I wanted to?"

She sighed. "Men think sex is so important. It just isn't." Her hair blew back from her face and her scarf lifted high in the breeze. She laughed in delight and rose up on her toes as if meeting the wind and said, "B-r-r."

Later, we ordered out from a gourmet food store for dinner. Then we called Patrick. Irene described the apartment, but soon she broke off and grew serious, listening.

"Here," she said to me, "talk to him. He says he's coming here tomorrow."

"What's up?" I said into the phone.

"Robert. They gave me no notice. I had to get out of my room and now I've moved into a nightmare, a place in which you can tell someone has recently died. Do you remember *Lost Weekend*? Ray Milland goes on that bender—"

"Patrick, aren't you under contract?"

"Don't you want me to come?"

"We want you to *come,* that's not—" Irene was signaling to me. "What?" I asked her. "Patrick, just a minute."

"He shouldn't stay if he's that unhappy, should he?" she said.

"Patrick," I said, "I don't think you should fuck yourself up with Derek. You said he had a lot of influence, not just there, but—"

"Robert, he's some kind of throwback to earlier times. I can't stay, the future is too hypothetical, I'm on the verge of nervous collapse."

As I hung up Irene said, "He's coming then. Do you think it's okay?

"I don't know," I said.

HE SHOWED UP the next night, thinner and harried, his plane having been delayed. I gave him a tour of the downstairs. At the doors to the pool I said, "Brace yourself."

He had to stoop going in, and when he saw it I thought he would swoon. "*No,* don't insist I go any further," he said. "I will dine in the Jacuzzi and sleep on a chaise lounge. There I am! Pisces. The fish," he said, straining to be cheerful.

Then we brought his bags upstairs and he chose a room. "Ah, this is nice, if austere," he said. "The Japanese room, must be Robert's."

We passed the Victorian opium den. "Irene's," he said, tipped off by her clothes on the bed. "Quite a bordello. Oh, look at this one. All frothy and white, fit for a virgin—well, that *isn't* one of us." Then, "Robert, I must." We were inspecting the room with the moose head, but I think what attracted him was the black panther bedspread.

"This will be mine," he said finally. "It's so butch."

I worked days at the restaurant while Irene and Patrick went shopping, to the movies, and one afternoon to the ballet. Evenings we swam, had dinner together, and drank champagne as the cases in the pantry dwindled. Each night we read in the library, with its heavy damask drapes shrouding the windows and carved wood paneling.

On the sixth night, Irene announced: "I've made a decision. I'm not going out of town anymore. What's the good of working where no one can see me? I have to work *in* town or I'll never have a career."

"That would depend," I said, "wouldn't it?"

"I don't think so. You know what I heard about de Kooning? Why he's a drunk? He and a lot of those abstract painters worked so long in obscurity that they were ruined. He was in his fifties when he was discovered and it was too late."

"But he kept painting, didn't he?" I said. "I mean, he's still this fantastic painter."

"Yeah, he kept painting," she said. "In a cold-water loft. They all had these cold-water lofts in SoHo. You could afford them then, they didn't cost anything."

"Faulkner," Patrick said, "started out in New Orleans, and supposedly he could live for a month on the money he made working some odd job for three or four days."

"Exactly," she said. "But an actor—even if you could afford to work without making any money, and for years and years no one knew about you, and you didn't care—you can't do it alone. It isn't like being a writer or a painter. You can't sit in a room doing monologues forever."

"We're so dependent," Patrick said. "It's so depressing."

"We should start our own theater," I said. We all laughed.

"I'm heartsick," said Patrick. "Here, have a cigar." Earlier he had unearthed a humidor in his bedroom.

We had on swimsuits and robes: Irene, the red satin; me, a conservative terrycloth in a pale bluish gray; and Patrick, a Cary Grant number, a brown-and-burgundy print with brown satin lapels.

"If we did have our own theater," I said, "what would we do?"

"*Philadelphia Story*," Patrick said.

"Oh God," Irene said, "that would be fabulous for us."

"I've always thought you should do Shaw's *Cleopatra*," I said to her.

"Really? Robert, that's so sweet, *thank you*. Oh, oh. The two of you should do *The Zoo Story*."

"*Yes*," I said.

"Can I be the man with the parakeets?" Patrick asked.

"Indubitably," she answered. "You'd be the psycho," she told me, "you love playing psychos."

"We should do all of Chekhov," I said. "And Tennessee Williams."

"And Ibsen," she said.

"Can we do Sean O'Casey?" Patrick asked.

"Sure," I said.

Down the hall a door definitely shut. "Someone just came in the front door," said Irene.

We all froze.

"What should we do?" Patrick said.

"I'll go see who it is," Irene answered, getting up. "You stay here. Oh, what a bore, betcha a thousand it's Floyd."

"Who's Floyd?" Patrick asked me.

"He lives here."

"Oh yes."

"Son of Dude."

"Floyd, *hi*," we heard her saying, "what a surprise."

"She's his guest," Patrick said. "We're not doing anything wrong."

But I didn't have a good feeling. In fact, suddenly I had a very bad feeling. We heard their feet, he appeared in the doorway beside Irene, and my bad feeling got worse.

"This is Floyd," she said to us. "Floyd, Robert and Patrick."

He wore a Stetson, an ankle-length duster, cowboy boots with silver tips on the toes; he had long reddish blond hair and a Fu Manchu mustache.

"Charmed," Patrick said, rising—which I thought wise. Floyd was short, but stocky as a bull.

"What's going on?" he said to Irene.

"Floyd, I told you, these are my friends."

"You're wearing my robe," Floyd said to me. "And *that*," he said to Patrick, "belongs to my father."

"How *is* Dude?" Patrick asked.

There was a pause. "We'd better be trundling along," Patrick said. "Pardon us."

But Floyd wouldn't move to let us get by.

"Stand clear, my good man," Patrick said.

"Those are my father's cigars," Floyd said, and he rolled back on his heels and hitched up his trousers.

"Oh Floyd, don't be a redneck," Irene said. She pulled him into the room, and Patrick and I started off down the hallway.

"He smelled like bourbon," Patrick said. "Should we leave her alone?" But then Irene came after us. "Don't worry, he's exactly like all these guys I grew up with, I know how to handle him—"

"*Irene*," he bellowed.

"Coming!" she called. "But I suppose it's good that you're going."

"You really topped yourself this time, Irene," Patrick said.

Floyd came out of the library. We went on to the entryway.

"*Hold it!*" he called to us.

"Floyd, don't be stupid," she said. "They're *leaving*."

"Did they stay here?" he asked her. "Did they stay here with you?"

"I don't believe this," she said. "Yes, they stayed here, what of it?"

"I don't like it," he said, "I don't like it one bit." He stood with his legs apart, hands on his hips. He was one of those little guys who picked fights.

"How long have they been here?" he asked her.

"Since the first day I came here," she snapped. "I slept with them both. I slept with him Monday and Wednesday." She nodded at me, and then at Patrick. "And with him Tuesday and Thursday. Over the weekend we all slept together."

Floyd couldn't quite compute that. "Ho-ho, that's a good one, Irene."

"I'm not kidding," she said, her eyes ablaze.

His face fell, and for a second I felt sorry for him. "You stayed in my apartment and slept with these men?" he asked her.

"Yes, Floyd, I did."

The wind had gone out of his sails, completely. "I thought you were okay, Irene. I thought we were together."

"You don't even know me. The one reason you *wanted* to know me was to sleep with an actress. You used me, Floyd."

"*I* used *you?*"

"Irene, let's just go," I said.

"He can't do anything," she answered. "There's two of you and only one of him."

"Irene, don't you dare," Patrick said. "Just be quiet, let's go."

She looked at him, then at Floyd. She was *outraged,* and with great effort said, "Okay, we'll go."

"Five minutes!" yelled Floyd. "Be out in five minutes or I'll call the police!"

We went upstairs and packed. When we came back downstairs he was pacing back and forth in the entryway.

"Floyd," Irene said, "we have too much stuff, so I've left my bags upstairs in the hallway. I'll come for them tomorrow."

"Bitch," he said.

"Watch your language," said Patrick.

"I'll have them *sent,*" Floyd told her. He stood fuming while she wrote our address for him on a slip of paper from her purse. He had probably envisioned a sexy reunion. "Bitch," he repeated.

"*Floyd,*" I said, "*watch* it." I had just had the astounding idea that a fight might be fun.

She gave him the address, saying "What time may I expect my bags to arrive?"

"Whenever I get around to it." His lips were ready but stopped mid-word.

"It's been fun," Patrick said.

"Get out," Floyd answered.

"Bye, Floyd!" Irene called. "Thanks for everything!" But then she turned to him once more—he was standing in the doorway—and said, "I guess this means I don't get an audition?"

He slammed the door shut. We clung to the walls of the hallway, trying to smother our laughter. "Oh, God," Irene said, "oh, God," wiping tears that ran down her face, "I can't stop laughing." She had a box of my belongings in her arms, I had my suitcase and Patrick's garment bag, and Patrick carried a trunk he had bought in Minneapolis.

We rode down in the elevator and went out to the street.

"Shit. Christ, *Jesus,* it's cold," Irene said.

"I can't even feel it," said Patrick.

"I don't want to go home," Irene said. "Let's get a drink." We took a cab to Third Avenue and got out at a singles place packed with drunk people in giant collars and Jordache jeans. We squeezed ourselves into a corner at the end of the bar and stacked everything on the trunk. Someone got up and Irene took the seat; Patrick and I stood crushed against the front windows.

"What's potent?" Irene asked.

We ordered stingers and relit our salvaged cigars, and Patrick said: "I have a confidence, friends." Another seat opened up. I sat down, and Patrick hovered between us with the clearest, most placid expression on his face. "On my thirtieth birthday," he said, "I will come into a legacy."

"Really?" said Irene.

"Oh?" I said, padding his dramatic pause.

"Yes. I will receive in the neighborhood of two million dollars from my mother's estate." We just looked at him. "I want to share it with you," he told us, "with you both, because I love you."

"God," I said. "Wow."

"Patrick, that's so sweet," said Irene.

He was very emotional. He looked at me, "Robert, you won't have to wait tables ever again." He looked at Irene. "And you can start sleeping with paupers."

"Ha-*ha,*" she said.

His eyes shined. "We can have a theater. Whatever we want."

10 Happy

The day after Floyd kicked the three of us into the bitter streets of Park Avenue, Irene and I picked up her cat in Fort Lee. I
hadn't collected him yet since my parents, against all expectation, had
become attached to the beast. He followed my mother around like a
puppy, so she couldn't help unintentionally trampling him at least once
a day.

"Oh, it wasn't a bother," my mother insisted, kissing him good-bye.
Irene gently settled St. Martin into his case, and then my mother knelt
down beside Irene and they clucked and cooed at him through the bars.

"What a darling."

"The baby."

They stood, and Marilyn took Irene's hands. "Now promise me
you'll come to dinner next week."

"We'd love to. Then the following week, you come to us. You can
visit St. Martin."

Ever after, my mother never neglected to ask about the cat when we
spoke on the phone. "Any work?" she would ask. (The restaurant was
my *job*, acting was my *work*, and I demanded that she refer to them
by their proper names.) Then, "How is Patrick? Irene?" Lastly, as though
he were my youngest and most precious child: "St. Martin?"

"Listen, Mom," I said repeatedly, "get a cat."

"No, I don't think I will . . . you know how they shed . . ."

"You said you didn't mind."

"Oh yes, but that was St. Martin."

St. Martin spent most of his time with Irene in her room, which was tiny—about the size of her room at Ruth's. But she said she liked it, and she would lie in there reading for hours, St. Martin sleeping beside her, and I'd think: two cats.

Irene was unusually free of attachments to possessions and places. For a woman she didn't have many clothes, the boots being her single indulgence. When she moved in, she borrowed a sewing machine from a friend and made curtains and a slipcover for the couch in the living room out of purplish blue fabric she bought at a shop on Orchard Street—but I think she did it more for Patrick and me than herself. This unsuspected talent of hers impressed me: I watched her busy at the curtains, her small white hands against the blue fabric—quick and skillful. Her mother had taught her to sew, she told me. She positioned the footlocker in her room exactly as at Ruth's, under the window, the photographs set out on top: the mother and the horse.

That first spring we all lived together, we remained poised on the brink of a change we could already sense, though not see.

I existed in a semiperpetual holding pattern to which I had almost adapted. The future was no longer self-evident, plastic, and surely better than the present. Gone entirely was the feeling I'd had at the beginning of that summer at Crispins, the feeling of satisfaction and marvelous ease—to *see* the fruit of my effort, with others I respected, and to think: this is how it will be. I hadn't been terribly young then, I hadn't expected a smooth stretch of luck onward and upward, but I *had* expected connections, progression.

Strangely, being deprived made me see and understand life in ways I would not have, otherwise: I would sometimes feel liberated into a perfect and complete present; the tiniest common details gained in intensity as they had as a result of acting, of art. But then I would see in

Patrick's eyes, or Irene's, that familiar anxiety, that disappointment, that wariness and defensiveness, and I knew that something had already started to dissolve.

So of course, things did happen, did change.

EARLY IN THE SPRING Patrick got a play at a regional theater in Kentucky, but was fired the third day of rehearsal. He glossed over why, just as we never really understood what had happened at the Guthrie. Irene was amazing in the lead in a showcase, but nobody came, and then again it was summer, and we were all in a similar frame of mind; not expecting anything to happen, and not even quite remembering what it was like when it had. Patrick did *The Importance of Being Earnest* in Brooklyn and was wonderful, but nobody came. I had had several near jobs that fell through. I continued to send out my pictures and résumés, although certainly not as hopefully as I once had. Nothing we did seemed to have any relation to what we got.

Patrick complained about pain in his knee and chewed aspirin like candy. He began using a walking stick when it rained, to take the pressure off his knee. He went on a radical macrobiotic diet and fainted one day getting out of the pool. He blamed his appearance for the difficulties in his career, which wasn't like him.

"If only I were handsome," he said. "In fifth grade I said a novena to the Blessed Mother to make me smashing and, as you can see, it didn't work."

Irene ran out of money and had to get a regular job. She started waitressing at a new restaurant on Seventh Avenue South, but she detested it and came home traumatized every night.

"I'm just no good at it," she complained, "I have no *aptitude*. How come what I'm good at is *negligable*?"

One day during the lunch rush she dropped a tray of food in the café, splattering diners with soup and pasta, and one of them, a well-dressed middle-aged man, as she described him, slipped her his card, saying "Call me as soon as you can." The guy was a shrink. On the card he had scribbled his home number, beside PLEASE! underlined thrice.

She explained to me what had happened while pacing and alternately smoking and gnawing on her nails. St. Martin worriedly circled her.

From my post at the doorway of the kitchen, well out of her way, I said, "He was trying to pick you up."

"Do you think?" Stopping and squinting at me through a tornado of smoke. "No, I seemed mentally ill."

"Irene, it's a come-on."

"It is?" She stubbed out her cigarette and, picking up St. Martin, sat down at the dining table; the cat sniffed at a streak of mustard on the collar of her blouse. "It's just that that tray on the floor felt like my life." St. Martin kept sniffing and she put him down. "Are you positive he's a jerk?"

"Yes."

"Then I better go cancel the appointment," she said.

"You made an appointment?"

"Yes. At the end of the day. I didn't call him at home or anything, I called his office."

"Why?"

She shrugged. "I thought it might help."

"Just like that?" I asked. "On the advice of a total stranger?"

She nudged St. Martin aside and got up, looking so weary—her fine shoulders slumped, and she emitted a faint aura of food, sweat, and faded flowery powder—that I wanted to put my arms around her and hold her, but I resisted. Occasionally, I let myself remember what I *could* remember about that night in the pool, or it came to me unawares and I didn't try to repress it—as she hung the drapes at the windows one warm sunny day, the blue bringing out the sheen of the blonde wood of the bookcases, muting the dinginess of the carpet. She stood up on the air-and-heat unit in cutoffs and my eyes skimmed her slim hips and her strong white legs and I wondered if that was what it would be like with a wife, always being in the vicinity of the woman you slept with, the woman you knew in that way, so that even the most banal household activities would radiate sex.

As predicted, she succumbed to Andre numerous times. She fought seeing him, but soon Patrick and I could read the signs of an impending lapse. Irene was so transparent—the opposite of Patrick. She would be quiet at dinner, then she would grow restless, switching the TV or the stereo on and off, and when we complained she'd defiantly state that she was going out.

Patrick always gave in. "Where, Irene?"

"Only out," she'd reply.

Then he or I would say we were going too and if she let us, we prevented another night of Andre. That spring, if she had been an alcoholic, Andre was the bar.

"Why?" I said to her one morning. "Just tell me why you do it."

"He's wise," she said softly.

"Wise, how?" I said. "Outside of the theater?"

She studied the rain tracing lines against the window and said, "He's definite. With him I know where I am. Whatever else he is, he is solid, substantial. Whereas my life—" her voice broke and she asked, "Well, what do I have?"

"You have me," I said, "and Patrick."

Yet the next night she was restless again.

She exploded out of her room. "I have to get out, let's go out. We never go out anymore."

Without looking up from his book Patrick said, "We went out last night to the theater."

"Doesn't count," she said, "I mean out. Walking, a café, a bar, on the *town*." Petulant, already dressed up in boots, a dress, her face made up; her hair, now long, piled on top of her head.

It was already eleven. I had an audition in the morning.

"You're afraid you'll get bags beneath your eyes?" she asked me, and she said it mean. "God, Robert, you're such an actor."

"Thanks a lot." I hated her, and looking at her, I thought she was ugly. She had gained just enough weight so she looked plump in the cheeks.

"Now children," Patrick said.

"Why do you have to be perfect?" she said. She threw out an arm, "You lift that damn barbell every day, you get an audition you always go and you *always* prepare. Don't you ever have a day when you just don't *care?*" she asked me.

"Don't be daft, my love," Patrick said. "Of course he does. He's only more practical than you are."

I had been sitting on the couch throughout her attack, which had materialized from thin air. I stood up. "I beg your pardon, but you don't give a fuck *what* I do, unless it interferes with something *you* want."

"Real-l-ly," she said.

"Really. I'm such an *actor?* You're such an *actress,* arrogant and temperamental and so fucking emotionally draining I've just about had it."

At that, she swept out the door—only Patrick made her come back and apologize, ruining the exit.

In July I got a message on my service from a commercial agency. I'd sent them a picture and probably eight hundred postcards, attracting the interest of an agent who in all likelihood would send me out once or twice and then relegate me to the "never works" file. I'd heard it took forty auditions to get one commercial, that *expert* commercial actors got one in twenty. To have any serious chance of working you had to audition all the time, and to audition *all the time* you had to know people—agents and casting directors. Each theater or production company, every advertising agency and soap opera, had a casting director—who would keep getting you in there. You needed a break to escape from the cycle of the catch-22. You needed some kind of notice to get noticed at all. I didn't feel optimistic.

I knocked off my shift early and, after a spit and a shine in the men's room, left for my appointment with Mr. Paul Joyce.

The secretary had said on the phone, "Mr. Joyce wants to meet you."

"Oh, fine," I'd replied, in an artificially casual voice.

Stay calm, I thought, in the agency's reception area, a stark corporate-type space, the unyielding fluorescent lights making me nostalgic for the clutter and closeness of Harry White's office.

A slim balding man in a tailored gray suit approached me from the mouth of the inner sanctum and asked if I were Mr. Holt.

"Paul Joyce," he said, "May I call you Robert?"

I walked with him past the secretary, who was told to please hold his calls. Normally my interviews with agents were conducted in the twenty-second intervals between calls from the Coast.

"Splendid, you match your picture," he said as we were seated.

His office was spare, but I preferred it to the office of another agent I'd recently met who had a wall behind his desk covered by Liza Minelli's face. He asked me a few questions, about Crispins and Carnegie Mellon.

"Well, Robert," he said then. "Bryan Johannes said I should meet you. He said you were extremely good-looking and talented and that I had better snatch you up before someone else did."

I stared at him, humorless without intending to be, and he smiled, displaying a perfect set of small even teeth.

"How do you know Bryan?" I said.

"I worked at the office that represents Bryan before I came here," he said.

"Oh." It was Patrick's office too.

"I only handle commercials," Paul told me, "an occasional soap, but Ms. Cohen and I have talked about adding another agent for stage, if that interests you. Are you open to commercials?" he asked. "I think you might do very well in the young daddy category, shall we try it?"

That was ironic, I thought. Some father I'd make. But thinking *that* hurt. "All right," I said.

He took a paper from his drawer.

"I'd like to sign you," he said. He handed me a contract. "Take it home and read it and call me in the morning, will you? I'd rather you didn't sign for less than a year—and I'll need more pictures, will you drop some by?"

We stood. "If you have any questions, call anytime," he said. "You might want to pay more attention to the commercials when you're watching TV than you normally do. The energy's high."

At home I found Patrick's address book and called Bryan.

"Oh yes," he said. "I saw your picture on his desk and told him he ought to call you. How's it going?"

"Oh, well, you know—um, it can be hard, so that's why—" No, I thought. Remember the unwritten rule: never sound negative. "Paul asked me to sign with him for commercials," I said.

"He's a very good agent. I never did commercials—well, one. It takes a knack, and I didn't have it. But they're good to do if you can, they can free up your time for the theater."

"I'll try it," I said. "Thanks again."

"Robert? Just keep doing whatever you can, and eventually it happens."

Patrick was thrilled.

"I must remind you," he said, "that Bryan was *very* impressed with your work on *The Rehearsal* and at Crispins."

"Have you seen Bryan since he's been back in town?" I asked Patrick.

"Oh, once or twice," he said, as if he wasn't quite sure.

Irene came home. I was already having doubts. "Listen," she said, "if he wants to sign you he wants to get behind you. It means that he'll really send you out, if he has the connections—"

"Bryan said he was good?" Patrick asked. "Then he must be."

She and Patrick agreed that I was a good type for commercials, whatever that meant.

We sprawled on the couch, our television on the coffee table, displaced from its usual, more discreet position in a corner of a bookcase, flipping channels as we watched commerical after commercial.

"Oh, I know Paul," Patrick said. "I met him, I know I did—snappy dresser, bald?"

"Yes, that's him," I said. "Good teeth?"

"Uh-huh. Nail polish?"

"Nail polish? No, I don't think so."

"It's subtle," said Patrick.

"Look!" Irene said, and we looked, and there was Clarence on the screen taking a shower slathered in *Coast* soap. Suddenly seeing him on TV was typical; you would think that an actor had died, and then out of nowhere their face would go by on the side of a bus, or their name would appear on a cast list in the paper. Actors were titans, I thought, as Clarence shot a big toothy grin at the camera and turned his face into the dazzling spray, *they never gave up.*

I STARTED GETTING commercials almost immediately. I watched TV constantly and read magazine copy into the bathroom mirror. At my first auditions I snuck out the scripts for further study at home. Some days I had as many as three auditions a day. In the humidity of July and August I carried changes of clothing from agency to agency or ran back to the apartment between young daddy calls—casual dress, or upscale "caj," depending on the client—and young businessmen calls, requiring a suit. Everything happened so fast once I met Paul that I hardly registered the initial rejections, or felt bothered by the continuing rejections—alongside the successes—that were simply a part of my new life.

Commercials called for an *essence.* I had to quickly convey the essence of daddyness and that was all. I'd arrive slightly ahead of my appointment, look over a monologue or dialogue, go in and do it and go home. Then wait for callbacks. When I got the booking, I got paid handsomely. Bookings took only a day, and often produced those fantastic bonuses, holding fees, and residuals.

It wasn't Shakespeare. All the acting I did was *happy*. I was happy because of this product—this shampoo! this diaper! this motor oil!—and you could be too! And *there was plenty of money*. Even the actors had a sheen about them, an air that said—up! happy! success! Everybody was nice: the casting directors, the smiling clients lining the long gleaming conference tables, the production people—only a little bit artsy, and somehow more polished, like the actors, than people in the theater. I had expected actors to be actors—thought I'd see the same people at a call for a Honda commercial that I'd see for an off-Broadway play. But the world of commercials, closer to modeling really, was its own unique place. I learned to be, on demand, a laser beam of enthusiasm. It was gravy, compared to waiting tables. I had a skill, I looked right, and now I could use all my time for paving the way to true success. Even friends of my parents were impressed. The doormen thought I was a star. I met gorgeous women. The checks mounted. I'd laugh when they came in the mail. Onward and upward, I thought. Bryan was right. It happened, and it wasn't really that hard.

I WAS COMING HOME one night and saw Irene jump out of a cab at Union Square. I was a block north, and by the time I got to the corner where she'd gotten out, the light changed and I had to wait. I watched her walk rapidly and disappear into our building.

At home she was sitting on the couch and had turned on one light, the lamp to her side. It was quiet except for St. Martin, meowing and pacing in front of her. She hadn't taken off her coat, and her purse lay on the floor.

"You okay?" She didn't look at me. "Irene?"

"Yes. St. Martin *be quiet*," she said, and he ran away and leapt up on the air-and-heat unit and watched her from there.

She said she had agreed to meet a producer that night in his office, he said he'd discovered Ali McGraw, but when she got there the building was deserted. He was casting a play she had read for, and so she hadn't been worried. He boasted about other work he had done, about the time he met Marilyn Monroe. Marilyn, he said, was waiting with him and another man for a table in a restaurant and someone came in from the street and, right there in the foyer, started fondling her, had her up against the wall with his hands on her breasts and she didn't do anything, like she didn't know how to defend herself or it didn't occur to her that she could or should, and he had to pull this stranger off her. It was a rough business, the producer said. Marilyn was great but she slept her way up, as most famous actresses did.

The producer was older. Short, fat, little red eyes, round stomach pushing at the buttons of his sweater, and after they'd talked awhile he told Irene that she was adorable, that he would use her in the play, and now could they fuck?

Irene took a deep breath. She said she didn't feel that way about him. He said he thought they had an understanding and she said he had misunderstood. Then he began to whine and kept asking and the room and the building felt even more empty. She started to feel that she was talking for her life. Finally, defeated, he said, not even a hand job? And she said no, she was sorry, and they went down together in the elevator and he unlocked the front door and let her out and she walked away casually until she was far enough away. Then she broke into a run and got a cab. Everything was okay, she said, she was only humiliated and felt terribly, gruesomely naive.

"Don't tell Patrick," she said.

"No, no I won't." I couldn't scold her, I couldn't judge her. Here was this great looking woman who should have been having a wonderful life, with this spectacular talent that no one cared anything about, and now she felt ashamed, as if it were her fault some pervert would grovel for a hand job.

She went to her room to change clothes and I made tea. I saw from the illumined clock on the Con Edison building that it was eleven. She came back in an oversized sweater and we drank the tea.

"I don't know what's going on with Patrick," she said. "He doesn't whistle anymore." She half smiled. "He and Bryan are seeing each other again."

"That's good."

"I don't know, Bryan sees women too." She was very small in the sweater; "And Sidney hasn't been sending Patrick out." Sidney was Patrick's agent. "In Mira's last week he did Shakespeare's Jacques"— she and Patrick were in a new class with Mira Rostova, who had coached, among others, Montgomery Clift—"and he was lovely, but his hands—they were shaking, he was all nerves for the longest time."

I tried to look concerned, but I felt annoyed. Lately Patrick seemed not even there, a bare slip of himself—and now this.

"I got the Mennen ad."

"Hooray, that makes nine.

"There's something else," she said. No, I thought, nothing else, let's just be ordinary now, let's be quiet. "I called Andre, I called him just— damn it, to get an *audition*—I didn't know what to do. He said to come over, we'd talk, he'd see about something. He was being very nice, said it was wrong that I wasn't working. But when I got there he didn't answer the door. I thought I had the wrong buzzer, I thought he had moved and I had forgotten, but of course he hadn't."

"I'm not crying," she protested, but I went and took her in my arms and held her against me like a brother maybe, a father; if fathers could be fathers, brothers friends.

"I sat down on the stoop, I was tired, and I knew why I'd let him do this *last thing,* why I'd let him do *everything*—because he was Crispins and the show on East Fourth, all of these wonderful things that had happened and weren't happening anymore."

THE VERY NEXT DAY, life being life and running according to its own schedule, not ours, I was shaving in the morning when Paul called. I walked into the living room and stood listening to him on the machine say, "Robert?" Pause. "It's Paul, call the office." Just say it, I thought, go ahead and say it. But that wasn't his style.

I went back in the bathroom and finished shaving. "It's okay one way or the other," I said to myself. "I hate this, I fucking hate this." I'd had a test for a part on a soap, it was down to two other actors and me, but I hadn't told anyone about it.

I dressed and went to the phone thinking, my work was good, and there was nothing else I could do.

Paul picked up immediately, "Robert, *okay! You got it!*"

"God."

He laughed, "Is that all you can say?"

"Oh God."

"Two shows a week guaranteed, fifteen hundred a show to start, but in a year—" I had trouble listening. Someone from the show would call this afternoon and contracts would be ready the day after tomorrow. I'd start work on Monday; a messenger would drop by a script. We'd have to discuss my commercial conflicts.

"Are you there?" he said.

We agreed on lunch later in the day. I hung up and stood stockstill. Funny, my first reaction was concern about how long I'd be away from the theater. Then I came to and ripped out of the apartment, slamming at the elevator button and sprinting across the street in the middle of the block and down Fifth Avenue toward Washington Square to find Irene. I ran out of breath and slowed to a walk at Eighth Street. Me, I thought, they want me. Then I got to the arch and thought, how can I tell her? But then she came running around the corner from the south side of the park—she'd taken up jogging—in her tank top, her hair in a ponytail, and she saw me and smiled this huge smile, and waved.

I let her run to where I stood under the arch. "What?" she said, reaching me, stopping, "what?" She was smiling so broadly, I thought, *I* must be smiling. I really couldn't feel it, my face felt numb.

"I—uh, got a part on a soap, I mean, uh—two years, a contractual role on—"

She screamed and jumped on me, wrapping her arms around my neck and her legs around my waist.

"*Hot damn!*" she yelled, "One out of three!" Leaves on the trees turning color in the park, people, cars in the street and that beautiful October light falling on everything.

"Irene," I said laughing, "you're sweating all over me."

"Come on."

She got down, taking my hand and pulling me back across the street.

"Where are we going?"

"To tell Patrick."

"He's at the gym."

"We'll have him paged, if we don't he'll never forgive us," she said, so excited she tripped and fell down, then jumped up, laughing.

We walked and then ran back up Fifth Avenue, she kept patting and hugging me, doing these funny little skips and hops. For a few moments I just let myself be completely happy. Only once that whole day did I ever think anything negative, fear this might not augur as much as it seemed to, might not be the break that would bring about the others. I could even fuck up and get fired, I thought. But I didn't think I would.

11 Success

My entire life changed just as that possibility had seemed most improbable. I started pulling in $20,000 a month, working long hours, adjusting to a different type of acting and much bigger stakes. Suddenly, I was there, it was finally real, and yet it seemed it could vanish again and never reappear. It seemed more than anything about belief, and keeping it together. There were no words to describe the degree to which I lived on my nerves.

My character was named Rad.

"As in radical?" said Irene.

"As in radish?" Patrick said.

Rad was short for Radley Rutherford, the bad boy son of a prominent family who'd fathered a child as a young lad and then promptly departed for the wide world; I was Rad six years later, when he returned to make amends. But he was still bad—thank God, I thought —and kept screwing up. When I relaxed I had fun with Rad Rutherford, though my mother was not amused by my premise that, basically, I was playing my father. In my first week on the show my storyline was expanded so that most days I was at the studio for twelve hours, then came staggering home to study the next day's scenes. Irene was a memory machine. We sat together nights working on lines and by the third or fourth time through a script she would know the whole thing. Not me; I hated working in what felt like a vacuum. Whatever rehearsal I had occurred on the same day we shot it. Then too, I had been trained to mistrust the surface, to get under the words. As a consequence I wasted time looking for levels that in soaps simply didn't exist. Unlike plays, in which entire lives were conjured in two or three hours, soap operas were slow, unfolding in long linear paths. In any scene hardly more than one thing would be going on; you just did that one thing to the hilt. It took Rad ten boring episodes just to get up the nerve to go see his kid.

Years ago I'd learned a technique called playing the opposite; where there is hate there is also love—whatever you are called upon to play, the other side must also come into it. Not so here. Colin, our director, had come out of the English theater and taught me to stretch it all out: if Rad was being bad I had to be *bad*. But don't worry, he'd say; another scene would soon appear showing the other side. His voice would boom over the speakers—a disembodied voice from the control room, like God's—"No, Robert, here he is confident through and through. But I assure you he will doubt himself a week after next." The scenes weren't written as they were in the theater: if you put too much into them they would grow muddy and collapse. In soaps there wasn't any major overriding theme, they weren't about "the success ethic" or "the immigrant's dream." They just took situations from contemporary American life and exaggerated them as far as they could. Soaps were *soap operas*, melodramas—about everything and nothing.

It used to be that a soap wasn't an awfully hard job to land. But when *Dallas* hit prime time the rules changed, and I found myself in a prestigious position as a soap opera actor. It came down to this: I became known, which was more than any theater job had done for me.

And I was doing real acting. I was treated with respect. A month into the job I told Irene I would support her, that she couldn't concentrate on acting while working full-time as a waitress. She accepted. Patrick had been siphoning cash to her since last spring, although the trust money he lived off when he wasn't working wasn't really very much, and expenses had risen. Our rent had burgeoned; and it seemed there was less and less work for serious actors.

Irene did another showcase in November, but despite being a splashy affair with a famous playwright, nothing came of it. Afterward she threw herself into the apartment, cooking and cleaning with a frantic displaced energy that reminded me of my mother. Irene seemed to think she needed to earn the money, I thought we had been friends long enough to be past such a shallow interpretation, and one night we got into a terrible fight.

"Look, it isn't the money," she said. "It's how you weren't there for me after what happened with the showcase. Whenever I mentioned it, you would *sigh.*"

"Irene, I feel—"

"Oh, don't tell me how you *feel*, Robert, you don't know *what* you feel half the time."

"You know how much pressure I'm under," I said.

"I guess so," she answered. "That's about all I ever hear from you."

"I'm *tired*," I told her, "okay?" At least, I thought, while she was doing her showcase it was fun. All I ever did was sheer downright work, and I was the one who was supposed to be supportive. In moments like these she brought to mind the downsides of having a wife, without the main benefit.

December was better. I began to adjust to the soap. She got a part-time job as a hostess at a restaurant near Lincoln Center and it worked out better than the waitressing had, and made her feel less dependent on me. She spent Christmas with my parents and me in Fort Lee. Patrick had gone again to LA or San Francisco or somewhere, who knew? He had become more evasive than ever. I tended to steer clear of him. It took too much energy to comprehend what he was feeling or doing.

Irene and I sat up late Christmas night by the tree in the white living room—in the darkness by the lights of the tree and the lights in the distance of the city behind falling snow.

Standing, she dragged her hand across the window and it looked like the heat of her hand melted the snowflakes that flew against the glass: "I am trying to absorb this," she said. She wore a thin gold sweater and I could see through it the shift of the delicate winglike bones in her back. "Patrick talks about it as though it's a matter of being good," she ran her hand high up the window, reaching. "Like you're supposed to take whatever comes and be content. He even *lectured* me about kissing the cross, but this isn't—I mean, it isn't as if I'm sick or homeless or my country's at war. I feel embarrassed for feeling so badly about any of it.

"How long can you keep doing something that nobody wants? I get so tired of essentially saying *Please, like me.*"

Toward the end of February I realized that she had stopped, that neither she nor Patrick had had an audition since the beginning of the year and that they had dropped out of the class they'd been taking.

PATRICK GOT A JOB as a bartender working afternoons at O'Toole's, of all places, the Fifty-seventh Street brasserie where I had been a waiter last year.

"Why?" I asked.

"For something to do, and my liquid assets are not what they could be."

Irene said as a bartender he had an audience, a following, which I said for someone of Patrick's talent was too pathetic a speculation to even entertain.

"Well, he can't audition anyway," she snapped; his nerves were uncontrollable. Every Sunday he brushed his stiff hair and put on a suit and went to Mass at St. Patrick's, or elsewhere—he did a revolving tour of New York City's cathedrals. Nights he went out, often didn't come home. He wasn't with Bryan; Bryan had gotten married in January.

I could see that Patrick was depressed, and I tried to be sympathetic. But even beyond his evasions and masks, I had begun to perceive another facet in his behavior toward me: I suspected not that he envied me, but that he looked down on me for the soap. He saw my success as easy and cheap, not what he would have wanted—he saw it as proof of the impossibility of his dreams.

As it happened, I had become a minor celebrity. People recognized me in public. I did interviews, I went to LA to shoot a pilot. For the first time I saw a continuum to my career: Andre had led to Crisipins, Crispins had led to Bryan, Bryan led me to Paul, Paul got me the audition for the soap. There *were* connections, it did come together if you hung in there, and I wanted Irene and Patrick to believe this too. I thought my success should encourage them. Patrick had done especially well—from *The Rehearsal* on, once he had met Bryan's agent: shows at the Goodman, the Guthrie, only Broadway or a hit at the Public Theater would have been better credits. Then there was Kentucky, although it fizzled. He auditioned for really superior jobs, and was almost always called back. But starting in the summer his auditions dropped off, as though Sidney had lost faith in him. I thought of the Guthrie, of his unhappiness there, and his abrupt departure. I thought of Kentucky, where he was fired. I called Paul and asked what he had heard about Patrick. "Who knows what happened?" he said. "It's a freaky business." I asked him to call his old agency, where Sidney worked, but all he said when he got back to me was that Patrick was difficult, and that the business was too overcrowded for actors who didn't cooperate—people just didn't have to contend with all that. He didn't say this presumptively, but I still didn't like it. And I didn't buy it either. Everyone said Barbra Streisand was difficult and she was a star. In this business, you'd be an idiot *not* to be difficult.

One morning in Makeup with Suzie Glines, who played my mother on the soap, Suzie said, "Hey Holt, you're supposed to be enjoying this."

"I am," I said. Suzie was my best friend on the show. Like Colin, she came out of the theater, but in her late-thirties she got her first soap and she'd been with them for twenty-two years; on our show for eighteen. She looked like an older, leaner version of my mother.

"You seem a little world-weary to me, and you shouldn't be."

"Suzie," I said, "if you were me, what would you do? Would you stay with the show like you did, or go back to the theater?"

"You've acted long enough to know it's pragmatic," she answered. "You take what you can get." She looked at me in the mirror. "But if I were a man? If I were young?" There were twice as many roles for men in the theater as for women; and twice as many actresses as actors. In commercials the quota was ten to one. Rotten odds.

"If I were you," she told me, "I'd finish out your contract, take the money and the exposure and run. Do *Macbeth*, do Chekhov, wherever you can. Oh boy, had I been free"—she had four children—"what I would have done."

She was sincere, though not bitter. Soaps had allowed her to do what she liked—act—and have a good, solid middle-class life. "Which it's tough to do without," she'd said, "if you've been raised in it."

"Robert," she said, "you have everything." I wondered why I couldn't feel it.

Outside the studio at the end of the day I walked to the subway. I hadn't taken the subway in months. I relished the ride, the hard plastic benches, the puffs of heat from the vents warming on my legs. It was Patrick's birthday, and I stopped off at a florist's and bought him an enormous bunch of red roses and walked to O'Toole's.

Herbert, Patrick's extremely short friend from the Guthrie, sat at the bar drinking a Budweiser. Herbert was cheap. But at the sight of my roses he was mortified. "All I got him was a package of Famous Amos."

"I like Famous Amos," Patrick said graciously.

"He told me not to get anything," said Herbert. "You liked what I got you last year," he said to Patrick.

"Yes, I did," Patrick said, "I like those Talking Heads."

"Oh, well a tape," said Herbert, "isn't much either. I can never think of anything good enough." Herbert had creases ironed down the sleeves of his jean jacket. The day was cold and sunny. Inside all the ceiling ferns and brass railings and the black-and-white tiles were lit up so cheerfully it was hard to believe it was winter. Patrick seemed happy, bustling about among his bottles, looking dapper in a big black bow tie.

"Hey hey hey *hey*," said Jeffrey, the boss, walking by, "Mr. TV."

"Hey Jeffre-ey," I called, waving my bottle of Guinness at his back. "I can't stand him," I said to Herbert. I turned to Patrick, "Why you voluntarily submit yourself to Jeffrey's managerial éclat I cannot understand."

"Jeffrey's jealous of you," Herbert said to me.

"Only because he imagines that I have a wider access to women."

"Don't you?" said Herbert.

"No," I said.

Alix finished her shift and joined us. She was also having it rough in the business. She had a new haircut; very short, very simple, very Alix; very nice. "You're fetching," I said, putting my arm around her and giving her a kiss.

"How's Irene?" she asked me.

"I don't know. Patrick, how is Irene?"

"In the ether," he told Alix, "everywhere at once. For all we know she could be watching us now."

"Irene?" Herbert said, peeking over the bar, "are you there?" Irene had taken a course on astrology at the Ansonia where she made friends with a medium who could purportedly communicate with Irene's dead mother. Of late, Irene had been reciting a prayer that had to do with white light.

"How are you feeling?" I asked Alix.

"I have nothing to live for," she said. "But I called Boston. I'll take the train up and audition. I'm opposed, you know, to auditions."

"A formality," I told her, "you'll knock 'em out of their chairs."

"I hate auditions," Herbert said. "I'd work for anyone who didn't make me audition."

Looking at Patrick more closely, I saw that beneath his veneer he didn't look good. He filled orders for waiters and waitresses, shook a martini for a customer, then slid his rag along surfaces, glancing at us with disinterest. Surely this was a phase and it would pass. I wanted to tell him something profound and encouraging. Better yet, something clever and bracing. But we had established such a routine of speaking to each other indirectly that I really didn't know how else to talk to him.

THE NEXT NIGHT Patrick and I went out to dinner. Coming home, he and I turned from Fifth onto Fourteenth and saw an ambulance and a snarl of traffic, heard a rise of voices above the regular din. As we entered the lobby they brought out a man on a gurney. I saw him beneath the bright lobby lights, being wheeled past Charles, the night doorman who must have been just coming on, and I had the absurd notion that Charles, a sad person already, should not have had to see this. His already ashy complexion approached dark gray and his expressive hands whirled at his sides.

Our intimate confrontation with the man on the gurney was so concentrated, and the man himself so brilliantly alive and wounded and prone there, stripped of his shirt amidst the lights and mirrors and running people in jackets and coats, it wasn't easy to register anything else. He was younger than Patrick and me, a bottle of glucose was attached to a tube in his arm and held aloft by the man running beside him in a crouch. A sheet was pulled up to his chest and on his chest was a pad lit up with blood of a color so red it verged on orange, not the dark red of a cut finger. It was a mortal wound clearly; yet his complexion was healthy, pink, he was well nourished, his shoulders and arms heavily fleshed, and his hair, carefully styled into loose brown curls, was so much the hair of a living breathing person, I had the impression of it breathing itself, in how it shined, in its contrast along with the color of his skin to the much more vehement, unnatural, and victorious color of the wound.

We didn't quite stop as we walked in, but we had to step aside for him to get by and outside to the waiting ambulance. Then there seemed nothing else to do but to go on upstairs.

"Is there anything in the apartment?" Patrick said.

"Only wine."

"Let's go back out."

We rode the elevator back downstairs silently, ducking into the hallway of the service entrance to get outside.

At the Cedar, Patrick went to get our drinks, and I sat feeling the bar and the streets and the night and the world filled with sudden death. Sounds were sharp, the smoke acrid. I watched a waitress serving food to four men: two burgers, club sandwich, a salad, the salad bowl patterned like a parquet floor. In the morning we would learn that the murdered man was twenty-three and recently married. He and his wife were eating dinner from trays and watching TV when someone knocked on the door. He opened it and was shot point-blank in the chest. The perpetrator fled and was not apprehended. There was evidence that the victim was dealing cocaine.

Patrick set down my beer and a shot of Bushmills.

"Thanks." He sat across from me with a vodka on the rocks and lit a cigarette. "Have you ever seen him?" I asked.

"No, have you?"

"No." Patrick had on a red V-neck sweater over a white shirt. "Did you notice the color of the blood?" I asked him.

"It's like that when it comes from a very deep place," he said.

"Yes?" The four men across from us laughed, then the laughter was drowned out by a new song on the jukebox and the ding of the pinball machine. I leaned forward, toward Patrick. "Whenever I see something dreadful, an accident, whatever, there is part of me standing aside and watching—myself. Thinking I have to remember this, everything I'm seeing and feeling. I also feel something like—gratitude, that if it's something that happens, well, I want to know about it." I sort of laughed.

"There are things I would rather never see again or even hear about," Patrick said. He stamped out his cigarette.

For a moment I didn't know how to react. Then I recalled Irene's letter. The accident. Benton. The knee. Somebody dying. But if he had made an allusion to that shady event, I did not even know whether I was supposed to *know* about it. He had already clearly removed himself from the conversation. He acted ready to go. I said nothing more.

Several nights later i awoke at 4 a.m.; there was a subtle but constant noise stealing my sleep and I had to stop it. I went out to investigate a ticking sound in the kitchen. I turned on the kitchen light and saw Patrick bent over the sink, dripping into it blood from his mouth and nose, and I had the impression that he was weeping.

"Turn off the light," he said.

Hearing him breathe and the blood falling into the sink, I said, "Are you all right?"

"Yes."

He is ashamed, I realized, *he doesn't want me to see,* and I went back to bed.

In the morning I found him sitting in the chair by the coffee table gingerly smoking a cigarette, one side of his mouth raw, his nose swollen, and Irene, in her tatty white robe, setting coffee on the table.

"Did you see this?" she asked. "He got *mugged.*

"I know what you do," she said to him, "Robert told me, you walk in the streets all night. You'll get yourself killed and how will that be?"

"Little mother," he said.

"*My ass*, Patrick. I hate you, I really hate you," she said and stalked to her room.

"Well," I said.

"She's upset." In a chatty tone.

"You should be more careful."

When he didn't answer I went back to my room and got dressed. I needed to get out. With no destination in mind I went down to Washington Square and then west. Maybe, as Irene had thought, he was only walking in places he should not have been walking, as we had walked that one night together, as he had maybe the night he'd been mugged before and came to my apartment, an incident of which Irene and I had never spoken. But after discovering him in the kitchen

I couldn't help but imagine worse things. For the first time since that icy morning at Ruth's I thought of him picking up strangers—cruising. His long walks, his sudden departures and nights out did not seem innocuous anymore.

I went past Sheridan Square and traveled west on Christopher Street. It was Saturday morning and gates were down over businesses, sex shops, and bars, quaint little restaurants that had been there for years. This was the heart of the gay scene; even this early men strolled the sidewalks, some of them dressed head to foot in leather, chains hanging out of back pockets, maybe on their way home after a long Friday night. Further on, near the West Side Highway, were the rougher clubs, desolate days and choked nights, the flip side you could say of Forty-second Street; gays certainly never having anything on straights in the vice department.

I stood on West Street looking out at the wharves and abandoned buildings by the river that I'd seen at night from a cab. I knew that even smart, ambitious gay men checked out the scene. It was simply part of our generation, our time. But you could be swallowed up by it too. And it could be ugly, the little I knew of the worst of it making my skin crawl.

I wondered if Patrick came here. Was he obsessed? Addicted to danger? *Why?* On the one hand: shame, violence, lies. On the other: the sweetness, the seeming openness. Now, I had to think, that openness was another kind of veneer.

I turned and walked back on Christopher Street, glaring at men who eyed me, as if by staring it down it would all go away.

I DIDN'T SEE Patrick again until the following morning. When I went into the living room I could see through the windows behind him the edges of the buildings flamed with the sunrise. He sat, fully dressed, reading the paper. Did he ever sleep?

"If you're getting up," he said, "there's coffee." I got a cup and came back and sat with him to drink it.

"Anybody die?" I asked. He was on the front page, undoubtedly he had already scanned the obituaries.

"No one for whom I've had to mourn," he said with some irony, "since Jimmy Durante."

"Going to church?" It was Sunday. He hadn't yet put on his jacket and tie.

"I'm trying a Mass in Riverside today," he said.

"Patrick." He looked up from the paper. "What's going on?"

He closed the paper and set it on his lap. He turned his gaze to the chair arm.

"I'm sorry if I've been remote," he said. He groped for words, "I was very fond of Bryan, as you know. . . ." I waited without expectation, though I wasn't as angry as I had been yesterday. I remembered that Irene had always been more up on Bryan. Lately, especially, I had observed a trust between Irene and Patrick that went very deep. I would never forget a night Irene was sick with a strain of Asian flu, and burned with fever. She was sure she was dying and, swayed by her fear, I was ready to call an ambulance when Patrick sat down on her bed, swooped her up into his long arms and said, "There, you're all right, it's about to break and you'll be fine in the morning." She calmed and slept, and woke up the next day nearly well.

"Oh, nothing's really wrong," he said finally. "I'm still young, and youth they say is everything, yes?"

He smiled, nothing harsh or mocking in his demeanor. Okay, I thought. His subtext said I'm not fine, but I'd like to deal with it in my own way. Perhaps Irene's outburst yesterday had been enough.

In any case, that concluded the confrontation. There was obviously not a thing I could do. In any event, I did not need the mess, the senselessness. If he was determined to wallow in misery, I thought, let him.

The next afternoon I came home from work and heard Irene in her room.

"Hi." I propped myself up with the door frame. She lay on her bed: fuzzy red socks, jeans, a T-shirt, the cat coiled up on the pillow beside her head. Her hair was in braids. "Cute," I said, pulling on one. "What are you reading?" She showed me the book: *A Mystic in the Theater,* Eva Le Gallienne on Eleanora Duse.

"How's the show?" she asked, still reading the book.

"Rad's falling in love with Silver."

"Is Silver a person?"

"So to speak." I took the book from her and closed it. "How you doing?"

"Okay."

"Irene, have you quit?"

"What?"

"Acting."

She sighed, "Do we have to talk about it?"

"Yes." What a bully I was—and lonely.

How come Patrick goes to church? I had recently asked her. That's easy, she had said, to recapture a sense of the sublime.

"I'm resting," she said. "I can get another job if—"

"No," I said, "I have plenty of money, I didn't mean—"

"I just thought if I wasn't acting then maybe it wasn't right—"

"I have plenty of money." I honest to God didn't care about the money. All I cared about was having enough so I wouldn't have to worry about it. "You're resting?" I said.

"Yes." She didn't want to talk. Her skin looked translucent, she lay there as still as the cat.

"Irene—" I wanted to talk about Patrick. Instead, I said, "Paul got a new agent for stage."

"Great."

"You want to meet him?"

"Not now. Come on, there wouldn't be any reason now. But thanks, really."

"Okay, well, let me know if you do." I got up, paused in the doorway, heard her reopen her book, and St. Martin began to purr again.

I thought I would read the Le Gallienne book after she did, and we could discuss it. But I was busy.

"What is the point of confession?" I asked Patrick casually one night, "Explain it to me."

"It's simple," he said. "It's to be released, to have a fresh start."

"Do you really believe in it?"

"I don't know, but I think it's a beautiful idea."

Beauty, ideas. Evanescent as mist. Oh, he was a stellar actor. It would have been laughable had it not been so sad. He had finally become a good actor, honing his talent in the years since we met. Only to better play that everything was fine, turning emotions and truths on and off at will. I was good at it too, pretending I didn't see anything odd in his reply.

I recalled a conversation we had had once about acting, how it was less about what you were feeling than what you did about it.

I<small>N</small> M<small>AY</small>, <small>WITH</small> <small>SCANT</small> warning, my soap went off the air. There had been rumors, but none of us on the show had believed them: ratings were steady and the show had run so long we deemed it invulnerable.

Suzie cried in her dressing room. "We've been canceled!" she wailed. I felt a quick loss of breath. So much for my two-year contract. I would have needed a couple dozen lawyers to get out of my end, but apart from the protection the contract assured me while my services continued to be welcome, what was binding on paper remained elastic for the network.

"Why am I crying?" she asked. "For months I've complained about wanting more time for my grandchildren. It must be the shock."

"You can get another show," I said.

"Oh no, *never*," blowing her nose. "Give me a minute and I'll feel relieved."

She explained what she knew, having to do with a corporate takeover, and then I went off down the hallway in search of Colin. Now in a turnabout I felt a heady sense of expanded possibility. I found Colin exiting wardrobe, marking his script with his automatic pencil, drinking coffee, absentmindedly listening to a last-minute comment called from the room he'd just left. Colin, like most people in television, could juggle an array of simultaneous tasks. Tallish and stout, with ripply bronze hair and aviator glasses, he cast an unswerving aura of absolute ease.

"You look pleased, you foolish young man," he said, as I approached. "Unless you haven't heard the news."

"Call Hugh," I said. "Tell him I'll do the play if I can direct one."

"Like a house afire," he replied. "Drinks, say—tomorrow evening?"

"Great."

"Come," he said then, "and we'll talk about Silver's childish demands on Rad's valuable time." We started together down the corridor to the rehearsal room, speaking of line changes. Ever the consummate professional, Colin wasn't easily disturbed. There remained a full week of shows to get onto tape and he would attend to them as he did any other week of work.

But my attention was profoundly split throughout the day between the work—I'd already gotten to the point where I could do most of the scenes with 60 percent concentration—and my altered, fabulous future. I was going back to the theater, or I was about to only *begin* in the theater, but this time, I thought, I would not be deterred. The soap had lasted just long enough to give me a name and a decent stockpile of money; the cancellation could have been part of a preordained plot to make my career in the theater possible. *What luck!*

Colin's brother Hugh was a professor of theater in a small college in Missouri, and the artistic director of a stock theater, where Colin directed a play every year. Colin had asked me to act for him this summer, and my new plan was to direct a play in which I could use Irene and Patrick.

But now that the soap was canceled, Paul wanted me in town for auditions. We snapped at each other through a lunch at Café des Artistes.

"I'll be gone six weeks or two months," I said, "it's nothing. I just— I could never do anything before the soap, I was afraid to go out of town thinking something might come up. I'm tired of living like that. I thought now I could do a little of what I want to do finally."

If you were viable as an actor in other mediums, Paul thought, why do theater? Even Broadway, realistically speaking, had become a blundering brontosaurus kept alive for tourists. But he rested his hands on the table—his well-manicured nails were, indeed, lacquered the palest shade of pink—and said, "I want you on Broadway if you want to do theater."

"Yeah, me too, but—"

"Robert." Paul was unusually intense today. "They're putting a hold on your pilot."

"Yeah?" I wasn't sure what that meant. When I'd shot the pilot I hadn't taken it seriously. The negotiations over what would transpire if it was picked up were so over-the-top, involved so much money that I had to banish it from my mind; the world I had glimpsed seemed to me more bizarre than a Beckett play. "Great," I said evenly, "but they didn't pick it up. What are the chances anything'll come of it now? Really, Paul."

"They like you very much in Los Angeles, *know* that, all right?"

I felt owned instead of complimented. "I just don't want to do another soap," I said, veering off the subject, "at least not right away." I knew very well that all of the prospects he'd been alluding to could dry up, and I sat there feeling mad when for years I'd imagined I would be practically leaping tall buildings at such a moment. Mostly I felt disoriented: *what the hell was going on?* And how did I know what to *do* about it?

I had to hold on to something. I figured I'd better hold on to my life—and my life, for better or worse, was Irene and Patrick. They would be fine if they could work. I told Paul I was going.

12 Second Chance

I read the play Colin had planned to direct me in while sitting at my desk. The windows were open and I heard a baby crying from somewhere outside, piercing through the other city sounds. The dark night outside, the circle of light from the small lamp on the surface of my black desk, illuminating my hands and the white paper of the script. Then the crying went away, and any consciousness of turning the pages vanished, until the script lay closed; I had been sitting there for I didn't know how long. Finally sounds—and the smell of something burnt—seeped slowly, by increments, into my awareness, and I got up and walked out to the phone in the living room and called Colin.

"It's—I love it. We're really gonna do this in a small town in Missouri?" After the soap, the complexity and richness of the play lit up regions in myself I had almost forgotten: every inch of me felt alive, rife with dimension and possibility.

He laughed, and I sat down on the couch, putting the phone on the floor. "The author is from that fair state," he replied, "which I'm hoping will bring them to us in a more, shall we say, open mind."

"I think he's more like me than anyone I've ever played," I told him.

"That's exactly what we need," he said, "passion, belief. To get away with this we must do it magnificently. The rest of the season, as you know, in balance, will be light: the musicals, and whatever you direct. Anything except for a comedy is out of the question."

"I like comedy, I'm up for a comedy."

He could have said anything to me. I took the script and went out walking, up past the Flatiron Building and over to Gramercy Park, finally landing in a coffee shop, where I didn't look again at the play but had it there with me at the table while I gazed out the window at the street and thought about my father. I had believed, incorrectly, that he was really dead for me. I had stopped thinking about him first ceaselessly, then every day, and at last practically never. But in reading the script he lived again in my body, because he was imprinted in my sensations, *in me,* and I thought, sitting there—my own ghostly reflection in the glass of the window—Okay, you son of a bitch, *let's go,* I'm ready for you now.

The name of the play was *Lemon Sky,* by Lanford Wilson. I was Alan, twenty-nine years old in his narration and seventeen in the action. It's the story of Alan's failed attempt to live with his father and his father's second family after years of living away from him. The play was about what it meant to be a man—a son, a father, and it touched on sexual abuse and homosexuality. I couldn't wait.

I WENT OUT TO Missouri two weeks before Irene and Patrick arrived. *Lemon Sky* was the first show of the season. People walked out, people cried, people waited to talk to us; there were nights of such a split in the audience that while some people jumped to their feet at the end, others actually booed and hissed. Every night I felt psychologically excavated.

One night after the show I got in the car—this *boat,* a green Buick with a black hardtop I'd been given to use—and drove, and then turned onto a road running through fields that went on forever. It was so flat, and the sky was immense. I stopped and got out right there in the middle of the road, in the center of those fields, and beheld the sky:

a black dome with more stars than I'd ever seen and in colors more various, silver, white, gold, orange, copper, and even red almost, *red stars*. I was full of my father and my mother and my whole life—it was all around me, in the faint breeze rustling in the field and in all that vast quiet of the sky, in the way that Strasberg explains van Gogh's painting of his shoes as a moment when you can look at your shoes and see *within them* your life.

I didn't think anything at first, standing there, but then words rose to my mind: *I will never be enough to make up to her for what he did* —large enough, good enough, strong enough, careful enough. It wasn't about my father at all, it was about my mother and me. I remembered her picking me up when I was very young and he was gone, had only just left, and what I had felt was her size, her strong neck and firm powerful dancer's back and shoulders, how large she was in comparison to me—and my thought, how will I comfort her? There was so much of her and so little of me. She was still that giant woman with that giant grief, and I was still small.

Then for the first time, hearing the wind in the field and smelling the sweetness of the hay, under the stars I felt pure sorrow, as though I were four again and he had just left.

The town wasn't much, a town square with an old courthouse and two rows of shops that closed before nightfall. There was a movie theater seven miles out, and a bar named Reno's. The one nearby restaurant that stayed open late was a Pizza Hut. The campus was pleasant, grassy with a couple nice old stone buildings. The theater was The Barn, having once housed farming equipment and mules, once owned, like much of the town and the campus, by an argricultural tycoon named Noble Nankin. At the college was a Nankin Hall and a Nankin Chapel, and contemporary Nankins, still living in the town, invested heavily in The Barn's summer season. The town remained surrounded by farms: I could smell hogs on the wind.

They put me up at the old Nankin Manse with Tony, the actor who played my father, and with the college librarian, Wally Press, a very strange individual. His looks weren't unusual, ordinary brown hair, medium height and build, medium age, early forties, I figured. A few clothes, maybe two pairs of slacks and three nearly identical shirts. But he had somehow missed out on the most rudimentary social graces; it seemed never to occur to him that he was supposed to make the person he was with comfortable, or to keep the more intimate aspects of his psyche even vaguely private.

He showed me around the manse when I got there and helped me choose a room. But first he confided, verging on *tears,* "They've fired me. I don't have another job, or anywhere to go." To my silence he sadly concluded, "I'm allowed to live here another month."

It was a big white house with columns circa 1890: beveled glass in the front door, a formal parlor and a wainscotted smoking room, a dining room, and a music room with a grand piano, where Wally said college receptions were held; across the back of the house was a large kitchen opening out to a patio and yard. It stood at the top of a hill, overlooking the town, the campus, and the valleys beyond. Upstairs, there were two bedrooms that were available. Wally opened one door and presented me with a drab, shag-carpeted room at the back, stripped of its original furniture. "The one next to it is mine," he said emphatically, and then nodded at the room opposite: "That's Tony's." Since Tony had only arrived earlier this morning—I hadn't met him yet—the easy way Wally had of referring to him was mildly disconcerting.

He just stood there—we were still standing at the doorway—with his bland eyes fixed dully on me.

"What about that one?" I asked, pointing at the closed door diagonally across the landing.

"It's haunted," he said.

"Yeah? By who?"

"Bella Nankin," he whispered, "his wife."

"Oh. Can I see it?"

He shrugged and started down the hall with an attitude I read as, suits me, pal, it's your funeral. When he opened the door I knew I would take it: four-poster bed, fireplace, and spacious windows with a view for miles. "She lay on that bed," Wally said, staring at it, "looking out at the town. Stroke," he explained, "paralyzed. Her and Noble owned everything then. . . . She could see it, but she couldn't move."

"Uh, hmn . . . well, I'll take it."

"One night before I moved in," Wally said, "three businessmen were here, to audit the college books—" visions of small-town graft, garnished paychecks, impounded cars "—and they stayed in the other three rooms." A tight pursing of his lips, his reaction, I surmised, to my singular foolhardiness. "In the middle of the night all three woke up at the same time and looked out at the hallway. They heard moaning and crying sounds coming from her room." He told me about half-buried tunnels in the basement that led to the campus, false stairways in the attic leading nowhere, the sealed servant's quarters to the rear of the second floor, behind Tony's room.

After our initial meeting I hardly saw him. He constructed little meals in the kitchen he carried upstairs. Once, when we passed on the stairs, he said ominously, "three weeks," and I didn't understand. "One week," he said, two weeks later, and I got it. He had been talking about the time he had left in the manse. He went away two days after Irene and Patrick arrived, packed his belongings into a rented Chevy van, quietly and, for a change, stoically, refusing our offer of help.

Bella Nankin didn't bother me. I slept well and peacefully, once I had dealt with my own personal phantoms. I pored over the scripts of *Lemon Sky* and *Same Time, Next Year,* the play in which I would direct Irene and Patrick. It was a two-character play about love spanning twenty-five years. The lovers, each married to someone else, meet one weekend and have an affair they repeat thereafter every year. It was funny, moving, sexy, and I knew we could make it the hit of the season.

Most of the actors were semiprofessional, from Kansas City or Nebraska and other neighboring states. Colin's brother Hugh had negotiated contracts for Irene and Patrick and accepted them as my cast without an audition. I'd been afraid of Patrick going to pieces under the strain.

A few days before they were due in, Patrick called in the middle of the night in a panic. "Oh, hi," I said, switching on the lamp by the bed; I picked up my watch: after three.

"You were asleep. I'm sorry, often you're reading—"

"It's okay." I lay back down and waited. He tried to pretend there was nothing going on: "I've been looking at a book about the state of Missouri. One major city at one side, the other at the other side. St. Louis, the last bastion of the civilized East. Kansas City, gateway to the West."

Jesus, I thought, is this what we're talking about?

"It says here that having put Jefferson City, the capital, in the middle of the state," he continued—"who *knows* why they did it, anyone could have *seen* it would cause problems. Well, nobody wanted to live there, all of the state officials were living in St. Louis and Kansas City and attempting to commute, and an ordinance had to be passed that *required* them to live there."

"Is this why you called me?"

"I'm sorry, I thought you'd be up."

"Is anything wrong?"

". . . Isn't it terribly conservative there?"

". . . It isn't like you're coming here to live, Patrick." It was hot in the room, I kicked off the sheet. "If nothing's wrong," I said, "I'm hanging up."

"Don't." His voice was suddenly urgent. I sat up, now completely awake and intent upon him.

"Patrick?"

"Please, I—"

"It's okay, I wasn't all the way asleep, what is it?" His *please* had plummeted to the pit of a tone that frightened me, and yet the word "please" itself was so formal. "Patrick?"

I had an intimation of his loneliness beyond anything I, or Irene, could provide; had a sense of that very distant plane from where he, increasingly, seemed to regard all of life.

"I—don't know that I can do the play," he said.

This I could deal with. "Listen," I said. "Nerves really aren't that unusual. Everyone has them sometimes. Stop overreacting."

"But think of a race car driver," he said. "He has to believe he can control the car, otherwise his career is over."

"What you need is to regain your confidence, that's why you're coming out here, okay?"

"All right," he said.

"The part's perfect for you, and it'll be just the three of us, no other pressures."

He seemed to feel better by the time we hung up. But I was plagued by the idea that he had been talking about more than acting, and his trouble with nerves disturbed me more than I had let on. It was too pronounced, such severe nerves signaled more than a response to rejection and a few bad experiences in the business—things we all went through—as if it all prodded much deeper wounds. And his allusion to race car drivers bothered me too. I lay in bed, pictures of smashed, smoking cars running through my head.

I sat in my underwear with the sheets twisted around my ankles. Too hot to sleep. I decided to put on the wheezing air conditioner that protruded from one of the windows, but I had to close another window first and it stuck, wouldn't budge. I put my forehead against the wall. Here, even so far from New York, everything felt difficult and painful again. He let everything hurt him too much; love, the lack of love, acting.

I tried the window again and it slid down. The air conditioner grunted and choked. I lay flat on my back in the darkness.

I felt something—a coolness. Something else. Someone. Bella. I raised myself up on my elbows. Said crazily, jokingly, urgently, "Bella, get out."

I PICKED THEM UP in the Buick at the airport. Irene wore a short skirt, a blouse knotted at the waist, her red cowboy boots. Patrick had on new Ray-Bans he said he had purchased to be inconspicuous in Missouri—which of course didn't work.

"*Look* at you," Irene said, hanging on to my hand after she'd hugged me. "Doesn't he look *good?*" she asked Patrick.

"Dare I say you look relaxed, Robert?" Patrick said.

"He's even smiling," said Irene. "No, it must be a twitch."

"I'm *smiling,*" I said.

"The Midwest becomes you," said Patrick.

"This is worse than the Midwest," said Irene, glancing at an old sunburned guy in a cowboy hat walking by, others from the flight meeting up with relatives; lots of polyester—"this is the Plains."

But in the car with the windows open and the warm bright air flying in, she said, "God, I feel like I'm home."

Patrick said, "I may prefer Paris," but I could tell he was excited.

"I'm not in the least relaxed," I told them. "The show's been fantastic and I'm sure tonight it will be a disaster. The weirdest thing has been happening to me. I don't get nervous anymore—I mean, I get nervous but I feel tired, like I'm about to fall asleep."

"I wish that would happen to me," Patrick said.

"No, you don't," I told him. "I'm guzzling coffee, I'm dunking my face in ice water. Last night I did laps around the parking lot."

"So when you *really* want to sleep," Irene said, "you should pretend you're about to play Hamlet."

"Yeah, ha." I told them more about the house, with its hidden tunnels and rooms. "The car's for all three of us," I said, pulling up the road leading to the manse.

"I don't drive," Patrick said.

"Don't you?" I said. "I didn't know that."

"Hate driving," he answered.

"I drive," said Irene. "I love to drive."

"There it is," I said.

"Gee, I feel like a star," said Irene.

"You are," I told her.

We left the luggage in the foyer while I showed them the downstairs. Patrick tested the piano in the music room and found it in tune; played three sonorous chords, and then, going back to the foyer to continue upstairs, Irene let out a shriek that lifted my scalp from my head. She had turned the corner first, followed by me and Patrick. "*God*," she said, clutching at us for support, "I'm sorry, but you scared me." It was Wally, standing perfectly still on the stairs at about the midpoint, in the center of a step, his hands folded calmly in a fig leaf position, gazing down at us. Triangles of light—green, yellow, red, blue—from the stained glass window at the top of the stairs played along the wall to his side.

He remained where he was, expressionless, while I made the introductions, then he disappeared into his room. "Oh boy," Irene said softly, "are we in Missouri."

"What a character," said Patrick.

Irene said, "I've got five or six cousins just like him."

THE NEXT DAY we began our rehearsals for *Same Time, Next Year*. Patrick was nervous, but his character was a nervous, careful guy and I told him to put his anxiety *into* the character. Very slowly, he did, and by the end of the first week he and Irene were finding exceptional ways to relate to each other. We got a lot of comic mileage out of their extreme physical relationship—we really milked it.

One day when we broke from rehearsal Patrick rushed off to a fitting and Irene and I stopped for a Coke at the machine just outside the swinging wooden doors of the auditorium. "You want one?"

"No, sip of yours."

"Good, I don't have enough change." I gave her the car keys. She had a fitting after Patrick's; I had to meet with the guy designing the sound. She took a long sip, handed me back the can. "Irene," I said, "I'm not sure how you feel anymore about acting. But if you want it, I know you can have it."

I wasn't only impressed with Patrick; Irene was sublime. Her work just kept growing. Her character was by now so interestingly developed that I couldn't take my eyes off her when she was onstage.

She seemed pleased. "You really think so?"

"Yeah. Oh yeah. I do."

"Thanks." We went outside.

"See ya," I said, and walked away across the blacktop, sun on my head, subtly shaken, thinking, if we weren't such good friends I would think I still had it bad for Irene. Of course I had invited this situation. I'd known what directing Irene and Patrick in this play would be like. Now, when he kissed her, all the old feelings came flooding back. I finished the Coke, followed the curving drive onto the short road that led to the campus apartments. I knew plenty of other women, that wasn't the problem. I just couldn't stop being in love with her.

I couldn't live with her day after day, learning her habits, her humor, the capacity for love she had that I so often saw in relation to Patrick —her energy, her evocative inwardness—and stop feeling it. Her acting made me feel callow and shy.

MOST EVENINGS WE drove out to Reno's for a drink after rehearsal. A perfectly square-shaped dark place, with an out-of-date Donna Summers still moaning to a climax on the jukebox. There were blue burlap curtains on the small windows, and greasy oilcloths on the tables. You could get dry sandwiches and slimy french fries at Reno's if you could talk someone into making them for you. There was usually just the bartender, Ben, there, or the owner, a loud, big-haired, middle-aged woman named Hildy, who liked to table hop when Ben was on duty, as though Reno's were the mecca of the Plains.

"What in the world is *he* doing here?" Patrick said, the first night we saw Ben. But for the next two or three nights, even though Ben was behind the bar pouring drinks, Patrick ignored him. Ben was thirty, a tall husky man with black eyes, gaunt cheeks, and a long patrician nose. He was quiet, rather stolid, and lived here, it turned out, instead of in Kansas City or Cleveland, cities he had tried and abandoned, because it was easier, cheaper.

One night during a pause in our conversation, Patrick decisively stubbed out his cigarette and said, "Excuse me." He went and sat at the bar and he and Ben started talking, and that was that.

"Well," Irene said, seeing Patrick was not in a hurry to get back to our table, "now life gets scintillating." She took a cigarette from Patrick's pack of Gauloises and lit it.

I watched her smoke for a minute and said, "Give me a drag."

"You're not taking up smoking at this late date, are you?"

"I don't know, maybe." I inhaled and, unexpectedly, liked it.

Irene and I left and went to the Pizza Hut for dinner where, anyway, the music was more up to date. Irene put on Diana Ross singing "I'm Coming Out" and we toasted Patrick and Ben with our water glasses.

"I hope it works out," she said. "Wouldn't it be great if he found someone he could last with?

"I had a dream last night about our theater," she said. "I woke up sure we should start by next summer." Since Floyd's, the idea had come up now and then between the three of us, and since coming here we'd begun to discuss it more seriously.

"I keep thinking it's the one way to do what we really want to," I said.

"It could really be good," she said, "we know all these really good people. We'd just have to worry about the business stuff, but not the quality of the work. We could maybe lure Alix back from Boston, you think?"

She picked the pepperoni off her slice of pizza and put it on mine; the air-conditioning was up too high and she got cold, and I gave her my jacket.

She bought a pack of Merits as we left, lit one, and gave me a drag, and outside the Pizza Hut she took my hand while I unlocked her door on the passenger side, but it didn't mean anything, she was always taking my hand.

PATRICK CAME IN the next morning and regaled us with the news about Ben: described the foundation and frame of his house, his trailer.

"Yes, a trailer. You can imagine my chagrin. As for the house, it's industrious of him, but I couldn't help remarking that it would have been more honorable to apprise me of the circumstances before inviting me there."

"Oh, come on," Irene said, "you didn't really care."

"He's a nice guy, isn't he?" I said.

"Yes," Patrick answered, "he's a very nice guy."

I'd appreciated Patrick's forthrightness.

"What," Irene said, "about Ben? Well, he doesn't have his regular options. Secret lives are harder to lead outside of the city. For one thing, he can't throw out an arm for a cab whenever he pleases."

I thought of my own secrets, of hers, and of all our secret channels of isolation. When the three of us were together and it was right, everything we had run from seemed to recede, and everything that we wanted stood on the bright verge of taking its place. It tasted and felt as if it were already there. More real than a promise, better than any dream.

THEN THE NEXT DAY in rehearsal, watching a run-through of the first scene, I had a horrible revelation: it wasn't funny. It was truthful, the moment-to-moment playing was exquisite, but it wasn't funny at all. We were five days from opening and it didn't even *look* like a comedy, it looked like two very good actors playing a scene in a soap. We had come up with *The Days of Our Lives*.

They finished the scene, looked praisefully at each other, and turned, smilingly, to me. Christ. I had to tell them. I sat thinking for what must have been a long time because Irene got up and walked to the edge of the apron and peered out at me: "So?"

This first scene, especially, had to be funny, brisk. If it wasn't, by scene 6 we'd be doing a dirge. Light, bright, *brisk*, I thought, they're supposed to be young, for Christ's sake.

"Let's try it again," I said, "double time. Everything you were doing, twice as fast." Patrick, good, soldierlike, headed for the bed, to his opening position. Irene stayed where she was.

"I don't know what you're saying."

"I said do it faster."

She looked back at Patrick, now sitting on the bed taking off his shoes, and then back at me, "Why?"

"It's not funny."

"Oh?"

Oh brother, I thought. I got up and walked to the stage. "It has the *potential* of being funny but it isn't. Let's just try a few things."

"This isn't ha-ha belly-laugh humor," she said, holding her ground. "It's not farce. These people have to connect in this scene or why would they keep coming back here every year?"

"You're connecting," I said, "now I want you to be funny."

"We've worked hard for the reality here," she said, "and I don't want to disturb it. We do the stuff hiding the clothes, that's funny, isn't it?" Patrick still sat on the bed, his shoes off, all ready to take off the rest of his clothes.

"What do you want to do, Robert," she said, "reduce the whole scene to low comedy?"

"*No!*" I shouted.

Patrick's eyes became huge. Kate, the stage manager, a sensitive young woman, delicately cleared her throat.

I walked away down the aisle of the auditorium, trying to steady myself. "Irene," I said, turning back, "I want you to do exactly what you've been doing, only faster."

"*I'm* telling you a speed-through will wreck it."

"Did I say *speed-through?*"

"Patrick," she said, turning her back to me, "What do you think? Do you see what I mean?"

"Yes, but we could try it—or," she was undoubtedly glaring at him, "if you really think it would jeopardize the truth of—" he looked at me. "I guess I shouldn't interfere."

"No, you shouldn't," I said. I walked back to the stage. "Irene—"

"*Robert.*"

"This is no biggie I'm asking," I said, Woody Allenish.

She looked ready to cry, but instead she hopped off the stage, grabbed her purse, and started for the doors.

"Irene!" I said. "What are you doing?"

"Leaving," she said.

I went after her. Great, I thought. I conducted the fucking rehearsals making sure we had a goddamn *democracy, sitting* on myself so they'd never take the situation wrong, God forbid, and the first time I *suggested* I'm the goddamn director, not even the reason they had *jobs* this summer, this was what I got.

She was heading for the parking lot, marching very purposefully in the direction of our car. I remembered she had the car keys.

"Goddamnit," I yelled, "will you come back and talk to me?"

She stopped and turned to me. "Come back to rehearsal," I said to her. "Now."

She turned away and started walking again, and like some damn buffoon I grabbed the back of her shirt, gave it a yank—this was supposed to stop her—and ripped it right off her. *Then* she stopped.

I was holding the back of her shirt in my hand. She looked at me like the jerk I was—well, I knew I was a jerk about the shirt but I continued to think myself right about everything else.

"Sorry," I said.

She ran to the car, unlocked it, got in, and drove away, while I stood on the strip of grass at the edge of the parking lot watching. Then I went back to the auditorium.

"What happened?" Patrick asked. He and Kate were sitting together on the apron.

"I tore off her shirt."

"You did *what?*" I had it in my hand even then; his eyes dropped to it, scandalized.

"Can I borrow your car?" I said to Kate, and she got me the keys. "Take a break," I told them, "have a Coke."

NO FIGHT IRENE and I had was about any one thing: we fought about the entire structure of our relationship, our past and our future, and as soon as we had any part of the relationship solved, there were other complications, including the major one now that was always coming up, the distinct possibility that I was about to get a lot of what I wanted and she would get very little.

I knocked on her door.

"Go away."

"Irene, you're being paid."

"Tough."

I tried the knob, found it locked. My anger had begun to break up, leaving a residue of righteousness and a sneaking suspicion that my underlying power, my noblesse oblige—*my* wounds—were precisely what had made her behave as intractably as she had.

And yet, *yet* goddamnit—I leaned against the door and as I did she must have opened it because I fell in, which made me furious all over again, though I wasn't about to show it.

She laughed.

"Okay," I said, meaning maybe it *is* funny, but don't.

She'd put on a new shirt. She went away and sat down on her bed.

"I'm sorry about your shirt."

"It's okay." She looked out the window, as if she'd lost interest in me and our fight. I smelled her perfume in the room, the Chanel that Patrick selected for her at Crispins three long years ago. What an ugly room it was. The light picked up stains and worn patches on the rug;

too many different, anonymous people had stayed here, the furniture was bland and haphazard and even her possessions—the bottles and jars on top of the dresser, a scarf draped across the mirror, her old white robe tossed on the bed like a person thrown there—didn't change its relentless lack of identity. It felt to me like an old train station, a place where no one ever stayed and never would, a place where you only waited to get somewhere else.

"I shouldn't have lost my temper," I said. I stood four or five feet from where she sat on the bed. I hadn't been looking at her, and when I did now I had this overpowering desire to hold her. She looked up and I felt a rush of energy between us, saw a dare in her eyes; but I wouldn't let her know how I wanted her, wouldn't give her that, I wouldn't give myself that.

"I—you know what this means to me. The play." She turned away again. "It's very important to me, and it's hard here. How everyone defers to you."

"That doesn't have anything to do with us," I said. Did she want me to apologize for my success, my reputation?

"I get—confused, Robert."

I sat down beside her, "You're going to be sensational in this play."

"I am?"

"You don't know? I've told you."

Not enough, her eyes said. I realized nothing would ever be enough. I wanted to say *Goddamnit, Irene, I'm not the one who let you down. I've never let you down. I didn't spoil your career, take it from you.* Though I had let her down, and sometimes, I knew, it all converged in me. Our lives and our work were braided together, and neither one of us knew anymore how to separate them.

"You're very careful in what you say," she said.

"I tell you you're brilliant. I tell you you've never been better than you are now. What do you want from me?"

"Oh," she said simply, "I've become one of those neurotic actresses I never wanted to be."

"Imperious," I said.

"Needing endless reassurance," she agreed. She took my hand. "Let's go back."

We walked like that down the stairs and outside, playing friends again, while I realized, *I don't want to be your friend.* I sat stiffly driving back, watching her in the rearview mirror driving behind me, glad the fight was over and I'd gotten my way but feeling no satisfaction, no resolution, only unspeakable tension and the desire to be away from her and this lying play about love. What kind of sicko was I, watching her kissing Patrick and wanting to kiss her myself?

I was right; the faster pace opened up the comedy in the scene. It sharpened what they already had and gave them the confidence to take steeper comedic risks, so that we ended up with more contrast, the broader humor making the poignant moments more poignant, the sudden moments of heat, of sex, stronger, more startling.

But I couldn't stop feeling nervous and angry. I drove them too hard the last days of rehearsal, polishing pieces of business that couldn't really be set until I saw the show played for an audience, going three, four hours overtime at the first tech and dress, exhausting them when I should have been conserving their energy: pacing them, pumping them up. My behavior practically screamed *I don't trust you.* I sat watching them together onstage and Patrick was every man she'd ever been with. I thought with comforting familiarity, I'm outside again, watching. What I want is everlastingly beyond my grasp. There were no more tantrums or fights; they were models of cooperation, knowing that *somebody* had to be reasonable. But on the morning of the opening, when I saw Patrick's pallor and bleary eyes, I knew he'd been up all night, worrying over his performance. I watched him pour a cup of coffee and saw his hand tremble.

"Good morning," I said. "How're you feeling?"

He presented me with a beaming artificial smile and said, "Fine, and you?" I mumbled an answer and he limped away with his coffee.

"How's your knee?"

"Fine, why do you ask?"

Before I could answer Irene came in. " 'Lo big guy, how's tricks?"

He smiled painfully, and left. I had noticed when they arrived in Missouri that he hadn't brought his walking stick—what he called the shillelagh from Cork—and took it as a sign that his confidence was up. I'd spent the last five days tearing him down. I was one of those directors who put his own insecurities ahead of the actors and the play.

"He'll be okay," Irene reassured me. "I know this play, Robert. I'll get him through it."

By 7:30 Patrick could barely walk or breathe. We drove to the theater with Irene saying, "Deep, from the diaphram," him saying, "I'm *trying*."

I sat mournfully in the greenroom while they made up, and all I could say at five minutes was, "Well, you'll be great." I added, turning to Patrick, "Don't get safe on me, huh?" He smiled weakly.

"Pace," I said to Irene, who then hit me. "Break both your legs," I said, hugging her. "Just do what you did in rehearsal," I told Patrick.

I'm getting out of this business, I thought, climbing the stairs. The rumble of the audience turned me to water. I hid around the corner from the lobby, then darted into the theater as the lights went down.

The music came up. I stood at the back of the theater listening to Tommy Dorsey and heard a crash. I knew what had happened: Patrick had tripped taking his place in the dark.

The lights rose, and everything looked good—the props, the furniture, the two of them in bed, sleeping. His side of the bed, the part of the sheet covering him, was going up and down awfully fast, but other than that, no problem.

He woke up, saw her beside him, sat bolt upright: " 'Oh, Jesus.' "

Laughter, first line! His energy was a bit high but, oh well, here he was supposed to be hysterical.

He grabbed his shorts from the floor, put them on under the sheet, trying not to awaken her—more laughter. Got out of bed, found his sports coat on a chair, put it on; looked around, taking in her scattered clothes with an expression of growing panic and dismay and said, " 'Jesus H. Christ.' "

Nervously he took a bottle of hair lotion and dumped some on his head, began combing his hair, back to her, as she awoke and sat up, watching him.

God, she looked pretty.

" 'That's a real sharp-looking outfit,' " she said, and he leaped about a foot in the air and then clung to the dresser, and they brought down the house. The laugh crested and he looked at her; she looked at him; and they stared at one another as if encountering foreign creatures.

Home free, I thought. With an audience there I saw things we could work on, but mostly I stood thinking to the back of their heads, how's this for acting? He jumped a page of text but she picked it up without missing a beat and nothing seemed out of sync. It didn't matter, the audience was falling in love with them, they were head over heels, I thought, ecstatically.

At intermission I found him slumped in a chair and Irene rubbing his neck and shoulders.

"Great!" I said, "It's going fantastic, how you feeling?"

"*Tired,*" he said. "I don't think I can get through act two, my knee's *killing* me." At least he was behaving like himself again.

"Sure you can," I said. "Good house tonight, huh?"

It wasn't *Lear,* wasn't even Anouilh, but it was theater and it had worked.

FOUR DAYS INTO the run Maria Valdez arrived from New York to see the play. She appeared in a white rental Ford, wearing a tight T-shirt, tight black pants, and high heels. Her thick black hair crackled in the dry August afternoon. Her escort was yet another good-looking Latino. We came out of the house to greet them.

"Hector!" I said. He'd worked in the employees' cafeteria at ABC. "How ya doing?" I held out my hand and he shook it, saying "Don't tell me—tuna on rye, double cole slaw, strawberry yogurt—"

"Perrier with lime," I said.

"His name's Robert," said Maria, affectionately. She cared about this one; her eyes sparkled looking at him. "You know Patrick," she said, "and this is Irene." He smiled, the sun glinting on his shiny black hair.

"Get a load of this place," Maria said, lifting the glasses she wore on a glittery chain and putting them on; she looked over the lawn and up the stone steps at the terrace, where we had been waiting for them. "I've done how many, O'Doherty, six national tours? They ever put me up in a place like this?" She said to me, "I hadda change agents to someone at William Morris to get into the Hyatt. Patrick, you don't know what I've been through to get here. I got my period this morning, I start rehearsal for that flop I've gotta be in day after tomorrow, are you good in this play?" She had taken his arm and they started into the house. If Patrick wasn't gay, I thought, they'd be married, a grand theatrical couple in the old style, touring the world, hobnobbing with Wallis Simpson and summering with Coward.

Reno's had gotten a face-lift for the party that night. Hildy set candles on the tables and shut off the overheads, someone had brought a tapedeck and played rounds of Motown, Cole Porter, and The Police. Maria dragged Ben across the dance floor, attempting to teach him to fox-trot, a losing proposition. A willowy kid named Larry, an apprentice who was over the moon for Patrick, sat in a corner watching his idol, face shrouded by cigarette smoke.

AFTERNOONS, PATRICK PLAYED the piano in the music room, Chopin nocturnes and popular standards, "My Romance" and "Everything Happens to Me." It smelled like a hothouse in there, roses from the opening were set in vases on the mantlepiece and the piano, but it was my favorite room in the manse: the roses, the silk-covered overstuffed chairs, the blue tiles around the fireplace, the small leaded windowpanes, his open music. Two days after Maria left was our day off, late August now, and Patrick had gone somewhere with Ben. Feeling the luxurious emptiness of the day, I took a book and sat down in the music room to read. Five minutes later Irene came in, rustling a newspaper.

"This idiot says I'm like a different person at the end of the play."

"The idiot's wrong," I said. "You're thirty years older at the end."

"It's hot in here," she said. She turned on the ceiling fan and Patrick's music sheets stirred on the piano.

I kept reading, but she sat down on the piano bench, and sighed.

"What?" I said, without looking up.

"How do you do it?" she asked. "Turn everything off?"

"I'm just trying to read. Are you talking about the review?"

"Forget it." She got up and started out.

"Hey," I called to her, and she turned back. She wore a gauzy white blouse and cutoffs. "Are you looking for a discussion?" I asked. "A fight?"

"I merely came in here," she said, "for an opinion. So sorry if I disturbed you."

"I gave it."

"It *bothered* me, Robert."

"What the idiot said? The moron? A guy who's probably been to the theater twice in his life?"

She collapsed on the couch by the door, dramatically. I was sitting in one of the overstuffed chairs near the piano, clear across the large room from her.

"Come here," I said.

"No." A pause, "You come here." I got up and crossed the room. It felt like slow motion, wading through oceans, the longest walk of my life.

"Don't be mad at me," I said, standing over her. "You're the last person I want to be mad at me."

"Why?"

The scent of the roses—the literal heat I felt in the zone between us. "Because I'm in love with you," I said.

She starting crying. "What?" I said, sitting down next to her. "Don't cry, I'm sorry."

"No, it isn't that. I'm in love with you too."

I sat there, my entire body an ache, and I couldn't move. She pulled her bare feet up beneath her and turned to me, put her arms around me, pressing her head into my neck—the feel of her, utterly known and entirely foreign.

"I don't know what to do," she said.

"Nothing. There's nothing to do," I said tenderly.

WE'D BEEN IN BED for the whole day, it seemed, when Patrick came back. He slammed the front door.

"What was that?" she said. We were lying on our sides facing each other.

"Patrick," I said.

He came up the stairs. "Irene?" he called. "Robert?"

"He sounds upset," she said.

"Mm, yeah," I wrapped one of my legs around hers, "We're not here."

"Where is everyone?" and he opened the door.

There wasn't anything we could do except move away from each other—I sat up, startled. We had the lamp on beside the bed so we weren't even sheathed in darkness.

"What are you doing?" he said. "I mean *why* are you doing it?"

"Are you waiting for an answer?" I said. He came to and left, shutting the door quietly behind him.

"Oh, no major trauma," she giggled, turning to me and hugging my legs. "He probably thought you were reading. Lie down."

"Why is he so weird?"

"He always was, lie back down."

"Not like he is now."

"Never mind." She straddled my legs.

"I'm distracted."

"Not much."

"Did you hear the door?"

"Yes, he left." She lowered herself down onto me.

IN THE MORNING we took a shower together and made love again. "This has to stop," she said.

"Yeah, let's go try your bed."

"No, I have a show tonight, remember?"

"We'll cancel it." I was kissing her again and it was almost two o'clock; the sun slanted in through a crack in the curtains.

"I'm hungry," she said, "aren't you?"

"All right." I released her.

We ate at a diner in town, thinking we'd run into Patrick and Ben, feeling badly by then about what had happened. The natural light in the diner brought out the spectrum of her hair, reds, golds and browns, and the clarity of her eyes, and I felt myself flushing all over with pleasure and laughing at anything she said and grabbing her under the table.

Still, we decided to drive over to Reno's to find Patrick before going home. He wasn't there, and neither was Ben. Only Hildy, bored and looking for company. As soon as we could we got away and drove to Ben's.

"He's probably home now," she said.

"Probably," I agreed.

Ben was working on the house, and he hadn't seen Patrick since early yesterday evening. They'd had a fight yesterday. "Will you tell him to call me?" he asked.

"I think we blew it," I said to Irene in the car.

"I think he was worried," she said. "He looked really worried to me."

"*You're* worried. Nothing *happened*, he isn't our son."

She slid over near me and rested her head on my shoulder. "Anyway, I'm sure he's at home."

He wasn't. She went to her room for a nap and I went to mine, sleeping the second my head hit the pillow. I woke to her knock on the door: "Robert?"

"Come in."

"He isn't back," she said. It was seven.

Oh well, we would see him at the theater.

But he wasn't there. She went ahead and made up—it didn't occur to us that he might not show.

At 7:45 she came out of the dressing room and said, "What'll we do?" I went outside and hung around the stage door a minute, circled the theater, scanning the road and the parking lot: nobody tall.

She was waiting for me in the greenroom. "I feel sick," she said, and went into the john. I couldn't play it, I probably could have if given twenty-four hours, but not tonight unless I did it on book. I was thinking we could delay, hold the curtain, when Patrick walked in.

"Hello there. Time for a quick cigarette before make up." It was 7:52. I followed him into the dressing room, watched him pat his pockets for a smoke and then take one from his cigarette box. He had misplaced his lighter. "I was with Ben," he said, extracting a pack of matches from a drawer. "We lost track of the time." I went upstairs and, crossing the lobby, was intercepted by willowy Larry, who held out to me a pack of Gauloises and a black Bic lighter, "Will you give these to Patrick?" he asked.

"Why?" I didn't immediately understand.

"Maybe he doesn't have any others."

I took them dumbly, saw Kate, and told her we were ready to start, and Larry was gone. Then it clicked.

I went outside to the steps and watched stragglers coming into the theater, turned my face to the darkening sky, the new stars, thinking, oh please let me make it with Irene, I cannot be alone anymore.

They played well, even got a laugh we'd missed every show all last week. The romantic parts seemed more passionate than usual but that may have been me. "Hot show," I said, sticking my head in the dressing-room door. She was in her slip hanging up her dress. Patrick had already lit his post-show cigarette.

"Come in and close the door," he said, and as I did, "Robert. Irene. I'm sorry." He sat on the edge of the dressing table, "Are you in love?"

"Patrick," she said, "you don't have to embarrass us."

"I'm being sincere," he said. "I'm inclined to suspect that it wasn't strictly recreational."

"It wasn't," I said.

"Well," he replied, "in New York we could have a proper celebration. As it is, I'll buy you a pizza."

Even so, it didn't feel right. Irene and I sat across from him at the Pizza Hut, being careful not to sit too close together.

"Do you plan on being the great love of each other's lives?" he asked us. "You've eaten practically nothing, that's a sure sign." He sighed. "I suppose playing the show from now on will feel doubly adulterous. Let's go see Ben."

We couldn't not forgive him; the show had gone well, no harm was done. I handed him the cigarettes and lighter. He took them, and that was the end of it.

"GALA NEWS," PATRICK SAID, near the conclusion of the run. "Sidney called. For the first time in months. But I can't hold that against him because in exactly one week I have an audition for a Broadway play."

"You're going to get it," I said. "I feel it. The tides are turning."

"Poor you," said Irene. "Now you won't be able to visit my father with us in Kansas."

"Oh, I'm dismayed," Patrick said. "You're really going? To Coffeyville? Robert, you must be in love."

Ben came to take Patrick to the airport the morning he left for New York.

"You *won't* be nervous," Irene said. "You'll go to Maria's masseuse in the morning and all day think of nothing but how good you were in this show." She held his arm, her fingers lightly stroking the skin just above the inside of his wrist, a gesture she had used in the play.

"If in return," he answered, "you both agree to finish the honeymoon in Coffeyville. I can't stand being around you anymore. And gain weight," he added, getting into Ben's truck. "I've never seen two people lose so much weight in a week, it's obscene."

We watched them back out of the driveway. "We're alone," I said.

"I'll miss it here," she said.

"Maybe we'll be here next summer."

"Next summer we'll have our own place to work."

I'd forgotten. I'd fantasized Patrick on Broadway, she and I doing fabulously well, no need for a theater after all.

"We'll do plays that matter," she said.

We were packing when Colin called to say good-bye and in the course of the conversation I learned that Wally Press had been discovered on campus the previous day, living in a storage room in the English department. The building had been closed for the summer but with the school year coming up the custodial staff had gone in to clean. Someone's suspicions were aroused by the strong scent of shoe polish emanating from the storage room off the main hallway. Imagine, living in a storage room for a month and still shining your shoes.

"How creepy," I said.

"How sad," said Irene.

Part III

13 Finding Irene

We took 29 South through Kansas City, then cut over slightly southwest to Coffeyville. It was hot, and dry. We'd come at the end of a summer of drought. Kansas, Irene explained, was a place of extremes; of long droughts and sudden floods, of blistering heat and blizzards, of long empty days and violent tornados. Sky was everywhere, a good three-quarters of the view in any direction, like buildings were everywhere in New York. I had a sense, driving in, of high, far, lonely distances.

"What's he like?" I asked her. "What's Ray like?"

"Looks like an old cowboy." She shrugged. "I don't know, I told you."

"You miss him?"

"Christ no. We'd both probably be better off if we never saw each other."

Her hair was tied back, but the heat had strands around her face wet and sticking to her skin. She'd knotted the tails of her shirt, so an inch or two of midriff showed above her jeans. She turned off the highway and stopped for gas. We got out of the car and I bought a bottle of Mountain Dew, grabbed her, and held the cool bottle against her bare stomach, making her scream, pulled her to the side of the soda machine and kissed her.

"Tired?" I asked.

"We're almost there."

The surrounding land was hardly broken by hills or trees: only fields, tiny cattle in the distance, a farmhouse and a silo, the road connecting to the highway and, everywhere, sky.

"What do they grow here?" I asked her.

She tucked a hand into one of my back pockets and we walked like that back to the car. "Mostly wheat, some alfalfa and corn." Many families had recently lost their farms, she said: inflation, developers like her father, corporate operations. Livestock had always been big in Kansas, but influence these days was more with the banks and power companies, even still with the railroads, than it was with the ranchers and farmers.

I watched the land stream away. As we came into Coffeyville she swung east around the fairgrounds and stopped at The Pig Stand, where I watched her devour two mean-looking barbecue sandwiches. I ate part of one, aware of two tables of families with young children, a table of teenagers on dates, and a group of farmers all enthusiastically eating.

She'd told her dad not to wait for supper with us. We went down Eleventh, which ran parallel to the Missouri Pacific Railroad, dividing Coffeyville proper from Southtown. "The Daltons are buried down there," she said. The Daltons were outlaws, shot robbing the old Condon National Bank in 1892. I'd been briefed on the Dalton Museum and the yearly enactment of the original shoot-out. We passed little row houses and bungalows stuffed between businesses, with short cement stoops and thin-armed girls holding babies in the waning daylight.

"The college is in the other direction," she said, "where I met Rose. I'll show you tomorrow."

Buildings gave way to more space again, larger homes set like ships on broad, parched, open lawns.

The house was bigger and blander than what I'd envisioned: ranch style, wood and brick, late fifties. One lonely tree on the whole big front yard. Silence, a distant buzzing of insects. No sunset, no clouds in the sky, just the unabating heat and a foretaste of darkness, like the light was getting tired.

She stopped halfway up the driveway and said, "You sure you want to do this?"

"Do you? You okay?"

"It can be real peaceful here . . ." She didn't move to get out of the car. "Or it can be a *tomb*." She shut off the engine.

"Where's his car?" I asked.

"Shut away for the night." I saw the double garage doors were closed. We got out our bags. "He's had his supper and his dishes are drying by the sink. The paper's been read and now he has on the TV." We heard it as we went up the walk. "See?"

"We could stay at a hotel," I said hopefully.

"Robert, he'll *hear*."

"You didn't even *knock* yet."

"*Hi*, Daddy."

"Irene Jane," he replied.

After an awkward moment of trying to manipulate our bags and ourselves through the narrow entryway, she put her arms around him and hugged him. He patted her once on the back, not coldly exactly, but as though he wasn't used to hugging anybody. I could see Irene in the fineness of his features and the width of his mouth, although not in his eyes, which were small and close set. He was wiry, with close-clipped gunmetal gray hair, his face tanned and lined, and extremely good-looking.

We sat down in a family room where he left the TV on, but turned down the sound. He was a smoker; I had heard it in his voice and smelled it in the room, a sooty peppery odor betraying a lack of ventilation and old curtains and carpeting that held it.

"You look good, Daddy," said Irene, positively beaming, perched on an arm of the couch.

"Had your supper?" he asked.

"Stopped at The Pig Stand," she said.

"First time in Coffeyville?" he asked me.

"Yes sir, first time. I'm originally from New Jersey." He kept looking at me. "Glen Rock and Fort Lee." He hadn't heard of them, evidently.

"Missed the fair," he said. The big Interstate Fair and Rodeo—Irene had told me about it as we circled the fairgrounds.

"I know," Irene said, "I'm heartsick."

Another silence.

"How's business?" she asked. He nodded.

How would I get through a week of this? She got him to talk a few minutes more by inquiring after people he knew with interesting names like Ivy Knotts and Opal Hall. I was beginning to relax when she hopped to her feet and vanished into the murky hollows of the home.

He sat in a bulky olive green vinyl chair and in it looked smaller than he was. Nonetheless, even considering the probability that I was prejudiced against him because he was laconic and had on a Western shirt, I didn't think I'd like to get on his bad side. He took a pack of cigarettes from the table beside him, lit one, and smoked.

"How's the weather been?" I asked.

"Dry." The room was all browns, mustard yellows, and greens. There was a stereo and mostly empty shelves; stacks of magazines and old Books of Knowledge.

"I thought you came from New York," he said.

"I do."

"You said New Jersey."

"I grew up in New Jersey, I live in New York."

He rose from his chair and turned up the TV. We watched a new dramatic series about a detective, which didn't seem to particularly interest him; he took in the commercials with the same quality of attention he gave the program. Irene returned for the climax of the show, interrupting it to ask her father whether he had someone in to clean.

"Bonnie Lorraine," he said, "same as ever."

"Daddy, she's eighty years old! Well, I'll clean up, but you're going to have to find somebody else."

He smoked, his face turned toward the TV, only his eyes drifting vaguely and lazily in her direction when she spoke. Presently, at five minutes to the hour, the conflicts confronting the TV detective were resolved and Mr. Walpers got up and went to bed.

I pulled Irene from the couch and onto the floor, saying "Help!" She kissed me and laughed.

"Where were you?"

"On the phone."

"Who's Bonnie Lorraine?"

"One of my aunts."

"Oh yeah, sister of Jean Rae and Wilma."

"What did you talk about?"

"We didn't. Oh, but we did attempt to untangle the contradiction of my growing up in Jersey and living in New York." Irene was the one person her father knew who was raised in Coffeyville and had left. People here, even the young who felt trapped in the town, were strangely rooted to it. It got under your skin, and people who lived here felt its pull inside.

She untied her hair and sat up, and I slid my hand under her shirt and rubbed her back saying, "Actually, that's kind of nice."

"It can be," she said.

Only days before, watching her onstage, I'd had the mistaken realization that I would be able to know her as I'd known, perhaps, only myself. But then she'd moved away from a table she had always moved toward before in the scene and focused on it with an expression I'd never quite seen on her face—something terribly pensive, shattered, and dark—and I felt confused and disoriented and distant from her. I saw how thoroughly she was herself, how I could never hope to know her as I had imagined, how much any concept of possession was in fact an illusion.

That first night in her father's house I felt similarly again, expectant as though the dark rooms around us, illumined, the rooms of her childhood, her past, would give her to me.

We got up and moved through the hot rooms, turning off lights behind us as we left. In the living room opposite the family room was her mother's piano, a squat brown spinet, on top of which rested the same photograph Irene had of her mother in the field, and her parents' wedding picture. I stared at Ray, years younger then than I was now, and could not see in his face the romantic Irene had described, a man who would spend his life mourning the neat, pretty woman standing beside him.

"Does your father have a girlfriend?" I asked.

"None that I know of. What my father does is work."

She put out the light and we got a drink of water in the kitchen and stood kissing at the sink. "I wish we could go somewhere," I said. It wasn't later than ten-thirty or eleven. We brought a blanket out to the yard and around to the side of the house farthest from her father's bedroom and lay down together in the still-warm night.

I slept in a small dusty room, separated from her by a wall. Ribbons papered two oversize bulletin boards across from her bed, for doing rodeo. Barrel racing—an event, she explained, of speed, nerve, and precision.

"Good training for an actress," she said. "Teaches you when you fall to get back on the horse."

IN THE MORNING I went to the kitchen and saw her through the window in the backyard. Her back to me, she stood with her hands folded behind her, wearing a faded print dress, thin enough that I could discern the outlines of her body.

It was just after nine, dishes were drying by the sink; Mr. Walpers was gone. She'd left coffee for me on the stove. I sat down with a cup at the table and looked at the *Coffeyville Journal,* read an article with the headline, KANSAS, THE DRY STATE, about liquor, not rain; an old-timer describing joints built on the border of Kansas and Oklahoma; when the cops raided, everybody ran over to the Oklahoma side.

I heard her boots on the back steps, the screen door, and she came into the kitchen. "Come here," she said, and she took me to the window. "That's the stable, where Mercury lived."

"You look sexy. Where'd you get the dress?" I recognized the four buttons on the front; it was her mother's, the dress in the picture of her mother in the field.

"In my closet," she said.

I put my arms around her and she put her hands in my back pockets. "I missed you last night," I said.

"Me too." She smelled wonderful, and felt warm; her hair was silky against my face. "What are we doing today?" I asked. "You want to go to bed?"

"Not here." She extricated herself from me. "You want breakfast?"

I leaned against the sink. "But he isn't here."

"I couldn't here, *ever.*" She opened a cupboard and pulled out boxes, turned back. "I have to tell you that my father—I don't trust him, Robert." There was actual hatred tingeing the words. I resisted the urge to say, why are we here then? You despise him, you love him? At least he wasn't my father, at least he stuck around. She shifted her eyes from me, sighed. "And besides, I've made other arrangements." She kissed me lightly, with a brief but effective tug on one of my belt loops.

"Well good. If I don't have sex three times a day I feel deprived."

"Oh, *ha.* You want cereal?" She set a dish on the table, her voice an odd mixture of vehemence and embarrassment. "It's only—this house is all him, even if he's not here."

"That's okay," I said.

She sat down at the table, dejectedly. "I'm sorry."

"For what?"

"Coming here."

"Oh hey, since we're here let's have fun. That *Coffeyville Journal* whetted my appetite for the sights." She laughed.

She had more coffee while I ate, and then we drove over to Sixth Street to visit her friend, Rebecca. Becca was married to Billy Wayne Boyers, and Irene had known the two of them since childhood. Billy Wayne was eight years or so older than Becca and Irene, and had held for both of them a certain glamour after he went to Vietnam and came back minus the first two joints of three fingers. But then Irene went to New York, and Rebecca married him. They hadn't done badly, had kids right away, but lived in a nicer home than the crowded boxes I'd seen on Eleventh, a tidy white house with a decent-sized yard.

Rebecca had long, straight, toffee-colored hair and red-rimmed brown eyes, and she answered the door holding a baby, another small child attached to her leg.

"Oh, Becca," said Irene, "this is him?"

"Yep, this is Lonnie, and you know Billy Junior. Come on, honey," she said to the boy, who was hiding his face, "show yourself to the nice people. He's shy." Irene got him to look at her, briefly.

"Oh, he's cute," Becca said, meaning me, and putting her hand to her mouth, she laughed and said, "I'm sorry, you're Robert."

"Yeah, this is the one," Irene said, taking my arm. The twang that had flavored her speech in Missouri was reaching its apex. Becca showed us the house—they'd moved in recently—and we sat down in the kitchen with glasses of iced tea. "I saw you on the soap," Becca said. "You look almost the same. . . ." She peered at me as though she thought that as an actor I was capable of physical mutation.

Becca put the baby into one of those slings and he slept while she and Irene talked. At first they tried to include me, but soon they were busy discussing local people and I sat back and listened until Billy appeared at my side, thrusting out to me a plastic toy soldier.

"Yours?" I said, taking it. "Spiffy. How old are you?" His eyes were light brown and red-rimmed like his mother's. He held up three fingers.

"He lives down in some sleazy hotel on South Walnut," Becca was saying.

"*No,*" Irene said.

"Got what he deserves, going back into those big professional shows at his age."

"How'd he get gored?" Irene asked. "Bulldoggin'?"

"What's that?" I said.

"Wrestling steers," Irene said.

"Oh."

"Hank's a fool," Irene said. The ex-boyfriend.

"Why, Billy," Becca said, "you've brought every single toy that you own from your room and put it out on this floor."

It turned out that Becca and the children were leaving and Irene and I were staying here.

We stood on the back stoop while Becca opened the garage and got the kids settled in the car. Next door an old man tended a lush green garden surrounded by sunflowers, big meaty faces buzzing with bees. The car pulled out of the driveway.

"So," Irene said quietly, "aren't you going to take me inside—?"

I did, bringing her back to the small master bedroom with the crib at the foot of the bed and the faint smell of sour milk, undoing the four large buttons at the front of her dress and lifting it, reverently, over her head, feeling vaguely nostalgic from the sight of the sunflowers and the old man in the garden for a life I'd never known. She took off my shirt, and I sat on the side of the bed and took off my shoes and socks, stood again, light-headed, heard the clank of my belt buckle hitting the floor, the hiss of my zipper; behind it, the whipping sound of the fan on a chair in the corner.

"You're not going to make a crack about the location?" she asked.

"Uh-uh, not now." I could think only of her hands, and the wetness of her mouth and the whip of the fan and forgot where else I was in the rest of the world, except with her.

THAT WAS THE RHYTHM of our days, visiting after breakfast with relatives and friends, or sightseeing—the infamous Dalton Museum, and the cemetery where her mother was buried. Afternoons we returned to Rebecca's house and that room. Becca worked afternoons at the five-and-ten while her mother took care of the children; Billy Wayne sold liquor in a package store.

In the evenings we saw Irene's father. He never asked questions, but Irene chattered to him about Missouri and New York, and he listened. We joined him for television after supper, our version of being gracious and showing an interest in his life. I started to think, what the heck, he wasn't so bad.

Our fourth day Patrick called to say he had gotten the show on Broadway. Irene and I sat at the kitchen table, smiling.

"You see?" I said. "You see how everything is going to be all right?"

"Everything's all right now," she said.

"Sure, but—"

"It's lovely. Let's wait and see, you don't have to make it mean something." Her face had gone tight, closed. The play itself was weak, his role small, but the role was a good one in which he believed he could easily shine.

"All I *mean*," I said, though I'd meant more, "is the one thing he needs is visibility."

"Careful," she said, "you sound like an agent."

"What does—?"

"Just leave it, okay?"

She sat silently in the car as we drove to Rebecca's, staring out the window. But at Sixth Street we made love, still at the stage where our bodies solved everything.

Afterward, lying on top of the sheets, listening to the clip-clip-clip of the fan, she ran her hand over my chest and then rested her fingers against my ribs. "In my next life," she said, "I want to be physically strong." She drew her hand over my stomach, "I guess I want to come back as a man."

"You really believe in that stuff?" I asked her. As I understood spiritualism, or the version of it she had studied, your being chose every aspect of your life according to the needs of your soul's development.

"Sure." She leaned over me jauntily, eyes bright, hair tangled; herself again.

"What's it like to be strong?" she asked.

"I don't think about it." I laughed.

"I bet it feels good." She ran a hand down my thigh.

"Okay," I said, "if you believe in it, how come I chose my father?"

"I don't know, maybe sometimes God chooses . . . maybe you chose your father, and then God gave you David."

I gathered her into me, loving her very much, and kissed her.

"You say nice things," I said. We made love again.

That night after supper, we returned to Rebecca's to meet Billy Wayne. Billy Jr. answered the door silently, his father behind him.

Billy Wayne was a short man but powerfully built, topped by a small round head set close to his shoulders. Dark hair and penetrating eyes. He wore Levi's and a belt buckle of a steer head studded with rhinestones. But he was in no way a Floyd—there was stature, substantiveness in him. Vietnam, I presumed, irresistably drawn to the partially severed fingers of his right hand.

Once we had exhausted the usual topics of weather and the fair, everybody sat sipping Coors while a breeze sighed in through the open back door. Cre-eak, tip went Billy Wayne's chair; he maintained a precarious balance by supporting himself with the toe of one boot positioned underneath the flat top of the table. Becca got up to give little Billy his bath, and feeling like a third wheel with Becca gone, I went to keep her company.

She knelt at the side of the tub, the ends of her long hair dragging in the suds. "You like kids," she said, "don't you?" Billy squealed, smacking at the surface of the water, "C'mon, honey, stop it. Maybe you and Irene will have kids someday." Then I heard Irene's and Billy Wayne's laughter.

In the hallway I heard it better, waves gushing out from the kitchen. Her head was thrown back, her throat arched; I could only see the back of his head, his broad back against the chair. *Slam*, the front legs of his chair. They stopped laughing and she was looking at me; maybe I had stood staring at them for too long. I summoned a demeanor of normalcy, fetched my beer and left. But I could tell she had slept with Billy Wayne. Once Becca and I rejoined them in the kitchen, the party was over. Irene said we should go.

"We could have stayed," I said at the car. "You were having fun."

"I'm tired," she yawned, getting in.

"Me too." At Morgan Street, in her father's driveway, she squeezed my arm.

"Know what? I love you," she said, and when we were in the house she got physical, but I couldn't help feeling that I could have been anyone, that she was just generally excited, maybe from seeing Billy Wayne again.

"Oh, come on," she said, trying to pull me from the entryway into the family room. "Let's put on the TV and fool around."

"I thought you were tired," I said. "Besides, I thought you had a thing about this house."

"What's wrong, grouchy?" she said, putting her arms around my neck. Ever since we'd come here she'd worn clothes that I didn't recognize—the T-shirt she had on tonight, her mother's dress.

"I'm tired," I said, wishing that she would mention something about *our* life. I made it a test in my head, which she failed.

" 'Night, love," and she went to bed.

I couldn't sleep. The more I tried not to think of what I'd been thinking the more I did. I convinced myself that if she'd told me the truth about Billy Wayne, that he had been more than a friend, I wouldn't be bothered. She *had* said she'd had a crush on him, but that didn't mean "sleep with." Or did it? Should I have assumed they had been lovers? If so, what did that mean? Who else was there in Coffeyville besides Hank and Billy Wayne?

Ages ago she had offered to sleep with me, no strings attached. In the era of Neal. Which meant she had *always* loved me but chose her *real* lovers according to other more mercenary needs. Or else we were all interchangeable. What would have happened if Neal hadn't been such a heel? If he had been even a halfway decent person? Or Andre? Or *Floyd?* What did it mean when she said she loved me? How could I trust her if I couldn't trust her actions?

I drifted off into that twilight world between waking and sleep, of flickering images that didn't track—when I jolted awake it was morning.

I'd decided: I had to know where things stood. She'd have to be honest with me. I recognized the doughy smell of biscuits baking wafting into my room.

"Hi!" She'd been looking out the window, drinking coffee. Huge smile. Why was she so happy today?

I got a cup for coffee, and she came up beside me.

"Well, kiss me." I did. "Oh, that was real good," she said flatly, so I kissed her again.

"Irene," I said, "I love you very much."

"I love you too. How come you're so serious?"

"No reason." I couldn't do it, couldn't ask her.

She opened the oven, inhaled the fragrance of the biscuits, and said, "There's a sale on at Weinberg's. The Western store, remember?"

I'd wanted to buy her some boots. I sat down and looked at the ad in the *Coffeyville Journal*. "I can't believe it's called Weinberg's. Makes me imagine a yarmulke built into a cowboy hat."

She said, "*Robert.* Can I buy you one?"

"What?"

"A hat," she sat down at the table. "Oh come on, if I bought it for you, you'd wear it, wouldn't you? No? Okay, then you can't buy me boots."

AT WEINBERG'S, AFTER choosing a gaudy pair of white boots with blue peacocks, she had me in front of a three-way mirror trying on hats. Stetsons. Straw. Gray, brown, tan, and black. She'd get one off the shelf and stand by me while I tried it on, to see all of us together: her, me, the hat.

"No, you're right," she said finally. "A hat isn't you, is it?" We put back the hat, the heels of my shoes and her boots knocking on the wooden plank floor.

"It wasn't that you didn't look good," she said. "You looked too much like these guys I grew up with." I had wondered whether that was the point. "You're my Eastern boy, aren't you?" She kissed me.

Near Rebecca's she wanted to show me the fairgrounds. She drove, under the vast cloudless sky. It wasn't too hot yet. The weather took its time and worked up to the heat, rarely cooling down before eight or nine o'clock. There remained signs of the big event at the fairgrounds, a gamey smell of animals mingled with dust as we drove by the empty holding pens, workers' trucks parked outside the permanent structures. We parked and got out behind the grandstand, one bank of permanent bleachers facing the ring. I followed her partway up, and waited so long for her to say anything while she looked around—squinting a little, smiling to herself—that I wondered what she saw. This corral was a theater to her, sets struck, lights gone, but redolent of worlds, emotionally dense and rich.

She'd only competed here once or twice, but the local riding clubs paraded around the ring every year on opening day, and the fair was such a central event in the life of the town, as marked and anticipated as the motions of the weather, I could imagine hundreds of smaller dramas enacted against the background of the fair, or overlapping with the fair. Dead dramas hovering here, written down in the books of minds, alive in consciousness, memory.

She leaned forward, and I thought she would speak, but then she sat back and relapsed into herself again, as a power saw growled into life in the distance.

"Getting hot," I said finally.

"Yeah . . . Robert," she said, looking at me, something in her eyes, "make love to me here."

"Here? You're crazy."

She smiled. "We could go down under the bleachers."

I scanned the area we had driven through just beyond us and saw a man come out of one of the buildings and get into a truck.

"No," I said.

"Oh, come on."

"No, we'd be too exposed." She stood and stomped down to the ground, unmistakably angry.

"Irene—"

"Forget it. Are you hungry?"

"Not really."

"So, where to?" She'd taken the keys from her pocket and they dangled from one of her fingers while she waited impatiently on the driver's side.

"Sixth Street?" I said. "Weren't we going to Sixth Street?"

She shrugged like good-as-anywhere-else and got in.

I barely got in—the car leaped and shot forward, dust rising in clouds. She had it up to sixty on the goddamn dirt road before I said, "Come *on*." She slammed on the brakes; the car bucked and jolted to a stop, and for a good twenty seconds we sat in a dust cloud.

"Okay, turn around."

"I don't want to now."

"Great." The dust cleared and she continued on to the stop sign with exaggerated precaution, drove like that until we were on Sixth, about four blocks from the house and on a straightaway, and then hit the gas again hard.

I said, *"Jesus, slow down."*

We squealed into the driveway and sat there, arguing loudly. I spotted the old man next door, approaching the fence to investigate.

"This is a *neighborhood*," I said, "you could have hit someone."

"There was no one *around*," she said.

"Shut up," I said.

"Don't you tell me to shut up."

I followed her in the back door, casting a short dour nod from the steps to the man in the garden. I watched her get a glass and open the refrigerator for the pitcher of ice water. I went and tried to take the glass from her but she wouldn't let me. I tried to kiss her and she resisted, standing against the refrigerator. I held the wrist of the hand in which she held the glass.

"C'mon," I said.

"No."

I pushed the hair from her face and kissed her neck. I pulled the tails of her shirt from her pants.

"You don't love me," she said.

"Wanna bet?"

I pulled open the snaps of her shirt, put my arm around her waist, lifting her as she raised her legs, and I carried her into the bedroom.

We kissed and got off our jeans, and as soon as our clothes were gone the tone changed, we grabbed and pulled and held onto each other hard and were fucking almost immediately, but kept changing positions like we wanted to do everything at once. We didn't bother to turn on the fan, so were soon slick and then dripping with sweat, our skin everywhere sliding against each other. She sat up and pushed me back on the bed and fell across me but I got her turned over again and with my arms under her back, holding her up, looking into her face I said, "Now." She put her hands against my chest pushing me away and then grabbed my arms, straining higher against me with her hips, and in a minute we were lying flat on the bed, soaked.

"Can you get the fan," I heard her say.

Somehow I got up and dragged the chair with the fan to the foot of the bed and clicked it on; then lay back down beside her and closed my eyes as the cool air poured across us. In a little while I turned my head and looked at her and she looked at me, and I kissed her, ran my tongue across her teeth. I could feel twenty different things about her at the same time and still want her, or twenty different things consecutively in twenty seconds and still want her, everything I had thought last night didn't matter, and I realized I was shaken by her anger. "Are you cooler?" I asked.

"Yes."

We took a shower together and put the sheets in the washing machine and went to the market for lunch, and even though she was very affectionate I thought her strange, as if she were still angry with me or had felt my unease more than I knew.

Back at the house we were startled by an explosion of sound— filling the neighborhood, coming near. The house rattled and shook and at last, when the source of the sound stopped in the driveway, I recognized it as a motorcycle. "Who's that?" I asked Irene, jumping up from the table.

"Oh, shoot," she said. "Billy Wayne. I forgot he gets off early on Fridays."

Without thinking I dashed to the bathroom, where there was a window over the bathtub that faced the driveway. He rode a Harley hog, naturally, and of course he didn't wear a helmet, he'd been to Vietnam, for Christ's sake.

"What are you doing?" Irene said.

I was standing in the bathtub was what I was doing.

"This is really embarrassing," I said, though I hadn't even thought to be embarrassed.

"Well, the sheets aren't dry," she said, "there's nothing we can do." I peeked out the window again and he opened the garage; he was wheeling it in.

"Robert, he has sex too, you know, *obviously*." I turned and looked at her. "And anyway, their sheets are so clean every day they must have suspected."

"I have to use the bathroom. Go out and close the door."

She rolled her eyes and left. I got out of the bathtub and went, just to kill time, washed my hands knowing I was acting stupid, part of me cognizant of the entire situation as comical, but the rest of me was deflated, illogically angry.

He offered us beer and pretended not to notice when Irene took the sheets from the dryer and went to remake the bed, while he and I sat at the table and talked about something.

"What is *wrong* with you?" she asked, driving home.

"What?"

"What's wrong?" To my "nothing" she rolled her eyes again, but dropped it.

I was in a foul mood at supper, though, and didn't try to hide it. Consequently, Irene's conversational steam petered out and she grew quiet. Never one to smooth anything over, Mr. Walpers opened the paper.

Later that night as she watched Johnny Carson, I sat down on the couch and she made a display of closing her posture, crossing her legs, hunching toward the TV as if she didn't want to miss a syllable of Joan Rivers. Fuck it, I thought, and waited for the commercial.

"Can I ask you a question?" I said.

A tremor of anger unsettled her brow. "Yes."

"Did you ever sleep with Billy Wayne?"

"Why?"

"I'd just like to know."

"It's none of your business," she said, and then left the room.

The back door was open; she sat on the steps. She'd gotten a pack of her father's Chesterfields and smoked, held a glass of bourbon. I wouldn't apologize. I wasn't the only one being unreasonable. I wouldn't ask why she'd said what she had at the fairgrounds, but I refused to apologize. I wouldn't mention the dress with the four buttons, her mother's dress. I didn't like it, this link to death and to longing and to me, lifting the dress over her head—this blending of loss and the past with the erotic. Who was I in the empty arena, what would it have meant to her, taking her under the bleachers, making love to her in the dirt?

She stubbed out her cigarette in the dry grass as I sat down beside her, and drained what was left of her drink. There was that keen relief night brings after hot days, and the light was beautiful and strange. Though the moon wasn't visible, light filled the sky, plunging the sloping ground and the small weathered barn into one soft plane. "Tomorrow Becca has off," she said. "We're driving out to some stables, a friend from high school boards horses I wanted to see. You don't have to come."

"I'll come."

"Beau is his name. Beauregard Dwight Eisenhower Gray," she shook her head in a mildly sarcastic commentary. I could tell she was discomfited, didn't know what to say.

14 Mercury Dying

Going to Rebecca's the next day she smoked, dragging deeply à la Bette Davis, and I knew we were in the middle of a struggle that wouldn't be quickly or easily resolved.

Becca came out to the car at the cue of the horn and as she got in I saw Billy Wayne behind the screen door.

"I wanna ride," Irene said.

"You ride?" Becca asked me.

"Not often," I answered. Twice in my life.

"You can ride if you want to," Irene said.

I didn't reply. Her tone said, "I dare you."

"First time I tried racing the barrels I fell and got kicked in the head," said Becca. "Scared the shit out of me and I never rode again."

The stables were down a dirt road at the edge of a ranch; cattle grazed off in a wider field past the immediate grounds. There were several small shelters, a pasture, a wired-off area where a few horses stood in the sun, and two corrals. In one a young girl with black braids held a lead, guiding a stocky brown pony around her in a circle. The larger corral opened on one side to the pasture. Everything had a run-down, unprosperous look, but that may have been the dust and the heat. Irene had told me the rancher, the uncle of Beauregard Dwight, was one of the richest in Montgomery County.

"Well, haidy hi haidy ho," he said as we got out of the car. I knew
I'd have to be really far gone to feel jealous of this one, rail skinny,
bright yellow hair. In an orange Western shirt sporting green pockets,
he resembled an exotic parrot.

"Hey, Beau," Irene said, grinning and slapping him on the arm like
a guy. "This is Robert."

"Haidy hi. You woulda told me you was comin' today," he said to
Becca, "I'd a had somethin' to ride. Pret' near everybody's out." Becca
said nobody wanted to ride but Irene. "Got a boy for Irene," and he
winked at me and Becca and beckoned with his bright head for us to
follow him to a young Appaloosa.

"Getcher butt over here, P," he said to the horse, and seeming thoroughly bored and put out, the horse advanced, his great head nodding
slowly up and down. He stopped before Beau, working his jaws, ob-
serving us out of one eye.

"This is Poker Chip," said Beau, taking hold of the halter and turning to us the mottled gray face. "Girl down in Caney's been teaching
him the barrels, but she ain't coming today."

Irene petted the horse's muzzle and he lifted his head and backed
off a few paces. Beau yanked him back, laughing what was almost a
cackle.

"He's feisty, you can ride eem, Irene."

"Got a saddle?" she asked.

"Shit, you wanna saddle?" He let go of the horse and headed off to
one of the wooden structures with unexpected fluidity and speed, his
gait consisting as it did of a short limp and compensating hop.

"Got barrels, you want to give him some turns," he called back.

"Just get me the saddle, Beau, I'm not messing with this girl's horse."
She was not having any of Beau's faintly inciting banter, but I saw
pleasure in her eyes, and a measured excitement.

"What are you and Beau trying to do," she asked Becca, "set me
up?" She ducked under the wire and approached the horse, talking
soothingly to him, this time reaching out and grasping the halter and
holding it firmly, and stroking him again. "Good boy, *good* boy."

Beau came back and saddled him, and Irene lifted a leg and put her foot in a stirrup, and in one agile motion swung herself over and was seated. The saddle creaked and he took a little leap forward. Irene pulled on the reins, caressing his neck. Beau opened an aluminum gate at the other side of the pen and Irene walked Poker Chip out and off to the pasture.

They trotted back and forth, testing each other, and when I noticed Beau again he was rolling this barrel the size of an oil drum out to the connecting corral. Irene caught sight of him and yelled, "Wasting your energy, Beau!" She swung Poker Chip around in an arc and took him into a canter, rode past the corral and out of the pasture and beyond another dirt road. Way out in the next field she opened him up, and they flew across the horizon.

"Nice to see Irene ride again," Becca said. "She had the prettiest sorrel horse, Mercury. Oh Irene, she was always wild."

"Wild, how?" I asked.

"Oh, you just always knew she'd do something different, you could always tell. . . ."

Beau had rolled out another barrel and set them both upright at the center of the corral, leaving eight or ten feet of space between them.

"He wanted to be a rodeo clown," Becca said, "but his uncle said he was too dumb," and she laughed, hiding her mouth with one hand. "Beau's a clown, but a rodeo clown's not a *clown*—they're brave. Anyway, he's got that one leg shorter than the other. But he kept on about it and his uncle couldn't stand hearing it anymore and sent him to rodeo school. First day there he grabbed hold of a bronc and got thrown in the weeds."

"Where is she?" Becca shielded her eyes against the sun and scanned the horizon. It didn't seem possible in all that flatness, but Irene was gone.

"You wanna go sit in those chairs?" Becca asked me. She went to get a cigarette from the car and I took a seat in one of the two chairs set up between where we'd been standing and where Beau was exhorting the young girl to make the pony go faster, faster. Beau's role in life seemed to be that of instigator.

"Whew, that feels good," Becca said, sinking into the chair beside me. She smoked, holding her hair off her neck with her other hand. "You want to talk about Irene, don't you?" she said.

"We don't have to."

"It's okay, me and Irene go way back." She dropped her hair and yelled, "You, Beau! Leave that girl alone!" Beau threw up his arms asking for mercy, then resumed his place at the fence, quieter, for now anyway. "You asked how she was wild," Becca said, "Why, when we were just kids, ten years old, we were having an overnight at my house and she got mad at me and left in the middle of the night, three o'clock in the morning! Slammed the front door and woke everybody up and my dad had to go find her in the car. She was already ten blocks toward home, and Dad said it took him forever to convince her to come back with him, this little kid!" Becca laughed at the memory, and sobered, put out her cigarette gravely by rubbing it on the heel of her sandal. "We've had our hard times. I was glad when she moved to New York. I was." She glanced at me. "She hadn't of gone I might not have had a husband. Oh, isn't so. Wasn't like it was serious, she was on the rebound from Hank, she tell you about Hank? But I already liked him and she knew it, and I was hurt."

So I hadn't invented it. I'd detected the leftover essence of a sexual history. I was too busy feeling smug to consider why Becca told me or whether she was wrong or lying, although she was clearly insecure and, on the evidence of their own shared history, conceivably jealous of Irene. Who knew to what heights of glamour Irene's life in New York had ascended in Becca's imagination?

"There she is," Becca said. Irene saw us and Beau and the barrels and came riding over in a flashy trot.

"Good horse, Beau." Her hair was messy and her color high; she looked down at me with an expression I recognized from bed.

"Nice boy," she told Poker Chip, and to Beau, "I'm not racing those barrels." She tugged at the reins and turned.

"How come she doesn't want to try the barrels?" I asked Becca.

"Oh, she will," Becca said. We watched as Beau talked Irene into checking out the corral. "You can try eem, Irene," he was saying, "this boy's been practicing barrels all summer, why would I lie? I got the gate open, you get your start in the pasture, there's plenty of room."

"Well, I'll see how he goes," she said finally and took off for the pasture. "Show yer boyfriend!" Beau called. He turned to me. "Irene, she's *good.*"

"She'll want to ride out to those barrels fast as she can," Becca said, "and get that horse around 'em. For speed you go close and turn sharp."

"I'll time her," Beau said.

"What's a good time?" I asked Becca.

"Oh, twenty seconds is not bad."

Irene appraised the corral then headed in, holding Poker Chip back, and went wide around the barrels in a clean S shape: "See there!" yelled Beau. Irene flipped her hair as she turned the horse back to the pasture, warming to the feel of her audience.

This time she charged the first barrel, cutting the horse to turn only in the moment it looked like they'd plow into it—but as she recovered from the turn and pulled the curve for the second barrel she reined him in again, and the side of his body passed maybe two feet by that second barrel as he went around it, much more of a cushion than there'd been on the first. Beau called as she rode by us, "*Twenty-four!* New York ain't helped your riding none, has it, Irene?"

She leaned in on the horse and tore out to the pasture and came back so fast that when they hit the dirt of the corral there was nothing but dust and the beating of hoofs on the ground. She took the first turn and coming out of it the horse almost went to his knees, I thought they would fall, but then he was up and turned to the left, and then back to the right again around the second barrel close enough it shook, dust pouring out after them in a shower.

"*Twenty-one, twenty-one!*" yelled Beau. She nearly crashed the far end of the fence.

"*You can do twenty, Irene, c'mon!*" But she'd stopped.

"What's a matter?" Beau said. Poker Chip's neck was dark with sweat. "That's enough," she said, and got down.

"You was just warmin' up," Beau said.

"Thanks for letting me ride him," said Irene. "Good boy, good horse."

Beau looked mad, "He's hot now, Irene, *c'mon!*"

Her eyes were glittering, she was elated, but said, "I don't want to. Y'know, Beau, it isn't good for the animals, really."

"Nothin' wrong with this boy," he said.

"I mean all of the animals, this—rodeo."

She stroked Poker Chip's mane and neck, and said, "They're so beautiful and so helpless, really, which gives us a responsibility, doesn't it?" To Beau, she may as well have been speaking a foreign language.

He took the reins, huffily, "C'mon, P."

"Oh, Beau," Becca said. He acted finished with us, and it wasn't until we were walking to the car and Irene yelled, "Bye, Beau!" that he forgave us and did a funny little show-off dance, spinning and wrapping himself in the reins, and climbed up on the horse, waving and calling "Bye, bye!"

"Deranged," Irene said to Becca.

At the car I caught Irene's eye and said, "Wow." She smiled and looked away. "The bozo," said Becca disgustedly as we pulled onto the road—still waving, his bright hair and shirt dabs of color against the dried landscape.

Irene and Becca made plans for the night, a sort of double farewell date.

When Becca was gone I said, "We have to see him again?"

"Christ," said Irene, through her teeth. She backed out of the driveway. "Don't come if you don't want to. That's fine with me." The car smelled of cigarettes, horses, dirt.

"I'm not fighting with you, Irene. Don't do this."

"Do what? What am *I* doing?" At her father's she parked and didn't get out, sat staring down at the steering wheel. I put my hand under her hair and held her neck, which was damp, leaned over and kissed her, felt her respond—except Billy Wayne was still there in my head.

"I just want to know what happened with him," I said. She shrugged me off and got out of the car.

Supper was grim. Ray read the paper, Irene and I had a contest over who could eat less and act gloomier, and then we dove for the TV. At eight she disappeared, came out an hour later reeking of perfume and wearing black boots—she had explicitly, I thought, not worn the ones I had bought her—and this red second-skin T-shirt. Makeup too, and artfully tousled hair one might describe as modified Country Western.

"You're dressed up," I said from the couch across from her father where I sat slumped, drugged by TV.

"Just jeans," she said, "you ready?"

"I'm gonna go change my shirt." She sighed impatiently and threw herself at the couch. Her father's eyes stayed nailed to the TV, where they were safe.

Walking out to the car five minutes later, her perfume—and it wasn't her own perfume, either—made me feel queasy, with the heat that still hung in the deepening night and the taste of her father's cigarettes in my mouth. The moon was huge and just rising, hanging over that one feeble tree in the yard as we drove away.

We traveled along Morgan for a couple of miles, out of the neighborhood and beside fields and the gurgling sound of a river. We turned onto a darker road, trees on both sides, made a few winding turns and came into a clearing where the moonlight came back; I heard music and saw a lighted building surrounded by trucks and cars. She didn't drive up to the building but parked at the mouth of the clearing and shut off the headlights.

"I don't need this caveman shit, Robert." I looked over and she was crying. "I love you, don't you know I love you?"

"Yes," I said, but did not move to touch her.

"Why are you doing this, especially here? Don't you know what it's like for me here? Oh goddamnit, *goddamnit*."

I put my hand on her arm then her shoulder, and she cried harder. "Oh God," she said, touched her cheek to my hand and I hated myself, hated her. "We're already late," she said, and jerked her shoulder, pushing me away.

"Irene—"

"Not now, Robert, please." I sought her eyes, silvery, smudged, in the dark. I had nothing to say, but I kept looking at her as she wiped her eyes in the rearview mirror in the interior light just to see if I could get her to stop. "Let's go somewhere," I said. "Let's go somewhere alone."

"No." She opened her door, "You're nuts."

Yes, and she was the Irene who ran off with Andre and the Irene I'd found at Floyd's apartment that night of the pool.

Billy Wayne and Becca had a booth against the wall opposite the bar. "I thought something happened!" Becca said.

"We're fighting," Irene said, sliding in on the other side. She would say it.

"Right now?" Becca asked, interested more than embarrassed.

"Uh-huh," Irene said, "I hate him, he hates me." She picked up Becca's glass of beer and gestured to toast me, then kissed me instead. Oh good, Irene, I thought, how disarming.

"Don't drink my beer!" said Becca, taking it back. "Billy says I only get two 'cause I'm nursing and this is my second." She wrinkled her nose at him and said, "Ogre." Billy Wayne glanced at Becca with a faintly amazed expression, as if to say, "You're not suggesting that *we* should fight, are you? If you are, I'll get up and leave." Maybe I overestimated what seemed his absolute mastery of their relations. But Becca smiled at him sweetly, submissively, adoringly, and he went to the bar for more glasses. There was a pitcher of beer on the table.

It was a small place, getting crowded, mostly men, a pool table through a square archway. Balls cracked through lulls in the music, when one of those country singers paused to bring home the depths of his despair.

Irene surveyed the environs hyperalertly, back over her shoulder at the pool table and down the line of cowboy hats at the bar. "I don't know anyone anymore," she said.

"Neither do I," Becca said, "we never go anywhere, do we, hon? We're always home." Suits me, he answered silently.

Becca drilled me about the soap. I told her about the time I was shopping at D'Agostino and from behind me this woman yelled, "Radley Rutherford! I know it's you! Turn and face me, or are you a lily-livered coward?"

"Geez," Becca said, "did you?"

"Sure," I said.

"What'd she do?"

"Nothing. We talked and she asked for my autograph. She wasn't that crazy." Becca looked delighted, Billy Wayne's forehead knit an inscrutable frown. Irene was down near the bottom of her second glass of beer, preternaturally bored, as though what I was saying inspired in her a yearning to kill herself with drink.

"What's it like kissing someone you don't know?" Becca said. "That girl—Silver!"

"Well, I *knew* her," I told her, and she laughed loudly.

"Excuse me," said Irene. I stood, and she slid out of the booth. "I'm going to the rest room." Did not deign to look at me; did a walk in the direction of the poolroom that turned heads at the bar.

"Billy Wayne, get another pitcher for the rest of you, will you?" Becca said. I was barely drinking, I wanted to keep my head clear. Irene may have gone to the rest room but her larger intention was to scope out the poolroom, and when she came back ten minutes later she had a tall cowboy in tow.

"Look who's here!" she exclaimed.

"Why, hi, Hook," Becca said.

"This is Robert," Irene said, holding Hook's arm.

"Pleasure," tipping his big-hatted head at me; the hat was one I'd tried on; tan, $19.95.

"Robert was on a soap opera," Becca said. That sank to the bottom of nothing.

"You don't say," he replied; he was top-heavy, a wedge balanced on poles.

"I'm gonna go shoot some pool," Irene said.

I had to be careful not to turn around and look at her through the square archway of the poolroom too often. The third time I did Becca said, "Are you and Irene still fighting?"

"Oh no-oo," I said.

Billy Wayne got quietly, steadily drunk; his eyelids hung lower and his round head sunk further into his shoulders. Becca's high spirits diminished once Irene left the table and she'd finished her beer.

Irene had been gone half an hour or so when Billy Wayne sucked back the last of the pitcher. I saw her at the end of the bar nearest the poolroom talking with Hook, who was buying her a drink. Becca and Billy Wayne got up to go and after the good-byes, I moved to their side of the booth so I'd have an unimpeded view of Irene. She came back to the table and told me we'd leave, as soon as she finished the game.

"Want to come watch?" she asked.

"No."

"Fine. Sit there and glower."

What was it about women and pool that was supposed to be so goddamned sexy? I thought. It was too obvious to be sexy.

At the end of the game, after downing a shot Hook had bought her, she came, reluctantly, I assumed, back to me. By then I'd had to give up the booth to a group of five. As I stood at the bar the man at my side, offended by my irresponsiveness to his boring comments about the weather, had discovered the object of my attention—it could not have been hard. He watched her walk over to me and his jaw dropped, as if he believed I had summoned her by sheer desire.

"Jesus, Robert," Irene said as we went out the door, "I *know* those guys, all right?"

"I thought you just knew Hook."

"Forget it."

"Hook, what sort of a name is Hook?"

"Oh, it's Hook now, is it?"

"All I'm saying is he has a dumb name."

"He's a roper," as if that explained it.

"You're drunk, give me the keys."

"I am not," but she was.

"He's a roper, so?"

"It has to do with the rope, what he does with a rope."

"That's stupid."

"*You're* stupid."

"Well, what were you doing back there?" I asked.

"What do you think I was doing?"

"You answer me that."

"Can we go?" We were sitting in the dark car, and someone blinded us with the headlights of their truck. "Tell me where to go," I said.

"Right at the end of the clearing. I wasn't doing anything for your benefit, I was trying to turn an absolutely miserable night into a little bit of fun. Just follow the road, I mean, what am I supposed to be now that we're fucking each other?"

That's a nice way to put it, I thought, aware that nice wasn't an adjective I could apply to anything I had said either.

"Why can't you adjust to me for a change?" she asked. "Why for once can't you accommodate me?"

"It is difficult for me to count on the fingers of one of my hands the occasions I haven't accommodated you."

We drove on in silence. I glanced at her and she was resting her head against the window looking tragic.

"I miss Patrick," she said, "I miss Patrick so much."

"Why did you say that?" I asked. She didn't answer.

At the house the leaves stirred in the tree and the sound, the invisibility of the breeze, and the corporeality of the leaves in motion made me think of the multitude of realities we couldn't see, couldn't know. I had to touch her, so great were the number of things I felt acutely conscious of and could never penetrate. I said her name in the yard and she stopped, let me put my hands to the sides of her hair, let me hold her head, though she didn't look at me.

"We need to leave," she said.

"I think so," I answered. I drew her into me, felt her weight letting go, thought I love you I love you.

"I'm tired, love, I want to sleep," she said.

SHE AWAKENED ME in the morning, knocking on my door; the bright light in the room blocked out whole patches, a bookcase, the closet door.

"My father wants to go out for dinner." Dinner was lunch, supper was dinner; I recalled where I was.

"When?" She wore the dress.

"Forty-five minutes?"

"All right. My watch read 11:30. Sunday. Tomorrow we would leave.

We went to Lester's Cafeteria on Ninth Street and sat among a veritable sea of gray heads and the shrill, sudden ringings of hearing aids. Mr. Walpers was a youth in this crowd, Irene and I children.

Mr. Walpers sat at the head of our table and neatly sliced pieces of ham, and took sips from his coffee. Irene had told me that apart from his shirts and jeans, he had a sharkskin suit for special occasions, a surprising revelation. What, I asked, would be a special occasion in his life? Invitations to weddings from employees he couldn't turn down; a holiday foisted upon him by relatives he rarely saw. But a sharkskin suit—the hint of a spark of vanity, riskiness, humor? The suit was a dark midnight blue. Irene got him talking about his development plans by an artificial lake. I looked around at the people who were born in Coffeyville's heyday.

There was a pause in the conversation. Mr. Walpers lit a cigarette and I watched the smoke veil his eyes.

"You say you've been to the museum?" he said. Days ago, but he hadn't even reacted when we told him. Now he was making one of his typical efforts with me, asking a question that I couldn't fathom, that led nowhere.

"The Dalton Museum."

"Robert loved the museum," Irene said.

He crossed his arms over his chest and smoked with his left hand. "They tell you they moved the hitching posts?"

"The hitching posts?" I said. "No—"

"The robbery was planned down to the second," he said. "Just enough time to get in and get out. But they moved the hitching posts the day before. They were caught because it threw off the timing."

Wow, I thought. He had a real little story going there, suspense, some narrative energy in his voice.

We traveled in a congenial silence back to the house, but Becca's place was off-limits today, and after we dropped Ray off we did errands as the heat soared.

My blood ran too thick and my breaths were shallow. There was a fragility about us both, both of us knowing we had to be careful and everything felt very taut, very intense, was just shy of too much to cope with.

After we stocked up Ray's kitchen and dropped off a cake Irene had made for her aunts, we pulled into a gas station to fill up the car.

Two old men in cowboy hats sat under an overhang, and one of them turned and spit into a can. While the attendant pumped gas Irene got out to clean the windshield, and the sight of her in that dress made me dizzy.

I closed my eyes, heard another car drive in and park. Then Irene said, "Rudy!" I opened my eyes to see her greeting a young guy sans hat, a more nondescript, conservative type.

I got out of the car. "This is Robert," she said. "Robert, Rudy."

Then she took his hands, and when she touched him my skin contracted across my face and I felt an equal tightening in my gut that went all the way down to my scrotum, and she perceived it, and our truce tumbled down like an edifice—this, *this* was the truth: she didn't love me, never had, never would.

"Why did you look at me like that?" she said in the car.

"I imagined you in bed with him."

"Why?"

"I imagine you in bed with everyone."

"I don't understand you."

"I don't understand you either."

One of the old men sitting under the overhang whistled, a sharp quick blast.

"Can we get out of here," I said, "can we please get out of here."

"Can you leave me alone?" she said. "Can you let me be until we're back in New York? If you don't, I'll start screaming and I won't be able to stop."

At supper, she sipped from a glass of whiskey and watched her father and me warily. Mr. Walpers asked a few cursory questions and picked up the paper. While she washed the dishes, I went to the family room with her father to watch TV, but I couldn't stand it for long and returned to the kitchen.

She'd taken the Wild Turkey bottle from the cupboard and was refilling her glass, spilling a little on the counter.

"If you would have told me, none of this would have happened," I said. She put down her glass, took the towel and mopped up the whiskey. "I know you slept with him, and it's okay, I just wanted you to tell me."

She looked at me, "Slept with who?"

"Billy Wayne."

"Goddamn you," she struck the counter with the towel and let it drop to the floor. "Goddamn you, Robert, Goddamn you to hell," and went out the back door.

I heard something behind me and turned, and her father had entered the kitchen. It occurred to me that after days of knowing she and I were having trouble he wanted to help, which was somehow shocking, sad, and repellent at the same time. His dry lined face and his sterile life reminded me of someone preserved and barely alive. He crossed his arms over his chest and shook his head slowly.

"That girl has never been contented and she never will be."

"Excuse me," I said, and went after Irene. She'd been on the stoop but now she went down the steps and out to the yard. It wasn't quite dark yet; I felt the presence of the sun and moon both, in the light and the suspension of the heat. I followed her.

"Irene—"

She pulled away violently. "Don't, don't."

We were partway down the slope and stood facing each other, but she moved side to side with small feinting steps, as if about to attack me, to hit me.

"I slept with Billy Wayne," she said, "I slept with Hook, I slept with a lot of people, not Rudy if you want to know." She pushed me, her eyes saying fight me, come on!

"Irene, I just—"

"I was *lonely*." She was crying. I reached out to her and again she pulled away, put her arms up over her face as a shield, her hands over her head.

"I'm—"

"They keep pulling it out of you—" she garbled. "They take it, they take it from you, and you take it too." She started further down the slope and I helplessly followed, but then she swung back around. "You don't know what it's like for a girl! To be young, to feel wild, you don't think we want to do every crazy thing you do? We do, but we're not *free*. You know what he did?" she said, pointing at the house. "He shot my horse! He shot Mercury! Because I left!" She looked up at the house. "He's watching us," she said.

We were at the bottom of the slope near the barn, and she went in and I followed.

The smell pricked at my nostrils—old wood, dry dirt, and moldering hay. It was divided by a partition, one side a stall and the other an open space. She leaned against the wall, slid down to the ground. I sank down across from her. A coiled rotted rope lay in the corner. She drew up her legs and wrapped them with her arms.

"I'm sorry," I said at last.

We sat quietly. "When my teacher Rose died I had to leave. I was seeing Billy Wayne then. He was good to me. I will always think well of him for that. I was going to—" I waited. "I'd arranged for Beau to take Mercury, he would have come the next day. My father didn't do it out of any real need for me, or love. He did it out of anger. I swore I'd never come back.

"When I was running around with men, he never said anything. Don't you think he should have warned me? Don't you think he should have told me I might get hurt?" She started crying again, terrible crying, hard to stand, and I went and hunkered down in front of her.

"I trusted you," she said, "and I've never trusted anyone really except you and Patrick—" and she took my hand, I think just for something to hold on to, and held it hard.

"You're hurting my hand," I said.

"Oh. I'm sorry." She loosened her grip.

"You and I," she said, "it's the funniest thing you and I, you weren't like a man, well, you were but you were my friend first and I never had that, and when we became lovers I thought, why didn't I know this is how it should be? It was like sleeping with a brother but it wasn't. You made everything okay somehow. It felt like equals. Even back that one time at the pool." I could barely see her, but I saw her rub her head, her eyes, and she said, "But then New York got harder . . . sometimes I wonder, is it wrong to love things too much? How I love acting. My God, to find your true thing and then have it taken away. To find out that nothing can ever live up to it again. It feels like a curse. . . .

"Now this, I don't know, I don't know what to do anymore. I don't know where I am."

A pale spill of moonlight came in from the doorway; otherwise it was dark. "I don't know anything," I said. "But I'll try."

"All right," she said.

"I know I love you," I said. I told myself not to keep saying it, that every day I would have to show her, and I wanted that: I did.

"Let's go in," she said, and we went out to that strange light and the

new milder air and walked up the slope through the rough grass. Inside the door we heard the TV, and the kitchen was dark except for reflections from the family room and the moonlight in the window above
the sink.

"Full moon," she said, looking at the window. "We're mad," and sat
down at the table, her face scraped of emotion, raw. "I feel so empty,
I'm hungry." I fixed her a sandwich and brought her some milk and sat
with her while she ate.

Looking at her father, enwrapped by the monotonous sound of the
television, I thought that instead of shooting the horse he should have
shot the TV. Soon he turned off the TV and went to bed, and the subtle, irregular sound of living things came in through the open window
—and his absence or the food revived her.

"Remember how I said after she died he was never any kind of a father?" she said. "Well, I don't know if he ever was. My mother was
everything. She wasn't special, well, I thought she was. She taught me
to appreciate music and books, and later I found that in plays there
was more than what I saw around me, that I could get away, there was
something else. . . . And, when I act, it feels like I have her again.
Maybe because I have myself.

"I don't really know whether he loved her or not. I don't know
what comprised his love for her. Only his anger over her death. I remember thinking, It didn't happen to *you, you* didn't die. . . ." Her
voice softened and filled with sadness. "Her sickness was never explained to me. I was told she had 'female trouble,' and when she died
I had the vague misconception that being female killed her." She
paused, and her eyes scanned the kitchen, the window.

"The first time I acted in a big play with an audience all I was aware
of was living my life as you do in a play, and can't in life—being completely there in the present. I was totally there. Then it was over and
there was this who-osh! of the audience. Clapping, just going wild. All
of those people. I had been *seen,* after being invisible in this house.

And it wasn't just about me. It was about all of us. Being together and sharing that story. Being alive together in that one moment in time.

"I'm sorry," she said.

We sat silently, washed by the moonlight.

"I'm going to bed," she said. I walked with her down the hall and she said good night without looking at me and I went to my room and sat on my bed while she was in the bathroom. Mine was a junk room but had been her mother's sewing room. There was an old Singer sewing machine in the corner, a mint green bookcase of poetry and American classics beneath the window that framed the tree in the front yard.

Then she came to my door. "Robert, come sleep with me."

We got in her single bed, spread the sheet over us, and she curled against me, her back against my chest, and fell immediately asleep. I basked in her, in her breaths, my mind swimming with thoughts of her father in the next room. She'd described him to me once as reckless and I hadn't seen that in him, not quite. Now I understood, knew the hardness and recklessness and definitiveness of his action in shooting the horse, how final an act it was against life, his daughter, himself. I thought nothing could be harder, deader, and with all my heart I didn't want to be that: that one midnight-blue sharkskin suit in the closet, all that was left of his life's blood.

"Make love to me," her voice; I'd fallen asleep. She was kissing me, it was warm, my skin filmed with new sweat. I was already hard and that didn't seem right, but I kissed her.

"No, no," she said, "like you love me," with an urgency in her. Her mouth was very hot.

Her nightgown was up around her waist but now she wrenched it off. She was breathing heavily, and started talking again. "Irene, be quiet," I said, and she stopped. Then she whispered to me, "Please, more," and then the bed was slamming into the wall and I didn't care and she cried out sharply, and I did too.

15 Back

In the morning I opened my eyes to her sitting at the side of the bed looking at me. She was dressed in her own clothes and rigidly solemn.

"You won't believe this," she said. "My father didn't go to work. He's in the kitchen and he wants to talk to you."

"To me?" I lay back down. I thought, He didn't have the gun, did he?

"Once you've talked to him let's just have coffee and go," she said. She stood and I caught her arm.

"Irene?" Her eyes were full of tears. "Irene," I said, "I love you better than anything."

"You do?"

I pushed her hair out of her face. "Yes, yes. Why are you crying?" I pulled her to me and cradled her head against my neck.

In the kitchen he was reading the paper. She poured me a cup of coffee. He put aside the paper.

"Good morning. Sit down," he said—not friendly but not breathing fire. "Come and sit down," he said to Irene.

She came, defiant, and sat down beside me.

"What are your intentions in regard to my daughter?" he asked.

I glanced at Irene, who looked appalled and then so amused that I hoped she wouldn't laugh. This was more than a bit of a travesty on his part, when by any important measure he had never been there for her before. But I didn't want things to get any weirder than they already were. As if it had long been decided, I said, "I'd like to marry Irene."

"Good," he answered. "I don't think it's proper for you to visit my house again if you're not married."

"*Your* house," she stood, nearly knocking over her chair. She had gone white at the lips from anger. "We're not getting married, Daddy. We never even discussed it," she said, and walked out of the kitchen.

"We haven't discussed it yet," I said, "but those are my intentions. Well, I ought to go pack."

Irene was packing loudly in her room. "Fuck him. Fuck him!" she said, "I'm twenty-five. At fifteen I would have had to be fucking somebody in his face to evoke a reaction." We almost had, I thought distantly, unconcerned. I was feeling this happiness spread through my body like a new color. I'd marry her, we would get married, why hadn't I known that before?

She sensed my mood, "What? Robert, *what?*"

"Let's get married."

"Oh." She went to her closet and on her way back I caught her hand.

"I mean it, come on, we should, let's get married."

"You really are nuts, you know?" she said.

"Yeah, but I have to marry you." I did this dumb nodding gesture and accompanied it with a sweep of one hand, imitating this actor we'd seen in a bad movie in Missouri. "Because you are the girl for me." She was laughing, "So what do you say, Irene, huh?"

"I don't know, *God,* Robert." She tried to pack again and I grabbed her around the waist from behind.

"Come on," I said—in a deep voice, "Oh my darling, my darling. So? Come on."

"Maybe I'd rather you ask me in New York over an expensive dinner." She laughed, "I'd like you to kneel."

"Oh, you'd love *that*," I said.

"Go pack. Can we talk about it later?"

"Okay."

I carried our bags out to the car and she followed. "Shouldn't we say good-bye?" I said.

"You can if you want to," and I went once more to the kitchen where he sat smoking. "Good-bye, Mr. Walpers," I said.

"Good-bye. Tell Irene good-bye." It was sad, even though you had to hate the guy.

She drove.

That heat, those fields spiraling away at each side of the road; the pale sky. We were on the highway heading south in the direction of Tulsa, Oklahoma, when she pulled up on the shoulder and stopped.

"I just passed the exit."

"Why?"

"I don't want to go to New York."

"Where do you want to go?"

"I don't know." She was looking at her hands in her lap. A car going by felt faster than a jet. I was afraid she'd start crying again.

"I'm going to say something stupid," she said.

"Go ahead."

"Don't—" she turned to me, "don't die?"

"I won't. I'm not the type to die young. You'll die first. I'll linger and become a burden to our children."

She smiled. "Can we just sit here a minute?"

We sat there awhile. I looked out at fields that weren't harvested and parched like others I'd seen. Tender green shoots sprung back from the road in hundreds and hundreds of vertical rows.

"What are they growing?" I asked her.

"Soybeans," she said.

Soybeans, I thought, how miraculous, and she pulled onto the highway.

16 Trevor McCann

Patrick was waiting for us in the apartment when we arrived. In the kitchen his bottle of Geritol and a fifth of vodka were set side by side on the counter, as though one was a chaser for the other. He told us the head doorman, Angel Jacome, had removed his mustache, and there was an audacious new artificial flower arrangement in the lobby, had we seen it? Someone was circulating a petition to have it incinerated. His play would go into previews in three weeks. His character's name was Trevor McCann, "a sympathetic chap," Patrick said, "but quite a queen." Meaning, unless he exaggerated—and after reading the script I saw he didn't—that his first important dramatic role in New York would effectively type him.

One night in bed Irene said, "Robert, you know that pact we made at Crispins? You know that it wasn't meant seriously, don't you?"

"It wasn't?"

"You don't have to worry about me and Patrick."

"I don't. But I *do*. Irene, it isn't the *pact*."

"I just wanted to tell you."

"Stop acting pessimistic," I said, dismissing the issue. But I knew she was talking about our plans for a theater. She knew I wanted out. Shortly after we'd returned to the city she'd researched stock and regional theaters, but as Patrick appeared to have lost interest and I was distracted, she talked less about it as the weeks passed. Clarence was currently head of casting on a soap, where a young female role was coming up. He told Irene he'd call her. But when a week went by and then another, she was convinced he'd forgotten her.

"So call *him,*" I said in exasperation, beginning our second fight of the evening, after one about money. ("So I'm *touchy?*" she'd shouted. "Just because if I didn't live with you I couldn't afford a goddamned Tampax?" We'd decided she'd go back to work part-time at the restaurant, and I would put money in a separate account and give her a checkbook. Always having to *ask* me for money, I reasoned, was what she most objected to.)

"It's *Clarence,*" I said. "Call him at home, you have the number." It was a beautiful night and we'd planned to go out but we stood in my room, glaring at each other.

"Wait," she said. "I want to show you the script." I sat in the chair in the corner, reminding myself to be patient. She smoked while I read it. The girl was a ditz, but it was a decent scene.

"So?" I said.

She sat on the bed, "I can't play it."

"Why not?"

"All the references to her chest."

Oh, please, I thought.

"I don't have big breasts, Robert."

"No? Really?"

"Don't laugh."

"Oh, come on, you're—"

"*What?* You can tell they want someone who's stacked for this."

"Then how come Clarence sent it to you?"

"He hasn't *called* me."

"Call *him,* he's probably busy." She remained sitting on the bed, indecisively chewing on a nail. "Come here," I said, and she came over and sat on my lap and I put my arms around her. "Look at the sky," I said, and we looked up through the open window together. "The line of that building," tracing it with my thumb.

"It looks pasted on," she said. "Like some kid cut it out of construction paper and stuck it on the sky."

"And see how the clouds are moving," I told her.

"The sky's inside out," she said.

The clouds were dark violet and the sky was a lighter shade of gray blue, a sort of reversal.

"All that," I said, indicating the script, "is just—all that."

"I know," she said. My hands rested against the warm skin of her back.

"You need to call him," I told her, "and do the audition. You know they don't know what they're looking for a lot of the time. They could see you and think, well, not stacked, but very *nice*."

"Shut up," she said.

"And then they might notice your legs and realize that was more what they meant."

She got up and went to call him and left a message.

"It just seems so *stupid*, so *small*, you know?" she said, sitting back on the bed. "I know it's not about me, the rejections—I don't take it as personally anymore. But it doesn't mean as much to me anymore. It's too arbitrary. How can I believe in something this random? It doesn't seem valid, or significant, and if it isn't—

"This is what I know," she said emphatically. "Nobody cares whether I'm an actress—why should they?" She smiled, "Apart from you and Patrick."

"I think you think too much."

"I do?"

"Maybe. Why don't I call Gabriel tomorrow and get you an appointment?"

"No, Robert, please." Gabriel was Paul's agent for stage. It wasn't that I believed Gabriel could solve the problem of her career, he would simply be someone else to try. I hated feeling helpless where she was concerned, but whenever I introduced a connection of mine, especially since we'd come back from Kansas, she refused it.

"I have to do it for myself, do it on my own. That's what I need and want."

"No one does it on their own."

"I can't have my entire life hooked into you, Robert. I've done that before."

"All right," I agreed, fed up.

"Please understand," she said, coming to me.

"You'll do what you want to, whatever I think," I began, but she kissed me, stroking my hair, and said, "Let's take advantage of Trevor McCann." She climbed onto my lap and I took off her T-shirt. Patrick, being Trevor McCann, had been home every night until the first preview. He was out days at rehearsal, but at night he seldom budged from the apartment. To have the place to ourselves seemed very luxurious. That night, after bed, we got dressed and went out into the freshness of autumn and walked down to Washington Square, and sat at a café on Thompson Street, eating Italian. It was the third week of October by then. I had met with a famous director about a feature; I'd turned down a soap. There was talk about other pilots and the pilot I'd already shot was suddenly back in contention. I knew—we all knew—that something big would come through for me.

Later, Clarence explained that the role on the soap had been taken by an actress who played a small role on the show the previous year. The three of us watched her one afternoon; she was, indeed, well endowed.

"Amazing," I said.

"The kind that defy all the forces of gravity," Patrick remarked.

"But her acting's okay," Irene said.

"She's not as good as you," Patrick said.

"Oh, I don't know. . . . Should I save up some money and—?"

"No," Patrick said.

"No," I agreed.

That week, Irene and I attended a preview of Patrick's play. It was not a good play, as he'd said, but it wasn't bad enough to account for the disparity of the performances, the mishmash of styles and abilities.

"But your part's flashy and you're doing it well," I told him over drinks at Joe Allen. "You'll be singled out even if it doesn't run."

He looked drained, his long face pushed against one big pale hand, the other hand decorated by scars from cigarettes he'd forgotten. A series of faint red burns, in graduated stages of healing, striped two of the fingers of his left hand. People bustled about; wherever you sat in Joe Allen during the late-evening crush you would catch snatches of ebullient theater talk—somebody's contract, or performance, or comeback. That night it made me tired.

Irene was being quiet. "How was I?" he said to her.

"I told you already, *good*." She wrapped her hand around his arm, stroked the pale skin on the inside of his wrist. He had come, already, to hate McCann.

"Well," he said, "*Miss* McCann, queen of the prom, is limited. About that, we agree. She's there for cheap jokes. Flashy? Well, yes, queens are. They're rather like children, aren't they? Or performing dogs."

"Patrick, don't," I said. "Don't hate him so much." It was starting to sound as though he hated himself. Nobody else thought of Patrick like that, and if he got typed, so what? If he was typed and he worked, he would at least have a chance to *break out* of being typed. I knew how he prided himself on being a person of dimension and grace, but he'd also always been someone who simply loved being onstage, playing *anything,* as long as he believed that he could. He'd said to me once, "I love all of it, Robert. Getting the call at half hour. Waiting back stage. Just spotting glow tape in the dark gives me chills." Now nothing but bitterness, edge. No humor, no lightness, no Patrick.

He rallied for the opening. His attitude buoyed, he grew excited. He was back on Broadway, and even if he was in a flop he hoped he was wrong.

He got heaps of flowers and telegrams— "Who *are* all these people?" I asked in his dressing room after the show on opening night.

"You fucker," I added, "you beat me to Broadway."

"Oh, I beat you a long time ago, Robert," he replied, gaily. Irene, Maria, Herbert, and I jostled each other in Patrick's small dressing room; glad shouts and greetings echoed from the hallway. At last Patrick shut the door and changed, and we waited outside in the narrow passage as others walked by.

"It's gotta run," Maria said, "he's king of Manhattan." She looked somewhat frazzled, after having administered to Patrick's nerves since morning.

"He was wonderful, wasn't he?" Irene said to the world at large.

"He was treee-mendous!" Herbert said so that Patrick could hear, banging on the dressing-room door and then laughing with his entire body, staggering down the hallway and back, bumping into a matron in mink who was not amused.

"Let's get drunk," he said, "let's get good and good and drunk."

The party was held at a disappointing steak house smelling of newness, where the five of us sat at the end of a long banquet table bearing only a shiny white cloth. But drinks were served and people talked more, laughing louder to compensate for the environment and for the play. A few smaller tables behind us began to fill with others. Herbert did get good and drunk.

"Robert," he said over the food, his magnified eyes bleary behind his thick glasses. "I'm not twenty-eight, I'm thirty-two." I tried to determine how I was supposed to reply. He looked twenty-four in his black turtleneck, striped scarf, and army jacket hanging across the back of his chair.

"My therapist says to accept my age. Everyone!" he said. "Patrick! Irene! Maria! I'm thirty-two."

"Oh," Irene said.

"I'm thirty-two," Herbert repeated. "How old are *you*, Maria?" he asked, taking a bite of roast beef.

"I'm not in therapy, you horrid man," Maria said. She was overdressed in a white beaded tunic. Irene wore a sweater and skirt and pumps, one of which kicked me under the table.

"*I* know how old Maria is," Patrick said. He didn't eat, he drank vodka and was progressively despondent. All of us feared for a few seconds that he would say it, but his cornflower-blue eyes observed us with a fixed glassy stare—then they enlivened and he said, "Or I *did* know, but in deference to Maria's timeless beauty I have forgotten," and everybody laughed.

"How come you're in therapy?" I asked Herbert.

"Oh, everything," he said.

After the dishes were cleared Patrick leaned across the table and said to me, "I want to go. Will you and Irene come with me?"

The cast was going to someone's apartment to wait for the *Times*, but Patrick couldn't abide those mass vigils. We took a cab to a coffee shop, where we could see deliveries arrive at a newsstand. We drank coffee; nobody felt much like talking. Patrick sprang up when the *Times* hit the stand, and returned with the paper and soberly handed it to me.

"You read it and tell me."

As soon as I saw the headline I knew the show was dead, but I read the review with Irene reading over my shoulder.

"Listen!" I said as I got near the end; a mention of Trevor McCann: "The tall Patrick O'Doherty was effective as Trevor McCann."

"How generous," said Patrick. "Effective. I feel like a spark plug, or a piston." We paid the check and walked home.

The next morning the stage manager called the cast to tell them to collect their belongings from the theater by 4 P.M. It was fast and harsh, but not unusual. Patrick left us over an uneaten breakfast.

Irene said, "I'm scared."

"I know," I said. Patrick's pallor had been deathly.

"He's getting worse," she said.

"This could blow over."

"He picks up strangers for sex—did you know that?"

"Well—sure," I said, deciding to underplay it. "A lot of guys do."

"But with him it doesn't seem—joyous. Do you know what I mean?" I nodded. "He's all but admitted to me that he's into rough sex."

I didn't know what to say. If she was trying to say he was self-destructive, I thought that was fairly obvious by now. I felt badly—and had felt badly for a long time—that the business was difficult for him. I felt badly that he'd lost his dancing, that his knee had been wrecked, that he had known someone named Benton—that he had to lie, that he couldn't *not* lie, that for reasons I didn't believe I would ever untangle he felt somehow trapped by the past and doomed. But where did it end? I thought of blood in the sink, pictured him stranded that night on the dark stairs of my apartment on West Forty-sixth, clutching the stained bar rag to his nose.

Whatever else I knew and suspected I did not want to discuss.

Several days later I came home to find Patrick on the phone, a glass of vodka on the table beside his blue cigarette box, the living room smoky.

"Yes, well," I heard him say, "having been through it myself I am deeply concerned. Yes, I had leukemia. I was seven years old."

"Who were you talking to?" I asked, as he hung up.

He looked at me without any real focus, as an animal can. "A charitable foundation."

"You said you had leukemia when you were seven."

"Yes, and that I recovered." He dropped the cigarette that clung to his fingers into the overflowing ashtray.

"You never had leukemia."

He hesitated, "No."

"So why did you say you did?"

"Because I understand. Occasionally, Robert, you are destitute of imagination."

"You're saying you understand what dying children feel like, Patrick? That's sick."

"I said what I did to *communicate*—" such a chore to explain to a soft head like me "—that I understand as much as if I had had the experience."

"It's not the same."

"Of course it isn't," he snapped. "But I *do* understand."

I don't know what bothered me more, the lying or the weird identification; it was disturbing in a way that his long-term reading of the obituaries and his hypochondria weren't.

SOON I WAS BUSY shooting commercials again. One day on a shoot for Avis I spent ten hours racing down a corridor at La Guardia Airport. I couldn't walk the next day. The clients had wanted the perfect amount of breathlessness at the Avis counter, and while I was tracked by a camera throughout my mad dash, it was of the utmost importance that my tie fly back over my shoulder with the proper degree of urgency and panache.

Patrick was the same, and whenever I contradicted his unremittingly negative state of mind, he turned on me and said something cutting.

"That's a fabulous part," I said to him one afternoon.

"So what? I'll freeze at the audition, or if I don't I won't get it anyway."

Getting up one morning and finding him gone, I went back to bed. I lay watching Irene, and then moved into the heated space around her body. She opened her eyes.

"You have any appointments?" I asked.

"No," she said, shifting herself up against me, "work at four-thirty."

"He isn't here," I said.

"Good." She rolled over on top of me under the covers. "You think he's at the gym?"

"Let's hope." He didn't go to the gym every day anymore, nor to church on Sundays, and we'd begun to encourage these activities that we used to see as compulsive. They seemed to help, yet only so much. He stayed out more nights.

"Your feet are *freezing*," she said.

"Ignore my feet."

"I missed you," she said; "I missed you." I'd been gone on another shoot the day before. After we made love I got up, and still in a light-headed daze put on my sweatpants and got us the paper and coffee.

We read, riffling pages.

"Patrick thinks I should go off the Pill," she said.

"Patrick does?"

"You know how he is about health stuff, and I've been taking it a long time, so I suppose he's right." She turned a page, continued perusing Arts and Leisure. "I'll get a diaphragm, okay?"

"Why were you talking about it with Patrick?"

She shrugged, "I don't remember how it came up."

"Don't you think it's a subject to talk over with me?"

"I am talking it over with you."

"A diaphragm's fine."

"You know, you've been busy, I see him more than you," she sounded defensive. "I can go back on the Pill after—"

"I said it didn't matter, didn't I?"

She kissed my shoulder. "You want to get breakfast?"

"Irene, you know, he's going to have to decide. If acting makes him this depressed he may have to quit and do something else."

She didn't answer for a second. "I know," she said, and then sat up, swinging her legs over the side of the bed.

"And where's Ben?" I said. There wasn't any family there for him, no Ben, no Bryan, only us. Were the three of us going to go on forever together?

"Ben's in Missouri," she said, "where he lives." Yes, yes, Patrick couldn't live there, and I was afraid she'd berate me, tell me that Patrick had genuine reasons to feel discouraged and torn.

Her back was to me and I put my hand on her shoulder, "I'm sorry." I slid my hand onto her chest and felt her heart beat against my palm. "I'm sorry about how things have gone."

"I know," she said. "I know you are."

17 Phantoms

At a phone on the street on the last day of November I learned that the network had picked up the pilot. I would be starring in a nighttime dramatic series that would film in Los Angeles, beginning just after the first of the year.

It was rush hour and drizzling and I couldn't get a cab; I walked to Second Avenue for a downtown bus. Where would I live? In a *house?* No, LA had apartments—and pools. I didn't know anything about it except for the barest generalizations. We'd done the pilot on a mammoth soundstage in Burbank in a couple of weeks. I'd seen the studio and my hotel; parking lots lined with BMWs and Mercedes. One night we'd gone out to dinner in a white limo to some place with bad food, big prices, palm trees, and celebrities I'd never heard of. But it was balmy and dreamlike, with these little lights twinkling in the bushes.

Didn't Patrick have friends in LA?

He wasn't home. Irene was in her room folding laundry, taking a shirt from the plastic basket on the floor and spreading it out on the bed. St. Martin lay amidst the clothes in the basket. For the tenth time, I'm sure, she said, "Scram!" and he jumped out and scampered away. I sat down on her bed.

"Is it raining?" she said. "What, the show?"

"Yeah."

"Hey, star!" she said, and hugged me. "Oh, God, this is it."

"I'm in shock."

"Of *course*." As always, at the advent of good news I felt goofy and emotional: the room looked so nice, the familiar old things, the pictures, the footlocker, the brick wall through the window bleeding with rain. I told her what details I knew and then I got nervous.

"You thought it was good, right? The script, the part—you want to read it again?"

"Robert, I told you, it's excellent, more like a play. To tell you the truth I'm impressed they've picked it up because of the quality, and you definitely have the best part."

We opened a bottle of wine. It looked like a first-season cycle of twenty-two shows, and according to Paul, everything was in place for the series to make it through this initial round anyway. Even if it wasn't a hit, he believed it would jump me onto another show, or into film.

"We're moving?"

"What do you think?" I asked.

"Wow." She finished her wine and set the glass on the table.

"It could be really positive for you," I said, "a new place."

"It's scary."

But she had considered Los Angeles as a base. People had told her that Hollywood was packed with tall blondes who'd never acted in the theater and that she'd be unique. Still, there was little theater *work* on the West Coast.

"Maybe Patrick should move out there too."

"I'd feel better about trying it," she said, "if he came."

"But he should get his own apartment. It's time."

She frowned. "Let's introduce moving there first and tell him that later."

Patrick came in dripping rain, sodden umbrella in one hand, the shillelagh from Cork in the other; he'd been visiting at O'Toole's, but he wasn't too drunk.

"I knew today was an auspicious day," he said. "I've felt it since morning."

We celebrated quietly at a small Middle Eastern restaurant, and he insisted on paying the check. It was warm, dimly lit; a flame flickered in oil on the table.

"We'll have to give up the apartment and move," Irene told him carefully. "Why don't you come too?" He smiled.

"Tell me you'll think about it," I urged, and he promised he would.

But days later he declared that he couldn't move to Los Angeles. He was a theater actor, and that was the end of it.

At the Equity office we checked out the "Apartments" section of the bulletin board to see if someone in Los Angeles wanted to trade, or had a sublet.

"Will you look?" I asked her. "I've got a crashing headache."

She stepped over to the bulletin board. I sat down on the worn couch that faced Broadway. Actors stood in clumps writing things down off the boards, drinking coffee from Styrofoam cups, clutching copies of *Back Stage, Show Business,* and *Variety.* People forty, fifty, even sixty years old. In the hallway people waited to be seen for an open Equity call; folding chairs banked the walls and a power-starved deputy in run-down shoes sat officiously at a table, barking, *"Number two hundred sixty-two!"* Three women at the far end of the boards were discussing a recent extra call for a Woody Allen film. People began lining up at three in the morning, they brought along *sleeping bags,* and the line snaked from West Sixty-first to West Sixty-ninth by nine o'clock. One of the women had a hole in the back of her coat as big as a tennis ball. Glorious life, trying to act in this town.

I got up and went over to Irene. "You ready?"

"Just a sec. You're upset, aren't you?"

"You could say that." We went out to the trash-blown street.

"You find anything?" I asked.

"A couple. Where are we going?"

"To lunch."

She wore a new duffel coat and black tights. Her hair blew in her eyes. She tucked her arm through mine and put her hand in my pocket.

"It's not a rejection of us," she said. "But Patrick won't change his mind, I could see that."

We walked up Broadway to Fifty-seventh not saying very much. I had expected to feel relieved if he stayed in New York. But suddenly I knew I had really wanted him to come.

The restaurant was crowded, a country-kitchen place, where Irene had a penchant for their eggs Florentine.

"Maybe we'll be back anyway," she said.

"Irene, I don't think we'll be back, I really don't think we're coming back. Or anyway, it'll be a while."

I ordered a carafe of white wine and then took her hand: "You know what I want to do?" She shook her head. "Take you to Europe, to Rome and Venice and Paris and Amsterdam and Barcelona. To Greece."

"When will you work?"

I laughed. Everything but the money was amorphous enough in my mind. I didn't know what else to fantasize about.

"What'd you have this morning?" I asked her.

"Oh, nothing. But I got an audition for that play I interviewed for the other day. Here, look at this scene." She took out a script from her bag and handed it to me.

"It's a revival," she told me. I skimmed it; it was a romantic comedy and the scene was very funny.

"You'd be great," I said. "When do you go in?"

"Two weeks from tomorrow. I could—if I got it, which I probably won't, but I could come out later, couldn't I?"

"Sure." I watched her sip her wine, about to say *everything will be all right*. But I was sick of saying that, thinking that. I didn't want to *have* to say it and think it anymore.

"It's tier one," she said, "so I'd have expenses anyway . . . you know? Maybe I can just keep doing showcases for years and years until I'm better than everybody, and finally someone will *have* to pay me." She set down her glass, "You think they have showcases in Los Angeles?"

"Forget showcases," I said. "You can do film, and quality TV movies. It isn't only sitcoms, you know."

"I know." Why wouldn't she look at me?

"Don't you want to go?"

"I'll just be so worried about him."

"We can't—"

"I know." We were silent a minute.

"Maria's here, and Herbert." I took her hand again, "*Irene*—" with all of the love and longing and hope I still had, "we're going to have a good life." She squeezed my hand back, and the density of all we had done and been through together vibrated between us; and Patrick.

"I want to go to Japan," she said.

"What?" I laughed. "Okay, how about China?"

"I'm sorry," she said. "This is supposed to be a happy time, isn't it?"

Patrick wasn't in the least infected by nostalgia. The next day he said, "You won't like the West Coast, Robert. I'm sure you'll be back."

"And I only have *one* friend in Los Angeles," he said. "My friend Roger." After all this time he's giving me a name? I thought. We sat sharing the *Times* and drinking coffee at the table. "Roger lives in Los Angeles because he's an attorney and his practice is there. Otherwise he would move here. He doesn't *like* it there."

"You're going for Christmas?" I asked.

"Yes, of course . . . He and I went to Europe together."

"You did?"

"Irene told me you're taking her to Europe," he said.

"Yes." I didn't want to distract him, just in case he had accidentally ingested a truth serum and was about to spill his guts.

But he sipped his coffee pacifically. "You'll do your television show, go to Europe, and come back to New York."

All at once I was furious; my jaws locked, and heat rose to my face.

"You go to LA for Christmas?" I said. "Not San Francisco?"

"Why, no. Why ever—"

"Nothing. Way back, this travel agent made a mistake." I felt outright hostile. "You went to Harvard?" I said.

"Why, yes."

He put down the paper and stared at me, bright and startled.

"Fuck it," I said, and walked out of the room.

The following day he had an audition, and the day after that he got very drunk. There was a pattern to it. On normal days he got slightly less drunk. I didn't much care. What had drawn us together before Irene, our commonality as actors and men, was for all practical purposes gone. What I had admired in him, his dignity and his belief in himself, was gone too. I'm sure he didn't think much of me. But we pretended a bit in the time that remained. We could always pretend. My flare-up, our stifled interchange, after all, had barely got off the ground. Just as it never had. Us and our phantom friendship, I thought.

JOHN LENNON WAS SHOT that week, and people gathered outside the Dakota with candles, chanting old slogans as though with his passing they had lost their own youth. But I hated the sentimentalizing of his death. For me his murder underlined the reality of the more dangerous world we all lived in now.

I started packing right before Christmas. I packed books, filling boxes in my room, and then going out to the living room to separate mine from Patrick's. We were taking nothing but clothes and books. Patrick would sublet our rooms furnished, he said, or claim the entire space as his own, make my room a gym until I came back.

The room looked set free, about to take its own journey. I cleared each shelf of books, wiping each one, then putting mine on the couch, and replaced Patrick's. That old Jackie Susann paperback was smack up against Patrick's Faulkner: *Valley of the Dolls, Absalom, Absalom!, The Sound and the Fury, As I Lay Dying.* I opened the book and confirmed the Benton inscription. I closed it, considered burning it, ripping it up. Then I went to the window, opened it, and hurled the book out. It fell surprisingly slowly, as if it weighed nothing, getting smaller and smaller, shifting a bit in the air going down to all of the real life below. I lost sight of it, even, just as it reached the pedestrian level and vanished, perhaps behind the parked cars. I went back to packing, feeling I'd done a good deed for the day. About four I opened a beer and sealed up the boxes, enjoying the snap and rip of the packing tape and the tidy finished packages; stabilized, solid, secure.

Night fell and I got another beer after stacking the boxes in the front closet, thinking I'd take a shower, then we should go out. Because of Patrick, everybody was acting so apathetic about our impending departure that it felt slight, unimportant. Suddenly nothing about this huge break in my life felt real. I sat on the couch drinking the beer, and then another. The apartment transformed, seemed neither free nor encumbered nor anything much: It was just an apartment, indifferent to me.

The key turned in the lock and Irene came in.

"Where've you been?" I said. Her hair was back in a ponytail and wasn't quite clean; she washed it every morning but today she hadn't. She sat down in Patrick's chair without taking off her coat.

"Call your service," I said, something already splitting in my throat.

"I already did, I'm called back for the play."

"Congratulations," I said, "when?"

"After New Year's." She wasn't looking at me. "I was walking," she said.

"All day?"

"Yes."

"Why? Why were you walking all day?" There was a hardness in my words, a sort of ringing in my ears, and she started crying.

"Don't," I said, "don't cry." I got up and took my beer bottle to the kitchen just so I could breathe, so I wouldn't yell at her. When I came back I sat again on the couch.

"Come on, we'll work it out."

"I don't know," she said. She had stopped crying.

Then say it, I thought. I wasn't fucking going to say it for her.

"I'm not going," she said.

I let out my breath and sat back on the couch. "Ever? Well, *say it,* Irene."

"Don't shout."

"We're talking about my fucking life—"

"My fucking life *too*. I can't do it, I *can't,*" and she jerked to stand up and walked away. "I've been trying to see myself, to believe myself doing this, and I can't. I can't see myself there." She turned back. "For a while I was able to see myself there if I didn't work, you know, in a house, just cooking and whatever, but I can't do *that*."

"I never asked you to do that."

"I can't see myself working there."

"You predetermined that for yourself."

She was so angry, her voice shook. "You have entirely forgotten what it feels like to be in my position."

"What's your position? Define it."

"Well, maybe I'm sick of smiling all the time and pretending I'm so goddamn happy."

"You're not happy?"

She sat down again. "I am so sorry."

"You're supposed to love me."

"I do. But I can't do this."

I looked around, trying to get my bearings; the room looked farther away, painted in watercolors, diluted. "Should I not have accepted the show? Is that what you're trying to tell me?"

"No, *no,* of course you have to do the show. But for me—it isn't only always being in your shadow, it's the work there, it's everything combined."

"The work there?" I repeated. "How much work do you have here? So you do this showcase, then what? Let's say it's a hit, then? You get an agent? You get a soap? How's a soap any better than what I'll be doing? Or a play, most plays? What is on Broadway, Irene? What is the longest-running show on Broadway? Other than *A Chorus Line,* a sex show, that's what. Actors doing ballet in the nude and telling dirty stories, am I correct?

"Is it that then, the theater?" I said the words with contempt; *the theater.*

"If somebody offered me a lot of money, as they have you, I don't know what I'd do. Maybe I can afford to be idealistic because it's never happened to me."

"You read the pilot," I said. "You said it was good."

"As good as it can *be,* Robert. *God,* what do you want me to say, it's Shakespeare?"

"It's not supposed to be Shakespeare."

"No kidding. Look, just tell me—" her eyes looked so hurt. "Your idea about us having a theater, did you mean it? Did you?"

"Yes," I was confused. It was hot, stuffy. "I mean—we can still do that, you know, later—"

"There won't be any later, don't you see that?"

"I can't not do the show," I said.

"I can't move to LA."

I got up, walked toward the door, turned around. "Why did you imply we'd get married? What did you mean when you did that?"

"I don't know. . . . I was saying I loved you, which I do, I don't know. . ."

"What if I were staying here, if I hadn't gotten the show?"

"I don't know," she said, and that's when I knew the finality of it.

She sat in the chair, still in her coat. The living room was no longer diluted but worn, exhausted, vague with uncertainty, sickly in front of the lights that burned through the window, the goddamned red and green lights on the Empire State Building. I heard the door and felt Patrick behind me.

"Oh! I'm sorry," he said, as if he *knew,* and I went berserk, every doubt I'd ever had about her feelings for me exploding in my head.

"You tell him everything, Irene?" I said. "*Tell him to get out.*" The door shut.

"Were you with him today?" I asked.

"No."

"It's him though, isn't it?" I said.

"No."

"It's always been him, he doesn't even have to take you to bed."

"It isn't him."

"I don't believe you."

I was drowning in chaos, at sea all over again about who she was. I had watched her so carefully since the moment I first saw her, studying her as if she was the key to my life. The depth of her cruelty was incalculable—of her duplicity and her *seeming*. Otherwise she had been an illusion. Don't let me believe it, I thought, as if she could hear. Stop me, stop this. She sat with her face in her hands, her hair falling over her shoulders. I imagined saying to her, *Just get up and come over here,* imagined her saying *No, then I won't be able to do this.* I would say, *Then why are you doing it?*

But I didn't speak for a long time, and when I did, I didn't say anything brave. How had I convinced myself that I could have such a love, such a life? I had been wooed by a false life, a sham, by impossible things. It was all sham, and I wanted to cut it all out with a knife.

I was going to be alone, but I was going to be famous, hooray. Was it Arthur Miller who said, "If you're not a success in America, you're dead"? What I would have said: you're a success, you're dead too.

Part Four

18 Despair

The light was too yellow, like the city was lit through yellows gels. The fabulous vegetation, the palms, the cyprus trees, poinsettias, birds of paradise, aloe, roses, and citrus trees all floated and glimmered in an aquarium of eye-straining yellow. The studio put me up the first weeks in a house on stilts overhanging a canyon on Sunset Plaza Drive, from where on clear days I could see the ocean. I thought incessantly of catastrophe—earthquakes and mudslides—and felt better when the apartment I'd sublet was ready: a low-ceilinged, dark three rooms near LaBrea and Hollywood Boulevard, the landscape pleasingly flat. There was an antiseptic pool at the center of the complex, enclosed on two sides by tinted glass walls. It felt like a hotel.

Early in the mornings I'd get in my car and drive to the studio, drinking my coffee on the way. Anything I ate, I ate in the car, wearing shades. I felt like a spy, an imposter, an émigré from a dark fallen country. Work seemed easy. Maybe because I didn't care. Well, I did care, but I was so busy measuring what my life was without Irene that there simply wasn't room in my psyche for my old over-enthusiasm. I gave the work just what it needed and no more. At night I sat in the bath drinking gin. Some nights I called her, telling her that I had to be able to talk to her otherwise I couldn't work. She tried to be cool, detached, as if it were possible for us to talk on that level. She accused me of attempting to manipulate her. She said I was making what happened harder than it needed to be—how could it possibly have been any harder? Often, I hated her. Sometimes I wished she were dead, and I told her so. It felt like she was. Our conversations nearly always degenerated into arguments that left me worse off, more bereft. I would call for a scrap of hope, for sustenance in my desert life, and received only a cutting shell of Irene, of love. She seemed to be teaching me—more finally and more painfully than she ever had before—the discrepancy between what I had thought we were and what we really were, which felt like nothing. She brought home to me the stupid, clichéd revelation that while I had thought I was getting closer to everything I had wanted, I had in reality gotten further away.

For Christmas, I flew back to New York, and Irene and I spent two days in our apartment, without touching, in silence, before breaking down the last night and indulging at five in the morning in a slow-motion feast of sex and regret. At the airport gate, I pushed her hair from her face, drinking her in. She had never looked as tired, as empty, as lost.

"You don't want me to go," I said, and she put her arms around me and held me, molding herself to me, and I believed that the separation wouldn't last.

But then there was Patrick. If I called the apartment and Patrick answered I'd curtly say, "Irene, please."

"Robert—" he'd say.

"There's nothing to say," I cut in.

"Whatever is going on between you and Irene should not affect us," he said.

"Irene, please," I repeated. For whatever part he had played in this, his intentions meant nothing to me. I didn't want explanations and would not have believed them. Whatever crumbs of affection that remained between us before Irene defected were now, on my side, irreversably gone.

One night I called Irene when I couldn't sleep. It was one or two in the morning on the West Coast and three hours later in New York.

"You answered the phone right away."

"I brought it into my room in case you called."

"You were sleeping." I could see her lying on the pillow—her hair —the receiver, hard, cold against her warm cheek. She had gotten the romantic comedy.

"How was rehearsal today?" I held the base of the phone in my lap, sipping gin.

"All right," she said.

"Tell me about it."

"There isn't really anything to tell."

"Tell me anyway, I can't sleep."

"Tell you what? No matter what I say it won't be right. If I'm up it's wrong, if I'm down it's wrong too, or should I ask about you?" Then she was crying.

"Don't," I said. "Wait a minute, I'm getting more gin."

"No, don't."

"Just a sec." I put a little more in my glass, taking my time, picking up the phone again like we were making love and I was drawing it out.

"Hi," I said.

"Hi," she said, calmer.

"I'll talk then," I said. "It's not so bad out here. Today I played a scene with almost nothing but my eyes. Of course, you have to know the shot. You can also strip everything out of your face and maybe do something with your foot, like you're anxious and you're trying not to show it and your foot can be flapping away. But then again you have to know the composition of the shot, the screen's small, so it depends what else they've got in the shot, whether what you're doing with your foot will even show. With the size of the screen you can really do detail. I'm telling you it's not all full of shit."

"I know it's not full of shit."

I waited, thinking of what to say next.

"You should go to bed."

"I know, Irene, look. What about, when the show's over, why don't you come out and just look around a couple of weeks?"

"Robert—"

"Okay, never mind."

"Can we—"

"I miss you. What am I supposed to do?" Silence. "Okay," I said, "I'll go to bed." I knocked back the rest of the gin.

"Why are you doing this to us? Grinding it in. Asking me over and over, making me say what I've already said and hate saying—"

"I can't get through to you!"

"It's my life," she said, "my decision. It isn't yours. You talk on and on about what we had—what did we have? I'll tell you what I thought. I thought there was so much between us, so much understood without even having to say it. Now I don't know who you are. You don't care what I say, what I think. It's only what *you* want, what *you* have to have."

"You lied to me," I said.

"Lied? Lied? Can you hear yourself? Ever, Robert? Let it go, please. Let me go."

"So passivity on my part would be what, a badge of honor? I'm out here alone and you're in New York with Patrick, and I'll be a noble figure? No, thanks."

"You're like all the rest, *you are,* like all the others. You have to *have* me, and if you can't, then I'm someone who—why do you even want me then, *why?* I thought you wanted to *be* with me, Robert, I really did."

"Am I with you?" I asked.

"Don't," she said.

"You're no one," I told her, "that's who you are. You did this, Irene, I didn't."

"I know what I did."

The next day I called in the afternoon and the machine clicked on. I knew they were listening.

"Goddamnit, Irene," I said, "pick up the fucking phone."

After that, I didn't call for a week, but couldn't help hoping that she would. Instead, I got a letter, my name and the address spelled out in her big loopy writing. I carried it through the quiet open walkway past the swimming pool to my door.

I didn't feel like going inside. The one thing in my life that felt real was this.

It was a check, folded up in a sheet of typing paper, made out to me for $2,207.43, what was left of the account I'd kept for her. She didn't want me, she didn't want my money.

I sat down on the sidewalk, my back against the door. Was it some kind of insane courage? Devotion to a lost cause, to the theater? If I had failed, like Patrick, would she have loved me?

Sitting down on the ground, I felt lower than I'd ever felt. I looked up at the sun, the lightness, the brightness so far away.

But it wasn't yet over. Adding insult to injury, a week later a real letter came, and this one was thick and black with her scrawl.

Dear Robert,

I know how you feel, what you think of me. But I know too, that you didn't mean everything you said. That's why I'm writing. I know the person I loved is still there, and I'm asking you to please put aside our problems because of Patrick. He needs you. Just call, just be there for him in any way that you can.

I'm realizing more and more that Patrick instigates fights. He puts himself in dangerous situations. And it's much worse and more frequent. I'm frightened, and in a small sense now I understand.

Here's what I got out of Patrick about the whole Benton affair. Benton was Patrick's choreographer in the last show he danced in, as I told you. A sour, envious, twisted man, with a small talent and large ambition. But Patrick fell for him hard, and you know Patrick—once he loves someone, he loves them. It was a national tour, and in St. Louis a new dancer joined them, a replacement for the boy who danced a duet with Patrick. His name was Jimmy, very young and unworldly, from a coal-mining town. He liked to imply he had hustled to get money for dance classes. Maria said he was wild and crazy, and that you could see that he wouldn't live long. But he could dance, better than Benton, could maybe have been as good as Patrick had he lived.

Patrick was drawn to him, and Benton saw this. But Jimmy and Patrick were only friends. Patrick was loyal, and was by then very much under Benton's spell. Benton got what he wanted by intimidating people, crushing them really, and people mistook this for power and talent.

Jimmy and Patrick danced their duet in the show's second act, and Benton, living up to his self-publicized reputation for ruthlessness in getting what he wanted from dancers, pitted Jimmy and Patrick against each other, made the dance a competition. And he seduced Jimmy, made him fall in love, with Patrick's full knowledge, and got what he wanted —a dance that was a fight without fists.

Jimmy began coming apart at the seams. One night, drunk, Jimmy smashed Patrick's window with a metal chair. Then he ran to his car. Patrick followed, telling Jimmy he was too drunk to drive. Patrick offered to drive him wherever he wanted to go. But Jimmy wouldn't move over to the passenger's seat, and Patrick got in the car.

They drove out beyond the city, Jimmy drunk and self-lacerating, Patrick trying to calm him. It was late, and miles away on a deserted part of the highway Jimmy drove into a tree, shooting across the other dark lane that led back to town.

It was hours before anyone found them. Jimmy died, Patrick's legs were both broken, the right kneecap smashed. He had the first of three operations, and when he was well enough he went back with Maria to New York.

But later, Benton kept coming around. It was as if Jimmy's death had bound them together. Maybe this was why Patrick couldn't resist, refuse Benton. There was no telling him not to see Benton, even though seeing him made him unhappy, reopened wounds, seemed the cause of Patrick's dropping the new plans he'd started to make. Patrick got into the culture of rough sex, whatever you call it, with Benton. Maria says they left New York together for many months. She doesn't know where they went. But Patrick came back alone. This would be just before he met you. She doesn't think—and I don't either—that Patrick sees him anymore. But he carries this, Robert. And I think that as the acting got harder, perhaps, he started acting out all of the stuff from the past again. And you see, *he's so ashamed*. Not about being gay, maybe not even about things he's done, but about being unhappy, despairing, he thinks it's a sin. *Patrick doesn't believe in despair, ever, and he is despairing.*

This is bigger than me, and he loves you so much. He's never stopped. He misses you desperately. Call him? I'm sorry.

Irene

I put down the letter and turned out the light. It was night but the blinds were open and the shadows of palm fronds sliced at the wall. They shifted in the wind. Such a strange sound, a rustle of cardboard, or sticks knocking together, not a sound of leaves that I knew. I lay on my bed, detached, floating somewhere on a new planet.

Too late, it was too late. But his wretchedness pulled inside me, pulling me down through the bed and into the deep dark center of earth.

19 The Visit

I bought a pearl-gray Alfa Romeo. I bought a house—
a Mediterranean villa-type house in Whitley Heights. I met a woman
who had several key characteristics that weren't anything like Irene.
Jenny was twenty-four, and she'd already done dozens of guest spots
and TV movies. She wasn't bothered by my success. Her father wrote
for TV and her mother was an agent. There was nothing tragic about
Jenny. She liked aerobics and windsurfing and outdoor concerts at the
Hollywood Bowl. She was quite tall, with long goldish brown hair and
green eyes. Unfortunately, she constantly used three expressions: "I
ask you," "major bucks," and "go for it." I couldn't help thinking that,
inadvertently, they revealed her worldview. But early in our relationship this didn't grate. I even liked it. Jenny got me to talk about why I
was sad, sadness being my outstanding characteristic, one I barely attempted to cover.

"You feel guilty about your success," she said. We sat on a beach,
and I had been gazing at the dark blue sky, the gray white-spotted water tossing underneath.

"I don't know," I said, "I guess." Breathing the fresh sea air alongside a lovely woman, any regret stood out as an indulgence. "Don't
you ever?" I asked her.

"Why?" she said. "I work hard at it, so do you. Why shouldn't you be successful?"

I laughed. "I don't know." From her lips, it was simple.

"I'd like to make you happy," she said, tipping her face.

"Why would you want to do that?"

"Oh, it'd be a challenge. . . ."

She had an amazing little house on Mulholland Drive with a view of the San Fernando Valley and an overgrown jungly yard. I sat outside the next morning at her redwood table drinking a cup of coffee and thinking, LA, what a beautiful, wondrous place. Then she got up and straddled me on the bench, her robe spilling open across her sturdy tanned legs. She wore leopard-print underpants and a men's white undershirt, and my spirits sank. She had only distracted me; now all I felt was the absence of Irene.

Everything Jenny said called up her ghost. Jenny was languorous—outside of her athletic exertions—and I yearned for Irene's purposeful energy. Jenny always exhibited a sort of sameness, a smooth consistency, and I longed for Irene's changeability.

From the beginning Jenny was intent upon showing me how few strings were attached, how easy she was, and in my rush to escape Irene's hold, I believed her. But that placidity in her disturbed me: she had no fire. I wondered whether it was the very lack of adversity in her life that did this to her, stripped her of any real passion, though this was the last thing I wanted to consider. I'd become repelled by the myth of having to suffer for art, to know life. I'd had enough of all that.

One day in mid-March I received a message telling me to call Irene, an emergency, she said. We were stopped between takes on my last scene of the day and I had a few minutes to think. What would be her idea of an emergency? She'd reconsidered, was about to catch a plane—no.

They would ruin me, I thought. She and Patrick together. She'd called about Patrick, attempting to pull me back in. She had sent the check ruthlessly, discarding me, but never Patrick. Now she hoped I would join her in playing, what, nursemaid to Patrick? Together they had embraced the past, nursing wounds and defeat. They had abandoned their goals, given in, sinking back into hopelessness and gray inevitability.

My eyes swept the set rapidly—lights, cables, actors, technicians— I had it, I worked. They pined and brooded and were cynical. I had succeeded not because I was a finer actor than Irene or Patrick, nor because I was smarter or stronger, but because I refused to give up. I had managed to accept the rules.

No. I stepped out of the lights, feeling sweat breaking out on my forehead. I was better off gone from Irene and Patrick, and as I always survived, I would survive losing Irene.

He was probably hurt, perhaps badly. But I wouldn't call him. Someone from makeup powdered me down, and I walked back on the set.

THE SHOW AIRED IN APRIL. Jenny and I had just turned off the upstairs TV after watching the second episode of the series, then a movie starring two of Jenny's friends. I was in the kitchen steeping tea—I'd quit drinking—when the phone rang and it was Patrick, sounding astoundingly well.

"Hello, Robert. You were excellent," he said, "by far the strongest actor on the show. Authoritative, that's what I said to Irene. I've seen you look better. Not on the pilot, I mean tonight." Tonight's show had been shot in January when I was a wreck.

"Watch again in a couple of weeks," I said. "I've regained my healthy good looks."

"You would. Pity for me, I lost mine in nineteen sixty-four," and we laughed.

His voice poured from the phone and thickened the kitchen—my spacious, well-stocked, revamped, state-of-the-art, handmade-cabinets kitchen; the cool brown Spanish tiles hummed with the weight of him.

My new home wasn't dense yet with anything in particular, and I'd thought I liked that, but when Patrick entered it—even with just his voice, it familiarized, leavened, was made replete with all of the nooks and crannies of myself that were indelibly marked by him. My past in New York was still so much realer than myself in Los Angeles and I felt something so much richer than resentment. What a classy thing to do, to just call me like this.

"What have you been doing?"

"Well, I'm doing Proust, Irene's doing Dostoevsky. The other big news is that I've been teaching for your mother."

"At the studio? She didn't tell me."

"It's dreadful putting those poor little girls up on pointe, but I'm loving the tap. Babies, miniscule three-year-old people. They act on me like a tonic. I no longer languish in bars afternoons. Thank goodness for your mother."

"That's great," I said, moved.

"Oh, here's Irene! Would you like to speak to her? Here she is." Goddamnit, I thought.

"Robert?" I couldn't speak; I exhaled.

"Hi," I said.

"We saw the show," she said awkwardly, "well, both shows, and—I liked what you did. Really."

I rescued her, "Thanks. How was your play?"

"Oh, fine. I enjoyed it. Well, here's Patrick again."

He put his hand over the mouthpiece and mumbled something, and then got back on.

"Her play was a disaster," he said quietly. "Yes!" he called to her, and she must have left the room. The production was weak, the director and several of the actors weren't good enough, although Irene's part was exquisite for her, she was gorgeous.

I wanted to smash something with the receiver—the entire New York theater, and the endless repetitious cycle of her noncareer.

"How is LA?" he asked. "Please say it's terribly glamorous."

"Well, it is. You should come visit," I said, loosely referring to the undefined future which served as a convenient catchall.

"I'd love to, when?" he said. Then he asked if Irene could come too. She might not want to, but what did I think?

I agreed, I couldn't resist. I needed their affirmation of my new life. I had twinges about the work, the place, the lifestyle that, especially during the call, seemed abrupt and too willed. I was exhausted from upholding my righteousness. I just wanted to see them.

I hung up the phone and stood looking at the kitchen that buzzed with new possibility. Jenny came clomping down the stairs.

"What's up?"

"We're having visitors," I answered, perversely intrigued by the idea of Jenny, Irene, and Patrick together, these dissimilar reflections of me. Agreeable as ever, Jenny offered to entertain them. The house had felt too big and empty, and Jenny had been glad to rent out her house and move here. It occurred to me for the first time, answering her, that this had likely been a mistake.

They appeared two weeks later. I went down to the street to meet the cab.

I'd forgotten her eyes; how the color changed according to her moods and to light—just then, navy blue lit with silver.

"Hey," I said. We stood awkwardly on the curb, neither one of us knowing what to do.

The house was on the southernmost flank of the district, a cluster of homes on a hillside north of Hollywood, planned in the twenties to resemble a village in Italy. We progressed up the stairs that ascended the embankment to the front door, passing the flagstoned patio. The house was a pinkish fleshy color with a tiled roof, and ivy growing up the walls.

"Isn't this nice," Patrick said.

"Ivy . . . gee, you have rats?" Irene said.

I had warned Patrick that I was living with someone, but encountering Jenny, he did a droll double take and then burst out: "You look like Irene!" For whom this comment was intended—Patrick was too discreet to utter anything he didn't want heard—I wasn't sure.

We sat out on the back patio with drinks among the fruit trees and the pots of cacti Jenny had lined along the wall. Irene and Patrick were both dressed in black with jean jackets; I would see, over the next days, how Irene had gone haywire chopping necks out of T-shirts and sweatshirts, hacking sleeves and collars off blouses. She'd adopted a dark, raggy, punkish look. It had even influenced Patrick; all of his clothes were intact and neat as ever, but tended toward dark grays and blacks. They looked like a couple: twin toughs, a man and a woman, one tall and one small. They were relatives come from that dark fallen country I had left, speaking a language I could still understand, telling me, by speaking it only together, that I could never go back.

She was thinner, and wan. I noticed the fingernails of her small lovely hands were bitten. Her hair curled over her shoulders, and her skin gave off such an impression of softness, suppleness, tenderly colored, delicate as a flower. The tough clothes only enhanced the effect: a soft, lost girl. She seemed older in her demeanor, though. Tired and impatient. But yearning somehow, hoping, longing. Sometimes she almost seemed to be listening to a voice inside, or for a signal from an invisible faraway place. In my own impatience, I had tried to make her a cipher, attempted to explain her intricacies to myself as a self-canceling flaw. Now her emptiness seemed only empty as water is clear. In my sentiment, in my lyricism, watching her eyes, I thought of deep, reflective pools.

The first evening Jenny and I took them to a party in Malibu, celebrating the launching of a new movie magazine. We went in Jenny's orange Bug, which she drove, with me and Irene squished together in the back, Irene holding both arms tightly over her chest, as though not entirely sure I wouldn't molest her. When we pulled up by the gatehouse at the entrance to the estate she looked so disdainful I thought she'd start sucking her teeth. Patrick was fairly perky. At least he appreciated the beauty of the party's setting: a great lawn flowing out from a Tudor-style home and ending in a pool overlooking descending cliffs and spectacular ocean. In the sky the last colors drawn by the setting sun were filtered by lights within paper lanterns strung in diagonals across the lawn to the pool. People held glasses sloshing with liquid and clothes rose and settled in the breeze.

Inside, it was mobbed. Bette Midler came over the speakers and people were draped along the white couches, the stairs, and the walls beside the huge windows and the bright abstract paintings.

"My, my, my," Patrick said contentedly. Well-built young men and women in skimpy swimsuits strolled through the crowd with trays of drinks.

A woman in a chartreuse crocheted number stopped in front of us and said, "Champagne?"

Irene took one, Patrick smiled at her and said, "Doesn't that look good."

"Oh, Robert," he whispered to me, "I think she would send someone for morphine if we wanted it."

I laughed. "It's good to see you."

"I've missed you, Robert. I think it's too exciting, your being famous. Traveling as you do in the upper hemispheres of—oh my God, there's that woman who had an epileptic seizure in the surf and drowned years ago on *Doctor Kildare*," and he drifted toward her.

I found Irene sitting outside on the steps leading down from the house.

"Hi," I said, standing over her.

She looked up. "Hi."

I sat down and together we looked over the lawn and the pool to the ocean beyond.

"What are you doing out here by yourself?"

"I'm not feeling especially social." She wore a black shirt with the sleeves gouged out, and as she raised a hand to push back her hair I could see the whole beautiful line of her arm, her shoulder, and glimpse the swell of the side of her breast. I thought, *Look, I'll go get the car keys from Jenny and if we take off from here at a dead run,*

*then drive fast, we can get as far as Tijuana before anyone knows
we're gone.*

She sighed. "He wanted to come."

"What? Patrick?" She nodded.

"It's hard seeing you," she said.

I put my hand on her arm, and she didn't pull away. It had been easier to distinctly remember her body than her face. I could still close my
eyes and exactly recall almost everything. I could see the exact shape
of her knee, like no other knee, remember her feet. Sometimes I'd lie
in bed nights remembering her body, amazed by how present it could
seem.

"Tell me how you've been," she said, and looked up at the sky,
speechless.

"How are you handling this?" she said finally.

This? "You do your work," I said, "you don't go for the hype."

"How do you do that?"

"You don't buy what people say about you. You don't jump every
time somebody calls from publicity."

"Oh." She wasn't much interested.

"Why don't we go," I said. I went to find Jenny and Patrick.

I spotted him sitting forlornly off by himself, tucked away behind
a table laden with cheeses and fruit and an enormous, abandoned gold
lamé purse.

Over the next three days I saw Irene and Patrick only for dinner, always at a restaurant, and was glad I didn't have to see much of them,
glad to have work as an excuse. In their dark clothes, thoroughly un-
impressed with anything LA had to offer, they made me wonder why
they'd come. Patrick tried to have a good time, even if Irene didn't.
Jenny showed them around while I worked. At night after dinner, as
we were settling into bed, I would (seemingly) nonchalantly quiz her
on the events of the day.

The first night, with a casual counterfeit yawn, I asked, "How was
today?"

"Oh, fine."

"You really had an okay time?" I asked.

"Is he always 'on' like that?" she said.

"Most of the time."

"He's gay, isn't he?"

"Sure."

"What's wrong with him?" she said.

"*What?*" Looking up from my script, my old protective instincts galloping forward.

"There's something wrong with him, isn't there?"

"There's nothing wrong with him, Jenny. What do you mean, there's something wrong with him?"

She didn't answer. My defensiveness lay in the air like a suspicious perfume. But lying there in the dark I thought, What is she implying? He didn't bring the shillelagh from Cork but he limped; was it his limp to which she referred? Of course not. I felt that old dragging inside. He had sounded revitalized on the phone from New York. Since he came, that impression whittled away. Yes, something was wrong.

To see that she saw without the least understanding of why, and of what he used to be, was awful.

The next night we both sat on the bed, me with my script, her with *Vogue*. "So?" I asked.

"What?" she said.

"How did today go?

"They're not what you'd call optimistic, are they?"

"No, they're not."

"Well, it's true, Robert, no wonder you were such a depressive when I met you, if these are examples of your friends."

"They're very good actors," I said.

"She sure is tense," Jenny said.

"Yes," I agreed, "yes, she is."

She put down the magazine.

"Do I make you happy?" she said.

My smile, my brief touch on her thigh were not reassuring. I kept comparing their faces, Jenny's and Irene's—there was a similar length to the upper lips, the same spacial relation between their noses and their cheekbones—and sneaking a quick extra peek as Jenny turned off the lamp on her side, I had the extremely unnerving fear that I slept with and made love to a woman with the face of Irene. The fear leaped beyond Jenny and I saw myself searching everywhere, always, only for Irene. When Jenny turned to me in the night I feigned sleep. She liked being held more than any woman I'd known; she liked being held more than sex. That night I couldn't. I couldn't stand her delicious musky smell in the sheets, her voluptuous body, her big hands, I couldn't stand how I knew I would hurt her.

The fourth night we went out to a Japanese restaurant. As we sat down at our table Jenny turned to Irene and Patrick.

"Tomorrow's your last night here, why don't we go to the theater?"

"No," I said too emphatically. With a few notable exceptions, LA theater was remarkably bad. That was all I needed, more ammunition for Irene.

"Oh, okay," Jenny said.

"We could go to the movies," Patrick suggested.

"I just thought you'd like to see theater," Jenny said. I gave her a look. The night didn't begin on an upswing, but it took a new dive over the menus.

"I think—yellowfin for an entrée," Patrick said.

"Major bucks," said Irene. I looked at her, then looked at Jenny; Jenny hadn't picked up. Then the waiter appeared and told Patrick the price.

"Go for it," Irene said. Jenny's brow wrinkled ever so slightly, evidence that she was possibly on the verge of perception. But she dropped it and smiled.

Patrick studied his menu while the rest of us ordered and finally said, "No, it's too expensive, I'll have the salmon teriyaki." The waiter disappeared, and Patrick said to Irene, with hauteur, "These prices. I ask you."

Jenny wore an expression that screamed, *I'm sure* there's a reference here I should know; then again I saw her decide not to pursue it.

I felt provoked. It could have been utterly good-natured—his teasing was conceivably his way of saying he thought Jenny was sweet. But I still didn't like it, and anyway, Irene started it.

The next day I was off work. In the morning, Jenny announced she was off to a triple aerobics class and lunch with a friend. "A long lunch," she informed me, "an expensive lunch."

Go for it, I thought. The previous night had been *mildly* funny.

Irene wasn't up yet. I smelled cigarette smoke and followed it into the living room.

"I am sitting in your chapel," Patrick said.

It was a long room with lines of arched windows at the sides, a false fireplace that looked like an altar, and light entered cut into pieces by trees.

"I like the minimalist effect," he told me, "you should never do anything else." He had a glass of vodka in his hand and a cigarette burned in the ashtray on the table. The burns on his fingers had paled.

"I'm off," he said, rubbing out his cigarette. He finished the vodka.

"Off where?"

He seemed not to remember, then did: "Roger has returned." Good old Roger, who had supposedly been out of town only three days before. How conveniently he'd reappeared.

"I'm sorry," he said. Our one full day together. "Of course it's my single chance to see him."

"He's picking you up?" I asked.

"I've phoned for a cab."

"Where does he live?" Come on, Patrick, *think*. But he couldn't even lie effectively anymore. He stood there blankly, so remote for a moment I thought he had entered into a fugue state.

He looked down at me and smiled; pleased, I was sure, to be capable of producing an answer:

"Silverlake."

I don't think he cared whether I believed him. Everything about him was unhinged, askew; his dark shirt, jeans, and jacket were neat, his coarse unruly hair was as tidy as it got, but somehow he tilted when he stood.

"I think it's come," and he went for the door—a slight lurch, a correction. I was struck by the effort it took, as if he were old.

He opened the front door and stepped out onto the stoop, looked down at the street, and of course the cab wasn't there. It was beautiful on that stoop, a spear-shaped cyprus rose up amid tangles of foliage I couldn't name, and there were three fragrant white calla lilies among the green. The narrow brick steps that descended from where we stood were bright with sun; and he lifted his face to the light.

"I've quit, you know," he said. "I am sometimes depressed. But really, considering everything, it doesn't matter. When one considers the good things." He smiled at the tree. "Anne Bancroft—always," he lifted his eyes to the sky. "Irene when she's angry, I think she's grand. You," fondly, "when you direct. Baryshnikov's dancing. New York in the spring." He closed his eyes, and held up a finger that shook slightly. "Irene," he said. "I've been meaning to tell you." He opened his eyes. "She is too subtle for most people, and probably too infuriating as well. But she isn't for you."

In a minute or so the cab came into view and stopped at the curb. I watched him start down. He tripped and then caught himself, reached for the wall to his side and recovered his balance. He lifted his arm in a wave without turning back.

Inside I saw Irene was in the kitchen through the archway; dark outfit, wet hair. On the counter beside her cup was the copy of *Crime and Punishment* she carried around. She'd been about to pour coffee but stopped.

"What is he taking?" I asked her.

"Taking?" She poured. "He takes something to sleep."

"What else?"

"A pain medication for his knee."

"Well, is he supposed to drink with it? How the hell much does he take?"

She set down the pot, "Look. If you and Jenny are into, uh—orange juice, okay. But don't judge us."

"All I'm saying—"

She turned to me. "He's in pain," she said. Tears came into her eyes and she went out the back door. I went after her.

"What is it with you? Everything's an assault on me, on Jenny, on our life here. He was high enough this morning, he practically fell going down the front steps."

"He left?

"Yes, he left."

"Where did he go?"

"I don't know. You aren't being fair," I said.

"It's hard to be fair. You don't know how it's been." A real martyr, I thought. Maybe she was competing with Patrick to see who could be more fucked up.

"Why, in your company over the last four days, do I keep thinking of a line from *The Country Girl*. 'That's a conceit with you. To talk like a veteran of all the wars.'"

"Don't be clever," she said.

"I'm not clever in the least."

"You know," she said evenly, "I'm really much more like Patrick than I'm like you."

"Don't say that."

"You used to admire him."

"It's not that, I still do—"

"I don't turn on people when they're down," she said harshly.

"No, as I recall, you turn on people when things are fine. You prefer to do it when they're very well."

"We only hurt each other," she said in a minute. "We've always hurt each other."

But that wasn't all, I thought, that wasn't all of it. There was love there, true love, for each other, for the theater—and *no one* carried the joy for it all that she did. I wouldn't negate it, I couldn't anymore. Not with her here in front of me, even like this.

"You've always had an idealized vision of me," she said. "I've felt such pressure from you because of what you seemed to expect."

"Should you not expect things from people you love?" I asked. "I've always thought that was the point. If you love someone you think the best of them, not the worst, you do expect marvelous things, for, to you, *they* are marvelous. What else is love?"

She didn't reply. She looked at the lemon tree and said, "I like your trees, I like that tree."

I went and picked one of the lemons and brought it to her. She was lovely in the sun. Her hair was drying, curling at the ends. I sat down across from her.

"I'm sorry your showcase didn't go well."

"I knew it wouldn't, I've been through it enough."

"Everything's gotten ruined for you, hasn't it?" I said.

"I think everything's gotten ruined for you."

I sighed, leaned forward, elbows on my knees. Then, a great fool, I asked, "Are you seeing anyone?"

She waited. "No. You didn't waste any time."

"No, I didn't." I waited; it was almost a dance. "What do you think of her?"

"She's fine, she's—very Californian, how can you tell what these people are like?" We both laughed, and then we were quiet.

"Why did you send the check?" I asked.

"It was your money."

I waited. "How are you managing?"

"I still work at the restaurant. I'm a receptionist too, for this monumentally wealthy alternative doctor. I read a lot there."

"What about work?"

"Work? You mean acting?"

There I was, the cheerleader for acting, as always. "Yes, acting. Well, what? You don't want to? Patrick?"

"I don't want to. Patrick. I don't have time," her face tense, holding the lemon in both her hands.

"When I called you, Robert—"

I didn't say I was sorry.

"When I called he was in the hospital."

"Yes. I suspected."

"It had happened once before since you left. But that second time I didn't know how badly he was hurt. He came home the next day, as it turned out, but since then he's been worse—disappears for days, or stays in bed like he used to. The teaching has helped. Your mother's been wonderful, patient and supportive. But I feel, lately, I have to watch him all the time . . . I don't know what he'll do." She put the lemon down on the table, looking off toward the door in that listening attitude she had.

"Now he's gone out," she said miserably.

"You can't always watch him," I said. "He isn't a child."

I paused. "Irene. You cut me off with the check. Never called until then. Why then? What could I do?"

She raised her shoulders, let them drop. "I just didn't know at first how to deal with it alone."

"You do now, though?"

"As well as anyone could."

"You don't make any sense to me," I said. "You don't give a damn about acting anymore, you go around like the walking dead. You're most busy, it seems to me, worrying over Patrick—"

"You don't even care, do you?"

"What the fuck can I do?" We both looked away from each other. The light was so steady and warm on the trees and flowers that it hurt. "I'm saying, since I know you and I've seen you do it before, that maybe you've immersed yourself too much in Patrick. Maybe to avoid yourself, your own problems, your work."

"I don't have any work."

"You could, if you would stop running away from it at the slightest provocation."

"At the slightest provocation," she repeated. Her eyes narrowed dangerously. "How dare you—criticize *me*. I wrote you that letter—it was like shouting into a *void*. You're—cold and heartless. You sit there and talk about acting. Go ahead, act, with your coldness. Pretend for money how truly you feel." She stood, in tears, and turned away.

"Explain to me," I said, "how your excessive devotion has helped? He isn't better, he's worse." I couldn't stand to see her like this, to see all of the brio I had loved in her transformed into this—even her darkness, the extremity in her that made her such a fine, deep actor, used only for this?

Wiping her eyes she turned back. "This isn't about pragmatism, I love him! Not in the way you seem to think, he didn't take me from *you*. God, even this asinine visit—he so wanted to come. Now I see he had some crazy fantasy of getting you and I back together."

"Yes."

"He's depressed and embattled, I'm—I don't know what I am. Depressed, over acting, over you. Don't say anything. I don't regret what I did. But he and I, together, we—rest in each other. I have a kind of peace with him I've never had. He accepts me as I am. I accept him."

"I think you and he bring out the worst in each other."

"No. You know nothing about it."

"I have eyes to see," I said. It wasn't the business that had brought her so low, it was him. "What I see is somebody who's going down, and he's taking you with him."

She started inside, and I grabbed her forearms.

I didn't know why I did it exactly, to bring her to her senses, to touch her, to establish contact for one last time before it was gone.

"What are you doing?" she asked, but she didn't try to pull away. I let her go.

"I want to go to my room. I should never have written the letter to you. I'm sorry. No, really. I am."

I stood in the brilliant sunshine, and then went in too.

The rest of the day and evening was a blur. When I returned from the gym Patrick and Jenny were preparing dinner. Patrick had taken a nap, roused himself for the longest dinner of my life: he detailed to Jenny a thorough fabrication regarding his billing in the last Broadway play, a fight to the finish with the producers for days until, facing them across a great evil conference table he said, "As the inimitable Faye Dunaway, playing Joan Crawford in *Mommie Dearest,* put it, 'This isn't my first time at the rodeo, *boys.*'" At which point he slammed down his glass, splashing most of its contents onto Jenny's good maple table. Jenny laughed at his stories, a touch hysterically as they went on, and Irene and I sat quietly. Couldn't she see? I thought, how absolutely he was set on his course, bound for a breakdown. Then what, Irene, I thought? What? How could she stand it? He may as well have been gone, leaving his body to a stranger. She had been fighting since her mother died, to be seen, to be *someone,* only to rest in *this, him?*

Jenny and I barely spoke as we undressed. She rolled to her side of the bed, I to mine, and lying there, listening to her even breaths, I thought I might die of loneliness. I reached for her, touched the sleek satin of her gown smooth across her hip, rested my hand against her.

I was awakened at four by somebody on the stairs. The numerals glowed on the clock in the dark. At first I was confused. Then I recognized the heavy tread. Patrick was going downstairs, probably for more booze. I got up and walked quietly to the top of the stairs and listened. He went through the kitchen and into the living room.

He opened the front door—it made a loud chuff. He closed it. Go, I thought. But I stood there. Go, I told myself. Time lengthened, the door did not open again. I went back to bed.

20 Hurt

The alarm rang at six. It was Sunday. I showered and dressed, preparing to take them to the airport. Jenny slept.

Irene sat in the kitchen. "He isn't here," she said.

Maybe he had forgotten the flight or the time, a man in such a state couldn't adhere to schedules. Maybe he did not want to return to New York. Maybe he wanted us worried about him. We should go out, down the hill. We would find him sitting on a bench, overcome by remorse about last night.

But then, he might call. Jenny could answer.

We sat, and it became seven, then eight, and though not a shred of myself had envisioned this, had intended what I feared, I began to expect the worst possible outcome. The world seemed to shift, to disperse and reconfigure all of its elements into a new world—one that I had made.

At nine o'clock we began calling hospitals.

"Does he have any identification on him?" I asked Irene.

"Yes, in his wallet, but nothing that would place him here."

"Where is his plane ticket?"

"Up in his room."

"Is there a Roger? Can we contact him?"

"No, he doesn't live here."

"Where does he live?"

"In San Francisco."

We sat at the kitchen table, light spreading over the floor.

"How do you know that?"

"He told me."

"How did you know what you told me in the letter?"

"He's been much more open over the last several months. He's been trying—I swear it, Robert—to get better." As if to justify him, and herself. As if she bore responsibility for this.

"I believe you," I said.

Periodically Jenny came into the kitchen, disturbing our vigil, and I snapped at her, or she saw our coiled singular energy—Irene's and mine—and quietly withdrew. Every so often we went out on the back patio. Irene smoked cigarettes, I watered the fruit trees and the pots of cacti on the shelf of the wall.

We discounted leaving and making the rounds of clubs. I didn't say what time he had left, but even if it had been earlier, when they were open, he could have ended up anywhere. Now, anyway, the clubs would be closed and the sprawl of LA dishearteningly daunting. He would either come back, or be brought somewhere eventually.

Just after two o'clock Irene tried Cedars-Sinai for the sixth time. As she talked her face composed, and her voice gained strength—"Yes, but you can't tell me anything? No, a friend. He doesn't have any family here, they're in Boston. All right. Let's go," she said to me. "They would only say he arrived in an ambulance twenty minutes ago."

How did a person walk out of a house and in less than twelve hours accomplish what I could only interpret, given the history, as deliberate? How had he so easily found someone to hurt him? What had he done to provoke it?

Cedars-Sinai loomed as we drove west on San Vicente, huge, black, with immense granite pillars. Smog hazed the sky. I knew the hospital, part of it called the Max Factor Family Tower. The street that led to the emergency room entrance was named for Gracie Allen.

At the hospital there was valet parking. The whole of it felt unreal, being here on a bright afternoon, not low-down New York, but LA; I suddenly realized how perfect it was—he had meant it for me. How ideal the setting.

The waiting room was practically empty. Blonde nurse. A middle-aged Hispanic man holding a hat stared down at the spotless linoleum floor. Yellow walls. Warm. A rich hospital. Several paintings, a glimpse through an open door of a white-sheeted gurney, empty and glaring.

I sat. Irene dealt with the nurse. She was told to sit down.

In a few minutes she tried again. We didn't talk, we only waited for maybe half an hour until a doctor appeared from behind double doors and approached us. "Friends?" he said. "No, don't get up." He joined us, frowning, youngish but graying; he wore Adidas.

"He's pretty badly beat up. Did you know where he was?" Irene shook her head. "West Hollywood, in the parking lot behind Musso and Frank's." An upscale, New York–style restaurant. "The police haven't spoken to you?"

"No," I said.

"They'll want to." The doctor's frown deepened. "The trouble is he'd been there awhile. What we've got is a skull fracture and quite a severe hematoma of the brain." Irene gasped.

"What's that?" I asked.

"It's an abnormal pooling of blood along the brain's margin. We have to remove the collection."

"Surgery?" Irene said.

"Yes. I went over the CAT scan with the neurosurgeon. They're prepping him now. Again, the trouble's the time interval after the trauma. We'll drain off the pressure and see."

Irene leaned down as though feeling faint, and started to put her head down between her knees but then just collapsed, dropped over her legs like a doll.

"Nurse?" the doctor said and stood. "I'll let you know," he told me, while the nurse came over to Irene.

"How long will it take?" I asked.

"At least a couple of hours."

"Honey?" the nurse said to Irene. Irene sat up. "You want to lie down a few minutes? Have you eaten today? Let's get you some juice." The nurse led her off through a door.

The man with the hat looked over at me. I focused on a planter as if it would hold me together. It felt like my heart would explode through my chest. For some reason I thought of a play I'd done in high school. Afterward, my mother, dressed to the nines and the typical center of attention, came back stage—it was hard for her to compliment me on my acting because an actor's life wasn't what she had wanted for me—and said, "Well, okay. I get it. I see," and then smiled with tremendous pleasure. "You're gonna be something. You're gonna be something good."

Gonna be something. Good.

The room tipped. I stood and walked to the door where Irene had gone, walked back, gathering myself.

In a little while she came out. We went down to the cafeteria.

"I'm going to call Patrick's sister," she said. She left and I surveyed the room: the people in white, the others like me, bearing up.

Irene returned, fuming. "She gave me his mother and father's numbers. I reached them both. We're to keep them informed."

"Nobody's coming?" I said.

"No," she said.

"Maybe a brother?"

"Fuck the brothers. I want a parent. I called your mother, she's coming tomorrow."

"Coming here?"

"She wants to. You know? He never missed one of his classes, not once. He had to be out in New Jersey three times a week and no matter what, he was there. The little kids loved him. She told me. He'd pick them up high in the air. They said it was like being up on a mountain."

Oh, Patrick, I thought. On a mountain.

"Are you okay?" I asked her.

"I'm fine."

DAY STRETCHED INTO NIGHT. At nine o'clock the doctor emerged and said time would tell. Patrick was being taken to Intensive Care. We should go home. He wouldn't wake up tonight.

"Can we see him?" Irene asked.

"If you have to."

There were tubes everywhere. Monitors. He looked so long and ugly, his poor hawkish face white and discolored against the sheets.

"Maybe we shouldn't go," Irene said. "Do you think he will die?"

"I don't know."

"I mean tonight."

"Do you want to stay?" I had to work the next day.

We went back to the waiting room and sat until eleven, when there was no change. We decided to go.

We drove home through a hot wind. Foreign smells of the greenery wended their way through exhaust.

"What happened?" she said. "Oh my God, what happened?"

"Irene—"

"What did he do? Where did he go?"

"We'll see, we'll find out. Take it easy."

"It's horrible, *horrible. How?* How could he do this?"

I didn't want her breaking down while I was driving. I took her hand, manipulating the steering wheel with the other. "Hang on, we're almost there."

I pulled up at the house and stopped. She burst from the car, went around it and into the street. I got out. The street was deserted and dark. The lights of the houses above and below us twinkled like terrible stars.

"Come inside," I said. She began weeping, then gasping and choking.

I got her up the steps and inside. Jenny asked what she could do. She brought Irene water. I sat with Irene on the couch in the living room.

"I'll be upstairs," Jenny said and disappeared.

"I don't understand," Irene said.

"He got lost," I said. "He got very lost. What he did—it was part of a culture that he got caught in. It escalated. Maybe the danger, the fights, were an exorcism. Or maybe that's how it started, a pressure valve for release. But then it spun out of control. It got worse, and it kept throwing him back in the past. Endlessly. Maybe by then the fights themselves were what he had to escape and when he couldn't stop, maybe he almost wanted to die."

I could hear the clock ticking.

"Maybe what you said about me is right," she said. "That I was hiding in him. I was desperate myself and I wanted just to forget, and that blinded me to what I should have done. How I could have helped him."

"You haven't done anything wrong," I said. "You did what you thought was right."

"I'm a coward," she said. "I always have been."

"No, you're not."

"Since my mother died I've been afraid. I've tried not to be."

"Maybe that's courage," I said. "The effort."

"How will I do this? If he lives, if he dies. My God." She put her head in her hands.

"I'm with you now," I said. "I'm doing it with you."

AT THE END of the next day I came out of the studio and the abrasive sunshine caught me as in a searchlight, a criminal caught. The metal of the car handle was warm to the touch.

How would she do this? she'd said. How would I? How would I ever do anything again? *Liar,* thinking of how in silence I had listened to her blame herself. How I had blamed him, deserted him, given up on them both. I *had* understood him, and yet I did nothing, and worse. I'd sickened at the sight of his failure, as if it were a contagious disease. I'd counseled him to face up! Buck up! Sympathy, I wouldn't even give him that. As if I did not know the word. And her. Beautiful her, to think of the qualities in her I had loved and been so threatened by. The sensitivity in her. The passion. Mercurial, quicksilver. An actress. Her ability to identify, to absorb. As if I didn't know what an actress was! Did not want, did not desire, what an actress would naturally *be*. Rather a bank clerk, a diplomat? Somebody *reasonable?* And as if I did not myself love make-believe, as if I had not learned as a child that for me—for Irene, for Patrick—it was the oxygen I needed to breathe. Who cared why that was? Oversized feelings, oversized needs, incidents in a life that needed to be reenacted, reinhabited, for a tenuous but new resolution. An attempt to transform. Or simply to see that the difficult, large moments in life, the fraught, deciding moments that made and broke people *meant* something.

Yet how precarious. How what we loved turned. How treacherous it had proved in the end. To live out of love and deep need instead of for money or, God forbid, what others thought, and to meet massive rejection. To be overlooked and alone. I recalled Irene wondering if it was wrong to love things too much. Could loving too little ever be *right?*

But she had become so unhappy. And he could die. And I'd given up everything to be here in a place where I didn't belong.

But diving down into the mess of it, life's complications, the tiny, worrying, contradictory whirl of a soul—did not this itself exact its own price?

It could.

But please, I realized. Where else was there to go?

I felt somehow glad. I thought he would live.

I'D CALLED IN TWICE during the day and there'd been no change. My mother was in the waiting room outside of Intensive Care with Irene.

"He woke up!" Irene said. "I talked to him," and they both laughed.

"What's funny?" I said.

"He—" Irene laughed.

"Sorry," my mother said. "It's been a long day. We're slaphappy."

"He asked for a priest," Irene said.

"Drama queen to the end," my mother said.

"Guess you had to be there," I said. "Did you get him one?"

"Yes, there was a priest here in the hospital," Irene said.

The laughter gave out.

"The news has been hopeful," Irene said. "There hasn't been any seizure activity, and they think tomorrow they'll be able to test for other things—memory deficits, vision, hearing."

"There could be that?" I said.

"The doctor is hopeful," Irene said. "A cop was here. But they don't know anything. Only what happened based on the injuries. The cop couldn't talk to Patrick, he wasn't awake long enough. I guess he'll come back some other time. I told him anything I thought would help. Was that all right?" she asked, doubtfully.

"Of course," I said, looking at her, at the haunting openness of her face, her tired eyes, the echoes they held of so many dreams.

"Go on in," my mother said. "You can stay half an hour."

I went in. He looked much worse. The discolorations from the impact of surgery and from the fight had intensified, but the tube in his mouth was gone.

I sat in the chair and thought about how I'd taken everything for granted. My stellar life. Believing in my intrepid will. When by the accidents of timing, gender, and fate, he and Irene had suffered more. Because he was tall and unusual looking. A child could have seen that.

He slept.

Where had he gotten the faith in himself that he had?

He was so fucking big.

When I went out Irene was asleep on a couch.

"Let her rest a bit," my mother said. "Coffee?" We went down the hall to the machine. My mother looked older. She'd cut her dark hair, and with it swept back from her face her features had a new elegance and fragility.

"How's David?" I asked.

"Just fine."

"Mom? How much do you know about this?"

"A lot."

"You knew he'd been—?"

"He told me. We were together a lot at the studio."

"You didn't even mention to me that he was working for you."

"You seemed to have problems with him. I thought you'd object."

"Christ," I said.

"Who cares now?" she said. "Let it go. Robert?"

"Yeah," I said. "Right.

"For instance, what did he tell you?" I said.

"Something I talked about with Irene today," she said soberly. "Most of it she didn't know, and you wouldn't either. After the accident, after he had come back to New York with Maria—he disappeared with Benton. They were in San Francisco."

I had been gazing at the floor. I looked up at her.

"I take it they were involved in more of what began in New York," she said. "But Patrick had a breakdown, and Benton deserted him. Patrick went into a psychiatric hospital for several months. I don't have many details about it, when Patrick told me I didn't ask any questions. When he told me it was almost—in expiation."

I could see that.

"But while he was in the hospital a man he had known casually started coming to visit and they became close. His name was Roger. A good man, a wonderful person, and when Patrick was better they were together for a while."

"So Roger is a real person," I said. "A lawyer?"

"Yes, a lawyer. And he said they traveled together and that Roger helped him with another operation on his knee, and I gathered that they stayed in touch after Patrick returned to New York."

"Yes," I said, "yes, they did," and then the reality of the hospital reasserted itself, the walls glared and screamed. I got up and threw away my cup, and came back. "I deserted him too," I said.

"He didn't think that," she said. "Will you take some advice? It's been my experience that most of us don't even know how much we can help. If he recovers, you may be the one person who really can. Or maybe not. But maybe you can. Remember that."

JENNY WAS GONE when we got back. There was a note on the kitchen table.

Hey, Robert,
   I'm over at my friend Kelly's. I thought I should give you some space. I hope Patrick's okay. I hope you and Irene can work out, whatever. Go for it, Robert. You should be happy. I'm fine. I have most of my stuff, so we'll talk in a couple of weeks? Good luck.
                              Jenny

There was a PS at the bottom, Kelly's number in case I needed it. That was the saddest part of the note. I folded it and put it in back of a drawer. My mother went upstairs for a bath and to bed. Irene went out to buy groceries. I sat in the kitchen attempting to study a script.

Of course Patrick had talked to my mother, and had trusted her. Like him, she was a dancer and had had to give it up. I had never considered how it must have been for her, I'd only judged her for not going back to it later. And I'd never considered in my swaggering ignorant youth what a tough life dancing, acting, show business could be. Or I'd dismissed its toughness with stupid faux sophistication. Yeah, sure it's tough, so what? So what isn't? I hadn't the vaguest idea of the consequences it could have.

I thought of Benton. The hardness that must have prompted his actions, the pain that had to have surged underneath. I thought of the dead boy, Jimmy. Patrick smashed up in the car.

Irene.

Me.

I wished that, just once, I had seen my mother dance.

I put down the script and went for the gin.

When Irene came back I sat in the living room in the dark. "Don't turn on the light," I said.

"I've got a chicken and—"

"I don't want to eat," I said.

She sat down on the couch.

"You have to understand," I said. "I had this—deep—conviction of being on the outside, of everything. I couldn't be there anymore. That's why I *had* to succeed, why I left. Why I took the job here when a part of me knew that I shouldn't. Not only because of you, but him." She didn't say anything. "And I knew why you didn't come. I knew the day you told me. But I couldn't accept it. Because I had thought I was finally—getting in, and I was more cut off and alone than ever." I heard a distant purring of traffic. "And when you wrote me the letter I felt like I'd died. It felt too late. To get over you, I couldn't call him. Then when you called in March, I thought that if I got involved I wouldn't survive. It was stupid, I *see* that, but I didn't *know*. You were ripped out of my life—the one person—I loved. The one woman. I loved him too. But everything had gotten turned—inside out."

"I know all this, Robert," she said.

"No, you don't." I smelled flowers. "I'd decided that my loving the two of you never helped, never made any difference."

"It wasn't all your fault," she said.

"Listen. On Saturday night we went to bed. I woke up at four in the morning and heard Patrick on the stairs."

I felt her attention in the dark.

"I got up. I stood at the top of the stairs and listened to him leave. I didn't stop him. I didn't think anything would actually happen. But I knew it could. I keep asking myself why I didn't go after him. Didn't talk to him. Wake you up. Whatever I needed to do. I thought he was ruining you. Did I think I was saving you by letting him go? No. *I couldn't have you, and he did.* That's what it was. That's it."

She was silent.

"If it didn't happen then, it would have happened another time," she said. "But don't ever tell him. Promise you won't. *Promise me, Robert.*

"When it got really bad, you know what?" she said. "Sometimes I wished he would die too. Because I couldn't leave him. Because that would have spoiled an idea I had of myself.

"You think I don't understand obsession?" she said. "You think I don't know what it means to have to do something with all of your might? Not to be able to consider anything else? That's me. That's me and acting. But it all got—mixed up. With men. With Andre and you and Patrick. Why the hell didn't I go ahead with starting a theater myself? If that's what I wanted. If that was the only way I thought I could have it. I was waiting for you. Always waiting for somebody else.

"Waiting for somebody else to say yes, I can live?" she said. "I'm *allowed* to do the only thing that I can?"

"You don't hate me," I said.

"No."

A coldness went up my spine and constricted my skin. "I think he will die," I said.

"No, he won't," she said.

THE FOLLOWING DAY he took a turn for the worse, and on that day of all days I got held up at the studio. Then, coming out, I couldn't face it. I wanted to escape from him and Irene and my mother as I'd never wanted to escape before.

I hadn't told them exactly what time I'd be there. I parked in a lot a couple of blocks from the hospital and went into a bar.

What did I want? For none of it to have happened. To get back. To not have to live with myself. To not know.

To not have done what I did.

But if he lived I could help, and only in that way could I undo it.

If he died? God knew.

A guy at the other end of the bar was having a conversation with his glass. Saying, "How are you tonight?" Listening. "Yes? I'm very well too." Listening. "Well, I'm usually free on Wednesdays."

I got up and left.

Between the buildings were hills in the distance, the scraggly outline of trees against the sky, the houses all lit up against the night, holding life.

Irene jumped up. "He's stable," she said.

It was ten o'clock and I had to convince the nurse to let me go in. But my legs shook.

I opened the door and stood just inside, not even looking at him. Just standing there, being with him. I finally approached, and then I saw that his eyes were open.

It seemed he could not turn his head. I couldn't tell from where I stood if he was looking at me, if he knew I was there. He had to know.

I stepped up to the bed. His cheeks were sunken, the purple and red colorations extended from his forehead down to his chin. But those eyes. Open and staring at me. I put my hand on his forehead, on the hurt, just lay it very softly there. His eyes opened a little wider.

"Forgive me," he said.

"Patrick, you don't—"

"Forgive me," he said again.

"I forgive you," I said.

Very faintly, he smiled. "I forgive you too."

21 Home

Irene and I stood in a loft in Little Tokyo, near downtown LA. Masses of wiring and boxes and rickety office equipment littered the space. Thick dust lay in clumps on the floor and coated the windows.

"Are they responsible for hauling this stuff out of here if we take it?" Irene asked.

"Could be we could use some of it," I said.

"What do you think?" she said.

"It could work." Walls could come down or go up. It was large enough.

Irene suddenly turned to the windows where rain that had threatened since morning began lightly smearing the glass. An unusual rain in California in May. "I hope he's enjoying it," she said.

Patrick had insisted on keeping the apartment in New York. "If for nothing else," he said, "but an occasional *break* from the weather here."

My mother had agreed to send Patrick's and Irene's things. Patrick rested at the house, attended by Herbert and Maria, who had flown in for the week. Physically, there would be no long-term damage, but we were acutely aware of the precarious nature of the psychic trip back. We could only believe, and take it a day at a time.

In the weeks before Patrick got out of the hospital, we saw what to do. One day I had a revelation.

"Once in a cemetery in Key West," I told Irene, "I saw these two grave markers. A man and a woman, a married couple. Two flat slabs in the grass, one above the other. And beside them was another slab, another guy, and his marker said, BELOVED FRIEND."

Irene considered. "Touching," she said. "But it would be nicer if, down the lane from our ramshackle theater—" we had not yet hit upon celluloid city as the place. "Perhaps a mile," she continued, "or maybe *two* from our house, he lived with a guy. Someone for *him*. I mean, in lieu of your rather macabre ménage." She shot to her feet. "I'm calling Roger."

We'd been at home. "I can't believe that his address book has been sitting upstairs and I never thought of it!" she said. "Betcha I find the number."

She had. Roger came down. Who knew whether Irene's matchmaking would take. But one thing we felt sure of was that Patrick's secrets had to be dragged into light. And Roger was, well, hope. Patrick had visited San Francisco every Christmas to see him. Irene and I were hope, and Roger was too.

So there would be Roger and Maria and Herbert and my mother and us, shoring him up.

"And psychotherapy," Irene insisted as part of the deal.

He shored us up too. As soon as he could sit up and take nourishment he had begun to complain. "So I *survived*," he said. "If I don't get out of this room by tomorrow I'll die of boredom."

On that irresistible, charismatic surface level of his, he remained the same.

"We wouldn't have wanted a totally different Patrick," Irene said.

As we began planning a theater, I remembered the inheritance Patrick should have received on his thirtieth birthday.

"He didn't get it, did he?" I asked Irene.

"Well, no," Irene said. "But he's supposed to come into a slightly lower sum when he's thirty-two."

"Yeah, right," I said. "We could have used that money."

We'd never imagined starting a theater in LA. But life was like that. You never knew. Rents were cheaper here, I had the house, and it seemed fitting that TV would finance the project.

It was daunting, impossible, and the right thing to do. Miracles happened. Who knew? We could fail. But nothing I'd ever done had felt as important.

Irene raced around the space marking out areas by dragging her foot through the dust. "Box office. Office. Reception. Storage. Dressing rooms. Light booth. House. Stage."

She stood stage center. She wore white and a big pair of shades, never mind rain.

"You know," she said, "Monroe didn't make it until twenty-six."

"You may have to settle for twenty-seven," I said.

"To be or not to be," she declaimed. "Can I play Hamlet?"

I stood in the house, watching her.

Dropping down to her knees she yelled, "*Stell-lahhh!* Hey. Good acoustics."

I laughed. "Not really."

"Come on, pard'ner," she said, "pull up a chair and let's talk." We settled into a couple of desk chairs. "Well?" she said.

I was letting it sink in. "It's the best space we've seen."

"I'm really seeing it," she said. "Little Tokyo. Gee. We'll make our own little New York."

"It's a start," I said.

She took off her shades and closed her eyes, feeling the place and listening to the rain. "When I was a kid," she said, "about nine, I was in a variety show at the Methodist Church. I was one of a bunch of little girls who got to dance in alpine dresses—in Kansas! In the middle of summer. But they set up these lights, and they put makeup on us. I got lipsticked and rouged. Like a woman. God, I looked and looked in the mirror. And I remember whirling under the lights. How I loved it. The brightness. The heat. I wanted to do it forever. I didn't want it to stop.

"After the show there was a picnic out in this weedy sort of desolate place. Everything that day looked so charged. I danced in the weeds, and everybody looked beautiful, these old funky cowboys who sat on the back of their trucks, the church ladies, a couple of dogs, and the sun beat down and after I couldn't dance anymore I walked around talking to everybody and then I sat down by my mother and I re-member seeing her like for the first time, separate from me. Somehow I felt who she was in a new way.

"The lights were still glowing inside me so that everything and everybody was intensified, set off, perfect. There. I'd never felt more connected and more apart. Later, acting in high school it clicked, you know, that feeling for the world, that love, and how I could express it. But I think I first felt it that day in the church."

She leaned back and the office chair creaked. "Oh, good," she said, "it reclines." She stretched back and yawned.

She ran her hand down her body, then looked at me from under half-lidded eyes. "Cleopatra," she said, "queen of the Nile. Antony, kiss me."

I did.

Acknowledgments

First and foremost, I would like to thank my brilliant agent, Julie Barer, and my equally brilliant editor, Kathy Pories. I would also like to extend special thanks to Steven Varni, and to the following friends and colleagues for their invaluable information and support: Jeff Allen, Risa Allyn Bell, John DeVito, Carol Dines Rothenberg, Andrea Frank, Oakley Hall, Sands Hall, Bob and Meg Harders, Erika Insana, J. Patrick Landes, D.O., Michelle Latiolais, Peter Mendelsund, Richard Millen, Frank Miller, Margot Norris, David Parker, Jonathan Rabinowitz, Dianne Ramdeholl, Suzan Sherman, Daniel Stewart, Lynn Varley, Ann Varni, Suzanne Varni, Katherine Vaz, Tom Wallace, and Jeannette Watson.